Perfect Night

PERFECT NIGHT

Peter Grimsdale

First published in Great Britain in 2008 by Orion Books,
an imprint of The Orion Publishing Group Ltd
Orion House, 5 Upper Saint Martin's Lane
London WC2H 9EA

An Hachette Livre UK Company

1 3 5 7 9 10 8 6 4 2

A CIP catalogue record for this book is
available from the British Library.

ISBN (Hardback) 978 0 7528 9042 5
ISBN (Trade Paperback) 978 0 7528 9043 2

Typeset by Deltatype Ltd, Birkenhead, Merseyside

Printed and bound in the UK by
CPI Mackays, Chatham ME5 8TD

The Orion Publishing Group's policy is to use papers that
are natural, renewable and recyclable products and made
from wood grown in sustainable forests. The logging and
manufacturing processes are expected to conform to the
environmental regulations of the country of origin.

www.orionbooks.co.uk

For Stephanie

Prologue 1995

There must have been a moment when I knew we were going to spend the night together. I've been over it more times than I can count. But it was like the tide coming in: before I realised what was happening, I was engulfed.

For a long time after, I told myself I'd made the first move. I was more of a risk-taker then. Later, I wasn't so sure.

They'd dispatched me from London with barely twenty-four hours' notice. It was my big break, the opportunity I'd been desperate for. As I left, the editor clasped my shoulder.

'We're relying on you.'

I was flattered that he put so much trust in me; I'd never even been in a war zone.

'And look after Greer: she's the best there is.'

When I arrived in Sri Lanka there was no sign of her. Just a message to say she was somewhere in the hill country, laid up with a stomach bug. I couldn't just hang around. I'd managed without reporters before, and I needed to find a story. Three days in, I got lucky.

It was another two before she showed up. The afternoon was furiously hot. Thick cloud pressed down on Colombo. I waited, sweating, in the office our local guide Anita had found for us, listening to the rasp of the traffic below. The door swung open and there she was.

Greer Harmon. I'd seen her often enough on screen, but never in the flesh. I felt my mouth go dry.

She smiled briefly. 'Well, here I am.'

Her combats were caught at the waist with a wide belt, tightly fastened. A bleached shirt with epaulettes completed the dressed-for-action look. Her hair, a dusty, golden blonde, cascaded over her shoulders. She took off her sunglasses. Her eyes were a shade of grey-green that I didn't think eyes came in. I stared back, unable to look away. There was a soft rumble of thunder. She glanced out at the darkening sky.

'Are you feeling better?'

She shrugged and launched into the story of her journey from the hill country. Her driver had been detained at a roadblock outside Kandy, so she'd carried on by herself until a puncture stopped her a few miles from Colombo. She had made the last leg in a tuk-tuk. Her famous voice was slightly husky – and entirely irresistible.

I decided it was time to cheer her up. 'I've got us a serious scoop.'

She frowned. I leaned against the desk and gave her the headlines. 'How often do arms dealers agree to spill the beans – and on camera?'

She froze. For several seconds she didn't speak. When she did it was in barely a whisper. 'What do you think you're doing? Who knows about this? Our visas forbid any contact with combatants. Didn't it occur to you that you could get us deported?'

'But you weren't around. I—'

'What the fuck has that got to do with it? This is *my* film. *I* do the interviews. *I* choose the story ...' Her eyes had gone a shade darker, and drilled into me.

Anita arrived, flustered and embarrassed. Greer ignored her greeting. 'Did you have anything to do with this?'

Anita looked suddenly diminished; the radiance she'd displayed before Greer's return had deserted her. I thought she might be about to cry.

I took a step forward. 'It was all me. She had nothing to do with it.'

Greer didn't look convinced. The heat in the office rose another ten degrees.

'At least have a look at the tapes. Rammal may still be there. I could take you to his boat ...'

The thunderstorm finally broke, drowning out the sound of the traffic, and, I hoped, the pleading tone I heard in my voice.

She picked up her bag. 'I'm going. I need to think about how the fuck to get us out of this mess.'

She swept out. I watched from the window as a car took her away. Her rage hung in the sticky air even after she was gone.

Anita came towards me, her eyes full of tears and confusion. She deserved an explanation, but I was in no mood to offer one. She collected up her things and left. I smoked a cigarette then followed her out into the rain.

When Greer rang my room that evening she couldn't have been more different.

'Nick! Will you have a drink with me and watch the sunset?'

I hadn't heard her use my name before and it felt good.

'I thought you'd left me for dead.'

She laughed, and I laughed too.

I showered for the third time that day, shaved and checked my teeth. To the west, a ribbon of light bled through the curtain of purple cloud that still hung over the ocean. On the vast lawn beside the hotel, a European woman was walking stiffly away from a local in a Hawaiian shirt. His arms were outstretched in an exaggerated plea. *Whatever happens*, I told myself, *try not to be too much of a prat.*

As I reached the lobby, the sun, which hadn't been seen for three days, blasted through the tall windows to give the humid air a dreamlike quality. The white-gloved piano player had just embarked on his umpteenth rendering of 'Strangers in the Night'.

A busload of tired and angry-looking Germans filled the lobby, dragging huge bags. An argument broke out at the desk. I stood to one side. I thought I might look as though I was standing to attention, so I unbuttoned my jacket and slid my hands into my pockets. But that made me feel silly. I did up one button, lit a cigarette and tried to make it last.

Greer was transformed. The severe military-style clothes

were gone. She was swathed in muslin so light that it seemed to float above her skin. Its whiteness exaggerated her tan. She was clutching a small bag, and flicked a wave of blonde hair away from her face. A couple of Germans noticed her and stopped arguing. When her eyes found mine they shone with a mixture of pleasure and relief.

She offered her cheek and I breathed in her scent. A British couple I'd chatted to earlier recognised her and clearly wanted to be introduced. I steered wide of them and led her towards the bar. I caught the waiter's eye and pointed towards a vacant table on the veranda, close to the water.

I had my back to the sea, but that didn't matter. The afternoon deluge had not long stopped and the whole façade of the hotel sparkled as if it had just had a much-needed coat of paint. The clouds glowered further inland, deciding where to strike next. When the sun dipped under the parasol at our table her face glowed gold. Freckles I hadn't noticed before made her look younger, and somehow more vulnerable.

I leaned forward to shade her from the glare. She looked down.

'I'm really very sorry.'

I shrugged, trying to disguise my relief. She took out a jade-inlaid lighter and shook two cigarettes out of a pack.

'Heat turns me into a monster.'

'You were tired.'

She looked down. 'You did the right thing. My fault for going AWOL.'

I lit our cigarettes with her lighter and she took a long drag. Her lipstick was pale pink. She was trembling ever so slightly.

'I'm so tired … I want to just stand still for a long, long time.'

'I know what you mean,' I said, and jettisoned my speech about the joys of being on the road.

'No you don't,' she said rather curtly and then added, 'Sorry.' She sent out another electric smile.

I turned and caught a waiter's attention. 'A bottle of Chablis, please.'

'And put another on ice,' Greer said. I raised an eyebrow and she giggled unexpectedly. 'I'm sure we'll manage it.'

The waiter glided away.

She picked at a thumbnail and her eyes focused on something out at sea. 'The Rammal tapes – are they safe?'

I nodded.

'Hidden?'

'Oh yes.'

'Did you get anything else from him?'

I smiled, my excitement returning. 'Plenty.'

Her brow furrowed for a moment and she fanned the air in front of her.

The waiter returned with a bottle and an ice bucket and filled two big glasses. She took a long drink and touched the cool glass against her cheek.

Her lips glistened.

'So, tell me . . .' She leaned towards me, elbows on the table, cupping her lovely face in her hands.

'What about?'

'Anything. Are you having a good time?'

Did she mean now? In Sri Lanka? In my life? I sipped the wine as I considered my answer. 'I am now.'

She accepted the compliment then gazed out to sea.

'Anita. Pretty girl . . .'

I picked at something on my cuff so she wouldn't see my blush.

'I imagine you can take your pick.'

'I'm sorry?'

Her expression was sphinx-like, but I chose to take it as a compliment.

'Thank you.' I blushed again.

'So, what were you doing – before this?'

I ran through the best bits of my CV. It didn't take long. She hadn't heard of *Destination*.

'It's a holiday programme. The Network uses it as a training ground for directors.'

'Must have been fun.'

'It's not long before you've had enough of shooing away the beggars to get a clear shot of a beach. But I can say "Please don't wave at the camera" in fifteen languages.'

She laughed and her eyes sparkled. Then I was off, plunging into an account of my entire life, as if it was all a preparation for this moment. She looked completely absorbed, but that was what Greer was famous for – drawing people out.

'Only twenty-three? You've done well.' She clinked her glass against mine. 'Welcome to *Human Face*.'

'It's the show I've always wanted to do.' I refilled our glasses. 'Getting great stories, scoops, exposing bad stuff. But you know all that.'

'It gets less clear.' Her face clouded. 'There are so many shades of grey.'

The second bottle arrived. This was turning into more than a drink.

'Your turn,' I said.

For a moment I felt her slip away somewhere. 'I'm not very good at talking about myself.' She stubbed her cigarette out emphatically, and then laughed a smoky laugh. 'You're very . . . refreshing.'

'I thought we were talking about you.'

She lowered her eyes. I became painfully aware of the rise and fall of her breasts beneath the muslin. 'A lot of the people I've worked with are pretty jaded. But you're very determined. I like that.'

I wasn't sure whether she was teasing.

'You'll go far.'

A small, dark girl appeared at our table, waving a clutch of dusty ballpoints. 'Pens, Sir Gentleman, Lady Madam?'

I could see the waiter speeding towards us.

'What's your name?' Greer asked.

'Shani, miss.'

She was dressed in a dirty green sari.

'Do you have a family, Shani?'

She reeled off a stream of names, counting them off with her fingers. 'Five, miss.'

I held up my hand at the waiter who was about to swat her away.

'And who is the oldest?'

'Me, miss. I look after them.'

'And what would you like to be when you grow up, Shani?'

'Rich, miss. Like you.'

I laughed and then wished I hadn't.

Greer was somewhere else. She stroked the girl's cheek and for a moment some current of identification seemed to arc between them. She produced a hundred-rupee note and we watched the girl skip away under the glare of the disapproving waiter. There were tears in Greer's eyes.

'God, I hope you don't think I'm one of those frightful celebs who cry on cue.'

Her lips were slightly parted and she blinked away the tears. Suddenly she looked vulnerable. Her armour had been penetrated. I let my hand fall on to hers.

A concierge approached and whispered something in her ear. A shadow moved across her face, then she squeezed my hand.

'Don't go anywhere.'

I watched her glide away between the tables. I lit another cigarette and examined her jade lighter. It was getting dark quickly now. Despite the collective effort of the sea and the cicadas and the rickshaw hooters, and the tinkling from the white-gloved pianist, nothing penetrated my consciousness now except her face and touch. I was too captivated to ponder what had taken her away.

She returned in a fresh cloud of scent. An almost finished cigarette was burning between her fingers and I wondered where she'd smoked it. But she was back and that was what mattered.

She settled herself in front of me. She smiled and her lips shone with a fresh coat of lipstick. Something was different. There was a flicker of what almost seemed like fear, as if I'd broken through to a more private, vulnerable person that few were privileged to see. I kept my eyes on her. Hers flicked up at mine and away. She took another sip and her breath rippled the surface of the wine. I thought maybe this meant something for her, too, that in spite of all the fame and attention, she was actually quite alone.

She looked at me again and I held her gaze. Whatever the rules were about how long two people could do that before it became significant, we'd broken them.

The tables were filling up around us. I put both my hands over hers. 'Let's get out of here.'

We set off along the sea wall, onto the green. A youth came at us with a huge portable easel. I waved him away. The resident snake-charmer took the cover off his basket and yanked a groggy cobra into a sitting position. I shook my head at him, as I had every evening.

We walked on in a silence that seemed to deepen with every step. The sky was dark now. The only light came from the streetlamps on the road that bordered the green. A screech of brakes somewhere in the city startled her. I drew her nearer as she tucked herself under my jacket.

The feel of her body under the thin fabric was thrilling. Her breast brushed my side. I held her close and she covered my hand with hers. The first cool breeze in days lifted her hair and it wafted against my cheek. I stopped and she turned. Her face glowed. I pressed her towards me.

'I need to kiss you.'

She touched my mouth with her fingertips. 'Not here.'

Instead of putting on the light, she opened the blinds, letting the reflections from the sea dance into her room. Tiny lights winked on the horizon and we watched the silhouette of a liner, with its rows of gleaming portholes.

I stood behind her, holding her, breathing in the smell of her hair as she leaned against me. We must have stayed in that position for a full minute, not speaking. Then she stepped away and turned. Her dress looked almost luminous. She put her hands up to her shoulders and let the fabric slide off them.

Then she took my hands and pressed them against her breasts.

The blinds were closed now but slivers of light squeaked through, enough to wake me from the deepest of sleeps. The smell of her was all around me. The perfect night came back into focus and I smiled for the last time that day. The sheets stuck to me as I rolled over. I said her name and it echoed around the the room. The empty muslin dress, draped over a chair, fluttered under the ceiling fan.

Her lighter lay on the floor. I scooped it up and pulled on my clothes. On my way to breakfast, I stopped at my room.

Everything in it had been moved. The catches on my case were open and the wardrobe doors gaped. The rugs had been pulled back and the bedding was piled in a corner. In the bathroom the air-conditioning grille behind the cistern was unscrewed. I felt into the space where I had hidden the tapes.

They were gone.

Outside on the landing I hesitated, listening to the sound of my heart smashing against the inside of my chest. I had to find Greer. She would have to know. When I reached the top of the stairs I saw Anita, waiting in the lobby, just as she had every day. Prim skirt, white shirt, black hair neatly parted, big black eyes, attentive. But her hair hung more closely round her face, as if to guard it. Her eyes looked swollen.

I tried to look away but she stepped in front of me. The knot in my stomach tightened. She had no reason to know where I had spent the night, but her face said otherwise. She gave me the full force of her silence before she spoke.

'Greer's already gone.'

'Where?' My voice sounded shrill.

'The meeting with Mr Rammal – it's all arranged. She said you should meet on the quay at eight forty-five. There's a car waiting.'

I was too distracted to question her further. A white Toyota stood in the forecourt. The hot plastic smell inside it was nauseating. The driver started the engine.

'Negombo Pier.' He announced the destination like a stationmaster and set off at speed, weaving through the Main Street traffic. The clouds had gone and the sun was clear and sharp. It should have been a perfect day.

Rammal's cruiser was moored beyond the other boats, as if deliberately standing aloof. Five boatmen squatting near the dock stopped talking and stared at me. There was no sign of Greer. I checked the time. Almost nine. I was late.

'Did you take an English lady?'

None of them responded.

'English lady? To that one?' I pointed at the cruiser.

One of them wagged his head. 'I take you. Fifty rupees.'

I was in too much of a hurry to haggle, so I stepped into the bobbing motorboat. He fired up the outboard and steered into the bay.

The cruiser was almost in open sea. A wind was getting up and our little boat bucked as it met the small waves. A family looked up from their breakfast on the deck of a nearby schooner. A tanned, silver-haired couple were putting up the sails of a weather-beaten ketch. Another ten metres to go.

Suddenly everything brightened. The sound hit me in the chest as a giant cauliflower of smoke and flame burst from the cruiser. The force of the explosion made a crater in the sea and our bow reared up towards the sky. I saw the upside-down coastline as I hit the water. When I found the surface, it was snowing silver splinters.

Then my world turned dark for a very long time.

1

The Eurostar slowed as it entered Herne Hill. For all its hundred-and-eighty-something top speed, the route out of London kept it to a feeble twenty as it picked its way along the antiquated tracks of the South East network. Yet its progress was still majestic, demanding that those of us waiting for humbler transport abandon our papers for a moment and look up.

I stepped behind the yellow line. At first I failed to recognise the bearded stranger reflected back at me from the mirrored windows flickering past. Was the tie a mistake? It was supposed to confer an air of professional pride; but what I saw was the head of a hippy grafted on to the trunk of a middle manager.

The doors of the Victoria train slid back to reveal a wall of passengers. Today of all days. Instead of arriving relaxed and composed, I would be hot and stressed. I looked at my watch. I couldn't risk waiting for the next one. On the third attempt I managed to get a foothold and lever myself into the unforgiving crush. Others pressed in behind me and my nose almost touched the cheek of a pretty girl with wide dark eyes. She stared right through me, lost in her own thoughts. I turned away to where another passenger was stubbornly reading his paper. Its headline flickered across my eye line: NORTHOLT HIJACK TRAGEDY: HEARING OPENS.

I closed my eyes and rehearsed my script. *I recognise the challenge; I welcome the opportunity to redeploy my experience.* Or should it be *to leverage my skills*? Wasn't that the phrase of the moment? I swallowed hard. The train lurched and I opened my eyes. The sky was brightening behind the dark carcass of Battersea Power Station. An indecipherable message crackled from the PA system. Someone next to me sighed heavily and I tried not to inhale his milky breath.

The concourse at Victoria was a sea of people. I wormed my way round to the side exit. The road was eerily empty of traffic.

'Keep back, please.' A policewoman gestured with her loud hailer.

As I stepped back onto the pavement the air was filled with a quartet of sirens. Two motorcycles curved into view, followed by a black Range Rover, two police cars and a coach. The passengers, mostly women, might have been tourists, except that their expressions were set and many of them wore black.

I examined my watch again. The policewoman jerked her head and I dashed across the empty street.

The Passport Office had just opened. There was already a long queue of anxious-looking people, penned in by tape.

Twenty minutes later I was at a counter. I pushed my ID and the form under the glass partition. The assistant wore a trainee badge, like a warning sign. She studied the paperwork. Then she slid off her stool and went to a filing cabinet. She flipped through a stack of envelopes and pulled one out.

There were two passports inside – old and new. She pushed the new one through.

'Would you like to check the details?'

The wanted-criminal expression that all photo booths seem to impose on their victims glared back at me, the beard adding to the look of guilt.

'TV director. Cool.'

'That's in the old one.'

She shuffled the papers. 'Arch – ar*ch*ivist?'

'"C" not "*ch*".'

She blushed and looked down. 'The old one expired in 'ninety-six. That's more than ten years ago.'

'So?'

'Haven't you had another one in between?'

Someone in the queue behind sighed heavily.

'Not that I recall.'

She held up the old one, its front cover clipped at the corner.

'Do you want to keep this?'

I looked at her.

'As a memento?'

'No thanks.'

She pressed the buzzer for the next applicant.

The 'Metropolitan' plaque was all but obscured by a TO LET sign. Not that it mattered; few people actually came to the archive any more. These days, business was mostly done by email. Occasionally, people turned up unannounced with salvaged material for donation or sale. Couriers on motorbikes came and went. When I started there, a small fleet of vans painted in Metro livery criss-crossed London, but they were long gone.

'Pass?'

The staff receptionists had been replaced by a succession of blank-faced security 'operatives'. Today's wore a uniform that looked several sizes too large. He glanced at my ID then laboriously examined a clipboard.

'You're to go to – Anot – Antot—'

'Antonioni. Don't worry, you'll get the hang of them.' I took the clipboard from him and examined the list. Everyone was on it; all the archivists, researchers, cataloguers, the VT handlers, even accounts. Darren's name was at the top, ahead of mine.

Naming the rooms after famous film directors had been one of a series of cosmetic management initiatives to try and sharpen up Metro's image. Colin, the previous senior archivist and the man who had hired me, had greeted this development – along with the smoking ban in the viewing rooms – with a long whistle of despair, his trademark reaction to any change. I had been with him on that one – it was a pointless pretension – but kept my views to myself. He'd been there the longest, had the run of the place. It was his territory, and he felt it was his duty to guard against any interference.

How futile all that seemed now. Colin was gone. Metro had

been bought by the competition. Alliance Image was in charge now. I had told myself to appear positive about the message we had all been sent.

> *On behalf of the management, it is my duty to inform you of the current role redefinition initiative. As a result of management changes Alliance are standardising roles and levels across the organisation. In light of this, we are inviting you to discuss new posts, opportunities and rewards.*
>
> *Suzette Hahn, Director of Operations*

The corridor was lined with grey trolleys stacked with tapes and cans, the overflow from Alliance. Keeping on top of them was going to be a challenge. I hurried past the VT suites, catching the draught of hot electrics. My best shoes seemed loud on the lino.

It was nine-forty. I walked into Antonioni without knocking. Suzette was talking to someone with his back to the door. She looked up, and there was a flicker of puzzlement as she took in my tie. She signalled with ten fingers and mouthed, 'OK?'

I nodded and shut the door. I felt foolish hanging around for her, so I carried on down the corridor, trying not to sound like a storm trooper, wishing I'd worn trainers.

'Got your passport?' Tracy, our PA, caught up with me. 'You are lucky. Sure you won't need a bit of help out there?'

She raised an eyebrow and grinned. She never gave up.

'Don't get carried away. Dresden's not exactly exotic. Two days in a theatre full of archivists, probably all talking German. Are the tickets here?'

'Suzette hasn't signed off on them yet.' She rolled her eyes and disappeared into the Ladies.

In the VT area, four of the junior cataloguers were crowded round a monitor.

'Fuuuck-a-doodle-doo!'

Gareth elbowed his way in front of Jason who seemed to be rocking on his heels to some inaudible beat inside his shaved head.

'That guy is literally toast.'

'Yeah, right. Bar-beee-cued.'

'Again, again.'

Gareth slammed the drive knob and twisted it anticlockwise. The image on the screen became a dogtooth check for a few seconds. He pressed Play.

There was a blur of chicken wire as the camera panned left and right. Eventually it settled on the hazy outline of an airliner, in the glare of what looked like searchlight. It was taxiing. The shot zoomed in on the cockpit but there was nothing decipherable so it pulled out again. The plane picked up speed. There was no sound. It looked like amateur video, probably Hi 8, from the late nineteen eighties.

Abruptly, the frame crash-zoomed out wide enough to take in the headlights of a Land-Rover, swaying from side to side as if trying to fill the vast runway with its tiny presence. As the vehicle closed in on the airliner it slewed sideways, almost tipping over.

Gareth blew a bubble of gum until it burst. 'Here comes the money-shot.'

The forward undercarriage wheels struck the side of the Land-Rover crushing the cab and dragging its remains a few yards before the nose of the aircraft hit the ground.

A fountain of sparks filled the frame before it went white with the explosion, and the group round the monitor whooped in unison. The picture jerked upwards, towards the night sky. Whoever was holding the camera must have been blown backwards by the blast. The next shot was wide, showing a tower of flame and smoke. I looked away for a few seconds. When I looked back the frame was tight on an open fuselage door.

'Heeeere's Johnny!'

A figure appeared in the doorway, his back and arms on fire. He made an attempt to beat out the flames before he jumped out of view.

'Nighty-night, rag-head.'

'Too bad it's mute.'

Gareth's hacking laugh faded when he caught sight of me. He elbowed the others who all looked round. I tried a smile and immediately felt like a teacher happening on kids smoking in the toilets. Gareth glanced at my tie. 'Darren picked it up. Just been re-mastered. Really sharp, isn't it?'

I remembered the newspaper headline in the train.

'What happens next?'

Gareth pressed Play. The still shot of the cabin door came to life again as more figures appeared. Then the frame whited out with another explosion. He was thrilled. 'Looks like a movie. What's going on?'

Because of my seniority it was assumed I knew everything.

'The plane was on its way to Oslo when it was hijacked. They landed at Northolt and demanded to be refuelled. The military stopped it taking off. That's all I know.' I picked up an empty cassette box that was sitting on top of the VT player. *Northolt 1989* was scrawled on the label. 'Where's this come from?'

Darren appeared at my shoulder and took the box from me. The boys gave him a round of applause and he nodded his thanks. His rapport with the juniors came naturally. He drank with them after work, talked football with them. He had a feral charisma all his own.

'Just a bit of salvage.' He kept his eyes away from mine.

'Where from?'

Darren rocked slightly on the balls of his feet. 'Harrop.'

Harrop was one of the 'bin men', amateurs and obsessives who hunted for old film. Although the 'treasure', as they called it, wasn't technically theirs to sell, Metro paid them a finder's fee and didn't ask too many questions. Darren knew what I was thinking – all acquisitions were supposed to come through me.

'Suzette said to just do it.' I looked away. He had gone over my head. 'Now the inquiry's started, every station's going to want it.' He unwrapped a stick of gum, rolled it up and popped it into his mouth.

A year ago I had hired him for his IT skills, to put the old card index online. He had no background in film or television. Within a matter of months he had more than proved himself.

His natural passion for detail and his capacity to retain it were awesome. And his gratitude to me for giving him the job quickly wore off as he bonded with the rest of the team in a way I never had.

There was a Post-It from Tracy on my screen – *Mutants du jour* – and a list of phone numbers.

A 'mutant' was any male caller who didn't give his name. The girls assumed they were all perverts touting cans of porn. I recognised Colin's number and dialled it.

He picked up after one ring. 'So, you're still alive then.' He didn't like it if he hadn't heard from me in a while.

'How are you?'

'Better, thanks.'

What recent ailment he was referring to I couldn't be sure.

'How's business?'

'Oh, you know …'

After being made redundant from Metro, he had tried to go back to the cutting rooms, but the world had moved on to video – which simply fed his disillusionment about falling standards and the decline of the craft. His passion for anything old had taken him to the salvage business, where he made a reasonable living decommissioning old cutting rooms and trading post-production kit, as well as handling the odd bit of treasure.

'Time for one of our sessions.'

'I'm busy this weekend,' I lied.

'How about tonight?' His voice had a tinge of desperation.

'Let me get back to you.'

'Do you ever commit to anything?' He knew my tendency to baulk at firm arrangements.

'All right. I'll see you about seven.'

Darren loomed over my desk with a printout. 'Know anything about this?'

I examined the stream of letters and digits. It was a list of project numbers and each film's project status. One was ringed with red felt pen.

ND89/HF17–GH

I felt my cheeks flush. 'Who wants it?'

'Everybody. The whole film's about the bloke behind the hijacking. They're all offering top dollar. We could have an auction.'

I stared at the numbers, waiting for him to say something else.

'But it's AWOL.' He jabbed the printout. 'Records show a salvage copy as part of an intake in early 'ninety-seven, but no sign after that. Not cleaned or VT transferrred. Got two cataloguers going through the top floor now, but if it's not with the other NDHFs ...' He raised his eyebrows. For a moment I thought he was accusing me.

'I've no idea, I'm afraid. Sorry.'

'Pity.' He didn't sound convinced. After twelve years here there weren't many questions I couldn't answer. 'Let me know if anything comes to you.'

I stared at the red-circled number.

'ND' stood for Network Documentaries, the department it came out of, though it was just known as Net Docs – once the best place in the whole world, if documentary was your vocation. '89' was the year of production. 'HF' stood for *Human Face*, the once celebrated series than ran for more than twenty years. In its heyday it reached eight million viewers on Monday nights. Its reporters were household names. Several of its directors went on to Hollywood. '17' was the episode number; 'GH' the initials of the reporter.

Episode seventeen was *Face of a Terrorist*: Greer Harmon's first film.

2

This time I knocked.

A round-faced man stood up. He was surprisingly short. His eyes were shiny and his smile well rehearsed.

Suzette smiled thinly. 'This is Nick Roker.' There was an unfamiliar formality in her voice.

'Perry Samuels, Alliance HR.' He offered a warm, meaty hand. He wasn't wearing a tie.

'Coffee?' Suzette's tone was artificially bright.

'It's still out of order,' I said.

'I'll go and check.' She seemed keen to get out of the room.

I sat down facing Samuels. He smiled broadly again then clenched his mouth together so his lips disappeared briefly before he spoke. 'Interesting background.' He examined the papers in front of him.

'I'm sorry?'

'Your television stint. Very exciting.'

If that was sarcasm it was well camouflaged.

I tried to smile back. 'A long time ago.'

He read on, then raised his eyebrows. 'Gosh. Lucky escape.'

I hoped that by saying nothing he'd take the hint. But he looked up and made a caring expression that might have been part of his HR training. 'Water under the bridge now, I suppose.'

I blinked. It took him a moment to realise what he'd said.

'Sorry.'

I folded my arms. He peered at me. 'Never tempted to return to the fray?' He made a ludicrous gesture of holding a camera.

'It wasn't an option.' *Get on with it.*

He shuffled the papers in front of him. 'You got a bonus for ... *Paths to Conflict.* Is that a film?'

'A TV series; it was made in the fifties. Twenty-six parts. The show prints were lost in a fire. Some of the negs survived. And with a crate of trims and cutting copies I put together a new version and re-mastered it. I – we – got an award.'

He nodded vigorously and raised his hand. Perhaps it was too much information for him.

'I'm a bit of a new boy here.' He laughed briefly. 'If you wouldn't mind, paint a picture for us' – he registered Suzette's absence – 'of your current role as ...' he looked down at a file in front of him, 'senior archivist.'

I absorbed his request and its alien language. He clearly didn't know anything about the job. I reminded myself to sound bright and engaged. 'As senior archivist, my responsibility recently has been to oversee the transfer of our back catalogues from card to computer.'

Darren had probably said the same thing. I felt myself flush and was glad of the camouflage of my beard.

'As well as overseeing the archive team.' That sounded like Suzette's job. 'With the objective of ensuring the future of the archive by providing an ever better service.' I hoped this sounded more managerial.

'Go on.'

I took a breath.

'Any central London repository of archive, whether it's books or tapes or cans of film, faces the rising cost of storage. At the same time, our survival depends on the need to react quickly to the requirements of our clients.'

'Carry on.' Samuels' enthusiasm was more appropriate to a piece of gossip than an explanation of the finer points of film and television archive storage.

'If a breaking news story relates to events that have happened some years before, like the Bogside, or My Lai, footage from twenty or thirty years ago is suddenly relevant for tonight's *Newsnight* ...'

He smiled like someone not admitting they don't know the language.

'Say Prince Charles dies. There will be sudden demand for all the footage of him and Diana. It's at times like these the archive makes its money.' I immediately regretted implying that this was the only time Metro made money. Scrabbling now, I added, 'But with the possibility of sending pictures and sound electronically, all this can be achieved in minutes and at a fraction of the cost, providing the material is digitised – transferred from film or tape to a digital form of memory.'

I left out my suspicion of new technology, my doubts about security and pirating and the deterioration of digitally stored images. Today I wanted to sound positive about the future.

'I see.' Samuels continued to smile broadly. He looked down at a page of close type with my name at the top.

Suzette reappeared with coffee.

Colin had loathed her, as well as the rest of the board. 'The *tosserati*,' he called them. Having started life in the cutting rooms of Movietone, he belonged to a world where female managers had been unthinkable. 'Us lot are all fucked now,' he'd warned me after one of her visits. 'Might as well just bend over, drop our drawers and spread 'em.' I had made a face of grim agreement, but that was all.

'Nick's been telling me about the project he's just finished,' Samuels continued.

Her expression looked tight. I started to correct him. 'Actually, we've only got as far as nineteen eighty-four.'

Suzette's professional manner slipped. 'Can we just get on with this?'

Samuels' smile came and went as if a fuse was going. He cleared his throat. 'The position is that, as part of the rationalisation following the merger with Alliance, we have been conducting a strategic programme of role mapping. There are a number of aspects to this process, such as competency development, skills assessment and rewards, with the goal of performance optimisation. As a result of this review, we have come to some decisions about the future organisation and,' he blinked rapidly, 'we are notifying you today that your current position is – following this strategic structural review – as of now, considered at risk.'

I looked at the coffee. I heard Colin's voice in my head: *Fucking told you, didn't I? Right up the arse.*

'What is "at risk"?'

'It means the post has ceased to exist.'

'I thought this was a job interview.'

Suzette glanced at Samuels. 'As of this morning, Darren has accepted the new post of Archive Manager.'

They waited for me to digest the information. I took the lid off the coffee and sipped. I thought about Colin again. *You watch, my boy – they get rid of me and they're fucked. They lose all this.* He'd tapped his head. *They don't own this, and can't do a fucking thing without it.* When he went, I'd wondered how we would cope without his intimate knowledge of the arcane Cinemasport numbering system, or his rapport with some of the dodgier dealers in 'lost' film. He could name every head of state in the footage of Queen Victoria's funeral, or all the Generals in shots of Potsdam. But we had managed, and they would manage just as well without me.

Samuels pushed a letter towards me. 'If you accept our terms, in view of your long service, and in light of your good work, we'd be prepared to offer you three months' notice, which you could take as gardening leave, plus . . .' he paused, as if he was about to announce a prize, 'a week's pay for every year you've served. As well as being paid right up to your last day and combined with your . . .' he consulted the papers in front of him, 'your considerable untaken leave, it tots up to quite a nice leaving present.'

'When does this gardening leave begin?'

Samuels blinked like an amphibian. 'Tomorrow.'

Whatever I was feeling, I didn't want to show it. If it was anger, I didn't want to shout; if it was sadness, I didn't want to cry.

'What about Dresden?'

Samuels turned to Suzette for an explanation.
'Darren will represent us.'
'He doesn't even speak German.'
The two looked at me. It didn't matter to them. Samuels put his friendly expression back on.
'And obviously, if there's anything we can do to assist you with outplacement, don't hesitate to ask.' He coughed and straightened the papers in front of him.
The meeting was over.

I went into the toilet and wrenched off my tie. I caught my expression in the mirror above the basin. I looked scared. Since Sri Lanka, Metro had been a safe haven, a place to withdraw, where I wouldn't be recognised or questioned, where people's curiosity was about old reels of film, not each other. I had embedded myself there, camouflaged among the stacks and cans and screens. All the job demanded was a good memory and a taste for order. I filled my head with the most arcane details, walled myself in with dates and catalogues and roll numbers. Now it was all about to be taken away.
The shirt was the sort that looked wrong without a tie. They might all notice I had taken it off. I put it back on, and then loosened it a bit. I walked purposefully back to my booth, avoiding any eyes, and sat down emphatically, as if to get on with pressing business. But it was unnaturally quiet. *Everyone knows*. The small world of the archive, once so safe, had turned hostile.
My eyes roamed over the desk: a joiner for cutting and fixing film, a fine precision instrument, hand-made years ago by a firm that had gone bust. Stuck to the surface were Sellotape shapes outlined with dust where the plastic had lifted. An unnecessary number of pens sat in a BBC Children in Need mug and the keyboard, I now noticed, was ingrained with grime and the patina of daily use. My image stared back dimly from the dead monitor screen.
Darren was leaning back on his chair, talking into his mobile. He reddened when I approached and ended his call. He would

know that I had been told. I decided to pretend it was business as usual.

'That film you wanted, *Face of a Terrorist*. It could be at Honor Oak.'

Honor Oak was the overspill store where older, less frequently requested material was kept. He frowned. 'How come?'

'Fresh intakes used to go there before cataloguing. Maybe it got onto the system but never made it here.'

He was silent for a moment, as if my authority over him had been briefly restored.

'I'll need the van.'

He opened a shallow drawer lined with neat compartments and passed me a jumbled bunch of keys. 'Go easy pulling away; it stalls.'

I turned to go then looked back at him. 'By the way, congratulations.'

He nodded, but didn't look up.

3

As a boy I had looked forward avidly to the future. Just the phrase 'Twenty-first Century' sounded so full of promise. Now I wasn't so sure. I'd been comfortable in the twentieth. I knew my way around it. Sometimes, after a day immersed in pictures from the past, it was almost a shock to find the present going on outside.

I stopped at a grim café in Vauxhall but found I wasn't hungry. I had a coffee and smoked a cigarette. I needed a moment on neutral ground. Bits of the morning swam in and out of focus. When Colin went I had wondered what it felt like. Now I knew. Outside, the traffic hissed in the rain. An unmarked car with a magnetic blue flashing light stuck on its roof fought its way down the oncoming lane. The men inside leaned forward, as if willing it to go faster.

If I wanted to see Greer one last time, this was my only chance.

I used to enjoy trips to Honor Oak. It was like visiting a well-tended graveyard where great historic figures had been laid to rest.

Until a few years ago, it was staffed by a trio of 'brown-coats', men from a disabled servicemen's home. You could carbon date them by their names: Reg, Percy and Arthur. So obsessed were they with keeping the stock in perfect order that sometimes it was difficult to get them to part with anything at all. I once had to go in person to collect footage of Churchill's funeral procession because they refused to give it to a courier.

'Well, it's not right, is it? Would you?'

'Would I what?'

Arthur had brought his face close to mine, enveloping me in a moist cloud of pipe smoke. 'Winnie's last journey? With some hell's angel?'

The inconvenience was a small price to pay for their dedication. I missed them.

Doug, a former cataloguer, was now in sole charge. An outcast from HQ whose move I had been responsible for, he was barely suppressing a smirk.

'Sorry. Can't let you in. There's a new clearance list.' He held up a fax like a trophy. ''Fraid you're not on it.'

It was my turn to be the outcast.

'Pity. Because there's a Code Red in there.' Code Reds were priority requests for immediate transmission. They earned the money. 'But if you need to go by the book ...' I turned, as if to leave.

'Tell me where it is then.'

'Sure. You know where the pre-'eighty-one Net Docs are in the colour group under the non-Empire military?'

The smirk had gone from his face. I knew the vault inside out. He didn't.

'Don't tell anyone I let you in.'

He punched a code into a pad on the desk. A series of bolts shot back and I heaved open the cold metal door.

Inside, it was a mess. In the central aisle a long shelf had collapsed, overloaded. A half-hearted attempt to clear a path had left pillars of cans lurched against each other. Opposite, another shelf curved under the strain of more freshly stacked cans.

Doug had followed me in. 'Alliance truck arrived. A dirty great artic. No warning. They just took the forklift and stuck the cans wherever. What could I do? I told them, "This is a Metro store." "Not any more," they said.'

'What happened to theirs?'

'Sold for development.'

I stepped in further. I needed to be alone. 'Isn't this your lunch break?' He hesitated. 'Don't worry.' I gestured at the mess. 'I'll leave it just as I found it.'

*

There were three aisles, each about fifty yards long.

I looked at the labels on the first shelf in Aisle 1. Funerals of the monarchs shared a shelf with the entire cannon of *Pop Pickings*, an early, excruciating response to the rock 'n' roll revolution. I pulled out some cans. *Birds of All Seasons* had been mixed up with Dunkirk footage and *Pampered Pets*. On the next shelf *The Philosophers* had been pushed in next to *Go*, a motoring magazine show, and *Children's Treat*.

I heard myself tutting, like a park-keeper inspecting a vandalised flowerbed. The waste of effort, all the hours Reg and his comrades had given to keeping things in order, so carelessly desecrated.

There was a crack like a rifle shot. I crouched down instinctively then snorted at the ludicrousness of it. There was another sound I couldn't place, like a cross between a drum solo and a waterfall. I peered round the corner into Aisle 2. A shelf had split clean in two, like a bombed bridge, and the passage was blocked by a heap of spilled cans and videotape boxes. Much as the sight pained me, it wasn't my problem. Not any more.

I checked that I was alone, went back to the rear of Aisle 2, crouched down and rolled onto my side. My face was level with the space under the bottom shelf. It was empty. A pulse started thumping in my temples. Perhaps I had make a mistake. I checked the next aisle. And the next. The spaces under all the shelves had been cleared.

'Lost something?'

Doug was standing over me.

'I thought it was under one of the shelves.'

'Pity. After the flood all the stuff on the floor had to be dumped. Most of it was junk anyway.'

'What flood?'

'Couple of months ago. A drain burst up the hill.'

My breaths were coming in short gulps. I looked away from him.

'What happened to all the ... stuff that was on the floor?'

'Dunno. Landfill, I expect.'

*

Back in the van I smoked a cigarette.

After her death, all copies of Greer's films had been destroyed or wiped. I didn't know why. I assumed it was an act of corporate vandalism by the Network desperately trying to distance itself from controversy. A few years after I'd started at Metro, a bin man came in with a crate of cans salvaged from the vacated Network cutting rooms. Most of the contents were rough cuts and out-takes, of little interest or use. But among them was one piece of treasure – *Face of a Terrorist*.

At that time I couldn't look at it. Seeing her again – hearing her voice – it was still too soon. But I didn't want anyone else to look at her either. So I hid the film where I thought it would be safe, until enough time had passed and some of the pain had receded. Too late.

As bad days go this wasn't my worst, but it felt close. Doug tapped on the window.

'There's those skips. Could have gone in there.' He grinned. 'But a lot else has gone in since.' He held up some thick rubber gloves. 'Only one pair, I'm afraid.' The light was already beginning to fade, but this would be my only chance. I took the gloves and climbed onto the first skip. There was a lot of crumbled plasterboard and builders' rubbish. Most of it was wet, heavy or sharp. I remembered what I used to say to myself during long days of cataloguing: just do it. Don't think about it. A fine rain started to fall.

After an hour Doug reappeared. 'Darren's on the phone. Wants to know where it is.'

'Tell him I'm still looking.'

'Why bother? You're not going to be around much longer.'

I ignored him. After an hour, the contents of three skips littered the tarmac. None of them had yielded any cans. I pressed on.

To unearth lost material is the archivist's dream. Old episodes of *Dr Who* had been found in Beirut; a missing Peter Sellers TV appearance turned up at the former Anglo-Soviet Cultural Institute. Perhaps I should have taken the film home when I first found it. But I had already lost one job and wanted to hang on to this one. Maybe I'd done well to last twelve years.

At the bottom of the fourth skip, under a folded mass of sodden carpet, was a black sack. The few cans inside were all badly corroded. One had a metallic sticker with a silver and red 'R'. *RESTRICTED: Not to be viewed or transmitted without the prior written approval of the Board*. I knew the blurb by heart. Once it had been applied to all politically sensitive material. The original label identifying the programme itself was almost obscured. No one else would have recognised it. I prised open the lid. Inside, it was pristine.

As I climbed into the van Doug emerged again and surveyed the mess. 'What about all this?'

I started up the engine and threw him the gloves. 'Thanks.'

'Hey.' He pulled at the door but I had already locked it. I waved the can at him.

'Code Red. Sorry, can't hang around.'

'Bastard. You're fucked, you are.'

It was raining steadily now, battering the roof. The van's perished wipers protested as they dragged themselves across the windscreen. The traffic was almost static. I lit a cigarette. The windows started misting up. I glanced at the sack beside me on the seat. I took out the can. Greer's name was just visible on the label. I traced it with my forefinger. This was something they needed and I had found it. I was indispensable after all. Not that it would make any difference now.

I stared at the label. This was a top story. News would want it asap. No time to make a copy – we'd have to bike them the original. That would be the right thing to do.

I pulled onto the kerb and turned off the wipers. The rain and the condensation cocooned me.

I'd had enough of doing the right thing.

4

The office was hot. The thermostats were down again, and the ceiling fans whirred as if it were summer, flicking the thin leaves of the fat directories that lay open on the cataloguers' desks. Darren intercepted me as I emptied the sack of cans on to a trolley.

'That it?' He plucked the top tin off the stack and examined the label.

'I haven't checked it yet.'

'No time.' He dropped it into a courier's bag and patted down the Velcro flap. 'BBC are screaming for it.' He took off towards reception without another word.

A lid of blue-black cloud was closing over the city. The four clocks on the wall used to give the time round the world: New York, Tokyo and Sydney. Only the London one still worked. It was four p.m. The courier would take about twenty minutes. Another ten for the can to get to a viewing room. Another five to be laced onto a machine and for whoever was there to discover they had been sent the wrong film. I had half an hour.

Despite the smoking ban, the viewing rooms still smelled of ash. I lifted the lid. Two rolls – picture and sound. Not just her face; her voice as well. I lifted the picture spool out of the can. Even though the end was taped, I spread my palm under it in case the centre core dropped out. It could happen with film that hadn't been touched in a long time.

I laid the roll on the far left plate of the Steenbeck and unpeeled the leader. My hands were shaking. I steadied my forearms on the edge of the machine. I put a core on the right-hand plate and taped the end to it, then laced the film through the sprockets. The machine came to life when I flicked on the lamp and the bright light bounced against the black frame that preceded the countdown. I pinched the speed control between a thumb and forefinger and the film started to move. I fast-forwarded through the *Human Face* title sequence. Then the programme caption appeared: *Face of a Terrorist.*

The opening shot showed Greer walking through ruins. The barren landscape offered no shade from the unforgiving sun but she seemed at home in it. She was wrapped in what looked like the same white muslin as when I had last seen her, but her hair was much shorter and her eyes were heavily made up. Although it was only a few years before I'd known her, she looked much younger. My chest tightened. I realised I was holding my breath.

Coming nearer to the camera, she pushed her sunglasses up into her hair. A light breeze lifted a few strands. Her thick mascara and pale lipstick rooted her firmly in another time. A tight shot began with her looking down, as if she was working out what to say. She lifted her eyes slowly to the camera and started to speak. *'Tonight you will hear the voice of Malik. It's the only interview he ever gave, two months before his death.'*

I slowed the machine to a stop, freezing her stare. I lit a forbidden cigarette to steady myself then pushed the control back to Play.

'He was believed to be one of a new generation of fighters whose chosen battlefield is the street, the station, the airport, whose enemy is not an army but ordinary people like you and me. Our meeting took place before the events at Northolt. What he would have had to say about it we will never know.'

Her presentation was the opposite of dramatic, but the way she made the words sound – as if she was thinking them up as she spoke gave her an intensity all her own.

'You won't see his face. It was a condition of the interview. But you will hear his voice.'

A group of assistants passed along the corridor, on their way home. I looked round and watched them through the glass. When I looked back Greer was seated under a tree, her face in profile.

'Could you begin by explaining your aims? Are you any nearer to achieving them?'

I lit another cigarette and looked for something I could use as an ashtray.

'What were the circumstances that set you on this road?'

It took me a moment to realise there was no answer between the two questions. No shot of the interviewee. No Malik.

I stopped the film and rolled it slowly back. The sprockets made a slight click. I let a loop of the film unwind so I could examine it. The picture had been cut and taped. I disengaged the sound and rolled the picture forward in search of the next shot change.

All the shots of Malik had been removed and Greer's questions edited together. The credits came up. Produced and Directed by Philip R. Edgington. The footage counter showed it running at fifteen minutes. Half the film was gone.

The door sprang open. Darren was in the room, leaning over me.

'You taking the piss?'

The BBC would have been on to him by now.

'I told you I hadn't checked it.'

'Fucking arseholes.'

'The cans in the crate were all mixed up. Honor Oak's a bomb site.'

He squinted at the screen.

'Is that it?'

'Someone's already had the shots of Malik out of it.'

He reached across me and flicked the control to Fast Forward, turning all Greer's silky movements into absurd jolting spasms.

'Bollocks.'

He threw the machine into reverse. Inevitably, the film snapped with a loud crack and the broken ends spattered against the machine.

I said nothing and sat, motionless.

'Fucking shite.' He looked at me for a moment then left without another word.

I stared at the blank screen for a while. The office outside had emptied. The sky in the windows was dark.

Every evening I had left the building knowing almost exactly what the next day would be like. I had banked on it, anchored myself to the certainty. Gardening leave. I didn't even have a garden.

I pulled out a loop of film each side of the break, butted the two ends together in the splicer, pulled out a strip of adhesive tape and brought the press down on it. I released it, turned the film over and repeated the process, then re-laced the picture and watched the join run through on the screen at normal play speed.

Each side of the cut were images of Greer. But the shot change seemed too thick, as if there was something in between the two frames. I rolled back the film more slowly this time. An almost white frame separated them. I rolled the join through again even more slowly, until it appeared on the screen, and paused the machine.

I must have stared at it for a full minute. The shot was very under-exposed – a silhouette. Apart from the outline of a nose and a fringe of eyelashes, the face was virtually invisible. But I felt my pulse start to race. I blinked. I looked away, and back. The image matched itself against another that I had filed away. One I hadn't planned on remembering.

I unlaced the picture, pinched the frame between finger and thumb, and marked each side with a Chinagraph pencil arrow. Then I slowly rewound both spools before dropping them back into the can. I held it in my hands, weighing it. Colin would have an opinion about this. But he'd want to know the full story.

The guard on the back exit spotted the can under my arm. I wouldn't normally take a film away. But this hadn't been a normal day. And this wasn't a normal film.

'It's OK. I'm authorised.'

I handed him my ID and he swiped it on the reader.

'Doesn't say that here.'

I laid the can gingerly on the counter and tapped the label.

'Fire risk. It shouldn't be in there.'

'What?'

'See this?' I pointed at the 'R' sticker on the lid. 'Haven't they warned you about nitrate?'

He looked reassuringly blank.

'Any can with this 'R' on should be *refrigerated*. It's a miracle it hasn't gone up like a firework.'

'You can't take it out of here without a clearance docket.'

I leaned closer. 'Have you ever seen a nitrate fire? After the initial explosion, the gas forms into sticky particles that penetrate the skin—'

'You'll have to fill out one of these.' He pulled across a pad of transit forms and began filling in the top copy. I took it from him, completed the boxes and signed. Then I stuffed the can into my backpack and walked out into the night.

5

'Not like you to be late.'

I'd been due two hours ago. 'Got any food? I missed lunch.'

'Thanks to the wonders of microwave technology, we might be able to breathe life into your half of the takeaway.' Colin turned and set off up the hall. The corridor was stacked with boxes of equipment and crates of video cassettes. Piles of technical journals and trays of spare parts jostled for space on each step of the stairs. 'I'm about to have a clear-out.'

'If I had a pound for every time I've heard that.'

I followed him, weaving between a couple of office chairs and another tower of boxes. Loose cables snaked across lino that dated back to when the house was his parents'. He had moved back in after his wife left him.

The kitchen was his main living room. A small TV sat on the dresser, permanently tuned to a news channel. He needed round-the-clock doses of current affairs to survive. The table had been given over to a project. A motorbike engine sat in a washing-up bowl. The entrails of a carburettor were laid out in a drip tray. There was a powerful smell of petrol.

'Don't light up just yet. I'm trying to clear the jets.'

He plunged his hands into a jar of Swarfega and rubbed them together vigorously until the green jelly turned black. Then he rinsed them over a sink full of dirty dishes and pressed a can of lager into my hand.

'Here, drink this.' He sounded like a paramedic at a pile-up.

The table was covered in bike parts and a stack of two-inch tape boxes marked *Confidential.*

'Don't ask. Unless you want to bear the brunt of the full story.' Colin's great redeeming feature was his ability to take the piss out of himself. 'Tikka Masala or Tikka Masala?'

He threw the small stack of takeaway containers into the microwave and stepped out of his overalls. Underneath was a collarless shirt that might well have been his father's. Colin had two uniforms: a boiler suit for working on his cars and bikes, and his white coat, a relic of his Movietone days. The woolly hat went with both. It was hard to get a good look at his face. Under a pronounced brow lurked deep-set eyes. The bags beneath them gave him an expression of permanent gloom. Even though he probably counted me as his best friend, he rarely looked in my direction when he spoke. When he wasn't engrossed in some close-up technical challenge, he preferred to look off into space, rubbing the stubble on his bony face with nicotine-yellow fingers.

Beside the tape boxes was a copy of the *Evening Standard*. NORTHOLT – DEADLY IMPACT was the headline. The picture was a screen grab, the moment when the Land-Rover hit the nose-wheel and the plane was engulfed in flame.

'That down to you?'

I shook my head. I knew he'd want the details. 'It came from Harrop.'

'Bit out of his league. Probably didn't realise what he'd got.' He tutted. 'If he found this one at work he could be in trouble.'

Harrop had a job in an MOD unit that dealt with offices and buildings. It brought him into contact with storerooms and filing cabinets where old footage got put to be forgotten about.

'What did the old fart get for it?'

'I didn't ask.'

Colin sniffed. 'He should have filtered it.' Filtering meant using Colin as a middleman to sell on the film, for which he took a small percentage. 'I'll call him and give him a hard time. Bit of a coup, though, for the first day of the inquiry.' He opened the paper and shook his head. 'Not that it'll make any difference. It's a hopeless cause.'

'How?'

'Trying to get the powers that be to own up – it never happens.'

'Own up to what?'

'You *ever* pay attention to what's happening in the world?'

He rolled his eyes and peered at a photograph of a line of elderly women. NORTHOLT FAMILIES – THEIR DAY IN COURT.

'So what's so hopeless?'

'Do you want the long version or the longer version?'

'I'll take the short.'

He took a deep breath.

'June 1989. An East Mediterranean Airways 737 en route from Tel Aviv to Oslo. Men with beards and guns hold up the crew. The pilot makes an emergency landing at Northolt. Shooting is heard inside. A couple of bodies are dropped onto the tarmac to persuade the ground staff to refuel. Then the plane starts taxiing. No one knows who's in charge in the cockpit. So a have-a-go military cop drives a Land-Rover into the nose wheel. Forty-five dead. Short enough for your attention span?'

'Were all the terrorists killed?'

He nodded. 'Except their leader: the mystery man, *Malik*.' He pronounced the name with a caricature Poirot accent. 'He didn't come for the ride.'

I waited for him to continue.

'So I've got you interested? OK, stop me when you've had enough.'

Colin was in his element now. For him there was no such thing as too much detail. It was what had made him so good at his job.

'Her Majesty's Government decided, in their infinite wisdom, to refuse to give any details of how it happened, pleading national security, etc. Basically it was a cock-up and they kept mum. But these ladies, the widows and mothers of the dead, they want answers.'

'What's the problem with that?'

'The official line's always been that this was a common-or-garden hijacking – hot-heads trying to force Israel to let some of their mates out of pokey. But one of the dead passengers was Erich Zarev.' He raised his eyebrows, waiting to see if I responded.

'Pass.'

He sighed at my ignorance. 'Self-styled terrorist hunter, ex-Mossad colonel. Made a bit of a name for himself busting the financiers and backers – some of them big-deal types with fat chequebooks. Big popular hero in Israel but regarded as a bit of a menace in the West.'

Colin moved his head from side to side, stretching his neck muscles, and prodded the picture of the bereaved families.

'Some people have gone so far as to suggest that this Malik bloke was after Zarev and the powers that be knew – and let it happen.'

'What about Malik?'

'Killed by British Special Forces a few months after. In an ambush in Germany.'

'You're sure?'

He looked pained. 'I wasn't on hand to check his pulse.'

'So what now?'

'At the hearing? Nothing. There'll be a few new bits of paper, declassification of some communiqués and none of us will be any the wiser. But the ladies will have had their day in court and let off a bit of steam. They've got one witness who's on tomorrow, a retired air traffic chappie who thinks he heard some radio exchanges between the hijackers. I'm not holding my breath.' He lit his cigarette and frowned at me. 'Normally you fall asleep at this point.'

I took the film can out of my bag and laid it on the table.

'Ah. Hello.' He grabbed it and put on the glasses that hung on a leather lace round his neck. 'Something excessively pornographic, I hope.' He started to laugh but stopped when he read the label.

He looked up towards me and down again, tapping the 'R' on the lid. 'You know you could be sacked for taking this out?'

'I already have been.'

He didn't seem to hear me. His mouth opened and he took a breath to speak but the microwave pinged. He lunged forward, fished out the containers, and slid them on to a tray. He rummaged in a cutlery drainer and pulled out a couple of spoons.

''Fraid we're fresh out of forks.' He nodded at the can. 'So?'

'I'd like your opinion.'

'It's a crap film. Next.'

Anything remotely personal – whether it was about himself or others – embarrassed him. And his first line of defence was humour, usually inappropriate.

'Something's happened to it.'

He nodded sagely. 'Step into my office.'

Colin's editing bench and Steenbeck occupied the front room. Unlike the rest of the house, it was spotless. Although he hadn't cut a film in it for years, he kept the equipment on standby, capable of being scrambled at a few minutes' notice. He swept the dust covers off with a magician's flourish and hit a green circuit-breaker on the wall. The machine lit up. A pleasant hum came from the fan that cooled the projector light. I took the film out of its tin. 'Shall I?'

He batted me away. 'No sticky fingers near the gear.'

Although we had known each other for over a decade he still liked to address me just as he had on my first day at work with him.

'Give.' I handed him the can. He lifted out the spools and laced them up. 'I'll drive.'

He pulled a cord that switched off the overhead bulb. The window blinds striped us with the orange glow from the street-light. He pulled up a stool and ran the film forward, pausing on the *Human Face* titles.

'Launched November 1963, axed 1994. In its heyday it got an audience of eight million. Scoop every week. Mrs Lee Harvey Oswald, Christine Keeler, My Lai, Simon Wiesenthal, Porton Down, Anthony Blunt, the Krays, Myra Hindley, the

Animal Liberation Front, Radovan Karadzic. Impressed?'

'Always.'

He grinned. This was Colin in his element. Opportunities to show off his encyclopedic knowledge were rare. He spooled on to the programme caption, *Face of a Terrorist*.

'Interesting day to be watching this one.'

'You remember it?'

'Don't you?' Then he rolled his eyes. 'No, you wouldn't. You'd have been in short trousers studying the art of masturbation.'

'Actually I was sixteen.'

'You were a late developer.' He turned away and emptied his food onto the dish.

'Go on then.'

'First ever on-screen interview with a terrorist. Not so much pushing the envelope as ripping it wide open. Huge stink, questions in the House. Transmission postponed—' He clapped his hands against his face and screwed up his eyes as he tried to recall the detail. 'OK, well more times than I can remember, which merely added to its notoriety. BAFTA for Best Documentary. Director: Phil Edgington.'

He let out a long sigh. Any award dismayed him. All he could see were the faults and imperfections. And underneath lurked his own professional jealousy.

'Interesting sequence of events. They filmed him before Northolt. Once Malik had been named as the culprit; that put the kibosh on transmission. But after he was killed the justification for banning the film went away. The Network bowed to pressure and showed it. Got record ratings. And Edgington took over as editor. Unimaginable today.'

'Why?'

He gave me one of his withering looks. 'A leftie like him? Forget it.'

He reached across and ran the film on. As soon as he saw Greer's face he let out his tuneless whistle – then checked himself. I suddenly felt uncomfortable watching with him. We had never discussed her.

'Look at this.' I leaned over and fast-forwarded to where the first shots of Malik should have been. Greer's head jerked like a demented puppet as the jump cuts ran through the gate. 'It's the same all the way through. Malik's been completely cut out. But there's this ...' I went forward again until I spotted my Chinagraph pencil marks and slowed the film to a halt. On one side of the single shot was a close-up of Greer. On the other, a barren landscape. The ghostly image was in between.

'Flash frame?'

I looked at him, waiting for an explanation.

'Oh no. Technically speaking ...' He cleared his throat and started constructing a roll-up. Any Colin sentence that began like this meant a lecture was about to follow. 'A true flash frame is when the motor of a camera stops before the shutter has closed, and you get a white frame because the light has burned out any image on the stationary film.' He paused while he applied the finishing touches to the cigarette. 'But like everything in life, the term's misused. When editors want to separate two shots, they insert a frame of something else, of white or black, contrasting with the shots before and after – whatever was hanging around in the trim bin – to act as a kind of subliminal punctuation. That's called a flash frame as well. It's a *cinéma-vérité* fad. Load of bollocks, in my humble opinion.' He rolled the shot through the gate again. Malik's silhouette flashed up on the screen. 'This isn't a flash frame. This is a frame of the interview.'

Usually these were my favourite times with Colin, when some query of mine tapped into his vast knowledge of the most arcane detail. Where one explanation would do, he would offer three. He scooped up some of his meal and waved a spoon in the air.

'This was how they shot him.'

I stared at him. He groaned at my confusion.

'With the fucking camera. Your man here insisted on being in silhouette. In-ter-na-tion-al terr-or-ist. Get it? Probably didn't want his gob all over the television.'

'But we can see his face.'

Colin closed his eyes. 'Surely you, with your glorious track record of filming tourists broiling on beaches, should know it'd be damn near impossible to film someone in actual silhouette when they're sitting under the fucking Mediterranean sun. Poor old cameraman would just have to do his best and they'd blot out his features properly in the final print onto tape.' He waved the can in front of my face.

'This came out of a cutting room. It's not the final version.'

'OK, just checking.' Colin rewound the film and went over each join again. Greer's image bounced across the screen. 'Whoever went to all the trouble of lifting out the shots of this bloke did a very good job. Almost.'

I tapped the screen. 'How can I be sure this face belongs in this film? Could he have been cut in from something else?'

'Blimey, I thought I was the pedantic one!'

'I need to be sure.'

'OK, OK. Have patience.' He unlaced the film to examine it more closely. 'The same print crosses the shot change to the landscape shot, so it's part of the original film. The negative of this chap was definitely joined before this copy was printed. A lab might be able to confirm that.' He looked at me over his glasses. 'Are we getting somewhere?'

I took a deep breath. 'Have you ever seen anything like this before – where a whole person has been cut out of a film?'

His eyes widened with mock surprise.

'Sure. Wankers of all kinds come along and fuck about with precious prints like they're a load of rushes, as you should well know. Not the slightest regard for the value of anything. All that's weird is that every shot has been taken out and it seems to have been done with some care. Except they missed this one frame.'

'Could it have been some kind of censoring?'

He waved the question away. 'Waste of effort. Easier to junk the whole film.'

'Well, it was – sort of. This was one of the Net Docs skip salvages.'

In the mid-Nineties the Network tried to get its franchise renewed. The documentary department was disbanded. No one wanted to be left with anything sensitive. There was a wholesale clearout of the cutting rooms – entire cupboards were heaved into skips without even being emptied. Only thanks to one of the bin men had this survived.

He relaced the film. 'Any other copies?'

'No.'

'Doesn't make sense. Originals from a landmark series like *Human Face* should have been preserved.'

'Not this one.'

We both stared into the screen. I felt a dull shake somewhere in my body, like an engine idling.

'So.' Colin emptied his can of lager and cracked open another. 'Before I self-combust with anticipation, what's the big deal about this one frame?'

I got up and walked over to the window. A steady drizzle was falling. A couple kissed as they passed under the orange streetlight. I turned back to the screen. The image was hard to see. But enough of his features were there. The arch of the eyebrows, the eyelids in their semi-somnolent position. The nose, with a shallow cleavage in its tip. The small, triangular scar under his left eye. Younger, his hair still black. Colin frowned at me. 'You all right?'

'Alliance has taken over. They've given me the push.'

'Welcome to the club.' He gave me a congratulatory pat on the back and gestured towards the tottering piles in the hall. 'Plenty to do here, if you need a bit of distraction.' He drummed his fingers. 'Come on. Put me out of my misery.'

We had an unspoken agreement that we didn't talk about each other's pasts.

'In 1994, in Sri Lanka, I interviewed an arms dealer.' I turned away and lit another cigarette. All my muscles were taut and aching.

'And?'

I pointed at the face on the screen. 'This man, Malik, looks just like him.'

'Rammal?'

I stared at him. 'How the fuck do you know his name?'

He took off his hat and scratched this scalp. 'From when we vetted you.'

I could feel my face heating up. 'You never said anything about a vetting.'

'It was standard practice – in the days when Metro had any standards. You had this exotic CV with a bit of hole in it. One minute you're an up-and-coming TV director, drafted on to a prestigious documentary series. Then all of a sudden you're a jobseeker wanting to be an archive assistant. A bit fishy, you have to admit.'

I stubbed out my cigarette and lit another. 'Go on.'

'I got hold of your Network personnel file. There was a reference to an Overseas Incident Report, drafted by the Foreign Office. *Details withheld*. That got me curious. Someone in the FO's archives owed me a favour. He slipped me a copy. There wasn't much to it. The name was just one of those slivers of information that stick in the mind.'

'What else did it say?'

'That you had a mishap.'He turned away and busied himself with a roll-up. 'Well, more than a mishap. You saw some people blown up.' He tried to look like he was absorbed, smoothing the narrow, dart-like cigarette. This was uncharted territory for us and he knew it.

'And?'

'The gist was that you'd set up a meeting for this Rammal chappie and your reporter.' Her image was still on the screen. He nodded towards it so he wouldn't have to say her name. 'You had pursued this bloke with a view to making him the subject of a documentary you'd provisionally called *Face of the Arms Dealer*. You were left with concussion, some memory loss, broken collar bone, sternum and left tibia.'

'Is there anything you forget?'

'No, unfortunately.' He closed his eyes. 'Potter laid it all at your door. That fair?'

I tried ignoring the question, but he wasn't going to let me.

'You set up the meeting?'

It's all arranged ... There's a car waiting.

The image of Anita came and went.

'I'm not sure about that. There's a few bits I still don't remember.'

We stared at the screen in silence. He'd crossed the line now.

'Can I ask something?'

I shrugged.

'Your CV said you were a director on *Destination*, which I recall was an entirely trivial holiday programme. What were you doing chasing arms dealers for *Human Face* all of a sudden?'

'They needed someone to fill in.'

'Lucky break.'

'Seemed like it, at the time.'

'You weren't exactly qualified. Couldn't they have got someone more experienced?'

These were questions I'd never asked. 'Perhaps they realised I was gifted.'

'Perhaps they were desperate.'

'Fuck off.' I pointed at the screen. 'Can we get back to this?'

He put his glasses on and started to make another cigarette. 'Malik dies in 'eighty-nine, then resurfaces as Rammal in 'ninety-four ...' He stroked the creases out of the roll-up, his lips pursed. 'Well, you did have a jolly good bang on the head.'

He patted his pockets for his lighter. 'Did they send you in to track him down?'

I shook my head.

'What was the story then?'

'There wasn't one. I had to find it.'

He blew out through pursed lips and picked up the film can. He was unstoppable now. Any caution he might have felt had been overwhelmed by his virulent strain of curiosity. He rubbed the label on the can with a surgical wipe. 'Edgington was in charge?'

I nodded. 'He sent me.'

He waved at an almost invisible image on the screen. 'And who found your man? Did she?'

I got up and moved around the room. All my muscles had tensed, as if I was preparing to defend myself. It was stupid of me to have imagined I could get away with just asking Colin about the flash frame.

'No. I did. It was nothing to do with her.' I had never avoided taking responsibility for finding Rammal. I wasn't about to start making excuses now.

'But you didn't get as far as filming him.'

'Actually, I did.'

'Without her? That was a bit out of order.'

'She was ill. I was afraid I'd lose him if I waited.'

'Ah, using your initiative. What happened to the tapes?'

My stomach lurched again. 'Stolen.'

He snorted. 'Careless. So, nothing to verify your claim. What happened when they met?'

I shook my head. 'I wasn't there.'

'So you never saw them together?'

'Am I on trial here?'

'Sorry if this is difficult, but if you had, then presumably you would have remembered whether they recognised each other.'

He made it sound so obvious. I sat down heavily. It was a long time since I had thought about what might have taken place, what happened when Greer got to the boat. I'd made a decision to put it all behind me. Nothing could be gained from going over it. Whenever I let myself imagine those last moments, a shooting pain sliced across my chest. I saw my reflection in the blank screen of one of the other viewing machines. *You look like shit.*

'Am I going to have to throw this away?'

He pointed at the untouched takeaway. No wonder I felt strange. I hadn't eaten since breakfast. I reached for another can of lager. I should have left this film where it was and walked out of Metro without a backward glance. Every question Colin asked was an indication of how fragile my grasp was of what had happened. I felt stupid and defeated.

'What would you do?'

He frowned at the question. 'What d'you mean?'

'If you were me.'

He looked off into the distance. His cigarette flared briefly. 'I'd let it go.'

'What does that mean?'

'It's a long time ago.' He took a long drag and picked flecks of tobacco off his bottom lip, which he studied. 'Leave it. Move on.'

'Why?'

'You take the lid off this, you'll never get it back on, take it from me. There's nothing to be gained from going over the past.'

A fug of smoke hung around him. He continued to examine the tips of his fingers but his expression was distant. His wife had left him a long time ago. Instead of dwelling on it, he had erased the whole experience from his consciousness. He had moved back in to his family home, and walled himself in with the things he loved, the undemanding bits of kit he'd acquired, his own archive.

'So you don't believe me?'

'Whether I do or not isn't the point. You've got no evidence. And that's probably just as well.' He glanced at me briefly and sighed. 'If you're actually right, but the official line is that your Malik chappie died in 'eighty-nine,' he stubbed his cigarette out in the film can, 'then I'd imagine suggesting otherwise could make you rather unpopular.' He put the machine into rewind.

'I'd keep your head down if I were you. Come and give me a hand round here.' He chuckled to himself. 'Remember *Paths to Conflict*? What a mess it was in? All we had was about a quarter of the paperwork and a crate full of trims and roughs. You looked at it and said, "Give me a month," and you had the whole lot sorted – probably better than it was before.'

'So? It was just a version. I did what I could.'

'You went about it like your life depended on it. Your trouble is you like things to be in order, neat and tidy. No loose ends. Don't take this on.'

An emergency vehicle sped past, its sirens wailing.

He pursed his lips and looked at me over his glasses again, shaking his head. 'I can see I'm not getting through.'

I lit yet another cigarette.

'Any how, they won't let you get near.'

'Who?'

He gave me another weary look. 'The powers that be, of course.'

It was one of his favourite phrases. Whether he was talking about the government or the Human Resources department of Metro, the 'powers that be' were the forces that had conspired against him, dragged him down. All his life he had found himself at odds with authority.

He sighed heavily and returned to the film on the Steenbeck, ran it foward again. He examined one of the joins where a shot had been lifted out, his face screwed up in concentration.

'The joining tape's pretty stiff. Not standard stuff. Do you want me to identify it? At least I might be able to date when this chap was cut out.'

For all his caution, he couldn't resist a technical mystery. Even if I'd said no, he would probably have done it anyway.

'Pay attention, boy, and you might yet learn something.' He unlaced the film and the face disappeared from the screen. He held it up at the cut I had fixed earlier and tore it open. 'See? Modern tape. Thin. Pliable. Almost invisible.' Then he attacked one of the joins where an edit had been made. 'Now this. Look, thicker than your granny's toenails ...' He turned the Anglepoise light towards him and held up the exposed half of the old tape. He frowned. 'It's gone green. Most unusual ...' He stared into space for a second. 'Can I hang on to this for a day or two?'

The spell had been broken now. Leaving the film with him hadn't been part of my plan, but I didn't have a better one.

It was late. I picked up my bag and started to reach for my jacket. But something was replaying itself in my head.

'What's up?'

The meeting with Mr Rammal. It's all arranged. Anita's words from that morning.

'In that report, did it definitely say *I* arranged the meeting on the boat?'

6

I caught the last tube home. The carriage was empty. My reflection stared back at me from the window, nodding to the rhythm of the carriage. The beard made me look older than I was. I'd grown it as a disguise. But from what?

When I'd woken up in hospital in Sri Lanka I hadn't even known who I was. Some things were still in sharp focus; others fogged, or just sounds without pictures. The young doctor who treated me tried to be encouraging.

'Not only have you experienced head injury, you've also witnessed a traumatic event.' A Tamil who had treated victims of the civil war, Dr Sivalingham knew what he was talking about. 'The unfortunate experience is seared into your brain. And because of the degree of impact it may overshadow other memories. Your mind is in shock. But you are a young chap. You will get better, but it will take time and patience – and determination.'

Back in England, I was sent to a special unit devoted to memory loss. My therapist began by asking hundreds of questions about the trip. I had to write down anything I recalled on a separate Post-It note, which I stuck on the wall of my room. They made a formless yellow jumble.

'What do you do when you edit a film? How do you start?' she'd asked me.

This much I could remember. 'It's called a paper edit. You have a shot list of all the filmed material, and transcripts of all the interviews. You literally cut and paste together the pieces you think are going to form a coherent story.'

'OK, so do the same with what you remember. Think of it as a film you're editing but haven't got all the material for. Put what you do recall in chronological order and see if it helps you remember what fills the gaps. Each time something comes back, add another yellow sticky.'

I started putting them in what seemed like the right order, and a few things jumped miraculously back into focus. But that just led to more pain. The twenty-four hours leading up to the explosion came back all too clearly. The days before were in pieces, as if they'd been smashed.

Interviewing Rammal was a blur. The days with Anita, before Greer appeared, were beyond reach. But I decided that I could live with that. I'd reconstructed a version of events that seemed to make enough sense. In any case these memories belonged to a part of my life that was over. And I'd told myself that perhaps they were better left that way. What I had was a story that would do. Enough of one to get me back on to my feet ready to face the world. But when I got out there, whatever had driven me before was gone. I wanted shelter, obscurity, a routine that filled the day with distractions.

I nearly missed my station. A chill wind knifed down the escalator as I jogged up to the surface. Outside, the low-flying cloud pressed down on the shiny, wet streets. I stopped at a fish and chip shop. The last edition of the *Evening Standard* carried more fuzzy pictures from the hijack film. Metro would do well out of this. SHOCKING FOOTAGE OF NORTHOLT UNEARTHED BY LONDON ARCHIVE ...

Ice coated the steps up to my flat and I nearly lost my footing. I shut the door against the gusting wind. It was a relief to be home.

Once I had been addicted to foreign travel. Now, finding myself anywhere but here at the end of a day seemed out of the question. At least I wouldn't be going to Dresden. I pulled off my gloves and scarf and folded them into the drawer of the hall table. I poured myself a Scotch, unwrapped the fish and chips and put them on a plate. I set a place for myself: knife, fork, napkin, vinegar, salt cellar. I wasn't going to slip into the same habits as Colin.

A wind-blown branch tapped the window, as if trying to get my attention. I closed the curtains to shut out the night. The orange glow of the table lamp gave the illusion of warmth. I ate slowly, sipping the Scotch.

I had used the insurance money from the Network as a down payment on the flat. It was a small place but it had a large cellar, which the estate agent said had 'great potential'. 'Handy for storing stuff you don't want to be staring at.'

When I moved in I made sure there was no visible evidence of my Network days. I didn't even own a TV any more. The books on the shelves were from my student days: history and politics, some first-edition James Bonds I'd started to collect. A huge tome, *Film Century*, which a girlfriend had given me, was still in its cellophane.

The only clue was the shelf of guides to each of the places I had filmed. But they were also my cover. If anyone I invited back got curious about where I'd been before Metro, I'd just say I'd been travelling.

I hoped the meal and the Scotch would calm me down. I sat for a while over the empty plate, then moved to the sink and washed up. I was tired but couldn't imagine sleeping, so I poured myself another drink, made a coffee and sat on the sofa. I put on the radio, but the late-night jazz seemed like an interruption so I snapped it off again. I took another cigarette and watched the wisps of smoke twitch and swirl to the invisible movements of the air around me. The room seemed to be full of questions.

Maybe Colin was right: I should just let it all go. What did I have to gain? I had no proof of anything. Just a memory of a face. I took off my shoes and sat on the edge of the bed for a while, flattening the creases in the carpet with my foot.

7

Around three a.m., I awoke to the face of a full moon at the bedroom window. The door of an ancient phone box in the street gave a low squeal as it swung in the wind. My mouth was dry and my heart and head were pounding. I had drunk more than usual.

I roamed the flat. Despite the cold, I opened the doors onto the patio to clear the lingering smell of smoke and whisky. There was no going back to sleep now.

I wrenched open the hatch under the stairs and shifted a guitar case, an exercise bike and several boxes of childhood annuals and magazines I had been unable to part with. The trapdoor beneath them was almost too small for an adult. I eased myself through it and switched on my torch. The air around me smelled of mould and damp wood.

The cellar stretched under the now defunct pub next door, which the flat had once been part of. I concentrated the beam on a small stack of old suitcases. I had to stoop right down to reach into the dark space behind them, to where I'd given the Air Lanka bag a final shove to put it out of reach.

I gave it a once-over with a duster and carried it back up the stairs and to the sofa. The zip was stiff and dull but it opened. Inside was a little Olympus pocket camera, corroded on its leading edges and with a sharp dent in the lens cover. There was also a small plain manila wallet stamped, *Witjerwarra Chemist. 310 Galle Road, Colombo 7. Enjoy your pictures.* It was badly water damaged.

I poured myself the remains of the Scotch and moved to the table. I took the stack of prints out of the envelope. Some of them were fused together. The top one was of a pretty

Air Lanka hostess I'd promised dinner to when I got back to London. Colombo from the air, grey under low cloud. A throng of children crowding round, hands outstretched, unsmiling faces engaged in the serious business of extracting cash from new arrivals still too polite to shoo them away. An antique Morris Minor taxi with its meter bolted to the bonnet, to maximise precious interior space. Then the Majestic Hotel at night, magnificent in floodlight, and a Hindu temple, painted in garish shades. Standing in the foreground was Anita, dressed in a crisp white blouse, clipboard like a shield protecting her bosom. Her huge dark eyes made her look so young.

There was one that she must have taken: Bernard Hinde, from the British Consulate, his hands on the shoulders of his young Singalese houseboy. The sequence was coming back to me. There were several shots of ruins, buildings razed in the anti-Tamil riots that were the pretext for our film. Several more were of destroyed shops and the charred carcass of a bus. Then the last shot. Anita again, standing against an ornate balcony, picked out by the evening sun against the backdrop of dark foliage. She looked quite different, dressed in a sari, her eyes edged with kohl. I shoved it quickly back in the stack and swallowed the rest of my Scotch.

I picked up the camera and examined the dent that had crushed the viewfinder. The glass was crazed and dull, its iris jammed. Salt water had eaten at the exposure button. The needle on the shot counter stood at thirty-three. Blood rushed into my cheeks. I tried the rewind. It resisted. There was still a film inside.

It was five a.m. It was raining and the streetlamps cast orange puddles of wet light. It was weeks since I'd used my ancient Volvo. The tax disc was out of date. The smell of damp leather was almost comforting. I pulled the choke right out and pumped the accelerator, dusting condensation off the windscreen with the back of one hand as I turned the ignition with the other. Just as the starter was about to give up the engine caught and

I gunned it hard to resuscitate the battery. The rev counter needle arced wildly.

The streets were empty except for a few lorries and the odd newspaper van. After Sri Lanka, I had briefly taken a night job in one of the few remaining film labs so I could hibernate during the day. Farrar's in Clerkenwell still stayed open round the clock. I handed over my single roll. The processor grimaced at the corrosion on the case.

'This is old stock. And the cassette's buggered.'

'It's from 1994. Can you give it a go?'

He clenched his lips. 'I guess we'll be able to drag something out of it. How soon do you want it?'

'I'll wait.'

'Contacts?'

'Prints. Ten by eight.'

'Be ready at seven.' His eyes flicked towards me. 'The caff by the bridge is open.'

A gang of night-bus drivers were having a post-shift breakfast. They fell silent for a moment as I came in. I ordered a bacon sandwich and a tea.

'You want?' The man behind the counter held a bottle of brandy over my mug. I shook my head. On the front page of *The Sun* was a face in silhouette with a question mark over it. Underneath was the headline, KILLER WITH NO FACE.

> *The sick terrorist behind the Northolt hijack in 1989 has no face – that's official. Government spokesmen said yesterday that there's no known photograph of 'Malik', who masterminded the atrocity.*

It was still dark when I returned.

The processor slid a stiff envelope across the counter and shook his head. 'This film's been in water. Lot of fogging. Have a look.' He started to open the tube.

I held up my hand. 'I'll take your word for it.'

He shrugged. 'Whatever.'

Back in the car I put on the interior light and felt inside the envelope. The sachet of negatives fell out and I tweezered my thumb and finger inside until I felt the prints.

The camera had been in my pocket when I was thrown into the sea by the blast from the cruiser. All the shots were grey and fogged. I fished a torch out of the glove compartment to get a better look. My hands were shaking again so I braced them against the steering wheel. The horn blasted briefly.

Only in the last three shots, the ones nearest the centre of the spool, were parts of the images undamaged. Number thirty-one just showed a brow and hairline, thirty-two, the lapel of his stone-coloured cotton suit. Thirty-three, the tip of Rammal's nose and his left eye, with its drooping lid and triangular scar. Just as I had remembered. And just as in the one frame of Malik.

It was getting light. On any other day I would have been getting ready for work. I slid the prints back into the envelope knocking the sun visor down as I did so.

My heart was pounding so hard I thought it would punch a hole in my chest. I caught sight of myself in the mirror and shared a small smile with my reflection. *At least your memory isn't completely fucked.*

I drove home as fast as the traffic would allow and rang directory enquiries for the Foreign Office switchboard.

8

Eventually an operator answered.

'Do you have a Bernard Hinde here in London?'

There was silence. I cleared my throat and tried to sound alert. I could hear a keyboard being punched.

'Mr Hinde's office.'

I summoned up an official voice. 'Is he there? It's Nick Roker.'

'Concerning?'

'Um … tell him Sri Lanka.'

The phone played some Vivaldi at me.

'Yes, who is this?' The tone was sharp, impatient.

'Bernard, it's Nick. Nick Roker – from Sri Lanka.'

I couldn't think of a better way of phrasing it. There was a pause. I heard a few asthmatic breaths. Then the phone went dead. At least I knew he was in.

The Foreign Office reception area was heavily fortified. Two middle-aged women sat behind a grille that reached to the ceiling. One wore half glasses. A pair of guards waved their wands over visitors and X-rayed their bags. The receptionist caught sight of the envelope in my hand. 'Packages to the Post room, on the left.'

I passed it across the counter. 'For Mr Hinde.'

The receptionist held it at arm's length. Under *Photographs: Do Not Bend*, I had written: *To be opened only by the addressee. Signature required.*

'It's for his immediate attention.'

'I'm afraid Mr Hinde has rather a lot for his immediate attention.'

'I can wait.'

'Take a seat.'

She dialled his office. One of the guards X-rayed the envelope then set off upstairs with it.

'Could be a while.'

'I don't mind.'

The last time I'd seen Bernard he was standing at the foot of my hospital bed in Colombo with a look of weary disgust. He was a junior in the British Consulate and the only person in Sri Lanka I ever saw wearing a tie. I remember a wave of relief because I recognised him, the first indication then that my memory hadn't completely gone. He didn't speak. Perhaps he didn't realise I was conscious.

The previous time was on my first day in Sri Lanka, at Anita's insistence. She had spoken of him in such glowing terms that I had assumed there was something between them.

We waited for him on his veranda in Cinnamon Gardens, Colombo's smartest district. I had expected a master-race type with a rowing-blue physique packed into a tight shirt, so it took a moment for me to adjust to a small man swathed in a kimono. Only a childishly smooth complexion gave away his age. His round shoulders and slightly bosomy chest reminded me of a teacher I had once got on the wrong side of. His eyes moved around restlessly, as if checking the exits.

He gave me a soft hand that could never have clasped an oar and murmured a drink order at the boy who hovered behind his chair. He turned to me, blinking rapidly. 'I thought about television myself, you know, but my father wouldn't have it. "Rocky road, son." Those were his words.'

Sri Lanka was his first posting.

I watched the boy disappear into the house.

'How much are you monitoring the war?'

'Yikes ... Well, we wouldn't call it a war exactly, would we, Anita?'

She maintained her smile, as if she was going to agree, regardless of what he said.

'Terrorist acts. That's all they are. Atrocities. We don't dignify them with the word *war*. Take a look around you. Where's the *war*? It's you media people who've hyped it. As I understand it, you're here to make a film about the peace process.'

'Well, you can't have a peace process without a war.'

Anita looked away while he launched into a speech about how our visas and filming permit, which he gave himself credit for arranging, precluded any contact with 'enemies of the state' and sat back, basking in his own satisfaction. At that point, the boy returned with a tray of drinks and small things in saucers to eat. Bernard ruffled his hair as he bent to serve him and patted his bottom to send him away.

What irritated me most about Bernard was that what he said was true. There were no visible signs of the civil war in Colombo – and nothing to film.

Big Ben struck ten. Forty minutes had passed since my package had gone upstairs. My first thought had been to put in the photos of Rammal, but then it occurred to me that they might mean nothing to Bernard. And if they did mean something to him, I would probably never see them again. Then I had another idea.

A woman with Margaret Thatcher hair appeared beside the receptionist and glared at me.

'Could you come through, please?'

The guard frisked me and looked inside the Air Lanka bag. He rattled it and turned it upside down. Something small fell out and skidded across the floor under the X-ray desk. Everyone froze for a moment.

'Sorry about that, sir,' the guard said, without meaning it. He gave a small groan as he stooped to peer into the shadow beneath the desk.

'Aha.'

I couldn't see what it was until he held it under my nose.

'Thank you.'

It was Greer's lighter. The chrome was corroded but the jade was intact. I put it in my pocket. The assistant pursed her lips and motioned me to follow. We climbed a broad staircase with a marble banister. She shook her head in a sort of shiver.

'I hope this won't take long; he's very rushed today.'

'I know how it is.'

She gave me a doubtful look. We climbed on in silence to a long wide hall with a narrow strip of carpet.

'Go through.'

I stepped into a huge office. Everything was twice the normal size: a vast Chesterfield, two wing-backed chairs and a great plateau of a coffee table. On the desk was a family portrait: a woman in pearls and two children in purple private-school uniform. Bernard had his back to me. He was leaning against a mantelpiece. Red braces were stretched across his fleshy back. He had my envelope and the photograph – of himself with his houseboy – in his hand. He didn't look up.

'Close the doors, would you?'

I pushed them to.

He wheeled round. 'Is this some sort of blackmail?'

Except for the almost total absence of hair, he looked exactly as I remembered him. He had finally reached the age of his physique. He blinked rapidly and his cheeks wobbled. He was pink with rage.

'It was the only way I could think of getting in to see you.'

He didn't react.

'You hung up on me.'

He gestured at my beard. 'Travelling incognito?'

He looked away again.

'Did you have any idea of the trouble you caused us? Aside from the fact that I was nearly recalled, you provoked a major diplomatic incident – which we only just put a lid on.'

He moved away from the fireplace.

'Your permits specifically forbade any fraternisation with terrorists or their associates. I believe I reminded you of that, myself.' He was getting into his stride now, heading for some moral high ground. He had forgotton the photographs for a moment. 'I was completely mystified about what you were trying to achieve. I did a bit of digging afterwards and came to the conclusion that this filming jape was no more than your reporter's excuse for a holiday, and you were sent in after her to make it look like there was a real job to do.' He shook his head with theatrical amazement. 'You media people have no regard for the damage you do. It's just a game to you. I'll tell you something else. When the Network tried to renew its franchise we made jolly sure our conclusions about your behaviour didn't go unheard.'

He had worked up a head of indignation. I imagined it was his default mode.

I felt compelled to come to Greer's defence. 'She was a very diligent journalist.'

He snorted. 'Not my impression.'

I moved further into the room. The coal in the fire shifted and a cloud of sparks disappeared up the chimney. 'I need some information.'

He raised his eyebrows.

'Some of it didn't come back.' I tapped my head.

'What were you planning to do with … this?' He looked down at the photo again. The boy would be in his thirties now. 'It proves absolutely nothing, you know.'

He moved towards his desk, slipped the photograph back into its envelope and dropped it in a drawer.

'I'll do you a swap for the negative.'

He looked away.

'I just want to lay it all to rest. Tie up the loose ends.'

'You know you're jolly lucky to be alive, don't you?'

I didn't feel lucky.

'Those local doctors really put themselves out for you.'

An intercom buzzed on his desk. He ignored it.

'I'd like some background on Rammal.'

The name didn't register.

'The arms dealer – who got blown up.'

'Out of the question. That would all be classified.'

I let my eyes fall on the desk where he'd put the photograph.

He flushed. 'What you're doing – it's quite illegal.'

The door opened and his assistant appeared. She tapped her watch.

'In a *minute*, Muriel.'

The door closed again. He stared at me for some time with a mixture of pity and disgust. I leaned against a chair. There was no reason for me to hurry. He sighed heavily.

'How shall I find you?'

I wrote my mobile number on a pad on his desk.

'If that's all, I'd like to get on with my day.'

I started to leave. At the door I paused.

'Anita Jayarajah.'

'Well?'

'Do you know what happened to her?'

For the first time, he looked me full in the eye then turned back to the fire. 'I dread to think.'

9

There was a different guard on Metro's reception. He didn't look at my ID, but when I swiped it the barrier refused to open.

'A minute, please. I call.'

Suzette let herself through the glass gate and stood in front of me. She looked drained. Sacking people had taken its toll. She diverted me away from the turnstile towards a side room and closed the door. Under her arm was a thick wad of files and papers, which she unloaded onto the top of a filing cabinet.

'I came for my things?'

She leaned wearily against a trolley. 'I don't want to make things difficult after all you've done here, but it seems you have removed some film.' I didn't respond. She sighed. 'You know the regulations better than I do. We come down very hard on rule-breaking.'

'Darren bought the Northolt crash film – from a public servant. What happened to *that* rule?'

'As it happens, Darren is at the Northolt inquiry, screening the footage. Actually, we have been highly praised for discovering it.'

She gave me a thin smile and slapped an official-looking fax down in front of me. The rest of the files toppled off the filing cabinet.

'Fucking hell.'

I bent to help gather them up. My own file was among them.

'Nick, understand this,' she lowered her voice, 'Alliance is in charge. Their MD is here right now, going through everything. I shouldn't even be talking to you. In fact, I'll be jolly lucky if

I'm still here in a month's time. They will take any opportunity to get out of paying anyone redundancy. Return what's gone and I'll see what I can do. Otherwise—' Her phone buzzed. 'Shit. Tell them to wait. I'm coming now. Yes, now!'

She marched out of the room. I was alone. Her stack of files was still there. I flipped open mine. It was full of overtime forms. In the back was the Foreign Office Report Colin had mentioned. It was a single sheet, very creased. I imagined it being passed to Colin over a drink. I scanned the text.

... a meeting between the party known as 'Rammal' and the Network reporter Greer Harmon arranged by Nick Roker ...

I folded it up and stuffed it inside my combat jacket – along with the Northolt fax. Suzette reappeared and scooped up the files.

'You have to go. As things stand, you will be dismissed without benefits. Your things will be sent to you. Please hand in your pass at the desk.'

She paused. 'I'm very sorry. You've done good work here. But we all have to face up to realities some time or other.'

She turned and walked back through the barrier. I looked at the guard. He was engrossed in trying to find an extension number for a visitor. I walked past him and out of Metro for the last time.

In the street I took out the report and read it again: *arranged by Nick Roker*. I stared at the traffic.

The Northolt inquiry was in an old assembly hall next to the Law Courts. The entrance was up a side street off the Strand. The road had been blocked off. The coach I had seen the day before took up most of the road, along with two police Transits.

'Public Gallery's full.' The policewoman spoke without looking at me.

I produced my Metro card and put on a weary expression.

'Technical support: the film screening.'

I waved the fax to Metro about screening the Northolt film.

She glanced at me and back at the fax, then gestured towards a door with her chin. 'See them at reception.'

'Thank you.'

Inside was a makeshift reception desk. Several people were crowded round it. I kept my ID in my hand and stepped through a security scanner. Everything looked temporary, as if the inquiry wasn't expected to last long. At the other end of the reception area was a series of signs; one pointing upstairs said Public Gallery.

I climbed some stairs and stepped into a narrow area of wooden benches. It was full of spectators; there was barely room to stand. I could just see down into the main area of the hall. There was a long U-shaped table covered in green baize. At its head, in a tall chair, was the presiding judge; a row of men and women sat on either side, each with several ring binders piled in front of them.

The group of elderly women I had seen on the coach the day before sat close by. Two were in wheelchairs. Their faces were blank, as if years of grieving and campaigning had fixed their expressions in a state of permanent resignation. Each one held a small, framed photograph in her lap, a portrait of a loved one who had died in the plane.

An old man and a younger woman sat at a smaller table, facing the judge.

'If you don't mind, sir,' said the woman, 'could the question be repeated?'

The judge gestured at the barrister, who adjusted his gown before continuing.

'I am just trying to clear up the confusion about your whereabouts, Mr Stevens. You were present in the control tower. Is that right?'

Stevens waved a finger in the air. 'In the control tower. That's where I heard it. I got a fix on their frequency. All in Arabic. I knew it from the war, you see. It was him, telling them to get him.'

The barrister nodded eagerly. 'Get who, exactly?'

The old man hesitated. 'The Jewish fella.'

'Could you clarify, Mr Stevens? Most of the passengers were from Israel.'

'It's all in my statement. From the time.'

The barrister looked at the judge and back to Stevens.

'Yes, I do understand that, but since there is no record of that statement, we are asking if you can recall what you overheard. Who was speaking to the men on board?'

One of the wheelchair-bound mothers gave an audible sigh and shook her head. Another clutched her hand and started whispering. The judge looked up at her sharply.

The barrister's associate got up and whispered in his ear. I had seen her picture in the paper: Esther Carr, the spokeswoman for the Northolt Families.

'Perhaps I might come at this from another angle, Mr Stevens,' the barrister continued. 'How were you able to identify exactly who was speaking?'

Stevens rubbed his mouth.

'The bloke they said did it ... it was him all right. I heard him telling them to get the Jewish bloke.'

No one spoke.

Stevens looked round. Esther Carr smiled at him encouragingly, nodding at him, willing him to keep going. 'Arabic. With an American accent.'

The judge cleared his throat and took off his glasses.

'Ms Carr, your clients have campaigned very hard for this inquiry. But it may be necessary for you and those representing the next of kin to review the evidence you are bringing before us and consider if it is serving your best interests. I have no doubt that Mr Stevens means well.' The judge smiled thinly at the old man. 'And I thank you, sir, for your contribution this morning. But I must reiterate that the aim of this inquiry is to shed light on the specific circumstances leading to the tragic deaths of passengers on the East Mediterranean flight *on the ground* at Northolt. It is *not* the aim of this inquiry to air conspiracy theories about the hijackers' motives and intentions, which can only be a matter of speculation since none survived.'

Esther Carr got to her feet but the barrister gently put a hand on her shoulder. There was an exchange of whispers between the elderly women.

Stevens struggled to his feet. He gripped the table with both hands. 'They were in flames – trying to get out – even the little ones.' His voice faltered. The room fell silent. One of the mothers swayed and an usher rushed forward to catch her.

My mobile rang. I made my way to the back of the gallery. It was Bernard.

'There's someone here who will speak to you. His name's Tanager.' He paused. 'He'll call you.'

'Thanks.'

'The negative?' His voice went up an octave.

'I'll drop it off.'

I hung up.

Seconds later, the phone rang again.

'Nick, it's Tanager, Bernard's pal.' The voice was older. The lack of formality suggested an easy authority. 'Thought I might be of help. I'm in your area – would you like a spot of lunch?'

'How do you know where I am?'

'You're with Metro, aren't you? It's quite near my club.'

I wasn't used to this sort of attention. Perhaps it was a slow day in Whitehall.

'Got a tie on? They'll find one for you if not.'

I wrote down the address.

10

The doorman's gaze drifted over my combat jacket.

'Mr Tanager will be in the library, sir.'

'I don't know him, I'm afraid.'

'Far left by the window is his usual place.' He handed me a dark, regimental-looking tie.

Deep carpet deadened the sound of my steps up the stairs. There were cases of swords and guns and a strong smell of floor polish that reeked of the past. The library walls were lined with books that looked as though they were more for decoration than reference. A long table was covered in magazines and journals. I wound my way through the forest of leather.

A man reared up from behind a *Financial Times* and beamed.

'Good of you to make it.'

Tanager pumped my hand. He seemed to be in no doubt who I was. He was tall and sinewy, the opposite of Bernard. His shoulders, though slightly stooped, were square. The double-breasted suit hung off him as if it wasn't his natural garb. He was tanned and weather-beaten; the lines radiating from his eyes reminded me of a cameraman's, from squinting into the sun. One side of his face seemed slightly frozen and his left eye moved more slowly than his right. Although his hair was thin and sandy grey the hairline had not receded. He could pass for mid-fifties but I suspected he was a lot older.

He oozed self-assurance. We entered a long dining room.

'Do you shoot?'

I looked at him. His accent was from another age.

'There's a shooting range under here. Only club in London to have one.' He looked at me as if I should be impressed.

'I'm afraid I've never handled a gun in my life.'

'Sensible man.' He laughed. 'Let's grab a side table before they all go.' He leaned towards me conspiratorially. 'Leave it any later and you're at the mercy of the crowd on the centre table. No telling who you'll end up next to.'

He made a grimace of extreme pain and propelled me forwards. Despite his age, his movements were brisk and athletic.

'Your job must be fascinating. This place is a bit of an archive in its way; some priceless relics. See that man over there? Gresham. Piloted a midget sub. And the chap with him, Ramsay, was on the Burma Railway. They'll be plotting their next escape.'

'From where?'

'The present: hostile terrain.' He laughed at his own joke.

The waiter arrived and shook out huge napkins with a flourish. Tanager leaned towards me. 'Everybody has his own great moment, don't you think? After which they go into mourning for its passing. Those poor chaps – the most interesting thing that happened to them was the war. What about you?'

'What do you mean?'

'What was yours? Your great moment.'

I looked at him for a while.

He smiled and shook his head very slightly. Perhaps he thought he was going too fast. He changed the subject. 'Steer well clear of the fish.'

He immersed himself in the menu, so I did the same. I needed a proper meal. He snapped it shut and stared off into the distance, though I felt his left eye keeping me in its sight.

'Greer Harmon. Fan*tas*tic looking girl. Impossible to forget. Don't you agree?'

I nodded. I felt I was being tested, but I had no idea what for.

'Nothing of her left in your archive?'

Was he asking or telling?

'Nothing? I know you chaps are terribly clever at turning up things from skips and whatnot.'

I shook my head. 'Nothing.' I had barely sat down and already I had told a lie. He was quiet for a moment. Perhaps he was hoping I would fill the silence. He offered me a cigarette. 'So, you were the witness. The one who saw it all.' He closed his eyes and made a shivering motion. 'Terrible to see someone killed. Even when it's not a loved one. I've known the hardest soldiers crippled with grief at the sight of their enemy dead. It's taboo, of course, but it's the truth.'

He looked at his hands. They were brown and spotted, suggesting he was well into his sixties. His nails were well bitten. Had he just happened to be free for lunch?

'It's kind of you to meet me. You work with Bernard?'

'Ah, *dear* Bernard.' It came out with a hollow condescension, as if he was recalling a well-meaning but disliked schoolmate. 'Where would we be today without the Bernards of this world flying the flag for us?'

'I thought you were colleagues.'

'Sort of. I'm more ... behind the scenes.' He patted his flat stomach and laughed. 'Fewer state dinners.' He treated me to the same grimace he had made earlier and laughed again, as if forcing some levity into the conversation.

The waiter reappeared and took our orders. Tanager glanced at the wine list and chose a white and a red. 'Not in a rush, are you?'

I smiled. I was intrigued by his attention. He looked more like a man of action, not someone with time to kill. He leaned in close. 'You rattled his cage all right. What've you got on him?'

'He owed me a favour.'

'He's still sore about your antics in Sri Lanka. Poor Bernard loathes the media.'

'He had given us instructions to stay away from terrorists.'

Tanager laughed again. 'Which you studiously ignored.'

It was hard to work out whose side he was on. I smiled and concentrated on the bread basket.

'So you're trying to fill in the gaps? You're pretty lucky to be here at all, aren't you?' He peered at me with what could have been real sympathy. 'You were, what, about ten yards from the *Por do Sol* when it went up?'

It was a jolt to hear the name of the boat. His eyes were on me now. 'Quite a big bang, apparently.'

'Rammal said it had a range of seven hundred miles; the tanks must have been full.'

He snorted, shook his head and repeated the name.

'So that's what he was calling himself then.'

I flushed at my naivety. I had never doubted it was his real name. Tanager stretched and leaned back in his chair, smiling knowingly.

'He had so many names he'd forgotten who he was.'

I had no idea whether that was a joke or a fact.

Tanager's smile was gone as quickly as it had appeared. He frowned, as if he was thinking of something else. 'And he was gone before you could get him in the can.' He studied a knuckle of bread and popped it into his mouth. Either he was bluffing or he didn't know about the tapes.

'You know a lot.'

He chuckled. 'Must be the same in your game. Bits of the most inconsequential info stick in the mind.'

I nodded and smiled. He seemed to swing between intimacy and detachment.

The food arrived. I was so hungry I ate the whole lot without noticing it. He kept my glass full but I avoided drinking; I wanted to stay focused. Suddenly he put down his knife and fork and pushed away his plate.

'Why now?'

'What?'

'What prompted you to call Bernard today?' Suddenly we were back on the main subject. 'After all this time?'

I paused for a moment. 'I've been made redundant. It felt like time to face up to things.'

'Ah.' If he was unconvinced he didn't show it. He was the sort of man who had complete control over how he came across. 'Funny thing, memory. No respecter of chronology.'

He smiled to himself. 'I could describe to you in minute detail the entire contents of my prep school tuck box, but I couldn't tell you what was on my desk this morning.' He laughed again. 'How the mind chooses what stays in focus and what becomes a blur …'

'I don't remember having much choice.'

'Course not. You had a nasty knock.'

He gazed at me, waiting for a response. I needed to move on.

'Can you tell me about … Rammal? What was his real name?'

He dunked a forkful of Yorkshire pudding in a pool of gravy. 'Fascinating character. Doomed, of course.'

'Why?'

'Well, I suppose he told you he was arming the Tamil Tigers?' He waved at one of the wine bottles. 'And you probably noticed he was a drunk.' He sucked in his lips and blew out his cheeks. 'Lethal cocktail, alcohol and ammunition. Bound to end badly.' He leaned back. 'The fact that he spoke to you at all – I mean, he had, well, delusions of grandeur, rather, and that's not so good if your game is things that go bang.'

'What are you saying?'

'How can I put this?' He dropped his voice, like a doctor conveying bad news. 'Did it occur to you he might have fancied delivering his obituary?'

I felt a cold pain in my chest. 'He knew he was going to die?'

No reply.

I stared. 'He killed *himself*?'

He smiled grimly. 'There's nothing conclusive, and it's true that plenty of people might have wanted rid of him, but the fact that he was willing to unburden himself to you. And you'll recall the boat was moored well away from any others. I'm sorry if this is painful …'

'And Greer?'

His eyes unfocused. 'Just jolly bad luck. Wrong place at the wrong time.'

He shook two cigarettes out of a soft pack and passed me one.

'Was he a terrorist – I mean, committed to a cause?'

He frowned and looked away. 'Maybe in his youth.'

'And he *was* dealing arms?'

'At times.' All Tanager's answers seemed incomplete.

'So what do you know, exactly?'

He looked slightly surprised at my impatience. 'Well,' he lifted his hands behind his head and leaned back, 'I know you'd been in Colombo a few days. I know you'd done the rounds of the elder statesmen who were trying to keep the peace process on track. It wasn't adding up to much of a story, so you decided to go to where the action was – up north. You took a train as far as you could, even though you didn't have a permit. There was a sticky moment when troops halted the train. You slipped a thousand-rupee note into your passport, but the young conscript was too dim to open it. Then you paid a driver to take you into Jaffna. You checked into the Ashok, the only hotel still standing. A boy took you on the crossbar of his bicycle to a deserted-looking building and left you to wait in a dark room. How am I doing?'

I was speechless.

'A man appeared from a hole in the wall with a curtain over it. He lectured you on the situation but refused your request to see Prabhakaran, the Tigers' leader. Then you heard a truck. A younger man in quasi-military uniform appeared and whisked you into an inner room where a third man sat at a card table. He was in a light cotton suit. He raised his glass to you.'

'How do you know all this?'

Tanager ignored the question. He was in full flow. 'They put you in the cellar where you crouched for some time while troops conducted a search above you. He introduced himself, this Rammal, and told you not to worry. When they'd gone, they hoiked your cellmate out but left you to the mercy of the mosquitoes. Eventually, you decided the coast was clear and found your way back to the Ashok. Feeling pretty sorry for yourself, I imagine.' Tanager lit another cigarette. 'After you'd got cleaned up, you went down to the bar. Your new friend was sitting in a steamer chair with a bottle of Scotch on the armrest. He offered you a cigar and lit it for you. Being the resourceful chap you are, you helped him finish the bottle and got him to tell you his tale. Then he whisked you off to his boat and you got a lift back to Colombo.' He folded his arms and sat back. 'There. Any gaps filled?'

'How do you know all this?'

'From your statement.'

'I didn't make any statement.'

'You reconstructed it all meticulously, on a large number of yellow Post-It notes.'

I felt the air go out of me. 'That was confidential. Part of my rehab.'

'Nothing's confidential I'm afraid, Nick.' He let his hand drop on my wrist. 'If it's any consolation, I don't think he would have been much cop.'

'What do you mean?'

'On camera.'

I looked at him. The theft of the tapes had been too painful to admit to, so filming the interview never went on my Post-It notes.

A low buzz came from somewhere in his suit. He ignored it. It sounded again. He patted his pockets and took out a mobile. He listened to it for some time.

'Coming.'

He snapped it shut, threw off his napkin, which was dotted with flakes of ash, and waved at the waiter. I didn't move. I needed to get my feelings under control.

Tanager was on his feet. He paused. 'Very bad luck you picked that moment.'

'What moment?'

'To introduce them.' He reached down and put a fatherly hand on my shoulder. 'But you mustn't blame yourself any more. It's all a long time ago.'

'I didn't.'

He frowned.

'I didn't arrange the meeting.'

He looked mystified. 'Who else could have?'

He squeezed my shoulder. 'Taking responsibility is tough. And the mind is a clever thing. It can be very selective when it needs to be.' He waved me forward like a traffic policeman. The meeting was over.

Tanager glanced at the Air Lanka bag as I retrieved it from the cloakroom. 'Some things are just best left behind. I'm sure you'll find another job. That'll give you something new to focus on.'

His phone buzzed again.

I returned the tie.

We were on the steps now. It was dark outside and a fine misty rain was falling. A cab swerved to a stop in front of me. I opened the door and climbed in.

'Thanks for your time.'

'I hope it's been of help.' He turned to go.

I had nothing to lose. 'You said he had a lot of names. Was one of them Malik?'

His reaction was almost imperceptible, no more than a narrowing of his pupils or a slight tautening of the skin above his cheekbones. But it was enough. For the first time in the afternoon, he looked off guard. His sense of urgency had vanished. He put his hand on the door, but the cab was already on the move. I watched him from the rear window, staring after me.

11

I travelled home, wrapped up in my own thoughts.

Rammal was a drunk, a suicidal con man. That was what Tanager wanted me to believe.

I started to doubt my judgement all over again. Was I, after all this time, still trying to absolve myself in some way for what had happened? If so, it wasn't working.

It started to rain again. My street was cordoned off with police tape. A police sergeant was directing people away. 'Sorry, sir. A suspect package in the phone box. Shouldn't be more than a couple of hours. Are you a resident?'

I gestured at my flat. The phone box was right outside it.

'The church hall is open, if you'd like somewhere to wait.'

I headed for the station.

Colin didn't seem surprised to see me.

'I've got news for you.' He had his white lab coat on. 'And something else to show you.' He motioned me into the front room. It was a blaze of light. A black-and-white print lay on the editing table.

'Much as I loathe admitting the virtues of new technology...' He sniffed and cracked open a can of lager. On the bench was an unfamiliar piece of kit, rather like a laptop but with a joystick.

'Image enhancement: picks up the finest traces of grain and bleaches the contrast until the shades reappear. So crap cameramen can stay in work, basically.'

I was staring at a blow-up of the flash frame. Malik's faint monochrome image had gained some shading. The ghostliness was still there, but his features were much clearer.

'Impressed?'

I took out the prints of Rammal and laid them down beside the shot of Malik.

Colin made a face. 'Where did you get these?'

'I took them in Sri Lanka.'

He frowned. 'Bit of a mess, aren't they?'

'The neg got a bit wet.'

His eyes flicked from the shot of Malik to the prints of Rammal. 'Twin terrorists, separated at birth? Only their mother could tell them apart ...'

'OK, OK.'

A church clock struck nine. He nodded at a stack of newspapers. 'I've had a closer look at Northolt.' Once he had latched on to a subject he was unstoppable. 'Nasty bastard, your man. Government seem to have caved in and released some details about him. Never actually did any of the dirty work himself, but took the families of his men hostage and killed them if they didn't deliver. No wonder the guys on the plane were losing it.'

I helped myself to one of his beers.

'There were three of them, not a word of English between them. They didn't actually take over the plane until it had been in the air for a few hours – too far for them to divert to somewhere friendly. They started arguing. It was completely shambolic. One of them helped himself to the contents of the trolley and got paralytic. Another started going through all the hand luggage, collecting whatever he fancied – toiletries, scent, sunglasses; anything shiny. He loaded it all into a kitbag too heavy to move.' He shook his head. 'Much good it did them.'

'How has this all come out?'

'Witness statement collected by the families. It's inadmissible because it's all from a survivor who died last year.'

I thought of Esther Carr trying to will some sense out of Stevens.

'It's in the terms of the inquiry, only testimony from the living. Kind of narrows the field.'

'What else about Malik?'

'First came to attention leading a breakout from an Israeli jail. Very ruthless and clever.'

'Any more about how he died?'

'Six weeks after Northolt. Apparently it was the only time he came out of his hidey-hole. Spotted in a Mercedes with a boot full of fireworks near a NATO base outside Frankfurt. SAS chased the car to somewhere not too populated and blasted him. Instant cremation.'

'What do you mean?'

'Because of the explosives in the car. No body to bury. It was hushed up at the time, because our boys aren't supposed to do that sort of thing in a friendly country.'

I gazed at the stack of papers. He would have been through every column inch and every relevant website.

'Has anyone disputed this?'

'What?'

'The assassination?'

'Only you so far, Tintin.' His eyebrows disappeared under the woolly hat.

I took a swig of beer.

He swivelled his chair in the direction of the papers. 'There's a reference in the *FT* to a claim around the time of the Frankfurt business ... He might have been giving information to the West about rival terror groups.'

I got up and looked at the prints again. What I knew was beginning to blur with what I imagined.

'I saw a man from the Foreign Office.'

'That was clever. What did you say? "Oh hello, I'm a redundant film archivist and I've got some footage proving that you're telling lies about a notorious terrorist. Would you like to see it?"'

I looked away.

'What was he?'

'He didn't say. His name was Tanager.'

'A spook?'

'I don't know. And didn't ask.'

'So you told him your theory?'

'No, not exactly.'

The room was filling with smoke. My head was throbbing. I needed to get back into fresh air.

'Can I hang on to these?' He nodded towards the prints. 'I might be able to combine them.'

'I've left the negs in the car.'

'Careless. Bring them next time. I'll do what I can with the prints.'

'Take care of them.'

He waved his can of beer at me.

'I think I need some sleep.'

He looked crestfallen. For all his awkwardness, Colin was someone who thrived on company.

I gave his shoulder a gentle thump and gestured at the prints.

'Thanks.'

'Don't be daft.'

He gave me a withering look. 'By the way, the tape the film's joined with. It's foreign.'

I leaned against the bench.

'Polyester. Hasn't been used for years. Dreadful stuff, but indestructible.'

'Who uses polyester?'

'Like I said. Foreigners.'

'Where foreign?'

'Dunno yet. Maybe East European. I haven't seen it since the Eighties.'

'Are you saying that the shots of Malik were stripped out of this somewhere abroad?'

He pursed his lips. 'I'm just saying the tape is foreign.'

12

Back at my street the police were packing up. Some men in overalls were taking down tall screens that had blocked off the road. The sergeant I'd spoken to was still there, looking chilled and stamping his feet.

'Turned out to be a bag of stolen phones.'

I gestured towards the screens. 'Isn't this overkill?'

He rolled his eyes in agreement.

I only realised how tired I was when I got inside. I put the shopping on the kitchen table and sat down on the sofa without taking off my coat.

The photo wallet was just where I had left it this morning, on the table. The cup and saucer I had forgotten to wash were beside them. The ashtray had three butts in it. The books on the shelf were all in the same order.

Everything was as I had left it, but nothing seemed to be in exactly the right place. There was an unfamiliar metallic smell. I felt my judgement was crumbling. I lit a cigarette. My head was hammering, so I foraged for some paracetamol and washed them down with a large Scotch. Then I remembered the negatives I had left in the car.

There was no space in the street. No gap where the Volvo had been. Tired and distracted as I was, I had no doubt where I had left it. The car had gone.

The police station seemed to be deserted. I pressed a bell on the counter and eventually an officer in shirtsleeves appeared.

'Sorry about that. Short staffed.'

'My car's been stolen.'

Wearily, he pulled out a thick pad of forms. I gave him the details.

'Is it possible to check if it's in the pound?'

He took his time to reply. 'I'll have to phone through.'

He was gone for a few minutes. When he returned, his expression was more alert.

'Could you come this way please, Mr Roker?'

He lifted the hinged part of the counter and I followed him down a corridor. He showed me into a bare room with a table, chairs and a tape machine. 'Somebody will be along shortly.'

13

I looked at my watch. It was nearly midnight. I badly wanted to lie down. There was a glass panel in one of the walls and my dull reflection stared back at me. My hair was matted by the rain and my beard looked slimy. I could have passed for a vagrant.

The door swung open and two men entered. One was in a suit, the other a bomber jacket. They were carrying a thick file. I got up.

'Sit down, please.'

They didn't introduce themselves.

'Mr Roker, there's been a report of a theft.'

'My car.'

One opened the manila file and started leafing through the contents. 'We're talking about a theft – from your workplace. A can of film was taken yesterday evening. By you.'

I could feel myself reddening.

'I came about my car.'

'Yesterday evening you took a can of film from the Metropolitan Archive Office on the pretext that it was a fire risk. That was not the case, was it, Mr Roker?'

'Can I ask who you are?'

'According to a witness, parts of a film had been interfered with by you.'

Darren must have thought I had taken out the shots of Malik when I tried to show him *Face of a Terrorist*.

The other man chipped in. 'The circumstances in which the film was acquired by the archive are also under investigation.'

There was nothing actually threatening about them; they were not even big men, but they had a directness and physical authority that was intimidating.

The younger of the two, the one in the bomber jacket, leaned forward. 'It's got to be recovered. All of it.'

I stayed silent. The file lay open at a photocopy of a form – the one I had filled out at Metro to get the film past the guard. I could see my signature. I wondered what was on the other pages.

'It would be best if you just took us to where you've hidden the material, so it can be recovered.'

I stared into the empty polystyrene cup.

'OK.'

The sergeant reappeared. They treated him with the same indifference.

'Just taking Mr Roker on a little run.'

They took no notice of his dismay. Whoever these men were, they weren't on his team.

They hustled me towards an unmarked BMW with its lights on, engine idling. A driver was sitting at the wheel. My two got in the back, one each side of me. Our shoulders touched. I stared straight ahead, painfully aware of the barrier of close-cropped hair and muscle that separated me from freedom.

'Where to, Mr Roker?'

'Home.'

The dashboard display glowed. The interior was warm and had the same metallic smell I'd noticed in my flat. The rain was still falling. No one spoke.

I hadn't given them the address, but the driver seemed to know where to go. He drove at speed, pointing the vehicle with precision into gaps that didn't look wide enough to take it. Why did I say home? They stayed silent. At least I had a moment to think.

We pulled up in the middle of the street. All the parking spaces were taken. A radio crackled briefly. As we got out I noticed that the driver seemed to be talking to himself. He wore a tiny cordless earpiece.

We brushed against the wisteria entwined around the railings alongside the steps to my flat. I disabled the alarm and held the door for them, but they wanted me to go first. The driver stayed outside.

They seemed to fill my living room, as if they were used to occupying bigger spaces. They looked at me in silence.

Why had I brought them here? The film and the prints were all with Colin. I didn't want to involve him. I'd taken the film; it was my problem.

They didn't look round the room. Perhaps it was already familiar to them. They were waiting. The plan made itself up inside my head.

'It's down below.' I pointed at the floor. 'You'll have to give me a minute or two.'

They showed no reaction.

'You may as well sit down.'

They complied, but stood up again when I moved back towards the hall.

'The trap door's under the stairs.'

The corridor was too narrow for us all. I swung the closet door open. The contents tumbled out, the exercise bike leading the charge.

A mobile phone went off and the one in the bomber jacket stepped back into the living room while his suited companion watched me.

'Sorry, could you ... ?' I gestured for him to move back slightly while I pulled out the bike. I hoped he wouldn't try to help. He didn't. He stayed put, watching. My face was covered in sweat, but that was all right. I was scared. I needed them to see I was scared. If I were to have any chance at all they would have to think I was under their control.

I pulled everything out, far more than necessary, and arranged it across the hall. It might give me a few extra seconds. I lifted the trap door. The suited man came forward.

'It's OK. It'll prop open.'

He stepped back again. We were on opposite sides of the barricade.

'Do you have a torch?'

He didn't. He retreated to the living room and returned with a small metal Maglite. I studied it, looking for the switch.

'You twist the head.'

I did so, and swung the beam towards the hatch.

'It's right at the back, under some other stuff.'

I sat down, my legs dangling into the darkness. He continued to watch. This wasn't going to work.

'Jez. Here a sec.'

The suit hesitated, and then moved to join his partner in the living room.

I dropped out of sight. This time, the smell of damp was so strong it caught in the back of my throat. A rustling sound near the door in the pub's partition wall indicated I wasn't entirely alone. The door had no handle. I had only opened it once, when I first moved in. I couldn't remember if it creaked.

I needed both hands so I put the torch down. The door was warped in its frame. I pulled on the remains of the bolt, and felt a flake of rust slice through the skin below my knuckle. Blood welled darkly and spilled across the back of my hand. I raised it briefly to my lips and tasted metal on my tongue.

This time it slid back, to reveal a solid wall of bricks. Someone had filled it in from the other side. Almost to the top. I wasn't going to fit. I glanced back towards the hatch. I had no choice. I took off my jacket and stuffed it through the gap, followed by my sweater. I grabbed the top row of bricks with both hands. The edges were sharp. I took a deep breath, wishing for a moment that I'd put the exercise bike to better use, then hauled myself up and leaned my head to one side to squeeze through the gap.

There was a different smell in the pub cellar, sharp and acidic. I held on. I pressed the air out of my lungs and heaved myself forwards. I was halfway there. My belt buckle caught against the brick. There were tears in my eyes now, not because of the smell, but because of the humiliation, the wishing I could rewind the last twenty-four hours. Bomber jacket's call will be over now. They'll start to wonder. They'll step over the feeble barricade. They'll peer in and discover the light switch beside thc trap door. And they'll see my backside sticking out of the top of the bricked-up doorway.

I wrestled my left elbow back through the gap, grazing it against the doorframe, unbuckled the belt and unthreaded it clumisly from the loops in my jeans. I let it fall to the floor and pushed myself through.

The floor on this side was a foot or so lower than in my cellar. My shoulder landed on something soft and sponge-like, releasing a fresh blast of ammonia. Perhaps it was an old mattress. I couldn't tell. It was completely black. I'd left the torch on the other side. They must know now.

I groped my way under the pavement, and crouched under the metal flaps where the beer barrels were once dropped into the cellar. The flaps were held down by a huge rod. At first it showed no inclination to move. I wrapped my fist in the cuff of my jacket and thumped it hard. On the third attempt, my knuckles humming with pain, it gave a little and I worked it back and forth until it started to slide, then came loose with a heavy clang.

I froze, ears straining for any sign of movement from above. All I could hear was the thudding of my own heart. Using the crown of my head I lifted the flap. Orange light glistened on the surface of the pavement. From this angle the BMW was completely obscured. There was no sign of the driver. *Please be in the car.*

There was no way of holding the flap open; the stays had rusted away. The edge scraped down my back as I crawled through, face down on the wet stone. I raised myself on my knees and lifted my head far enough to see the BMW through the windows of the other parked cars. The driver was still at the wheel, but his door was open.

I eased my right leg forward, then felt my left caught in a vice-like grip. I kicked out furiously. A burning pain shot up my leg. My ankle was caught under the hatch. A car door slammed. I dropped flat onto the pavement.

The interior lights of the car parked immediately in front of my flat came on. The BMW revved and slid back towards me to let it out. Its headlamp beams swooped across me. I twisted my foot free and moved into the shadow of a Land-Rover, folded myself into a crouch again and tested my ankle. Another flash of pain. *Ignore it.*

Bent double, dragging one foot, I started to put some distance between me and the BMW, but it started to reverse in my direction, making way for the other car. The street was too narrow for two vehicles to pass.

Now the BMW driver was on the street, looking up and down. I crammed myself down alongside a Transit van, three car lengths from the junction with the main road. I forgot about the pain and hobbled to the corner. I looked back. The three of them were on the pavement. I crouched behind the last parked car. There was a dull rumble above me. A helicopter.

A night bus cruised to a halt on the main road and disgorged a group of shrieking, tipsy women. I half crouched, half ran towards it and fell into the door as its rubber jaws slammed shut. The driver had no option but to open them again.

'Sorry.'

I went up the stairs and sat down, momentarily cocooned.

The bus pulled away, past the junction with my road. My building was caught starkly in the glare of the helicopter's searchlight, like the bleached-out frame in Greer's film.

Some time later – I'm not sure how long – I wiped away the condensation on the window. I looked at my hands. Blood seeped from my knuckle, and from under broken nails.

I tried to slow my breathing and concentrate on the road ahead.

14

'Fucking hell.' Colin rubbed a hand across his face.

'I'm not sure I should be here.'

'Where else would you go?'

I took another sip of tea. The heat of the mug stung the gashes on my fingers. Somewhere in the house a clock struck four. He let out a long sigh. 'I did warn you.'

I didn't answer.

'Did they try to follow you?'

'I don't think so.'

'Is your phone on?'

'No.'

'Good.'

'Why?'

'What century are you living in? As long as it's turned on, you're connected to a network. They could track you.'

'How would they know my number?'

He rolled his eyes. 'I'm not even going to answer that.'

I drank some more tea. It tasted wonderful.

Colin smoothed out a cigarette paper. 'Why did you run?'

I didn't have an answer.

'They'll think you know something they don't want you to know.'

He passed me the roll-up and started on another for himself.

'I don't think I should stay.'

He flapped his hand. I stayed seated and he lit my roll-up. 'Get some sleep then tomorrow, turn yourself in. Say you're sorry you took the film, you just wanted to examine it. Maybe they'll tell you what it's all about.'

'That's not even funny.'

He leaned forward and made rare eye contact. 'You're in real trouble.' He took a long drag and blew a cloud of smoke into the air above me. 'Because it means ... that you may be right about your chum Malik.' He glanced at me over his glasses. 'Remember the film about "shoot to kill"?'

'What about it?'

'The reporter, Cope, suffered a very bad mugging. And the director – his daughter got run over.'

'For fuck's sake.'

He shook his head. 'Bath for you, then bed.' He sounded almost paternal. 'Then we'll try and work out how you're going to get out of this mess.'

I slept fitfully in the unfamiliar bedroom, unable to distinguish between dreams and my racing thoughts. Images from last night and long before came and went in no particular order. All over again, I was struggling to get out of the cellar, my clothes torn as I scrambled through a series of tight gaps. When I got outside there was water all around me, and bright sunlight. Rammal's boat exploded again and the sky filled with fluttering yellow Post-It notes. I came to in Tanager's club. Anita was there, looking up at me, from the bottom of the hotel stairs.

I woke up covered in sweat. A cobweb, laden with dust, swung between the overhead bulb and the doorframe. I turned on my phone to see the time. Eleven-fifteen. There was a text message. It had been left at four-thirty a.m.: *Nick, think we should talk. Give me a call. Tanager.* I turned off the phone quickly.

A siren came and went. I started to get up, but my whole body ached. Why was I bothering? I had no job, no home to go to. I looked down at Colin's pyjamas. I wasn't even in my own clothes. In two days and nights, all the carefully assembled components that had shored up my life since Sri Lanka had been stripped away. My cover was blown. All the years I'd put between myself and that time had dissolved into nothing. Time had healed nothing. I knew I had no choice but to go back to the beginning and revisit every detail, like a detective reviewing a cold case.

I lay back down. I was still tired but any more sleep was out of the question. My pulse was racing. *Get a grip, for fuck's sake.* I needed to arrange my thoughts. I went back to the weeks of convalescence after Sri Lanka. I tried to conjure up the yellow Post-It notes in the order I had once assembled them.

On the first I had written *Asylum.*

It had been my third year on *Destination.* The novelty of working in TV was long gone. I had been filming a Club 18-30 holiday on a Mediterranean island.

On the last evening I had driven the crew bus up the coast to escape the relentless beat of the disco. I stopped at some cliffs that overlooked a bay and took a walk. It was a moonless night, the sky full of stars.

On my way back I passed a concrete structure in an olive grove. I heard a muffled howl. I followed a track to what looked like a small prison. Barred slots were cut high into the walls. Standing on an oil drum, I peered inside.

None of the children was clothed. Their faces craned up at me from cots. One raised his arm and it strained against something. They were strapped in.

I found the crew in the bar and told them what I wanted.

'What're you going to do? Intercut it with the disco?'

They saw I wasn't going to be deterred.

'OK, you're the director.'

I parked in the same spot. Pete the cameraman surveyed the sky and shook his head.

'Perfect night.'

'What?'

'When it's too dark to film. All you can do is remember it.'

'We have to try.'

I rattled the gates and yelled. Eventually a man appeared in a vest, pointing angrily at his watch.

'English tourists. Car no go. Phone?'

He waved us in, oblivious of the crew's bags. They hung

back while I followed the guard into an office. I managed to close the door behind me. A woman in something that might once have been a nurse's uniform was playing cards by herself. She didn't look up.

As the dialling tone purred in my ear, I had a long and involved conversation into the mouthpiece. A child let out a prolonged scream. My concern that we might be in trouble was immediately replaced by disgust that neither of them reacted.

We drove back in silence. I dropped the crew at a bar and went to find a phone. On my sixth try I got through to the Network switchboard and asked for Phil Edgington, Editor of *Human Face*.

15

Colin was stacking film cans in the hall. He glanced at his watch. 'Sleep well?'

'I need to find Phil Edgington.'

He shook his head. 'For fuck's sake.'

He walked off towards the kitchen. I followed him and sat down at the table. My clothes were drying on various radiators. He must have washed them after I went to sleep. On the table was Greer's lighter. I picked it up and fired it.

'Just needed a clean and some fuel.' He gave me a look, which said *what's that doing in your pocket*? But he didn't ask.

'Edgington sent me to Sri Lanka. He was in charge of *Human Face* by then.'

Colin paced about, randomly adjusting the positions of the various items awaiting his full attention on almost every surface, then put seven or eight rashers of bacon under the grill.

'How can I get through to you? You were once a director of harmless holiday programmes. Then you decided it was your personal mission to change the world. Next minute, you're this far away – ' he indicated the distance between his finger and thumb ' – from becoming fish food. I'd thought you'd learned your lesson.'

'What lesson?'

He made an explosion gesture with his hands, accompanied by the appropriate sound effect.

'I was unlucky.'

'Or very bloody lucky. A few more yards and you would have gone up with the boat.' He wagged a finger at me. 'And think about this: whoever blew it up – maybe they meant you to be on it.' He nodded sagely, as if he had it all worked out.

'You said the meeting on the boat wasn't your idea. So whose was it? Who sent you?'

He was waiting for an answer. I stared at the wall. *It's all arranged.*

'The researcher.'

'Who was he?'

'*She*. A Tamil student.'

'Ah.' He raised his eyebrows. I looked away.

A siren broke the silence outside. It grew in volume then died away down the street.

'She helped you find your man?'

'Not exactly.'

'What does that mean?'

'It's not relevant.' I could feel my face heating up.

'Everything's relevant.'

Tanager wanted me to believe it was suicide. *An accident waiting to happen*: that was his description of Rammal. And Greer just happened to go there at the wrong moment. The more I thought about it the less credible it seemed.

Colin waved a spatula. 'And another thing; the tapes.'

'I told you. They were stolen from my hotel room.'

He pursed his lips. 'For God's sake!'

'It was a burglary. Other things went as well.'

'First the tapes you hope will launch your brilliant investigative filmmaking career vanish; then your interviewee goes up in smoke. Have you never thought of putting the two together?' He rubbed a hand over his eyes. 'You are *way* out of your depth. Look at this.'

He pointed to the *Sun* headline: KILLER WITH NO FACE.

'*They* couldn't find a picture of him.' He jabbed the paper. 'Not a photo library in the world has him on file. All the copies of *Face of a Terrorist* have disappeared – except the one you nicked and that's been stripped of every shot of him. Someone wants his face to stay hidden, and badly.' He tapped the prints of Rammal. 'And where are the negs of these? In your car. And where's your car?' He looked at me sadly. 'If you're planning on a crusade, you've not made a very good start.'

'I have to do this,' I said quietly.

'Just like you had to join *Human Face*? No, you don't. You know something the powers that be don't want you to know. If they faked Malik's death, that's a big lie – so there'll be a big reason for it.'

Colin put a bacon sandwich in front of me. It was unnerving to have so much eye contact with him in one day. 'If they haven't come for you by now, they can't know you're here. So lie low. Stay put. At least for a few days, so you can get things into perspective.'

'I'm getting you in trouble just by being here. Listen, I am really—'

He cut me off. 'Just finish your sandwich.'

I ate, staring at the brick wall outside the kitchen window. Colin was right. They wanted the film. They had my car. They'd have found the negatives of Rammal by now. And by making my escape, I had crossed a line. Going back wasn't an option. Forward was the only way.

Colin paced about.

'Sit down.'

He sat and tapped the table. 'I'm not going to get through, am I?'

'I'll find Edgington. Then I'll turn myself in.'

He put his head in his hands.

'I'd better get dressed,' I said.

16

I sat beside Colin at the monitor. He sighed heavily as his fingers pattered over the keyboard, working through an elaborately complex security code. A page appeared on the screen: *Networkers*. I leaned forward. 'What's this?'

'It's for ex-Network people. A sort of Friends Reunited for distressed production folk.'

He entered my name. It asked for a password.

'I haven't got one.'

'You've never looked in here?'

'As you say, better not to look back.'

'What's your ID?'

I looked blank.

'Your old employee number?'

'24018655.'

It recognised the number and we were through the homepage. He clicked on *Find fellow Networker*.

'Shall I?'

He ignored me. He didn't like other people too near his equipment.

'OK, here we go.' He typed Phil Edgington's name and clicked on *Find now*. The screen went blank. The *Search* icon flashed. My pulse accelerated. After half a minute a message appeared: *Details withheld*.

'He's probably dead. Thank Christ for that.' He turned away and started on a roll-up.

I stared at the message on the screen. 'Try Carrie Marron. M-A-R-R-O-N.'

'No.'

I leaned across and entered the name. There was a pause,

then her face gradually appeared. It was an old picture. The background was probably the *Human Face* office.

'Who's she?'

'Edge's PA.'

There was an address in Hove. Beneath, it said, *Life Coaching and Career Development. Discount for ex-Networkers*. I took down the phone number.

'This is my final warning.'

I took out my mobile. He snatched it from me.

'It's just a phone call.'

'Use the landline, for God's sake.'

I dialled the number. My hand was shaking. I hadn't spoken to anyone from that part of my past for a very long time. An answering machine. I started to leave a message but Carrie cut in.

'My God, is it really you?'

I couldn't tell whether this was good or bad.

'I'm sorry to bother you after all this time.'

'Don't be silly!'

I hadn't expected such enthusiasm.

'I just wondered if you might be able to help me. I'm trying to get in touch with Edge. Do you have his number?'

'Slow down a bit.' There was laughter in her voice. 'It's been years! Tell me how you are. What are you up to?'

'I'm fine. You?'

'Oh, you know, battling on.' Her cheerfulness sounded fragile.

'Are you in touch with him?'

There was a pause. I could hear her breathe out.

'It's a very difficult time.'

'I only want to ask him a couple of questions.'

'His wife's very poorly. He's not taking calls. Is it something I can help with?'

She was still his gatekeeper, even now. For a moment I hesitated. Perhaps Colin was right. I should lie low. I took a breath.

'Can we meet? Today?'

‘Always in such a hurry. You haven’t changed at all.’
I didn’t know what she meant.
‘I’m tied up this evening.’
‘I could come earlier.’
Colin put his face in his hands.

17

'How long do you think I've got?'

Colin was already immersed in another project. He had the back off a computer and was poised with a soldering iron, like a surgeon about to make an incision.

'If you keep your mobile off, don't go to a cash point or use any credit cards, avoid all places with CCTV, and try not to steal anything else?'

'Yes?'

'A few days.' He sipped his coffee. 'Depends how badly they want you. If they're desperate, they could put your picture on the news and warn the nation that a dangerous archivist is on the loose.'

'Could I borrow a car?' He had several in a row of nearby lock-ups.

He sighed. 'I suppose you'll want some cash as well.' Again he raised his hand like a policeman. 'No gratitude, please. I might start to blub.'

The Beetle coughed out a cloud of blue smoke. He revved the engine until all the cylinders had clattered into life. I stood back while he reversed it out of the garage.

'Am I taking my life in my hands?'

'Right now, this car is the least of your worries. Stay in the slow lane and don't make any sudden movements. Let me try the wipers.' They groaned arthritically and struggled to make an arc. He shrugged. 'You could hitch-hike.'

He got out and held the door for me. I threw in a bag. Inside were some spare clothes, washing kit, a notebook and in a stiff card envelope, the screen-grab of Malik, and the prints of

Rammal. There was also five hundred pounds in cash that he'd want back one day.

'Remember me in your will.'

I gave him a V-sign and pulled away. As I got to the end of the street I could see him in the rear-view mirror, standing there like an anxious parent. And for all his caution, I sensed some small part of him wanted to come with me.

The rain set in somewhere outside Croydon. The wipers, already struggling, now had walls of spray from passing trucks to contend with. A black BMW with all its lights on came up close behind then flashed past and away into the distance. The speedometer seemed reluctant to go above forty. It was going to be a long drive.

My last sight of Carrie had been waving me off at Gatwick. I had tried to grill her about Greer and what to expect. She hadn't been keen to talk but I had pressed her.

'Stick to your guns.'

I had asked her what that meant.

'If she gives you trouble, don't expect Edge to back you up. She does what she wants.'

Before I could ask her to explain, I'd reached passport control, she'd kissed me and the crowd had swept us apart.

By the time I reached the outskirts of Brighton, my head was pounding. The Beetle lurched to the left whenever I braked and I had to keep the windows open to stop it from misting up inside. But once I hit the seafront and turned west, a wedge of blue parted the clouds. The sun came out and the road surface sparkled, along with the façades. Carrie's building was in a square a couple of streets inland. I rang the bell and the front door unlocked itself.

She was standing at the top of the stairs. She looked no different. Her top and skirt were formal and resolutely middle-aged. Her almost black hair was bobbed as it had always been.

I ascended into a cloud of scent. The freckles that had once made her look younger than she probably was were now submerged under a generous layer of foundation, and her smile made tiny lines radiate from the corners of her pretty hazel eyes.

A small dog was yapping at her heels. She held out both arms and drew me in. I had known her for no more than a few days over a decade ago, yet she greeted me like a long-lost lover. I hesitated, concerned that my beard might remove a layer of make-up but she kissed me full on the lips. Then she stepped back and held me at arm's length. 'Is it really you under there?' Her eyes were shining.

She scooped up the dog and led me through the flat and into a sitting room. Two large sofas faced each other across a long glass coffee table, like guests waiting to be formally introduced.

'What does a Life Coach do?'

She came towards me and pointed at my forehead. 'I look into this and show you how to unlock your potential.'

'Might be a bit late for that.'

'I help people who are stuck in certain mindsets to be more effective.' She grinned and raised an eyebrow. 'Maybe I can offer you my services. Tea? Or can I tempt you with something stronger?'

'Tea is fine.'

A collection of framed photographs stood on a piano. A lot of them were of pets. There was one of Edge in a dinner jacket, clutching a BAFTA and grinning triumphantly. Whoever was beside him had been obscured by another snapshot of him slotted into the same frame. I lifted it back with a finger. Next to him was Greer, statuesque in a strapless gown, also holding a trophy and looking slightly shy. On the mantelpiece was a shot of Edge and Carrie on a hillside in walking gear.

'That's my favourite of us.'

She returned with a tea and a large glass of wine, which she set down on the coffee table.

'He took me to watch some filming. We stayed on after.' She touched the glass of the picture. 'Anyway …'

She sat down and smoothed out her skirt. I turned away

from the pictures. 'I hope I'm not keeping you from your work.'

'Tuesday's a kind of day off. But I'll have to kick you out to get ready for tonight.'

She patted the cushion next to her and I sat down. The dog settled itself on a hearthrug. The room was timeless. There was nothing of the present in it.

'So, bring me up to date ...'

I told her about Metro, or most of it. As I talked she continued to give me her professional listening smile, though I wasn't sure what she was really taking in.

Eventually she looked away and took two large sips of her wine. When she looked back at me her eyes were full of tears. 'God, I'm so pathetic.' She pulled a tissue from a box on the coffee table. The little dog came over and pawed at her legs. 'It was such a terrible time.'

She made two fists and pressed them against her lap. I wondered if I should put my arm round her. The clock on the mantelpiece chimed three-thirty.

'I remember a man ringing from the consulate. He was really quite rude. And the line was terrible. Edge wasn't around and at first he wouldn't tell me why he was calling. He sounded highly inconvenienced. Because of his tone I assumed that you'd just got yourselves arrested. That sort of thing happened quite often. Eventually, I persuaded him to explain. He said Greer was dead. He handled it so badly I felt like making a complaint.'

She sipped her wine.

'With her I'd always half expected something like this. So my first thought was, What the fuck has she dragged you into?'

'How do you mean?'

She blew her nose and moved some hair off her face. 'She was a law unto herself.' Her make-up had run slightly. She shrugged. 'All the way to the airport I was thinking, Warn him – tell him what she's like – but I kept quiet. When I heard what happened, I hated myself for it.'

'What would you have said?'

'That she was impossible to work with. That she didn't take anybody's advice; that no director ever worked with her twice because she was a nightmare.'

Her expression was full of pity.

'Anyway, you were so keen I thought you'd be deaf to whatever I said.'

'I'm not sure what difference it would have made.'

She took a cigarette out of a box on the table. She tapped the end on the glass. It was years since I'd seen anyone do that.

'The last time Edge saw her they had a blazing row. I couldn't help hearing it, even though his door was shut. He liked a good shout, but this was different. Real anger.'

She took another sip of wine.

'He'd stopped her from going to ... Dubai, I think it was. She'd got some story about trade in endangered species and he'd said it was too soft for us. It was the first time he'd stood up to her, and she was livid. She said she'd had enough and threatened to go over to the BBC. He said he'd warn them off – tell them she was a loose cannon. Anyway, she stormed out and the next thing we knew she was in Sri Lanka. That was a couple of days before you appeared.'

She let her hand fall on my knee and laughed conspiratorially. Her eyes had become dreamy. 'In your shorts, all tanned, brandishing a can of film. All us girls were terribly pleased.'

'Why?'

'The other directors ...' She grimaced. 'You were rather gorgeous. Still are probably, if you'd come out from behind that hedge.' She tugged part of my beard.

'Standing in the middle of the office, insisting on seeing Edge "Right now!" Let me show you something.'

I followed her into the spare room that doubled as a study. She opened a drawer in the desk. A set of old Network diaries was stacked in a neat row.

'It's all in here – all the secrets.' She giggled girlishly and took one out dated 1995. 'Here we are: *Nick R waiting in office. No appointment, but E knows. Remind switchboard not to give out E's home number. EVER.*'

She shook her head. 'You slipped right under my radar. Half my job was protecting him from the likes of you. Everybody and his dog wanted to get on that show.'

She showed me the page. On the next it said: *N to Sri Lanka to RV with Greer. Gd luck to him.*

And underneath: *Call to Anita.*

I reached for it but she slapped my wrist playfully and slotted it back into its place.

On the desk was a big photo album. She sat down on the bed and lifted it onto her lap. 'You're in here as well.'

There were pages and pages of shots of people from the production team. The hair and clothes left no doubt which decade this was. I recognised some of the other reporters who had once been household names. Most were taken in the office. At the time the mess had astonished me. Piles of film cans and tapes jumbled with lever-arch files. Each desk had at least three different coloured phones. Beer mugs and plates of half-finished shepherd's pie fought for space with pictures, posters, books and big electric typewriters.

She giggled again and leaned close. 'Here's you. See: Irresistible.'

It took me a moment to realise what I was looking at. A fresh face grinning at the camera. The linen suit had been bought that morning. Beside me was a Samsonite bag – also brand new – and the backpack for a lightweight camera I'd persuaded them to let me take. A look of suppressed impatience – raring to get going.

'You were so keen. You couldn't get on the plane fast enough.' Her look had shifted from sad to dreamy. It was hard to gauge her mood, but I sensed she was the keeper of Edge's secrets.

'Do you know why I got the job?'

'Edge liked giving people breaks.' She didn't sound convinced.

'There was a whole team of directors on the show. Surely one of them could have gone?'

She picked a couple of dog hairs from her lap and sighed.

'None of them would. They all knew how difficult she was. How she always chose the story. It caused a lot of friction, the way Edge let her carry on.'

'Were they close?'

She looked away. 'He practically invented her. Greer Harmon. It wasn't even her real name.' She closed her eyes and breathed in.

'Her death ... Did it affect him?'

She rolled her eyes. 'He thought she was immortal.'

'How is he now?'

'He doesn't see anyone from the old days.' She let out a long sigh. 'He was so stupid about her. Letting her do what she wanted. Until that row, he never crossed her. And yet he was so tough on the others. But by then he was coming under pressure. A few years before, it wouldn't have mattered. But things had changed. Ratings were falling. The Board were getting all nervous about franchise renewal. They'd made him pull a film about suicides in the military. He was furious. And another one, about Myra Hindley wanting parole, that caused more trouble. But he knew he couldn't afford to have one of his reporters swanning around abroad without good reason. So he dispatched you.'

Listening to this, looking at Carrie's photos, it was all flooding back.

We're relying on you. That's what he said to me.

'He'd seen the asylum stuff you'd done while you were supposed to be shooting disco-ing teenyboppers. That's what he liked – people breaking a few rules to get what they wanted.'

She closed her eyes. Eventually she spoke again. 'But the controllers were on his back. They saw him as a loose cannon by then. Greer getting blown up was just the excuse they'd been waiting for. I came in one morning and found him at his desk, just staring into space. I think he'd been there all night. A memo had gone round from the Board: *After careful consideration by the directorate, it has been concluded that the funds allocated to* Human Face *would be more effectively spent on* ... I forget what. And that was it. Game over.' She dabbed her eyes. 'He thought people would rally round – have a protest outside the gates.' She ground her cigarette into an ashtray and shook her head. 'Nothing. There wasn't even a final wrap party. The team just melted away into other programmes. A few weeks later the office was taken over by *Crimefile*. After all he'd done for them.'

I turned to the next page in the album. It was blank.

She reached over and took it from me. As she flipped through the pages, her eyes filled with tears again. 'Such wonderful times; I was so lucky.'

'How did you get the job?'

She leafed back through the album. 'Saul. He shared a flat with Edge's old secretary, Ellen. We were all in the same crowd. She went off somewhere, very suddenly. I was working in an estate agent's. Hideously dull. He persuaded me to apply.'

She was about to show me a page of pictures but changed her mind.

'I wasn't very confident then, just a silly girl. Saul talked me into going for it. He groomed me, told me what to say. I was terrified when I went in. Edge just looked me up and down and said, "When can you start?"' She smirked and tapped the album. 'He's why I'm busy tonight. I'm having a reunion.'

'With Saul?'

She nodded shyly.

'Did you go out together?'

'For a time, I suppose.'

The dog got to its feet and wagged its tail. She patted its head. 'Shall we get some air?'

She disappeared into the bathroom. Her bag was on the table. Beside it was a leather-bound notebook. Another big diary lay on a desk by the window. But I knew Edge's address would be in her head.

18

We walked through a garden square towards the sea. She came close so I could shield her from the wind. I let her slip her arm under mine. 'Were you there for *Face of a Terrorist*?'

She let the dog off the lead and it galloped around the flower-beds.

'1989. Edge had just come back from the shoot when I started. I was terrified.'

'Of what?'

'Well, dealing with irate vendors was one thing; government press officers were something else. And that was *before* Northolt. Afterwards, when Malik was named as the ringleader, all hell broke loose. The more flak Edge got the more stubborn he became. Everyone wanted to find Malik. He said he'd go to prison first rather than give out any contacts. He loved all that – the notoriety; said if he wasn't making trouble, he wasn't doing his job.' Her eyes shone. 'We all thought the film would be banned, no matter what Edge said. But then with the news about Malik being killed ...' She shrugged. 'They couldn't stop him, he got his way.'

'What did you think of it?'

'Me? No one cared what I thought.' She breathed deeply and closed her eyes. 'I never told him, but I really didn't like it. All those innocent people ...'

'Did Edge talk about him?'

'Not to me. I think he'd guessed I didn't approve. But all that lot, they'd grown up in the Seventies. Edge was a real lefty in his youth.'

'And you?'

'I don't understand politics. But a killer is a killer, in my book. If Edge had a failing – and I'd be the last to criticise him – he could be a bit of a romantic.'

We sat on a bench, facing the sea. A bank of cloud hovered above the horizon. Big, grey waves dumped water on the beach.

'I was pretty scared of him at first. But when I got into trouble and I thought I was for the high jump, that's when I found out the sort of man he really was.'

'What sort of trouble?'

'A few weeks before Northolt, I borrowed a print of the cutting copy. You weren't supposed to let a film go out of the building without signed permission.' She groaned. 'I was so green.'

'Why did you take it?'

'Saul was a post-grad in international relations. He begged me to let him see it. He had it for ages. Then a few days after it was broadcast Special Branch seized all the copies, and all the paperwork. It was scary. They came right in and started going through the filing cabinets. Well, I was in a complete panic – I just handed in my notice. Edge pulled me into his office. I really thought I was for it. He could be terrifying when he was cross ...' She smiled to herself. 'But you know what he said? "I can't do this job without you. I need you by my side. You're staying put." And he told me to leave the film in the stock room.'

'Is that what you did?'

She nodded. 'He never mentioned it again. After that, I couldn't do enough for him.' She turned her face away. 'Still can't.'

The sea air whipped around my face. I looked at her, lost in her memories.

'He always said we were a team. He looked after me when I got into trouble, and I looked out for him. He called us "the firm".'

'You still meet up?'

She looked at me warily.

'I keep an eye on him. Shirley's MS is very bad. It came

on right around the time he lost his job. I help out, do his admin. Sometimes, when the nurse is there, we sneak off to the pictures.'

'Is he nearby?'

'Not too far.'

Still the loyal gatekeeper.

'I do need to see him.'

She shook her head sadly.

'Even if I told you where he was, he'd most probably shut the door on you. Nothing personal. It's just the way he is about it all. Especially now.'

'How did he and Greer react when Malik was killed?'

'I don't remember.'

'When Special Branch came ... What was the pretext, if Malik was dead?'

'I haven't a clue. Does it matter?'

She was starting to tire of my questions. I glanced surreptitiously at my watch. Four-fifteen. 'Can I buy you a drink?'

She leaned against me. 'I thought you'd never ask.'

We turned and walked back into the wind. She took my arm.

'How did you get on with her?'

'Edge always said you have to love the talent.'

'That's not an answer.'

She shrugged. 'She wasn't exactly one of the girls. She was always nice to me, probably because I worked for him. Even gave me a Cartier watch that some hapless admirer had pressed on her. And her clothes! All hand made. No labels. It was as if she existed in her own parallel universe. I went to her flat once, in her car. She had one of those classic sporty Mercs with the concave roof. Her place was amazing. Silk curtains, white floors, a black marble coffee table; very minimal. Lord knows what she was paid. But it didn't look lived in at all. Not even a coffee cup on the draining board.'

She giggled. 'Did you ever play four-minute warning? A nuclear bomb's about to go off. You've got four minutes to live. Who're you going to fuck? You have to be pissed, of course.

The production team always used to play it at wrap parties. She never came to those – except once. No one suggested it. You didn't do that sort of thing in front of her. She was always the boys' first choice.'

'Was there ... anybody?'

'No one got near. Even the lechers were in awe of her. If there was anyone, we never knew.'

She went quiet for a moment. 'She wasn't what you'd call happy. Even though she seemed to have it all.'

'Her and Edge?'

She gave me a withering look.

'He only had one affair, a long one – with his job. He couldn't get enough of it. That's why he's so remorseful now. Thinks he should have spent more time with his wife.'

The wine bar was empty. Carrie greeted the owner with the same enthusiasm she had me. He smiled thinly.

'This is my long lost friend, Nicholas.'

No one called me that. I realised I hadn't eaten, so I ordered a burger.

'And a bottle of something strong and red please, Gerard.'

We sat by the window. The rain had come back. Gusts of it splashed against the glass.

She put her elbows on the table and cradled her face. Then she took out a compact and checked herself. The wine arrived but Gerard didn't bother to pour it. Carrie filled the glasses and raised hers. 'To old times.' She drank half of it in one go and leaned across to me. I didn't feel part of anyone's old times, and I guess my expression must have said so.

She set down her glass and put her hands on my face. 'You're very tense. Relax. First rule of coaching. Forget the pressure. Lower those shoulders. Be calm.'

She closed her eyes and took some deep breaths.

I ate my burger. She continued to drink steadily and started reminiscing about some of the others on the *Human Face* team. It was well over ten years ago, but the way she spoke, it might as well have been last week.

'Don't disappear.'

She got up and went to the lavatory. Her bag hung on the chair. The dog whimpered and tugged at its lead, which was wrapped round one of the legs. Gerard sat behind the bar, reading a magazine. I reached for the bag. The dog got up and the chair toppled back and crashed to the ground. Its contents spilled out onto the floor and the dog started yapping. Gerard looked up. I mouthed *Sorry* and gathered everything up. I pressed the menu button on her phone, then *Contacts*, then *E*. I scanned Edge's number and put it back.

When she returned, some of her primness seemed to have worn off. She wove unsteadily between the tables and sat down heavily on her chair. She refilled her glass. 'So good to see you again.'

I nodded. I wanted to call Edge. She peered at me. 'I can tell a lot about people. What are you hiding from? Mmm?'

I didn't respond.

'You're on your own, aren't you?' Her voice had got louder. 'No Mrs Roker waiting at home.' I put a finger to my lips. Gerard refolded his paper noisily. I didn't feel like telling her I didn't even have a home.

'I know! I could give you a makeover; re-brand you. It's my speciality.'

She reached over and tugged at my beard.

'We could get rid of this. That would be a good start.'

Her face veered closer to mine. She tilted it slightly to one side and touched my hand. Her breath smelled of the wine. I didn't want to kiss her.

'I thought you had a date.'

She frowned and then laughed, slightly embarrassed. She rummaged in her bag and pulled out a half-flattened pack of cigarettes. I lit one for her and she inhaled deeply. Then her eyes focused on Greer's lighter. 'I remember this.' She plucked it from my hand and turned it over in her palm. 'Ah. Now I get it. Memento?'

'Not exactly.'

She fired it up and held it in front of my face.

'Old flame ...' She snorted at her own joke. Then she closed her eyes and shook her head with theatrical slowness. 'You as well ... I never got what it was about her. She had trouble tattooed right across her forehead, and none of you could see it.' She leaned across the table. 'You really want to know why he sent you, Mr Great-future-ahead-of-you? Sure? Because you had no fucking idea. That's why.' She paused while she emptied her glass. 'The others – they refused to go. No one would work with her. She was out of control. She destroyed Edge. That's a fact.'

She called loudly for another bottle. Gerard didn't respond.

'Don't ignore me, for fuck's sake.'

Two men had sat down at another table. They pretended not to notice.

Gerard came towards us and put his hand gently on her shoulder.

'Time to go, Carrie.'

'Don't touch me!'

He looked at me, appealing. I nodded and took out my wallet.

'Excuse *me*. I'm still talking.' Carrie's face had turned red. The dog started barking under the table. She pointed an accusing finger at me.

'And what about Anita? Eh? Forgotten about her?' She shook her head in disgust. 'Well, serve you fucking right.'

I looked away, my face burning. I paid the bill and half manhandled Carrie out onto the pavement. She shook herself free and leaned against a car, boiling with indignation.

Her eyes filled with rage then her face crumpled. 'I'm so, so, so sorry. Really I am.'

I held her while the tears shuddered through her.

'It's just so unfair. His wife's been at death's door for years. She barely notices he's there. All these years, wasted. She should be in care, but he refuses.'

I put my arm round her and steered her home.

She couldn't find her key.

'Don't look.' She bent down and reached under a pot plant by the mat. 'I think I need to lie down.'

'Shall I make you a coffee?'

She nodded meekly. 'I'm such a fuck-up. Why are you being so kind?'

I held her for a moment, and caught sight of us in a mirror. We made an odd couple.

When I brought her the coffee she was already asleep on her bed, the dog curled up beside her. They looked comfortable together. I eased off her shoes then set the bedside alarm for six so she would have some time to get ready for her date.

I dialled Edge's number, my heart thumping. It rang for a long time.

'Yes?'

'I've a package for a Mr Edgington from a Miss Marron, but can't read where it's going.'

Edge barked the address and hung up.

19

Rain lashed the side of the car and it rocked in the wind. The headlights were feeble. The road needed all my concentration but my mind was swirling. I could still smell Carrie's scent, as if some of her sadness had rubbed off on me. Even through the fog of alcohol she had seen further inside me than anyone had in a long time, seen things I hadn't yet admitted. What was her connection with Anita?

I turned inland and headed towards the Downs. The country roads were greasy. Farm equipment had left a slick of mud and the camber dragged the car towards the verge. I missed a sharp left and went straight through an open gate into a field. *Relax*, I heard Carrie say. I wondered if her date had turned up.

The village was tiny. There were no streetlights. Nine o'clock. Not a great time to call. There was a row of cottages, and, beyond, a larger house behind a high brick wall.

A solitary lamp over the door glinted through the drizzle. I ducked under the branches of a willow, taking care not to dislodge the droplets hanging from its leaves. The gate groaned painfully as I unlatched it. My heart was hammering. Part of me was resisting every step. I rang the bell.

'It's open.'

The voice came from upstairs.

I turned the handle and pushed the door. Warm, musty air enveloped me. A wheelchair occupied most of the dark hall.

'Upstairs. Hurry up.'

It was an old house. The stairs were narrow and curved round to a wide landing. One wall was all bookshelves. I could hear the blood pumping through my head.

A frail figure was curled in a fetal position on the bed. Her scalp was visible under wisps of silver hair. She had a mask on her face and wires and tubes led from under the covers to a machine on a metal trolley. Edge was in a chair pulled close to the bed. He was hunched over her. He didn't look round.

'Where the fuck have you been?'

I didn't respond.

'She's not been moved for eight hours. Let's get on with it.' He was suddenly on his feet. 'Move that trolley – you know the drill.'

I moved to the other side of the bed.

Edge pulled the covers back, liberating a mixture of medical smells and the unmistakeable odour of decay. She lay there, tiny and insubstantial beneath her white nightdress, as if there was nothing separating her bones from the cotton fabric.

'This arm first. Mind the drips.'

I put my knee on the side of the bed and got my arms under her shoulders. Edge grunted as he lifted her legs.

'Now. Gently.'

She was shockingly light.

'Don't trap those tubes!'

His breaths came in short bursts. I could see his face now, much older. The intensity still there, but superseded by anxiety. As if he was finally in over his head. We settled her into the same curled position, facing the other way. He smoothed out her hair.

The doorbell went. He looked up at me for the first time and frowned. A cheery male voice called from downstairs.

'Shall I come up?'

Edge rolled his eyes.

A tall man in his early thirties appeared in the room carrying a small case. He smiled brightly, as if it might make a difference, and put out his hand to Edge. Then he noticed me.

'Ah, jolly good.' He nodded eagerly. 'Help is at hand, I see.'

I didn't say anything.

'Sorry about your carer; he got caught up with an emergency.'

Despite the gloom, I could see Edge's face redden. 'I pay through the fucking nose for these people.' He pointed a finger in my direction. 'It's not bloody good enough.'

The doctor frowned. He put his case down on the bed and folded his arms. Despite his sunny demeanour, there were clear limits to his compassion. He looked wearily at Edge. 'Mr Edgington, you know what I'm going to say.' The doctor glanced at me. 'Only so much can be done at home. The level of care—'

'She staying put. You know bloody well it's not long now.'

Signs of exasperation were showing on the doctor's face. He put a hand through his hair. 'We can't do cover tonight; we just haven't enough staff. She'll have to go in. I've ordered an ambulance.'

I watched fury do battle with panic across Edge's face. It was painful to see – someone who had once made things happen through the sheer force of his personality, struggling to stay afloat.

'Well, what's he then?'

They both looked at me. I held their gaze.

'I can stay,' I said.

Edge frowned at me, confused, but didn't speak.

The doctor sighed. 'Right. I'll cancel the ambulance.' He picked up his bag and fished out a phone.

Edge continued to stare at me.

If he was thinking, *Who the fuck are you?* he kept it to himself while the doctor was still there. Whoever I was, I was the reason he could keep his wife at home one more night.

20

'You've got a bloody nerve.'

I sat at the kitchen table. He paced about as if he had energy to burn.

'I could throw you out.'

'How often does she need to be turned?'

'Every four hours.' He shook his head. 'Carrie's going to get a rocket.'

'She doesn't know I'm here.' I sipped the Scotch he had poured me. Eventually he let out a long sigh and sat down. I looked at him. 'I'm sorry about your wife.'

'Yes, well ...'

The kitchen was a mess. While Colin's was the mess of activity, this was the clutter of confinement, of inertia. There was a tray of pill bottles on the counter, along with a pack of syringes in transparent sachets and a box of disposable plastic gloves. A bunch of wrinkled grapes sat in a fruit bowl on the table. Beside it was an ashtray full of butts and a small pile of paperbacks. A stack of newspapers lay on the only other chair. At least he was still in touch with the world.

'Would you like me to make something to eat?'

'Be my guest.' He had resigned himself to my presence.

I found a packet of spaghetti and some tinned tomatoes in the larder. I held them up. He nodded.

'Carrie said you don't keep up with anyone.'

'Better that way.'

'So you wouldn't have agreed to see me.'

'Bit late for that now.'

I offered him a cigarette. He hesitated and then grabbed it, kicking the door closed with his foot. I didn't use Greer's lighter this time. He smoked in silence while I prepared the meal. The only other sound was the low hum from the machines in the bedroom, keeping his wife alive.

'I promised.' He glanced up at the ceiling. 'She begged me to let her die at home.' He drew heavily on the cigarette. 'And I've broken enough promises.'

'I know.' The comment escaped before I'd thought about it.

He looked bewildered.

'Like when you said, "I promise you, you've got a great career on *Human Face*" ...' I surprised myself with my sudden vehemence.

He looked stunned. He stared at me for a while as if he was waiting for his memory to engage.

'You couldn't get anyone else. You thought I'd get you out of a jam.'

I could see his fear and regretted my outburst. His expression changed. 'You did come over rather well. Like you'd give it a hundred per cent. Maybe you don't remember.'

'That's not why you sent me.'

'OK, you turned up at the right time. But I knew I could trust you.'

'Why?'

He held out his hands. 'Because you reminded me of someone.'

I waited for an explanation.

'Of me.' He smiled for the first time. 'The way you got to us. Just the sort of thing I would have done. You called the switchboard at, what, half nine at night? Even though they were sworn not to give out my home number, you got it out of them. You didn't even apologise.'

He helped himself to another of my cigarettes and lit it from the butt of the first.

'You showed up next morning with your asylum rushes. I even remember the label on the can: *Teen Dream Break*.' He laughed. 'You'd used up three rolls of *Destination*'s precious film stock, at about four hundred quid a roll, which could have got you sacked. You took the risk.'

I struggled to recognise the person he was talking about.

'You had what it took. It was obvious.'

I washed out a couple of soup bowls, drained the spaghetti and shared it between us. 'You liked to give people breaks, Carrie said. Spotting talent.'

He nodded.

'Especially when no one else would touch the job?'

He avoided my gaze. 'If it's revenge you want, this is a bloody funny way to go about it.'

I poured the sauce over the spaghetti and put a bowl in front of him. I found the cutlery and some parmesan in the fridge.

'There's a bottle in the study.' He nooded towards the next room.

The walls were lined with yet more books. There was a large desk. Behind the chair, a one-eyed BAFTA trophy stared down at me. I took a claret from a half-empty rack. He looked famished, but he had waited for me to return before he started. I uncorked the bottle and poured him a glass. He held it up to the light. 'Well, I got my comeuppance. It finished me and the bloody show.' He took a sip of wine. 'Anyway, it's all in the past now.' He didn't sound convinced.

His expression changed. The colour was coming back into his cheeks. His eyes refocused.

'You don't look a whole lot better than the last time I saw you.'

I waited for him to elaborate.

'I was the one who identified you. You were out cold. Despite the racket. There must have been about fifty in the ward.'

'In Colombo?'

I had no memory of him in Sri Lanka. The only visitor I could recall was Bernard Hinde.

'The man from the Consulate. Nasty little shit. He tried to stop me seeing you.'

Barely coherent images from the hospital flooded back. I was conscious, but trapped in a body that couldn't see or hear, thinking, *This is how it feels to be dead.* It was the smell of powerful disinfectant that made me realise I was alive. Then I became gradually aware of sounds, a distant murmur at first, like a theatre audience waiting for a show to begin. Sometimes there would be several faces looking down at me; then they would disappear. Sometimes I just felt hands, gentle on my shoulders, kneading or pulling as if I was a misshapen piece of clay. No one tried to speak to me. Then a ceiling fan came into focus. I gave myself a memory test. Could I count the number of times it revolved? I made it to nine. Later I managed thirty-eight. When I got to a hundred and ten I cried. Then I was moved away from the fan. I was in a cast, which kept me on my back. All there was to amuse me was a long, threatening crack across the ceiling. I wanted to warn someone about it, but couldn't find the means to speak.

Edge finished his food. He looked stronger. I wondered when his last decent meal had been.

'It was Hinde's idea to call it a boating accident.' He grimaced. 'He was more concerned about the impact on his career than anything else.

I refilled his glass.

'I thought I was coming to bring you both home. I waited two days before he would see me. I just wanted to find you both. There was a lot of waiting in corridors, to see various officials of equal uselessness. Just when I was about ready to punch someone, they told me ...'

Edge stopped talking, as if trying to get his breath. He was sweating.

'They told me that there wasn't a body to bring home; that the blast – there was nothing.' A forefinger went up to his mouth and his face tensed. 'Shit ...' The finger started to tremble. His other hand remained on the table. I covered it with mine. He looked at me again, his eyes full of tears. His voice rose an octave. 'You'd think it would get easier, with time.'

He wiped his eyes and tried to lose himself in his wine-glass.

'So I went to the hospital and demanded to see you.' Edge gripped my hand. 'I wanted you to tell me what had happened, but you didn't even know who you were. I met a young consultant.'

'Sivalingham?'

'Maybe. I said I'd sit by you, but he warned me it could be a very long wait. Weeks or months. He said he'd keep me informed.'

'And did he?'

He looked at his hands. 'He might have tried, but when I got back they gave me the push.'

'Did anyone mention the theft?'

He frowned.

'My hotel room; there were papers, photographs. And the tapes.'

'You'd *filmed* him? Without Greer?'

'I didn't know where she was. Didn't know if I'd get another chance if I waited for her to turn up. You were relying on me, remember?'

A buzzer went somewhere in the house.

'Come on.'

I followed him up the stairs and into the bedroom. His wife was exactly how we had left her. We performed the same manoeuvre, putting her onto her other side. Her limbs flopped lifelessly.

'How long have you been together?'

'Since we were seventeen.'

He smoothed out her hair.

Forty years.

'I've not been a good husband. She spent all her active life waiting for me to come home. Soon as I got the boot she went downhill.' He sighed heavily. 'Let's have another glass.'

My bag was in the hall. I took out the envelope.

'What's this?' I put Colin's print of the flash frame in front of him. Malik's face was ghostly pale but all the features were there. Edge swapped his glasses to examine it. When he looked up, he was red and shaking. 'This some sort of stitch-up? Who are you with?'

I put my hand out but he moved away and banged against

the counter where he had left the pile of newspapers. 'Is that what you're after? *Face of the Northolt Butcher, by shamed TV man who fell under his spell*?' Saliva had gathered on his lips. He wiped it away with his sleeve.

I didn't move. I held his stare.

He glanced back at the print. 'The whole world wants this picture. You could sell it for a fortune.'

'I just wanted to be sure.'

'Of what?' He had a hunted look on his face.

'That it was him. Malik.'

'Why? What's this got to do with you?'

He took a series of quick breaths, and his anger subsided. He nodded at the pile of papers.

'It's crap. What they've been saying about him, it's lies.'

I waited for him to continue.

'Northolt. It couldn't have been him.'

'Why?'

He didn't answer at first. His shoulders sagged. He took off his glasses and rubbed his eyes. 'Not him.'

I moved the chair out and gestured for him to sit down. He looked at the picture again and his eyes glazed over as if he was having trouble focusing. It was a few minutes before he spoke again.

'He wasn't a terrorist. I hated that word …'

'How do you know?'

'I'd done my homework. There was nothing directly linking him to any atrocities of any kind.'

He took a deep breath and rubbed a hand over his brow. 'Sometime after the Six Day War, all the men from his father's village were interned in a camp in the desert. Malik and his older brother missed getting rounded up. The mother wasn't Palestinian so they got exempted. Or maybe he was too young. I forget. But the brother was a hot-head, bent on revenge. Wanted to hijack a plane, take hostages. Malik had a better idea. He recce'd the camp. No one noticed him. He was just a teenager at the time. It wasn't very well defended. He came up with a plan. He sprung them – four thousand – without a drop of blood being spilt. It was a huge propaganda coup and emboldened a lot of those who'd been cowed by the Israelis. That's what brought him to prominence. Overnight he had a whole movement behind him. A lot of things started to happen in his name, though there's no evidence he had anything to do with them. But he'd become a hero, and for that he was considered dangerous. And a target. There was pressure, not to let anyone down. They wanted him to lead. He'd shunned publicity, but that just added to his mystique. We went after him thinking he was going to be the next Arafat. It was hype.' He tapped the photograph. 'After we'd filmed him, you know what he said? He'd had enough. He was going to get out. Disappear.'

'Did you believe him?'

He shrugged. 'When we first heard his name connected to Northolt, I laughed. It just wasn't in him. Nothing about it. He didn't do coercion. Those men who took that plane had been threatened with their families' lives. Greer agreed. They didn't know what they were doing. They weren't organised. Completely out of control.' He shook a finger at me and then tapped the pile of newspapers. 'I called them – the Northolt Families people. I told them who I was and that they were being misled.'

'What did they say?'

'They said they'd send someone to speak to me.' He sighed and shook his head. He was staring into space, lost in his memories. I could feel tiredness creeping over me, but I needed all I could get from him.

'If he was framed for it, then why?'

Edge sighed. 'A scapegoat? An excuse to take him down? I don't know.'

'Weren't you curious?'

He looked stung by the question. He stared into his lap. 'When he'd been named as the ringleader, it meant the film couldn't be shown, regardless of whether we thought he was innocent. I kept going, cutting it, but I wasn't hopeful. I thought it'd have to be canned. But then when the news came through that he'd been killed ...'

'It meant you could broadcast.'

He took a deep breath and nodded. 'They couldn't stop us any more. It's what we all wanted.'

'And the title?'

'The Board insisted. I didn't have a choice. But we scripted it so it wasn't judgemental, so people could make up their own minds.' He grinned and I saw a flicker of the old fire in his eyes. 'That upset a few people.'

'Why were all the copies seized?'

'They took everything they could find to do with that film – all the prints and transcripts, every scrap. Even the trims.' He shook his head. 'A mystery. We asked for an explanation. Nothing.'

'You never doubted he was dead.'

He shrugged. 'Enough people would have wanted him out of the way. I didn't have a reason to doubt it. Why are you asking?' Suddenly he was suspicious again. 'What's it matter now anyway?'

I'd held off showing him the other photographs. I wanted his version first. I reached for the envelope.

'Christ. No more, please.' He got up and moved to the sink. He produced a bubble pack of pills from his pocket and washed a couple down.

I laid out the three shots of Rammal beside the picture of Malik. The light in the kitchen wasn't very bright. He bent down and examined them. Another wave of doubt swept over me. I looked at the small triangular scar under the eye. What could be seen of his hair was much greyer than in the frame from the film. I waited, my heart smashing against my ribs.

Edge changed his glasses and studied the pictures. He took his time.

'Where did you get these?'

'I took them. In Sri Lanka.'

His gaze moved between me and the table. 'Impossible.' He put his hand up to his chest and took a couple of breaths.

I prodded the photographs. I wanted confirmation. 'Are they the same man?'

The heavy lids, the cleft in the tip of the nose, the same line of beard.

'I don't understand.' Edge looked frail and hunted.

'It's him, isn't it?'

He stared at me.

'Well?'

His mouth hung open, trembling, as if he couldn't find the words. He seemed to age in front of me. He bent down closer to examine the pictures and let himself drop into the chair.

Eventually he nodded. 'Has to be.' He tapped the picture. 'The one on the boat?'

I nodded.

'The arms dealer?'

A frail old man struggling to comprehend. He had lived with his version of what happened, just as I had, trying to come to terms with it. Now there was another. The story had changed.

I passed a cigarette to him and lit it. Then I poured him another glass of wine. He downed most of it and the colour started to come back into his cheeks. He sat for a while, savouring the cigarette, glancing at the pictures and staring off into space, deep in thought, then shaking his head.

I refilled his glass. 'Could Greer have known?'

'What?'

'That he hadn't been killed after Northolt.'

His eyes narrowed. 'When we heard, she was devastated. She disappeared for a while. I let her be. When she came back we never mentioned it. But she never wanted to look at the film. She didn't watch it when it went out. Wasn't going to collect the award – until I ordered her to.'

'Could she have known and not told you? Could they have stayed in touch?' He looked frail again and stared off into the distance, gnawing at his bottom lip. 'When you filmed Malik, what was she like with him?'

'She got him to agree to speak. Not me. I'd gone out to Lebanon to find him. Took me about two weeks. But he turned me down, very politely. Just said he didn't want the attention.

I was back in Beirut sitting in my hotel, wondering what to do next. That's where I first met her. She was a freelance then. Barely twenty-one. She offered to help.' He paused, his eyes far away. 'I went back to him with her. She asked me to introduce them and then stay out of the way.' He smiled at his own memory. 'I was a bit hesitant – after all, she was just a kid, but she winked and said, "Trust me." After a couple of hours alone with him, she came back. He'd agreed – as long as she asked the questions. He was pretty impressed. She had that effect. When we filmed ...' He shook his head. 'I'd never seen anything like it. She didn't push. That was her style. She just created this sort of vacuum into which people spoke. She just sucked it out of him. I think he said far more than he meant to.'

'Did you have any contact with him after that?'

'No.'

'And her?'

'If she did, she didn't say.' He looked away. 'She was a very private person.'

This wasn't going anywhere. He was drifting off into his memories.

'Why did she go to Sri Lanka?'

He studied his hands. 'She travelled a lot. I let her. She was good at finding stories.'

'Carrie said that she got difficult.'

He reddened. 'Carrie doesn't know a bloody thing.' He checked himself. 'They ... didn't exactly get on.' He looked away to the window. It was black outside. The curtains were still open. 'Greer said she wanted to do something about the peace process with the Tamils. I couldn't see it myself.'

'Could she have known he was there? Could she have been looking for him?'

I saw something of the old firepower in his eyes. He jabbed the air between us. '*You* brought them together remember. *You* were the reason she was on that boat.'

I opened my mouth to defend myself.

It's all arranged. There's a car waiting. Was Tanager right? I was starting to doubt my own memory.

As quickly as it had come, his fierceness left him. He put up a hand. 'I'm too old for this. I've got enough going on.'

The buzzer went again upstairs.

'Injection time.' He looked at his watch. 'This is where I turn in. You can use the sofa in there.' He nodded toward the study. 'Next one's at six. And after that, I'd like you to go.'

He scooped up a sachet containing a syringe and moved heavily towards the door. I started after him but he put up his hand again.

'It's just a jab. I can manage.' He glanced at me one more time. Then down at the prints. 'What you've got there – it's dynamite.'

Then he went upstairs.

21

The sofa was musty. I didn't care. I lay staring at the artefacts of his illustrious career ranged across the shelves.

My sleep was brief but deep. It seemed only moments after I'd dropped off that he was standing over me in a dressing gown.

'Come on.'

It was six fifteen. We turned Shirley over again. I wondered how much longer she had to go. She looked like most of the life had already seeped out of her. I caught sight of a portrait of the two of them, very young, laughing at the camera.

He went over and picked it up. 'Don't do what I did.'

'What's that?'

'Forget what matters.' He stared at the photo. 'At the time, it's like a drug – getting the scoop. I was an addict. I lived for the rush. She waited at home, never complained. And the minute I got the chop, bang ...'

Edge put the picture back in its place and steered me out of the room. I went downstairs and into the kitchen. I put a kettle on and started to clear up. There was a scattering of Post-It notes on the fridge. *Tax car. Shoes to menders. Pruning. Hoover bags.* I straightened a pile of post: building society statements, rose catalogues, a brochure of holidays for the disabled. Under the pile was an ancient answering machine, its red light winking, and, beside it, a scribbled list of messages and numbers in childish handwriting. The kettle boiled and I made a pot of tea. I put the rest of the dishes into the sink and ran the tap. I reached for the washing-up liquid but my hand stopped in mid-air. I moved back to the list.

Next to one of the phone numbers was written: *Tan?? Will call again.*

I took out my phone, switched it on and checked received calls. The number was Tanager's.

'What is it?'

Edge was standing in the doorway. His wiry hair was flat against his scalp and his cheeks were pink from the shower. Sleep had restored him. Like a creature coming out of hibernation, he seemed to fill his skin again.

'This message.'

He moved towards the teapot. 'Not my writing. One of the nurses.'

'When would it have been?'

He shrugged. 'There are all sorts of calls. I can't be bothered with them.'

'Does the name Tanager mean anything to you?'

He shook his head. 'Lots of things don't mean anything to me. It's called getting fucking old.'

He sat down and I brought him milk and sugar for the tea. He surveyed the tidy surfaces with a look of relief.

'I was sharp with you last night.'

'It's OK.'

'It's a lot to take in.' He drank the tea down in one go and poured himself another. 'I sent you, after all. You were only doing your job.' He watched me while I carried on straightening the room. 'It matters to you, doesn't it?'

'Greer. In Sri Lanka. What was she doing?'

'Recce-ing. As far as I knew.'

'Suppose she knew he was alive, and that he was there? And she'd been looking for him. But I was the one who found him. That could explain why she went to the boat.'

He waved his glasses at me. 'Your girl.'

'What?'

'The one with the long name. Very pretty.'

'Anita Jayarajah.'

'She said it was *you* who arranged it – the meeting on the boat.'

'You *met* her?'
'She was there when I came to the hospital.'
'What was she doing there?'
He shrugged. 'Visiting you, I suppose. Didn't know what to make of her. She was sort of frozen – like she was still in shock. I thought she was taking a big risk coming to see you, after what had happened.'
'What did she say?'
'She didn't want to talk to me, tried to leave. But I wasn't having that. We'd paid her, after all. I had to know what had happened.'
He sat down. His eyes roamed around the room as he rifled through his memory.
'She told you *I'd* arranged the meeting? You're sure?'
'I needed to know how Greer came to be on that boat. The girl was very clear, like she had rehearsed it. She said you fixed it, that you were going to make the introductions.'
'Did you believe her?'
'I didn't have a reason not to. Except …'
'What?'
'I thought there was something else going on with her.' He waved a finger at me. 'Were you … involved?'
I reddened. 'Why?'
'Something Carrie said.' He wrinkled up his face. 'It's all coming back now. Carrie found her for us. They had some family connection. She'd stayed with Carrie's parents; a student exchange or something.'
He looked at me. 'Carrie said you might have … raised her expectations.' The intensity I had remembered from our first meeting had come back to his eyes. 'Is there something *you* haven't mentioned?'
A cold pain spread across my chest. Anita's face – her expression when she confronted me in the hotel lobby – hovered in front of me.
'I need to find her. I don't even know if she's still alive.'
'Carrie should know.'

'She may not want to tell me. She was very cagey about you.'

He smiled. 'Tell her I told her to. She usually does what I say. How was she, by the way?'

'I thought you were in regular contact.'

'She's not been good.' He frowned and raised an imaginary glass to his lips.

I wondered if she had woken up in time for her date. 'Do you remember her boyfriend, Saul?'

His eyes narrowed.

'From the time she first worked for you.'

Eventually he nodded. 'American, I think. Pushy. Wanted to do an internship with us. I didn't take to him. Then he cleared off, without any warning. She was devastated. Why do you ask?'

'Carrie borrowed a copy of *Face of a Terrorist* for him.'

He looked blank at first. 'She got a bollocking from me.'

'The copy of the film this came from.' I held up Colin's print of the flash frame. 'Apart from this, all the shots of Malik had been cut out of it. As if someone was trying to erase him.'

The toast sprang up and we both jumped at the sound. Then he stepped forward and gripped my arm.

'We were told he was ambushed and killed a couple of weeks after Northolt. I was sorry, but I didn't question it. Frankly, what I really cared about was getting the film shown. And his death made that possible.' His grip tightened. 'Nick, I don't know what use I can be, but ...'

It was the first time he'd used my name. He looked younger, more alert, as if this was suddenly bringing him back to life.

'Carrie's got all her diaries. God knows what, but there may be something in them that helps.'

I put the envelopes back into my bag and put on my jacket.

'You should show those to the Northolt people. I'll verify that's him. They said they needed evidence. That would be a fucking bombshell.'

My eye fell on the winking light of the answering machine again. 'Can I?'

Three messages were from concerned neighbours and friends asking about Shirley and offering help. The fourth was from Tanager.

Sorry to bother you again. Wondered if I could call on you. I'm in your area tomorrow.

The message was from yesterday. It was the same matter-of-fact tone he'd used with me, as if he was just popping round to borrow some hedge clippers.

'Be careful. He may not like what you have to say.'

Edge snorted. 'At this stage I'm pretty much past caring.'

I needed to leave. 'If he comes, do me a favour: don't mention me.'

I moved towards the hall. He nodded at the bag. 'You're the one who needs to be careful.'

22

It was still dark.

There were no spaces in Carrie's street, but there was a small car park belonging to a bank in the next road. Seven thirty – too early to call. The rain had stopped, so I walked down to the seafront and found a small café that was just opening up. I ordered eggs, bacon and a mug of coffee.

A paper lay on the counter, I flicked through the pages. There was the picture of Greer and Edge holding the BAFTA award. Under it, a comment piece with the headline THROWING PETROL ON FIRE attacked 'naive left-wing TV producers' who 'romanticised terror' and glorified 'killers and psychopaths masquerading as revolutionaries': *giving airtime to the likes of Malik and his kind gave them just what they wanted – the world's attention, spurring them on to ever more hideous atrocities*.

I shut the paper and ate my breakfast.

A full grey dawn was spreading out over the sea. A flock of gulls swooped over a pile of rubbish on the beach. I dialled Carrie's number from a payphone in the café. It was engaged.

The rush hour had started. I crossed the road along the seafront and walked up through the park where we had strolled the day before. There was no answer when I rang her bell. A carton of milk stood on her doorstep.

I rang the bell again and bent down to look through the letterbox. There was an acrid smell. Urine. And a whining sound. The dog was standing outside the door to her bedroom, one foot poised in the air, as if uncertain which way to turn.

I lifted the pot and took out the spare key. The dog didn't move, but the whining increased. There was a damp patch on the carpet by the door and up the skirting board. I glanced into the sitting room. An unopened bottle of champagne in an ice bucket stood on the coffee table. Beside it were two glasses. The ice had melted. The water was room temperature.

There was another sound: the wail of a phone left off the hook. I put my hand down to comfort the dog, but it ran into the bedroom.

Carrie had changed into a low-cut dress; her make-up and lipstick looked fresh. Her hair had fallen across her face. As I moved it back, the tip of my finger touched her cheek. The strength went out of my legs. I sat down on the bed. She was completely cold. An empty water glass and an empty packet of painkillers sat on the bedside table.

The alarm would have woken her. She probably hadn't felt great, but she'd got herself ready. Made an extra effort. Laid out the champagne. And waited. And begun to wonder.

Perhaps she started making excuses to herself. He's got lost; he's missed the train. He's been detained at work; he's stuck in traffic. As time went on she would have felt the mounting disappointment, perhaps humiliation. Sitting alone with her little dog. Maybe he had called with an excuse. Or not called at all. And the ice in the champagne bucket melted. Perhaps she'd had enough waiting.

The dog was yelping, so I opened the kitchen door to the patio. I went back into the bedroom.

She looked so neat and tidy, just as she would have wanted to be found. So composed.

Too composed.

The dog. Would she have taken her life without letting it out? I looked at her face again, then at the water glass. There was no lipstick print.

I left the front door on the latch and ran back towards the car. On my way I stopped at the phone box and dialled 999.

23

Traffic lights, zebra crossings and right-turn lanes all seemed to come at me faster than I could cope with them. The Beetle was full of sound. I clutched the wheel and pushed my face closer to the windscreen, as if that would make a difference. A pedestrian stepped out into the road, saw me and leapt back. I glanced down at the speedometer. I was doing sixty.

I slowed to thirty, and Carrie's face forced its way back in front of me. She was everywhere, in shop windows, on posters, in oncoming cars, smiling at me, contorted with drunken anger, composed and still on her bed. Her scent was on my jacket. The space on my shoulder where she had buried her face and cried seemed still to bear her imprint. I rolled down the passenger window to let in the air coming off the sea. It didn't help. I pulled off the road, opened the door and threw up.

The tide was right out, uncovering a wide tract of wet sand. I stood at the water's edge. The sea was a pale grey froth. A hard wind was blowing. I let the clear sharp air fill my lungs. The sun went behind a thick bank of cloud hovering offshore and the sea turned a darker grey.

A woman came towards me, tugging an elderly dog. She altered her direction so she didn't have to get too near. As she passed, she frowned down at me. I turned my face away. I had dropped to my knees in the wet sand. The cold water was soaking up into my jeans.

Saul.

I didn't even know his last name. Why kill her? *Had* he killed her? I turned away from the sea. The adrenalin raging through my body started to subside. I felt sluggish and wrung out. I tried to bring my thoughts under control. I took out my mobile and switched it on. Then remembered what Colin had said and switched it off again.

The smell of urine in the phone box stung the back of my throat. I dialled Edge. I wanted him to find out about Carrie from me, not a newspaper. His answering machine was on.

I dialled Colin. He picked up after the first ring, as if he was waiting for my call.

'So you're not dead yet?'

'So it seems.'

'Where are you?'

'Somewhere on the south coast.'

'That woman any use?'

I didn't answer.

'The tape used on those cuts on that film, I was wrong about it.'

'That must be a first.'

'It's American made. Not sold commercially.'

'Meaning?'

'It's known as Reconnaissance Tape. Used on military survey films. Supposed to withstand damp and extremes of temperature better than domestic stuff. Last used in the late eighties before they switched to video.'

'What should I make of that?'

'That those cuts were probably done not long after the film was made. That the people who used it also do killing. That it might help me in my lonely battle to convince you that you're way out of your depth, Tintin.'

He was right about that.

'Are you OK?'

'Sort of.'

I could sense his frustration down the phone. He was torn between warning me off and wanting to know everything.

'Car all right?'

'Perfect.'

'Is there anything else?'

'Yes.'

'But you don't want to talk.'

'That's right.'

'Stay out of trouble.'

'It may be a bit late for that.'

I drove east along the coast until I reached Shoreham and stopped at another café with a payphone. I called Edge's number again. It rang for half a minute before he picked up. He was breathless.

'Can't talk now. They're taking her in.'

He had lost his battle.

The FOM – Film Operations Manager – at the Network used to scrutinise the daily rushes on two screens at a time. He wasn't watching the images, but looking for camera faults or imperfections in the negative. Sometimes, when there was a lot to get through, he ran them at double speed.

'Doesn't this drive you mad?' I once asked him as I waited for my rushes to appear.

'That happened long ago.'

He explained to me how he did it.

'You don't look at the centre. That's what the cameraman's concentrating on. You have to look into the corners – negative scoring, hairs in the gate, that sort of thing.'

Rammal and Malik occupied two separate frames in my head. I felt as I had convalescing after Sri Lanka, trying to order shards of memory into a coherent pattern. The interview on the boat. I knew I'd done it. There were faint details, like the impression a chair leaves on a carpet. I remember the boat rocking as we filmed and worrying that it would show on the screen. I remember the clouds from the cigar he insisted on smoking – in spite of my plea that it would cause continuity problems. His face was so sharp I could draw it – but nothing of what he said was there. Not even the sound of his voice. What else had I forgotten?

'The Salvation Army's down the road.'

My tea was cold. My head had settled on the plastic table. A woman with white-blonde hair stood over me.

'Sorry. May I have a refill?'

She returned with a fresh mug. I didn't want it but I didn't want to move either. I felt for my cigarettes. The wallet of photographs from Sri Lanka was still in my pocket. I held it in my hand for a moment then flipped it open. I pulled out the shot of Anita in her sari.

She had let out her ponytail and her long black hair swung around her shoulders. A pair of sunglasses held it away from her face. Her lips were slightly parted and her dark eyes shone. Behind her was an intricate pattern of ironwork.

From the moment she had skipped towards me, clutching her beloved clipboard, at Colombo airport, almost everything about her had irritated me. She explained that Greer was 'up country' but not to worry. She had planned my recce down to the last detail.

All I wanted to do was get to my hotel and rest but she wouldn't hear a word of it. The itinerary seemed to consist entirely of meetings with elderly men who had some connection with her family.

'They are learned men, all striving for peace. From them you will be able to understand in detail about our country.'

Over the next two days she delivered a continuous monologue on the marvels of the island and her faith in the peace process as we criss-crossed Colombo by tuk-tuk. After the sixth meeting I called a halt. I grabbed her clipboard and drew a line through all the other appointments.

'No more old farts. I can't make a film about peacemakers if I can't see the war.'

Her face burned with embarrassment. She didn't speak for the remainder of the journey back to the hotel. The next day she appeared in the same uniform but the clipboard was gone, and so had her puppyish enthusiasm. I noticed the small fray on her cuff that I had spotted the day before and realised she must have laundered the shirt overnight. Her sandals had split. We stopped at a roadside shoe-mender. They had been stitched several times before.

She didn't explain where we were going. She just said she had something to show me. We stopped in what looked like an affluent suburban street. She told the taxi driver to wait. The sun had come out and the road was heating up. She beckoned me towards the shade of a large eucalyptus.

Sprinklers spat water across the lawn of an immaculate bungalow. A gardener was clipping a hedge.

'Very nice.'

She motioned with her chin to the neighbouring lot, where the burned-out carcass of a Peugeot sat on its wheel rims in an overgrown drive. Behind it was a large pile of charred wood.

'So?'

I waited for her to speak.

'My family home.'

Her parents had been killed by Tamil terrorists. Her father was a moderate, involved in the peace process. It made him a target for extremists. Her brother had disowned him, fled to the north and joined the Tigers. She hadn't heard from him since. She had stayed on in Colombo, living with her godmother, whilst her medical school, where she had come top in her first year, had suspended her 'pending a review of the ethnic mix of the student body'. Her life had come to a halt.

'Why are you doing this – helping us?'

She stood in the shade, her head bowed.

'Trying to make a difference. What my father wanted.'

I stared at the photo. Location romances were one of the many perks of filming abroad. For some crews on *Destination*, who spent their life jetting from one holiday location to the next, they became almost routine. Few of them lasted beyond the shoot. Tearful promises made at airports were seldom honoured. They were a distraction that I'd tried to avoid.

In any case, Anita wasn't the type. At first glance, she seemed young for her age, and only focused on doing the right thing. A strict upbringing and a devotion to study had given her an overdeveloped sense of duty. Even when the world around her was in flames and she was left with almost nothing but the clothes she stood up in, she was still clinging to the idea of making the world a better place.

But seeing her among the ruins of her house, keeping her composure while I tried to digest what she told me – nothing had been done to find her parents' killers – I realised the veneer of girlishness was just part of her coping strategy, that underneath was a vast reservoir of pain.

I went to a newsagent's and got a handful of change, then found another phone box and dialled international directories. The connection for Colombo General Hospital took a few seconds.

'Do you have a Dr Sivalingham?'

'Who is calling, please?'

'A former patient.' I gave my name.

'Please hold the line.'

Sivalingham was the name on the hospital notes that travelled back with me from Sir Lanka. They were written with a fountain pen in a fine longhand.

> *This patient has suffered significant extradural haematoma and displays some degree of memory loss. There are fractures to the left collar bone and left tibia. However, he is a strong young chap with a good appetite and we anticipate full recovery if he is permitted to rest adequately.*

Sivalingham's face had been the first I saw when I came to. It looked as if he was sharing some private joke with himself. Maybe it was his defensive shield against the cacophony of suffering that swirled around him. Although we were about the same age, he addressed me as 'young fellow' or 'young man'. His laughing eyes danced over my face when he spoke.

'You are being treated by the youngest surgeon in Sri Lanka. You'll have the full benefit of my minuscule experience.'

Now I heard his name being shouted down an echoing corridor. Someone shouted back. I listened to footsteps four thousand miles away coming towards the phone. I explained who I was.

'Good God!'

'You remember me?'

'Of course. And you remember me. Excellent. My treatment was successful. Are you wanting a check-up?' He laughed heartily at his own joke. 'Where are you calling from?'

'England.'

'Shame. I am most interested in long-term recovery. Are you completely well? Did you get all your memory back?'

'Most of it. I am trying to find someone. Anita Jayarajah. She was a medical student. She helped me when I was there.'

'The young beauty who sat with you? She came the first few days after you were admitted – when you were unconscious.' There was a long pause. 'I am very sorry. Oh, I can ask my wife. She worked at the hospital at that time. They may have spoken.'

'When could you ask her?'

'You *are* in a hurry.' He laughed again. 'She'll have been snapped up by now.' He gave me his home number. 'Call me in an hour. I will be at home by then.'

The tide had come in. Waves slapped against the shingle. I left the café and walked along the seafront, hoping the sharp sea air would help me think. A mass of gulls swooped over the remains of a fish on the beach. I watched them fight over the scraps.

When the hour was up I went back to the call box. A woman answered. She passed the phone straight to Sivalingham. His tone was different.

'Yes, I am sorry, I am afraid I can't help you. The lady you were asking about left some time ago, for study abroad.'

'Where? What country?'

'Tamils go to many places. Canada, Australia, USA.'

'England?'

He hesitated, and I heard the woman's voice mutter something unintelligible. 'I am very sorry, I cannot help you further.' There was another murmur in the background. 'Goodbye.' Then, as an afterthought: 'I am glad to know you are fully recovered.'

There was a disappointment in his voice, as if he would have liked the exchange to have gone differently. I held the phone for some time until I realised he had rung off.

Carrie had found her. I cursed my cowardice for running from her flat without looking for her diaries or an address book. I went back to the car and ran the engine to get the heater going.

I took out the photographs again and spread them on my lap. *Look into the corners.* In the shot of Bernard Hinde, you could just see Anita's bag on the ground. It was almost out of the frame. I remembered the logo: *CFE*. I'd asked her what it stood for: *Commonwealth Friendship Exchange*. She had spent a summer term in England. It was a long shot, but I didn't have anything else.

24

I drove around the town until I found the public library. A woman in her fifties stood at the desk, flipping through a drawer of cards at impressive speed.

'I'm looking for information about Commonwealth exchange programmes.'

She screwed up her face as if she'd encountered a bad smell then slowly raised a forefinger. 'Bear with me.'

She disappeared behind a counter and returned several minutes later with a look of triumph and a stack of old books without dust covers. 'We don't have much demand for these.'

She laid them out. *The Almanac of Commonwealth Institutions*. I opened the copy nearest to me and examined the contents. Two pages were devoted to a list of Commonwealth Friendship Exchange offices around the country.

'Could I borrow this?'

'I'm sorry, it's strictly for reference.'

'Photocopy?'

'It's out of order.'

'Can I use a mobile in here?'

She smiled warmly and shook her head, taking perverse pride in her own unhelpfulness. I took a notebook from my bag and started copying out addresses. She looked over my shoulder as I got to the twentieth.

'They were disbanded, I believe, in 1995.' She smiled again. 'What is it that you need, exactly?'

'Someone who was a CFE exchange student.'

Her finger went up again. 'The university may have CFE yearbooks. They may have addresses of alumni.'

'You couldn't telephone them for me?'

She looked slightly shocked at the suggestion, as if I had asked her for a date.

'I'm sorry to ask. It's just that I'm in the most awful hurry.'

'Bear with me.'

She went behind a glass partition and picked up a phone. A younger woman in a parka arrived, puffing and out of breath, and slipped behind the counter. She lifted an elbow to release the local paper tucked under her arm. It dropped to the desk and she dumped a bag of shopping on top of it. The headline was obscured, and so was most of the accompanying photo-fit, but I could make out a murky screen grab from a CCTV camera, taken from somewhere high up. The shape of Colin's Beetle was unmistakeable.

I looked away. The woman hung up her parka and put the shopping on the floor.

'Yes?' She looked at me.

'It's OK, I'm being helped.'

I smiled in the direction of her colleague.

'Olga, you can go on your break now.'

There was no point trying to hide my face. I kept my eye-line up and my smile going. Wanted murder suspects probably didn't smile. Olga returned to the counter. She took off her glasses and let them swing on a little plastic chain.

'They think they might have some yearbooks but they're in the basement. Might take a while to dig them out.'

I didn't have a while, but I didn't have a better idea either.

'Are you a student?'

I shook my head. She filled out a small form headed *Inter-Library Viewing*.

'You won't be able to borrow anything.'

'That's OK. Thanks very much.'

'Wait. You'll need directions. The campus is very fiddly.'

The other librarian was looking down at the paper.

'I'll do you a little map.'

'I'm sure I can find it, really.'

She wouldn't be deterred. The other woman turned away for a moment and sneezed.

'Sorry.' She looked at me.

Olga started on the directions. 'Be careful on the roundabout that you don't take the turn for the Halls of Residence.'

I said goodbye and made for the door.

'Hold on ...' It was the other woman. I kept walking.

'Sir!'

I didn't stop.

'*Sir!* Your bag ...'

A traffic warden had just tucked a ticket under the Beetle's windscreen wiper. I pulled it out and stuck it in my pocket.

'You not gonna swear at me?'

The car started on the third go. I tried to make my getaway as orderly as possible and pulled out into solid traffic. All my instincts told me to hide. But where? What was the point?

The traffic crawled forward. A light blinked on the dash. The fuel needle was on *E*. Perhaps a have-a-go citizen would heave me out onto the tarmac. I locked the doors as a feeble precaution. All the faces in the oncoming traffic seemed to stare at me. My heart battered against the wall of my chest. I could feel a strong pulse in my temple.

A burst of dual carriageway deposited me at the slip road for the university. At the gate I showed the slip the librarian had given me. The guard waved me through without even looking at it. The car park was a vast sea of vehicles. There were several Beetles among the ageing Fiestas, Saabs and Novas.

'No bags or phones inside.' A librarian with a cardigan draped over her shoulders bore down on me. 'Combo lockers to your left.'

She gestured towards them. I put my phone into the bag and stuffed it into a locker. The combination number was stamped on the inside of the door: 7474.

I showed the slip again at the reception desk.

'Top floor.' She gestured at some lifts. 'See Jeremy.'

'I believe what I'm looking for is in the basement.'

'Top floor will have to get them for you.'

Jeremy had the face of a teenager and the stooped bearing of a pensioner. His shoulders were curved around him, as if for shelter. A large mole on his upper lip wobbled as he sucked in his mouth. He examined the slip.

'What dates?'

Anita was twenty in 1995. She could have been here any time from twelve to eighteen.

'Can I have 'eighty-five to 'ninety-four?'

Jeremy gave me a withering look then examined his watch.

'They're not catalogued. We'll have to get them all.'

'How many's that?'

He studied a computer screen. Along one wall was a large window that looked out over the car park. 'We've got them from 1924. Have to get the whole batch up. Hope you know what you're looking for.'

I didn't even know for sure that Anita's name would be there, or what use it would be if it was. Jeremy disappeared into a service lift. It took me a while to pinpoint the Beetle in the sea of cars. Nice and anonymous. Someone walked past it, stopped and walked on.

I looked at my watch. Three fifteen. Six hours since I had dialled 999. The crime scene would have been secured, photographed, scanned and swept for any trace of other humans. Someone would be looking after the little dog. Carrie would be on a slab. How much did they need to cut open? How did she die? Was it poison or a clever blow that took her so much by surprise that she was dead before her face showed what was happening?

Edge would be in the hospital. Better there than at home. He would probably have seen the paper as well and drawn his own conclusions. Perhaps he had already alerted the police. What would he have said? When I looked at the car again, two people were examining it like prospective purchasers, one stooping to look at the interior while the other backed away a few steps to peer underneath.

The service lift whirred and Jeremy hauled back the gate. He pulled a trolley, which contained several stacks of dark-green tomes. He looked put out.

'They've all been rebound. Amateurs! Nothing on the spines to say what year.'

I shared his frustration. Poor preservation: the bane of the archivist's life. 'Any chance you could help me find the years I'm looking for?'

'I should be on my break now.' He looked as if I'd asked him to lay down his life for me, then his expression softened. 'I'll pop in after.'

'Thanks, that's good of you.'

I plucked one volume from the middle of the top tray and worked through them, opening and slamming the covers until I found the most likely years. Then I started with 1985. The opening pages were packed with statistics; the number of students and countries travelled to and from. *Helping Hands Across the Commonwealth* extolled the virtues of *the practice of exchange*. I flipped through, hoping for a list of students. There wasn't one. Visitors were listed by school only. Eight hundred and forty secondary schools in the UK had foreign students that year. *Shit.*

I glanced back at the car park. Four people were standing around the Beetle. One was talking on a mobile phone. There was only one way to do this properly, and that was to start at the beginning, take the first book and work through. But properly wasn't possible. I plumped for 1990. She would have been fifteen. I opened the UK school list in the middle and worked back and then forward. There were no first names, just initials. Lots of the surnames were multi-syllable – little chance of Jayarajah sticking out further than the others.

What did she tell me about being here? I had asked her what most impressed her when she first arrived, expecting her to say Buckingham Palace or colour TV. 'Cars going along with only one person inside. And overweight cats.' She liked the Beatles – who didn't? Her favourite book was *Wuthering Heights*.

'Talk to me, Anita,' I heard myself say out loud.

A police car had stopped in the lane between the rows of parked cars. Tape cordoned off the Beetle. I wouldn't be driving out of here. *Keep going. Think, think! What else did you talk about?* I told her about my school in Sheffield and she was shocked by my description of the violence. Her English school was well behaved. Maybe it was in the country.

I was halfway through 1990 and twenty minutes had gone by. *Keep going. Don't think about it. Think about things she said.* She and Bernard had had an argument. About Sherwood Forest and how far north it stretched. No help. She loved the moors – it had to be somewhere north. Haworth! No school listed, not that year anyway. I remembered thinking she was right and he was wrong. It must have been something I knew about as well. The Sheriff. Nottingham! No. Maid Marian? Friar Tuck?

Far away a church bell was ringing. *Something about a gravestone.* Two more police vehicles had arrived. The lift doors opened. Jeremy was back. He was very tall. That's why he was so bent over – he wasn't old, just tall.

'Little John!'

Jeremy looked at me sharply. 'You trying to be clever?'

Buried in Hathersage, in Derbyshire. Bernard told her she was talking rubbish because Sherwood Forest didn't stretch up that far. Anita and I insisted. She'd stood at the long, narrow gravestone. So had I.

'Would you help me find all the references to Hathersage schools?'

He read the desperation in my face.

'Just open them at that page. Please?'

Jeremy stopped, his curiosity aroused. 'Who are we looking for?'

'I'll tell you when we find her.'

'Oh. A girl.' He snorted.

The phone at his desk rang. He moved away to take the call. My head was hammering now. The small print was almost impossible to scan. As well as all the exchange students, the 'host families' they had lodged with were listed under each school.

A. Jarayrajah. She was one of about ten. It must have been busy at Hathersage High. There was a beeping sound and a PA system squawked into life. 'Would all library staff contact the main desk.' No one else was in the room. Jeremy was still on the phone. He didn't respond to the announcement.

I stared at the page. There was no photocopier in sight. In *Chinatown*, Jack Nicholson coughed loudly to cover the sound as he ripped a page out of a ledger in a public record office. I did the same. Maybe my cough wasn't loud enough. Jeremy dropped the phone.

'You can't do that.'

The speaker on the wall crackled. 'Would all library staff contact the main desk.'

'You just tore out a page.'

He came towards me. I looked out of the window. The doors of the Beetle had been opened.

'Shouldn't you be contacting the main desk?'

'Give me that page.' He stood up straight, which put him above six-five. He blocked the gangway.

'See the police out there in the car park?' I gestured towards the window. 'They're looking for me. They think I committed a murder.'

He craned round towards the window.

'Right now I don't think you should be worrying about a torn page.' I started walking backwards, towards the stairs. I kept my eyes on him long enough for him to feel that I meant it.

25

I jumped the stairs three at a time, until I realised I was better off moving slowly. Maybe I could mingle with the students. There were lots of beards and combat jackets.

Two policemen in luminous jackets stood at the turnstiles next to the lockers on the ground floor. I headed for the basement. A corridor with overhead pipes led to a small tea bar. A woman sat behind a counter stacked with cakes and cans of fizzy drinks, bent over a magazine. Daylight seeped through a door propped open behind her. Outside, a narrow brick trench surrounded the building. My head was at ground level. There were more police, two with dogs, just yards away.

I hopped up onto the grass and joined a stream of students moving up the campus, away from the car park. Not knowing where I was going, I tried to look as if I did. A policeman stood outside the entrance they were all heading towards. This wasn't going to work. I took a sharp right, towards a round building with coloured lights that could have been a chapel. It was locked. I turned back in the general direction of the library then turned left and up an incline.

The wind was blowing hard, letting what was left of the late afternoon sun through the clouds. I skirted round another building. A path led up through a line of trees to a road. I followed a group of students through a small pedestrian gate. They turned left and I followed. On the right was a row of shops. Parked cars lined both sides of the street. One was occupied by a man and a woman. Its lights weren't on but the engine was running. As we walked past, I heard doors open and close, then the peep of remote locking. They didn't appear to be in a hurry, but there was something purposeful about their movements. I glanced over my shoulder.

They started to follow. I kept going. The sun came out and my shadow jogged along beside me. I heard a siren ahead. A police car, lights blazing, slewed to a stop in the middle of the street. The traffic came to a halt. Two uniformed men got out.

I was parallel with a café on the other side of the road. I turned and dashed through the traffic, straight inside, past the counter, ducking as a waitress came through a passage from the kitchen.

The back door opened onto a small yard. The wall was a couple of feet taller than me. There was a small wooden table beside it, and two chairs. I climbed onto the table and hauled myself up onto the wall. Several threads of rusty barbed wire were coiled around a bar that ran along the top of it. Part of the wall started to crumble under my weight. I lost my balance and landed on a pile of pallets and rusty drums. The barbs embedded themselves in my clothes. I tore myself free and ran towards an open door. It was the kitchen of a takeaway. Two Chinese women looked up and froze. I went straight between them, towards the front of the shop, and slammed against the front door. It was locked. I ran back through the kitchen and into the yard. A head appeared on the other side of the barbed wire wall.

I leaped the wooden fence into an adjacent yard. It belonged to a newsagent. At least they'd be open. A rack of sweets exploded onto the floor as I vaulted the counter. Someone screamed. The front door was wide open. A customer flattened herself against the shelves as I came past. I was travelling too fast to pull up before the narrow pavement gave way to a road. A motorcycle, snaking wildly as it braked, slid inexorably towards me. As I swivelled to try and avoid it, I saw one of the policemen inside the takeaway pulling at the locked door. Then I saw nothing at all.

26

My chin was clean-shaven. I could tell without even touching it. Something about the way the air moved around it.

I ran my fingers across the unfamiliar smooth skin. Part of it was covered with a dressing. There was bright light above, but my eyelids felt too heavy to open. I drifted away again.

Anita was on the Colombo station platform. There was a vast scrum of people with children, baskets and boxes. Everyone was bathed in horizontal, early-morning light. Some were still trying to get on as the Jaffna train started to pull away. She walked alongside as I leaned out of the carriage window, her eyes shining.

'I want to come with you.'

I shook my head. 'I'll be fine.'

She caught hold of my hand. Her face was contorted with anxiety.

'If anyone asks, I've gone to meet Greer. And if you hear from her, just say I'm recce-ing.'

She looked more doubtful. The thought of lying bothered her even more.

'Don't worry. I'll call when I'm back.'

She touched my hand fleetingly to her cheek. I watched her until the crowd on the platform engulfed her.

A dull ache pulsed across my jaw. I tried to open my eyes. The lids were sticky and I couldn't focus. Then the corners of the ceiling came into focus. I was in a small room.

'Don't try to sit up yet.'

I felt the soft pressure of hands on my shoulders. The silhouette of a nurse blocked my eye-line but I craned round far enough to see the plain-clothes man who had chased me leaning against the far wall.

'Is he compos?'

The nurse didn't look round. 'Just wait, please.'

The man came forward.

'Can you hear me? DS Skinner, Sussex CID. Can you identify yourself?'

The nurse moved towards him. 'I said wait. The doctor'll be here in a minute.'

I closed my eyes again.

I had no idea how long I had been unconscious. The curtains were drawn and there was no light behind them. I heard the door open and the sharp click of women's shoes. I let my eyes open again and stared blankly at the ceiling.

The woman's white coat hung open, revealing a floral T-shirt. She lifted my arm and felt my pulse. A stethoscope was draped over her shoulders. Behind her were the blurred faces of two men.

She touched my chin. 'Can you tell me your name?'

I didn't respond. She lowered her face closer to mine. It was young and alert, full of confidence. Then she turned away.

'This'll have to wait till morning. You've got his prints – which, by the way, you should have got permission for before you took.'

'Look, love, if he's awake, he needs to know he's under arrest.'

'He won't have a clue what you're saying. All the indicators are he's concussed.'

She shone a small torch into my eyes. I tried not to flinch.

'You can post someone on the door, but he has to sleep. We'll do a review in the morning.'

'We need something now. We're looking at a suspicious death. Probable murder.'

'We could have a suspicious death right here if you start heavying him. And it won't be his.'

'His prints don't show any previous. We've got no ID. Without a name we can't start checking him out.'

'Why don't you go through his pockets?'

I heard air escaping from pursed lips. All my stuff was in the bag in the library locker. 7474. My brain was still working.

She bent over me again and smiled.

'Looks like a perfectly nice young man to me.'

'We've got CCTV of him leaving the phone box where the 999 call was made, and his prints on the body. Pretty conclusive.'

'Well, until I've done my job, you can't do yours. Don't worry. He's not going anywhere in this state.'

I must have been pumped full of something to make me sleep because the next time I opened my eyes I was alone. A digital clock on a monitor of some kind read 02:45. I hadn't slept so well in days. There was a steady throb in my jaw, but my mind seemed sharper. I tensed the muscles in my arms and legs. I waggled my toes. I felt around my groin. They'd put a catheter in.

The doctor appeared again at seven forty-five. Her name badge said Emma Stark. She came in alone, apparently unbothered that I was a murder suspect.

'Can you hear me?' She smiled. 'Just nod if it's easier.'

I nodded.

She smiled again. 'Good.' She leaned closer. Her scent was mixed with a tinge of tobacco. 'I'm not interested in what you've done. That's not what I'm here for. My job is to keep you alive. We've done a scan and there's evidence of a previous head injury. Yes?'

I nodded.

'You had no ID on you when you were … admitted.'

I looked at her.

'So we can't access your NHS details.' She paused as if to let this sink in. 'It would be a great help if we could contact someone who treated you before. Do you have any names?'

I stared at the ceiling.

'Anything? Any name or address or …?'

All the moisture had gone from my mouth. She brought a glass of water up to my lips.

'Jayarajah.'

'I'm sorry?'

I repeated the name.

'Is that a doctor?' I nodded. 'I don't know him. Is he local?'

I managed a shrug.

'I'll look him up. Was he neuro?'

'She.'

'The best thing is for you to rest. You're not badly injured on the outside. The gash on your chin will be fine.' She pointed at my forehead. 'I'm concerned that the impact doesn't cause any pressure internally. Last time, was there a haematoma?'

I didn't respond. I closed my eyes.

'Can you repeat the name of the doctor?'

I spelled Anita's surname. She wrote it down.

'I'm going off now but I'm on again at noon, for my sins. Nothing'll happen till then. So just rest.' She bent down closer. 'And don't try to think too much. Just let things float back.'

She smiled briefly and was gone.

I eased myself up onto my elbows and looked round the room. My head had stopped throbbing. I was dressed only in a hospital gown. There was a reflection in the dark screen of the monitor beside me. It took a moment to recognise the face. I remembered the photo of me in Carrie's album. The beard had been my disguise. I'd been unmasked.

It was daylight when I surfaced again. A WPC sat on a chair by the door, reading a magazine. When she noticed I was awake she left the room. A few minutes later Emma Stark reappeared. Her white coat was gone. She was dressed in a smart suit.

'There's no one with that exact name practising in the UK. Best I could come up with was an A. Jay, somewhere near Canterbury, but it's a GP surgery.'

'What does she look like?'

She frowned. 'I've no idea. I can't even tell if it's a she. Why?'

I looked into her face. She was young, but her manner seemed older; dealing with the sick had given her a crash course in human experience. She didn't seem to mind that I didn't answer.

'You look a lot better today. I'm sorry about your beard. Do you remember your address?'

I looked blank.

'What's your occupation?'

I shook my head. At least that was an honest answer. She leaned on the side of the bed.

'They want to talk to you. They're waiting outside. I don't have a choice. But I'll kick them out after fifteen minutes. OK?'

She opened the door.

I recognised one of the men from the day before. The other was older, with close-cropped hair and a thick neck. He had a pin-stripe suit on. The collar of his shirt had a pin running through it that pushed out the knot of his tie.

'OK, chum. What're we going to call you?'

He pulled his chair closer. I stared into his face. His breath smelled of eggs and coffee. Why didn't he know who I was? They had me on CCTV and a reasonable photofit. Wouldn't Tanager have alerted them?

'I'm Detective Inspector Woodward. I'm investigating Miss Marron's death, which I believe you reported. Can you describe what happened immediately before you dialled 999 yesterday morning?'

His features were shiny. A slight indentation ran upwards from his left eyebrow. He looked like someone who might have used his forehead as a weapon.

'We have a tape of your call from the phone box near Miss Marron's residence. Your fingerprints are in every room, and on the deceased. Do you want to tell us what happened?'

I stared at the ceiling.

'The Volkswagen Beetle. We've been speaking to the owner.'

My heart skipped a beat.

'According to him the car was last seen in his garage in London three days ago.'

Police came high on Colin's list of hates. He would have been only too glad not to help them with their inquiries.

'The car was observed in Miss Marron's street the afternoon before she died. According to another witness, a man answering your description ...' He glanced at the Doctor. 'With a beard, was seen having a heated discussion with the victim outside a wine bar. Any of this sound familiar?'

Carrie's face, so still against the pillow of her bed, came back into focus.

'Am I jogging your memory, sir?'

I caught the gust of coffee breath on my newly naked cheek.

'Not too close please.' The doctor was still there.

I worked back over the forty-eight hours up to the incident with the motorbike. My memory was clear, but they didn't know that. I was getting this special treatment because the scan had shown up the evidence of the last injury. I had an excuse to remain silent.

There wasn't much point in speaking. If the time of Carrie's death could be pinpointed to when I was with Edge I might have some kind of alibi, but my behaviour over the last few days wasn't going to help me.

'Can we get the heat turned down?' Woodward's forehead was beaded with sweat. His eyes stayed on my face. 'If you speak to us now, it could make things a whole lot easier for you later on.'

The doctor stepped forward and touched his shoulder. The detective jerked it away. His face reddened. He smelled guilt. He wanted his scalp.

'We've got you taped. Yards of it. In the wine bar, outside it. Walking the dog. Picking your nose. This isn't going to help you.'

I wanted the fifteen minutes to be up. I thought about Carrie, lying on her bed; her closed eyes, perfect make-up, rich, red lipstick. I could smell Woodward's breath. I turned back towards him. He sprang back as I threw up onto his shoes.

'Fucking arsehole!'

'Excuse me.' Emma Stark bent over me with a cloth and dabbed my face, smirking.

Woodward snapped his fingers at his colleague who passed him some tissues. He turned back towards me. 'I'll see *you* later.'

He marched out, slamming the door behind him. The other detective hesitated then followed.

'Sorry about that.'

The doctor waved away the apology. I pointed at the catheter.

'Can this come out now?'

'Sure. It may make your eyes water.'

I inhaled sharply as the tube slid out.

'We'll leave the drip. But it's on wheels for when you need the loo.'

'Where am I?'

'The West Sussex. You're under neuro care but because of your ... special status, you're upstairs with the geriatrics. It's the only spare room.' She smirked again. 'The constabulary will pick up the tab.'

'Are you always this nice to murder suspects?'

Her smile faded. 'I'm here to fix your head, not your life.' Her movements became brisk. She gave me two pills and a tumbler of water.

'Am I still under guard?'

'There's a plod outside who'll come in when I'm gone.'

'Can memory be recovered after a bang on the head as well as lost?'

'What do you mean? Is there something you've remembered?'

She stared at me for some time.

'What do I do if I need the toilet?'

'Buzz the nurse and we'll provide an entourage.'

She swept out.

27

We made a strange trio. The nurse went first and slightly to the right of me, steering the drip. On my left was the policeman, whose main role seemed to be to draw as much attention to us as possible. Everyone in the corridor stared.

I stood at the nurses' station while the policeman went into the lavatory to check it was empty. A staff nurse tapped at the keyboard of a computer. The NHS home page filled the screen. *Directory* featured about halfway down the options menu.

A hand gripped my elbow. The nurse moved me forward. The lavatory was a staff facility, inside a changing room walled with lockers. In the middle was a large basket. Sheets protruded from under the lid. They didn't let me close the stall door and remained in front throughout. They had a long wait. The morphine had made me constipated.

I asked to go frequently, for something to do and to get a bit of exercise.

It was after midnight and the corridor was deserted. A WPC and a male nurse were with me. They were discussing a club on the seafront that had lost its licence. A door opened further down the corridor and two men emerged. I recognised the shorter of the two instantly. He started down the corridor towards us. Then he stopped. It was natural to be curious about a patient with a police escort.

He must have known about Carrie by now. The nurse kept me moving. Edge's face looked drained. I didn't meet his gaze. My escorts were still in conversation. I stopped and put a hand to my forehead.

‘Saul.’ I directed the word at the floor but made sure it was loud enough for him to hear.

The nurse stopped.

‘You all right?’

I looked up at the ceiling. The WPC gripped my arm. ‘OK, keep moving.’ She turned to Edge. ‘Sir, could you step away please?’

We continued down the corridor. When we reached my room I looked back. He was still there.

28

The drip had a tiny plastic tap that varied the flow of morphine. I had shut it off four hours ago and pulled out the line without anyone noticing. I still felt light headed. I had slept for most of the day. I had eaten a meal and dissolved all the sachets of instant coffee into one beaker. It killed the wooziness.

I had made a small fuss about having the light off. A dull night-light burned but it was too dark for the PC sitting at his post by the door to read. He played a game on his mobile until I glared at him and he shut it down. The nurse had left the remote thermostat on the bedside table. I turned it up as far as it would go. Then I watched him struggle to keep awake. Around two a.m. his head flopped against his chest and stayed there.

I unclipped a report sheet from the clipboard hanging on the side of the monitor. Woodward had dropped the pen when I threw up over him. It was too dark to read what I was writing so I used capitals in the hope that they would be more legible. There wouldn't be time for a conversation.

It seemed a very long way to the floor. I was damp with sweat. My feet felt clammy against the lino and the sound when I picked them up seemed to tear at the silence like unpeeling sticky tape. I shuffled my backside closer to the edge of the bed until I had both feet on the floor. *Take your time*, I said to myself, over and over.

It was the first time I had stood up unaided, and a wave of vertigo swept over me. I lurched and caught the side of the bed with my thigh. The policeman raised his head but it flopped down again. His eyes didn't open. Perhaps he had already had a long day. I stood for a full minute, breathing deeply, trying to summon the energy to move.

I pushed out into the space between the bed and the door.

I was parallel with the policeman's chair. His head was bent over his chest and his mouth hung open. A small bead of saliva dangled from his lower lip. The only sound was his steady breathing. I gripped the door handle and pulled.

The corridor was much cooler. I half ran, half stumbled to the end and pushed open the door where I had seen Edge. He was asleep in a chair. Shirley was in the same position I had seen her in at home. I put my hand on his shoulder. He woke with a start. I pressed my finger against my lips and held the sheet of paper in front of him. He read it, eyes widening.

'Are you *serious*?'

29

I twisted strips of paper towel into crude firelighters and made a small pyre of them. I lit as many ends as I could with Edge's lighter. The flames coalesced into a sturdy inferno. Before it burned out, I added a sheet from the basket, draping it gently over the flame so it caught without dousing it. It was damp and gave off a lot of useful smoke.

I tore off my hospital smock and put on one of the cleaners' overalls. It was too small but it would do. In another bin were some disposable slippers. I added another sheet to the fire. By now the room was filling with smoke. I left the door open and moved back to my room as quickly as I could.

The policeman was still fast asleep. I turned off the heat, slipped under the covers and lay back, feeling the adrenalin careering through my body. It had given me a savage headache. I stared into the dull gloom. I didn't have long to wait.

At 03:12 the digital display I had been staring at started flashing. For a moment there was complete blackness. Then a low hum kicked in somewhere below and an emergency light came on near to the floor. A series of shrill electronic bleeps sounded somewhere in the corridor.

I didn't move. Outside, someone was running.

The policeman jerked awake.

'Stay there,' he barked. He opened the door and the room was filled with the sound of the alarm. Several more people ran by. There was a distinct smell of smoke. He looked back at me, hesitated, and set off down the hall.

I got up and moved to the doorway. The corridor was lit by ghostly green emergency lights. Sprinklers had been activated. I watched the policeman lose his balance as he tried to avoid a bed that was being wheeled the other way. He disappeared into the gathering throng.

The corridor filled with people, some of them barely clothed. A porter with a fire extinguisher struggled to get through. Someone was shouting. 'Do not use the elevators. Use the stairs.'

An old woman shouted, 'Fuck off.'

Edge came towards me with surprising speed. He pressed a small wash bag into my hand. His eyes twinkled through his glasses. He pressed his mouth to my ear and engulfed me in cigar breath. The alarm was so loud he had to shout.

'Level D3, Bay 44. Blue Jag. Shirley's phone's in the glove compartment.'

He looked down at my bare feet.

'There's some boots in the back footwell and some spare clothes in the boot. You going to manage? You look dreadful.'

I nodded. 'Thank you.'

'Get going.'

I tried to hug him but he batted me away. He handed me his overcoat and turned back towards Shirley's room. I put on the coat as the crowd carried me along towards the stairs.

I paused at the nurses' station. A computer was still on. A man in a fire warden's vest glared at me. 'Keep moving.'

The emergency door at the bottom of the stairs was wide open. The slippers did nothing to insulate the soles of my feet from the icy tarmac. Edge's coat barely reached my knees, but it was useful camouflage. Several others were dressed in an odd assortment of night and daywear. Staff with luminous bibs and megaphones directed them to various gathering points. The exterior lights were still working, but left pools of darkness between them. I retreated into one while I tried to get my bearings.

By the time I found the Jaguar my feet were stinging. I had stumbled several times, still unsteady from the morphine. My shins were gashed and bleeding. I unzipped the wash bag and took out the keys.

The car was well worn. Moss had taken root around the window rubbers. I lifted the boot and extracted a fishing sweater with elbow pads and a short pair of jeans. The interior smelled of cigars. The leather was crazed and cracked. The back seat had disappeared under a jumble of maps, coats, gloves, a couple of fishing rods, a wine box and a crate of gardening tools. I found the boots. They were a tight fit, but covered the gap between my ankles and the bottom of the jeans.

The engine fired and the car rocked on full choke. I engaged reverse and it leapt back. After Colin's Beetle it felt like a rocket. Gingerly, I manoeuvred out of the bay. The interior started to warm up.

The barrier at the bottom of the exit ramp was down. I hesitated then accelerated. It gave easily against the Jag's radiator grille and disappeared under its wheels with a light bump.

30

I tried to keep the car at a sensible speed. I watched the mirrors but there was nothing following. After a few miles I was in open country. I pulled over and took Shirley's phone out of the glove compartment. Edge's number was the only one in the memory. He answered after the first ring.

'You OK?'

'I think so.'

'Police are all over. You better get as far away as you can.' I could hear his rapid breaths. 'You sure about Saul?'

'Carrie said she was expecting him. That's all I have. Is there anything else you remember about him?'

'I've told you all I can.'

'There must be something. What was he doing when they were together?'

'Some sort of International Relations Ph.D. at an American university, so he said.'

'He was American?'

'Don't know. He had an American accent, but it didn't sound like English was his first language.'

'What else?'

'He was shortish, athletic. Thick black hair.'

'When exactly did he dump her?'

'God knows. Carrie didn't send me a memo.'

'After Northolt? After Malik had been ambushed?'

'No idea.'

'What about borrowing the film?'

'A lot of people wanted to see it – student groups and so on – when we thought it wouldn't get shown.'

'Did you ever look at it again – the print Carrie borrowed?'

'Nope.'

'If she'd known he'd taken out the shots of Malik, would she have told you?'

He sighed. 'She was so loyal.' His voice was cracking. 'I can't believe ...' I could hear talking in the background. 'I'll have to go. They're moving her to another ward.'

'One more thing: did Carrie ever mention seeing Anita again?'

'You're not letting go of this, are you? Not that I can remember. It would be in her diaries.'

'Can I hang on to the car for a bit?'

'I'd like the fishing rods back one day. Keep the phone. Wait. Something else: I called Rolt, the man who put me on to Malik. He was a radio stringer round southern Europe and the Med. He was in with the spooks down there.' He paused to catch his breath. 'I fed him Tanager's name. Said he'd gone from the Service years ago. Left under a cloud.'

'What sort of cloud?'

'He wouldn't say.'

'Anything else?'

'Worked mainly in the Middle East. Old school, ex-special forces. He was a maverick, a lone wolf, protective of his agents – and not to be messed with. I told Rolt he was looking for me.'

'What did he say to that?'

'Made him go a bit quiet. Tanager's being very persistent. He's left more messages.'

The temperature in the car seemed to drop. 'Him and Saul. They could be ...' There didn't seem to be a way of finishing the sentence.

'I know what you're thinking.'

'Don't see him.'

'Well, I'm here with Shirley. I'm not going anywhere.'

I kept to a lane that hugged the back of the Downs. The Jaguar seemed to occupy the whole of the narrow road. Eventually I hit the A23 and headed back towards Brighton. The streets were still, bathed in orange sodium light. I parked close to the seafront, within earshot of the unseen waves.

Carrie's flat had police tape across the front door. The shutters had been closed. The lock had been sealed, but I'd put the keys back under the flowerpot and they were still there. I headed down the road and took the first left. A line of garages gave onto a passageway that ran behind Carrie's terrace. The entrance to her patio was bricked up. I took some deep breaths and on the third attempt hauled myself over it and onto a garden table. The longest of the three keys fitted the back-door lock. It rasped loudly as I eased it open, so I left it ajar.

The place smelled strongly of chemicals. It took a while for my eyes to adjust to the gloom. Layers of white dust spread across most of the surfaces gave off a dull glow. Carrie's bed had been stripped to the mattress. In the living room the bottle of champagne was gone, and the cooler. I went into the spare room, sat down at the desk and pulled open the drawer where the diaries had been. It was empty. I wasn't surprised. If Saul hadn't taken them, the police would have.

A clock struck five. The desk light cast a giant shadow of me against the back wall. I scanned the wall unit behind the desk. A row of shoeboxes lined the top shelf. On the bottom shelf, sandwiched between some atlases and a coffee-table book on photography was a blank spine. I pulled it out. The photo album. My tiredness evaporated. I lifted the cover and scanned the pages in search of Saul. Most of the shots were of groups, at work, at parties. Short, athletic, black hair ... Plenty of young men fitted Edge's description.

All the captions were cryptic. *Off our 'Faces'. Too much of a good thing. Working all hours.* There were several of Edge with other members of the *Human Face* team, though none of Greer. One photo near the beginning of the section had been removed. The caption was still there: *The One that Got Away*, but above it, only small strips of glue remained. I stared at the page for some time, as if the vanished image might have left some discernable shadow.

A gust of wind from the back door nudged the calendar

on the wall. It clattered as it fell back. I flicked forward to where she had stuck my photo. It too was gone. I listened to the pulse pound in my head. I turned to the first page of the album. She must have started it in her last term of school. The first picture was from a prize-giving. Carrie receiving a scroll wrapped with ribbon: *Recognition at last* below it in neat fountain pen. A crowd of teenagers in fancy dress: *The gang at play*. Cheering girls beside a sign: Hathersage Grammar School. I leafed through a couple more pages of group shots. *Our sporting heroes. The thespians. Too much cider.*

Another page was devoted to smaller, single portraits. *Cheerful girls about to step out into the world*. At the bottom was one of a teenage Anita, eyes alight with laughter. *Our visitor from Sri Lanka ...*

I went round the flat pulling out all the drawers and opening cupboards, destroying the neatness and order with which Carrie had tried to disguise the emptiness of her life. I turned over cushions and pulled books off shelves. As the flat turned into chaos the search became more frantic.

Sweating now, my heart hammering, blood pulsing through me, amplifying the screaming ache in my head, I came back into the spare room. My head swam for a moment. *Focus*. I was here to find Anita. I looked round the room. Nothing.

I sat down at the desk again. Each of the shoeboxes on the top shelf had a label. The one on the far right said, *Xmas '04*. I stepped onto the desk and reached for it. I lost my footing as it slid out and I ended up on the carpet in the midst of a cascade of Christmas cards. Carrie must have been more popular than I imagined.

I looked at each one as I put them back in the box. One from Edge wished her 'a better New Year'. The biggest was a photograph of a crown cut into a chalk down. Inside was just a bold *A* in blue ink with an *x* beside it. I turned the card over. *Brook Health Centre, Nr. Canterbury, Kent.*

31

It was starting to get light. I drove a few miles across Brighton, watching the mirrors. I pulled over and took out Shirley's phone, got the number for the Health Centre and dialled it. There was no one there. It was too early, but the message about surgery hours listed a Dr Jay.

I dialled Edge's mobile. He would want to know. It came up as unobtainable. I tried the home number with the same result. And again. I called Colin. When he heard my voice he gave a long sigh.

'This is early, even by my clock.'

'Sorry.'

'Well, I'm awake now. Fuck was all that about with the car and the filth?'

'They think I've murdered someone.'

'Tell me that's a joke.'

I couldn't think of what to say next.

'You still there?'

'Yes.'

'You're in very deep shit, aren't you?'

'Edge's assistant is dead.'

'Fucking Jesus. You're not on your own phone, are you?'

Talking to Colin was good. It felt less like I had imagined it all. 'I need a favour.'

'I'm fresh out of favours.'

'You had a contact at the Foreign Office. The one that got you the report that was in my file.'

'Rendall. He'll be gone from there now.'

'Could you find him? I'd like to know if he's ever heard of Tanager. Anything about him.'

'If you're going to get killed I'd prefer not to be involved, if that's OK.'

'Please?'

He snorted. 'I spoke to Harrop.'

'And?'

'Told him I'd heard the Northolt crash footage had come from the MOD. Put him into a bit of a panic. He's terrified it'll go further and he'll lose his job and his precious pension.'

'Did he say anything else?'

'Wouldn't talk over the phone. I'm meeting him tomorrow night.' I heard him take a puff of a cigarette. 'Where are you now?'

'En route to Kent, to see a doctor.'

'About time.'

I drove to the university campus first. It was almost deserted. The student population hadn't yet risen but the cleaners had opened up the library. I went to the lockers and retrieved my bag. I tipped the contents onto the Jag's passenger seat. Everything was still there: my phone, the shots of Rammal and Malik; Greer's lighter, my passport, my wallet and the envelope of photos. I looked again at the pictures of Anita, her face glowing in the setting sun.

The route from Brighton was across country. The Jaguar was unwieldy on the narrow roads but there was little traffic and I welcomed its power. On one straight stretch I looked down and saw I was doing over a hundred.

I tried the surgery number again. A receptionist answered.

'Is Dr Jay in?'

'She's not seeing patients today.'

'But she is in?'

There was a pause. Being put through could jeopardise my chances of her seeing me. I rang off.

I tried to disentangle my thoughts about her. The fact that she had lied to Edge raised all kinds of questions. She had sent me to the boat. Did she know what was about to happen? Was I meant to die as well? Why did she visit me in hospital?

The picture of her – the way she looked into the camera – seemed to project itself onto the damp road ahead. If she'd wanted me dead, I could understand it now. And yet she'd sat at my bedside …

It was late morning when I reached the village. Frost still lay on the ground, turning the countryside monochrome. There was a long wait at a level crossing while a train sat in the station. Someone behind me started hooting pointlessly.

I dialled the West Sussex Hospital. The extension for the Geriatric floor rang for a long time. 'Can I help?' The voice was bright and female.

'I'm a friend of Shirley Edgington's. I was just ringing to see how she is.'

There was a pause.

'Are you in contact with Mr Edgington?'

'Why?'

'We need to contact him.'

'Has she died?'

There was a pause.

'I'm afraid I can't give out that information, but we aren't able to find Mr Edgington.'

The train finally moved and a railwayman ambled out to open the gate.

'Can you tell me where the doctors' is?'

He gestured with his chin at the road that led up the hill.

'Left fork at the top.'

I pulled up outside a modern building surrounded by a neat lawn. Morning surgery was under way. Colin's warnings replayed themselves in my head. *The one thing you can say about the past is that it ain't going to change. What happened, happened, and if you fucked up, you fucked up. Don't look back, else you'll turn into a pillar of shit.*

All my rehab had been about dealing with the trauma of the explosion. They said it could block other memories. I'd accepted that. What happened with Anita remained unexamined. I'd left any mention of her out of my Post-It notes. Tanager didn't refer to her. Her picture hadn't been removed from Carrie's album.

But I had to know. *Just do it. Keep it simple – check what she said to Edge. If she lied, why? If she doesn't answer, well at least you asked.*

I tried Edge's numbers once more: no answer.

Numb and ill-prepared, I mounted the steps to the health centre. There was a queue at the reception desk. A young woman with tightly braided hair looked up.

'Is Dr Jay here?'

'I'm afraid this isn't her surgery day.'

'But she's here?'

She looked at me doubtfully.

'I just need to speak to her. It won't take a minute.'

There was a passage to the right of the reception desk. The first door had another doctor's name on it.

'Are you a patient of hers?'

'I just need to ask her a couple of questions.'

'Unless you're a patient, it's not possible to see anyone without registering first.'

A phone rang. The receptionist picked it up. Dr Jay was the name on the farthest door. I set off towards it.

'*Excuse me!*'

32

I opened the door without knocking.

At first she didn't look up. She was bent over her desk, writing on a pad. I was about to close the door when the receptionist appeared behind me.

'I'm sorry, Doctor, he just barged past.'

She raised her head and her eyes met mine. Almost nothing about her appearance had changed. At first she didn't react. Her pen hovered in the air then she clicked it closed and laid it neatly down on the pad.

'It's all right, Lucy.'

Lucy looked from her to me, then at the clock on the wall.

'Primary Health Board's in twenty minutes.'

She left the door ajar. I tapped it closed with my foot.

Any words I had prepared evaporated under Anita's steady gaze. Eventually she spoke.

'What happened to your chin?'

'I cut it on a motorbike.'

'That dressing needs changing.'

She moved her hair off her shoulder, and tucked a strand behind an ear. Her eyes held mine. They were just as large and dark as I remembered. The lids were edged with kohl. Her mouth parted slightly. She took a long breath before she spoke.

'Sivalingham's wife was at college with me.'

'He didn't exactly guide me to you.'

'They called first.'

'You didn't want to see me?'

She sighed. 'Well, you're here now.'

She folded her hands on the desk. I took a step closer.

'Aren't you going to ask me what seems to be the trouble?'

It was a stupid remark and she ignored it. She looked groomed, professional. She exuded authority. I stood in front of her, in Edge's spare clothes, with a dirty dressing on my face; someone off the street feeling sorry for himself. She studied her hands.

'I saw you once when I was up in London. About five years ago. You had a beard.'

Neither of us spoke for a few seconds. She kept her eyes down on the desk. I caught a hint of her scent.

'You looked straight through me. Do you remember?'

I shook my head. Looking at her now, it was hard to imagine not noticing her. 'Why didn't you say hello?'

'I assumed you hadn't fully recovered. Or maybe that was just how you wanted it to be.'

Whatever she was feeling, she was keeping it to herself. I struggled to think of what to say next. 'How long have you been here?'

'A long time.'

The room was so spotless and tidy it looked barely inhabited. There was nothing on the walls – no certificates or photos. No hints about the rest of her life.

'You got away.'

She allowed herself a small smile.

'Have you been home?'

'This is home now.'

'You changed your name.'

'It was a bit of a mouthful.'

She closed the file on her desk.

I took a step closer. 'Are you in touch with Carrie?'

'Not much. I tried to help her with her drinking. How is she?'

'She was about to have a reunion with a very old boyfriend.'

She frowned. 'Saul?'

I nodded. 'You *knew* him?'

'He was around when I was here as an exchange student. I

saw him at her parents'. He let her down. She was very upset. Women are funny like that.'

She stood up, smoothed the creases out of her skirt and opened a door behind her desk that led onto a porch.

'Would you like a cigarette?'

'But you're a doctor.'

'No one's perfect.'

She made slow considered movements, as if at pains not to surprise me. If she was scared she didn't show it.

In the porch there was a bench and a small table with a vase of flowers. It had started to rain. The water running down the windows warped and twisted the view of the fields and leafless trees.

'Where you come from this isn't real rain. Do you remember the downpours?'

She sat down on the bench and let her gaze fall into her lap. She wore a black suede skirt and knitted jersey. A defiantly crimson silk scarf was draped around her neck. A sports watch and some silver bracelets clung to her wrist. No rings on her fingers.

'It got much worse. The Tigers control the north now.'

Her coldness occupied the space between us. Her hand shook as she lifted the cigarette to her lips. But when her eyes met mine they had no expression.

'Did everything come back?'

She watched the rain running down the window while she waited for my reply.

'How do you know what you don't remember?'

'Is that why you're here?'

'I just need ... some information.' I sounded like a policeman. 'I need to clarify a few things. Phil Edgington. You met him once ...'

She waited for me to go on.

'You told him it was me who arranged the meeting on the boat. That wasn't true.'

She stared into her lap again. Her scent mingled with the smoke.

I moved closer. '*You* sent me. You told me to go there. You had a car waiting for me. Was I meant to die as well?'

She recoiled, as if this hadn't occurred to her. Another doctor appeared in the doorway, his face full of concern.

'Is everything all right, Anita?'

'Yes, fine.' He seemed reluctant to leave. She smiled at him. 'Really, Steve, it's OK.'

He tapped his watch.

She nodded. 'I know.'

He gave me a long, appraising look and left slowly, without shutting the door. She took a few breaths before she spoke, her eyes focused on the floor in front of her.

'It was Greer. You were just meant to meet her on the dock.'

'She told you that?'

'For you to wait for her there. On the dock. She didn't say anything about going to the boat.'

'*She* arranged it?'

'I presumed you knew.'

'When did she speak to you about this?'

'That morning, when she left.' She gave me an empty look. 'Before you ... got up. She told me to wake you if you hadn't appeared by eight.'

She turned her face away from me and stared out into the rain. The look she'd given me in the hotel lobby still haunted me. She had known where I'd spent that night.

'So why did you lie to Edge? Greer was dead. It didn't matter if you told the truth.'

She didn't answer. She took a long drag on her cigarette.

I moved closer to her. 'Did you think about the consequences? That I would be blamed for sending Greer to her death?'

Her eyes swept over my face, full of contempt.

'Consequences? *Consequences?* Do you have *any* idea how compromised I was for helping you?'

Her anger had even taken her by surprise. She breathed out, adjusted her shoulders and flicked back her hair with a sweep of her hands.

An image of another time flashed inside my head, but it was gone before I could capture it.

Her expression softened. 'You don't look very well.'

I glanced at the face staring back at me from the rain-stained window. It was unkempt, hollow-cheeked; an alcoholic, maybe, or a drifter; someone who hadn't paid attention to his appearance in a long while. I barely recognised myself. The accumulation of tiredness and hunger and lingering pain gnawed away at me.

She stood and came towards me. Her eyes moved across my face. Her poise and grace were mesmerising. She must have had a lot of people making an appointment just to look at her.

'What *do* you remember?' The question was almost inaudible.

I opened my mouth but the words didn't come. The tiny muscles around her eyes stirred as almost imperceptible lines of moisture formed along her lower eyelids. I swallowed hard to steady myself and shook my head. 'We don't have time ...'

She stepped away and stared out at the winter wasteland. 'You're the reason I'm here.' She closed her eyes. 'I was still almost a teenager. I'd lost my home and my place at college. My parents were dead. I'd never met anyone like you or Greer before. I had such hopes for your film – that it would tell people what was really going on.' She smoothed out her skirt and shook her head. 'As if it could be that simple ...'

She leaned her forehead against the window.

'We'd just left Dr Chapra, Director of the Communal Friendship Institute, my dead father's best friend, a very eminent man. You listened politely while he lectured us for an hour and a half on his vision for peace and friendship in Sri Lanka. I had grown up hanging on this man's every word. Then, when we came out into the sunshine – remember what you said?' She laughed. '"No more old farts." I didn't know where to look. It was like an electric shock. All my life I'd been told to listen to my elders and betters, telling us how things would be and to study hard and do as I was told and serve others. I thought the whole world revolved around good grades and obedience. They'd suspended me from college for being a Tamil and I still hadn't got the message. I was such a *fucking goody-goody*.' It was a shock to hear her swear. She looked back at me and shook her head in disbelief. 'You were right. They *were* old farts. They had no idea what was happening, or what was to come.'

She lit another cigarette. 'You said, "How can I make a film about peacemakers if I can't even see the war?"' She was silent for a moment. 'I wasn't going to show you my house. I had only been back once. You just stood there. I could see the anger in you, as though you were feeling it all for me.'

She came up close. I could feel her breath on my face as she spoke.

'I hadn't cried properly. Not even when I was told about my parents. I thought if I did I'd lose my … dignity …'

She lowered her head until it was almost touching me, the force of her sadness arcing across the space between us.

'How long did I go on? I don't know, but you held me. I had barely touched a man before. I had so many tears stored up and once they'd started, that was it. I couldn't stop. After that, everything was different.'

When she lifted her head her eyes sparkled with tears.

'You said I had to get away or I'd die of hope – for something that would never get better. Remember?'

I was rooted to the ground, my muscles frozen.

'You gave me a cigarette. I stood among the remains of my family house *smoking* and laughing guiltily, like it was the worst thing I'd ever done. And then you said, "Where's the best shoe shop in Colombo? We'll start with a new pair of sandals." The rest of the day it was like I was high on something. As if I'd been released from a terrible prison of pain. Everything was speeded up. Sometime that evening, you made your offer …'

She stepped closer again. 'You held my face in your hands. Like this.' She touched my cheeks with her fingers. '"Get me to the North, get me to Jaffna, and I'll get you to England."'

She stepped away and smiled sadly.

'After that, I didn't want to let you out of my sight. Like a stray animal who'd been offered food by a stranger. When I got the train tickets—' She broke off. 'It hadn't occurred to me that you wanted to go alone. I had this terrible sense of foreboding, that I shouldn't have let you, that something would change. All the time you were gone I didn't know if you were OK. I went to meet every train coming back from the north.'

She let her hands drop and looked away. Rain thrashed against the windows.

'Would you have kept your side of the bargain?' She saw my hesitation. 'No, don't answer that. Let's just leave it that you weren't in a position to. So we'll never know.'

There was a long silence while our eyes conducted their own conversation.

'Are you alone?' My voice was hoarse.

She straightened up. 'I'm surrounded by good people here.'

'That's not what I meant.'

She turned and watched the rain.

'Why did you come to see me at the hospital?'

'Stupidity, naivety, I don't know.' She spoke without looking back. Then she got up, clutching her upper arms. 'Because I didn't know what else to do. I needed to talk – but you couldn't hear.'

The receptionist appeared at the surgery door. 'Cab's here, Anita.'

She moved back inside the surgery, scooping files into a briefcase. A doctor again.

'I hope I've been of some help.'

I stepped in front of her.

'I haven't finished.'

'I have to go.'

'Who told you to lie? Who told you to say *I* had arranged the meeting?'

I clasped her arm. Our faces were inches apart.

'Don't.'

I dropped my hand.

She reached for her coat.

'Carrie's dead.'

She stopped and looked up at me, eyes wide.

Steve appeared at the door.

'I have to go.'

I took the pen from her desk and wrote down the number of Shirley's mobile.

She paused at the door and turned back towards me, as if she wanted to add something. Then she was gone.

33

I watched the taxi take her away. Then I sat in the Jaguar, smoking and listening to the rain pelting against the roof.

How little of myself I recognised in her account. In the version of those days that I had reconstructed, I'd cut her part to little more than a walk-on, not even worthy of a Post-It note. The rest I'd pushed out of reach, just like the Air Lanka bag in my cellar.

The world I found waiting for me when I'd recovered was a terrifying place, ready to punish me for bringing Rammal into Greer's life, or remind me of my failure to come home with a film. I cordoned everything off – like a bad accident to be kept from view. I *had* seen Anita in the street. By then my determination to ignore anyone from the past was almost instinctive, though it was no defence against the stab of guilt and regret her face provoked.

I switched on the wipers and watched them sweep away the rain. I knew now that I hadn't just been looking for the truth about Malik. *Would I have kept my side of the deal?* I saw her at the carriage window as we waited for the Jaffna train to leave, blinking back tears, breathing quickly through slightly parted lips.

I squeezed her hand. I have to do this first. This is what I came to do.

I'd told her it was too dangerous. The worst that could happen to me was I'd be deported, but if she was caught she could be thrown in prison, or worse. The truth was: this was my big break. I couldn't compromise it.

I let my head fall against the steering wheel.

The car horn blared. I straightened up.

Greer arranged the meeting on the boat. She knew who Rammal really was all along; recognised him straightaway from my description.

Why did she want me to go to the quay? Why did she sleep with me?

The more I learned, the less I understood.

I was drained and hungry. I drove into Ashford, found a b. & b. and paid cash in advance for a single room with a bath.

I bought a small bottle of Scotch and a kebab, which I ate sitting on the bed. I turned on the TV news, then turned it off again when I realised I couldn't take anything in. I undressed and lay in the bath, drinking the Scotch, hoping that it would soothe the cuts and scars I had accumulated over the last few days.

When I woke, my head had almost slipped under the water. I shot upright. The bath was completely cold. Shirley's phone was ringing. It was Sivalingham's number.

'I am very sorry to bother you at this hour. Also for my previous evasion. But I have a message from Miss Jayarajah. Are you hearing me? She asks that you come to the surgery first thing tomorrow.' I stood dripping and shivering in the bedroom.

'Is she all right?'

'That is all the information I have. She was most emphatic though. Be there at seven a.m.' I looked at the phone. Four thirty. 'Can I tell her you will do that?'

'Will she be there?'

'I can't say.'

'Can I speak to her?'

'I have no number for her, I'm afraid. But she will call me back for confirmation that you are coming.'

'She may be in danger. There are things I need to explain to her.'

He didn't respond. My voice echoed in the earpiece, as if I was speaking into a void.

'I'll be there.'

The night was bitter. The car had grown a pale stubble of frost. I scraped at the windows with my sleeve. The tyres spun on the slippery road, searching for grip. At six fifteen I passed the surgery. It was all dark. I drove up the road, turned and reversed the Jag up a narrow sunken track almost opposite the entrance. I was out of sight but could see anyone entering the building.

The road was completely quiet. A silver Audi came past very slowly. A few minutes later it returned but didn't stop. I got out and walked down to the road. My breath billowed in the dim streetlight.

Another half hour went by. A Mini appeared and parked in the surgery car park. A woman got out. A big scarf obscured her head and she clutched what looked like a shoulder bag against her chest. She walked up to the surgery door. I was out of the car and running before she'd let herself in. When she heard my steps she wheeled round and shrieked, dropping a large Jiffy bag on the ground.

It was the receptionist, Lucy. I stopped a few feet away from her.

'Sorry.'

I picked up the Jiffy bag.

'It's for you. From Dr Jay.'

'Where is she?'

Lucy swallowed hard and clutched herself against the cold.

'I don't know. I don't know anything. Please don't hurt her.'

'Is she at home?'

'She rang my bell late last night and asked me to give you this. She—' Lucy broke off, choking on tears. 'She didn't say anything else – but she hugged me. She's never done that before. What's happening?'

'Where does she live?'

She glanced down the road.

'Where exactly?'

I stepped towards her. She put up her hands as if to shield herself.

'Glebe Cottage. After the pub.'

I set off down the road. An icy wind blew off the fields. The road curved as it passed the pub. Next to it were two houses then the cottage, standing apart. Beyond were open fields bordered by hedgerow.

None of the curtains in the front windows were drawn. I waited. Nothing moved. There was no sound other than the wind. There was a small lawn around the front and up the side of the house. A gravel path led from a small wooden gate. I crossed the lawn and approached the front window. I stepped onto a wooden planter so I could see into the room.

There was a loud crack as it gave way. I waited for a few minutes but no lights came on.

I went round to the front door. As I reached for the knocker, the door moved slightly. It wasn't quite shut, as if someone had forgotten to push it to. There was no sign that it had been forced. I stepped inside and called her name. I shut the door behind me.

I stood there for a few seconds, hoping my racing pulse would slow down. I mounted the stairs, a drumbeat smashing so hard at my temples it felt like my head was going to explode. An image of Carrie's body, still on her bed, flashed in front of me. *Please don't be there …* The bathroom was on the left of the landing. Two doors led off to the right. I pushed open the first. It was a box room, stacked with files. The second had to be the bedroom.

The bed hadn't been slept in. I breathed deeply and wiped my face with my sleeve. Although it was freezing, I was damp with sweat. The room smelled strongly of her scent. A large framed photograph of what must have been her parents stood on an otherwise uncluttered dressing table. A cupboard door was open and clothes were draped on a chair. A couple of tops had slipped off their hangers and lay on the floor of the wardrobe. She had left in a hurry.

I sat down on the bed and examined the Jiffy bag. There

was no label. I put on the bedside light and pulled open the stapled end. Inside was a note.

> *Nick, I don't know if you've caused all this, or were just trying to warn me. I've decided to believe you meant me no harm. Perhaps I was harsh yesterday, but even after all this time my feelings are muddled. You'd think these things would fade over time. I am returning to you what is rightfully yours. You risked so much and I still believe you wanted to make a difference. It's a small compensation. However ashamed I am of my part in all of this, believe me when I say I was given no choice. Ax*

I upended the bag and a package fell onto the bed. It was heavily bound in brown paper and Sellotape that had dried and shrunk. I picked it open and felt inside.

I pulled out a notebook, one I had shared with Anita on our recce. Some pages were fused together. There were also two Beta videotape boxes. Each had a Network label, filled out in my writing. Project number: ND95/HF29-GH. The *Human Face* that was never completed.

Next to *Title* I had written *FOAD – Face of the Arms Dealer*. And in the space for *Director* – my name.

The tapes were labelled: *Int Pt 1 and 2*.

My interview with Rammal.

I must have stared at them for about twenty minutes. It was like meeting someone you had been told was dead. I picked them up and turned them over, one in each hand, weighing them, as if to be sure they were really there. On the bad days after I'd been brought back from Sir Lanka, I sometimes thought I had imagined the whole thing. That there had been no film, no Rammal, no night with Greer, no deaths.

I shook a cigarette out of the pack and took out Greer's lighter. The first time I had handled it was the evening on the terrace at the Majestic. The thrill of the scoop had obliterated everything else. *Edge will be pleased with me*, I had told myself at the time, for putting the job first.

Anita had got me my introduction to the Tamil Tigers, but I hadn't wanted to take the risk of trusting her with the news about Rammal. I breathed the air in the room, her air.

It was dark downstairs. The message light on the phone was blinking. There was one message. I pressed Play.

Anita, are you there? It was Steve from the surgery. There was a long pause while he'd waited in vain for her to pick up.

34

Colin was still in his pyjamas. A duffel coat doubled as a dressing gown. He gave me a weary look. 'Cut yourself shaving?'

He shut the door behind me and glanced at the Jiffy bag.

'Sure you haven't been followed?'

All I could think about was the tapes. 'I need a Beta player. Twenty minutes. Then I'll be gone.'

I shook the tapes on to the table. He picked them up and examined them.

'What have we got?'

'Look at the labels.'

'Shit! Is this for real?' He stared at me.

'Have to look.'

'OK, but breakfast first.'

'I shouldn't be here.'

'Yes, well ...'

I sat at the kitchen table listening to the welcome hiss of bacon in a hot pan. The motorbike engine was gone. Newspapers were stacked on a chair.

'Don't suppose I'll be seeing my Beetle again.'

'Sorry about that.'

'I was extremely economical with the truth when the cops came. You should be very grateful.'

'I am.' Gratitude was something we didn't do.

'It was my mother-in-law's car, you know. It's all I had to remember her by.'

'So I've done you a favour.'

He snorted. 'So what was all that about? No doubt something else that's going to cause me to question your judgement?'

What was I going to say? That everyone I had seen in the

last few days had either disappeared or died? I was taking a big risk coming back to Colin's.

'Can we talk about that later?'

He sighed. There was silence while he concentrated on the breakfast.

'There's more in today's papers.' He appeared in the doorway to the scullery, brandishing a spatula. 'It's all going pear shaped for them. The Northolt Families say they're not being given enough time. One of the widows has been taken ill. She's been flown home to Israel. And one of their legal team's resigned.' He let out a derisory snort.

I followed him into the back room where a Beta-tape player stood among shelves of equipment and cassettes. He slotted in the first tape, spun through the colour bars until the first frame of picture and paused. Neither of us spoke.

Rammal's face was shaded by a wide-brimmed hat. Colin pressed Play and the first voice was mine, asking him to remove it. Rammal swept it off and threw it out of shot, grinning at the camera. He was clearly drunk.

If you don't mind, can I ask you not to look at the lens?

Whatever you wish.

And if possible, try not to brush the microphone.

He looked down at the clip mike I had attached to his tie. The frame jerked slightly as I adjusted the lens.

You always work alone?

I couldn't hear my answer, only a polite laugh. He reached out of shot and took a sip from a tall glass.

OK. Let's start. Can you begin by telling me about your work?

He launched into his answer in a language I didn't recognise. I interrupted him. He laughed heartily.

Oh yes. English. Of course.

Thanks. Tell me about your trading with the Tamil Tigers – and how you came to be doing this.

He listened to my question, his eyes almost closed. There was a long pause before he spoke.

You must understand it is extremely difficult for these

groups. They're preyed on by the very worst sorts, charging them a fortune.

He shook his head emphatically.

One kind of charlatan offers items that have fallen off Soviet trucks; another swears their weapons have fallen off American trucks. But they are trouble. And so are the goods. They refuse to go bang when they're supposed to, then they go bang when they shouldn't, or they don't go bang at all – which is most embarrassing.

He laughed and slapped his knee.

They all want a better class of weapon and a better class of supplier. They don't care who they get them from. So if you are a great big power like America or even Her Majesty's Government, you don't want your opponents getting friendly with them. You want to keep an eye on them. Know what they're doing, what they're buying. And you know the best way?

He wagged his finger at me.

You become their supplier. Become their friend.

He spread his arms wide and laughed.

The frame went black for a moment.

Colin cursed. 'Drop out. Tape's damaged.' He ejected the cassette, opened the front and studied the tape inside. 'Damp. Probably been kept somewhere airtight. Always fucks them up.'

'Try the other.'

'OK, OK.'

He pushed the second tape into the slot. There were several minutes of black then Rammal's face appeared again, taking another sip from his drink. The level in the glass was much lower. His other arm was outstretched.

Colin blew through pursed lips.

'I hope that's water.'

Rammal was in full flow, stabbing the air with a finger. His voice was slurred.

'You are going to die.' That's what they say. 'You will surely die.'

There was a long pause before he spoke again.

I tell them, 'We are all going to die. Sometime.'

He laughed silently and wiped his eyes.

And they say, 'You are going to die soon. You are a wanted man. There's a big price on your head. And if they don't kill you, your rivals will. And if you don't agree to work with us, we will probably have to kill you.'

His head flopped forward. He shook it from side to side with theatrical slowness.

Colin reached for another cigarette.

'Work with us and we will try to help you stay alive.'

More head-shaking. Then he held his arms out wide.

I had no choice.

An explosion of laughter.

Who made you the offer?

He seemed not to have heard my question.

Colin sighed loudly. 'You've got a right one here. He's shit-faced.'

I held up my hand to shut him up. Rammal was leaning forward in his chair, one finger raised. He took a deep breath and leaned forward, his hands clasping his knees.

They set me up with Emma, and then they killed me.

He made a gun with his fingers and pointed it at his temple. He repeated the line. Colin looked at me and shrugged.

Could you explain?

Rammal shrugged.

I gave them Amerair. Not one casualty. Three forty saved. Then they set me up. And then they killed me.

He stared unsteadily into the camera like a caricature drunk. There was a lot of rustling as he felt in his pocket for a cigar. The picture went again.

Colin ejected the tape and disappeared. He came back wielding a hairdryer. He blasted the tape with hot air.

'Sometimes helps.'

He shoved it back in and fast-forwarded through more black. I felt for a cigarette. When the picture came back, Rammal was holding a flame to his cigar. The rest was black. Colin ran the tape forward and back to the last shot. He jabbed Pause and the frame froze, then he turned and nodded at the lighter I was holding. Greer's lighter.

'Present from him?'

It was identical to the one in Rammal's hand.

I didn't answer. I stared at it in my palm. There was a small chip on one side where the jade had come away. I reached forward and rolled the image back and forward. The same chip.

'Give me a second.'

I went up to the bathroom, ran the cold tap in the basin. There were three hours between my meeting with Greer in the office and our drink at the hotel. I had told her about the boat, where it was moored.

I leaned over the basin and splashed some water on my face.

They *had* met.

Colin and I had once gone to the flat of a man who claimed he had the masters of Marlene Dietrich's first screen tests. The stack of pitted tins was neatly bound in wire with the wax seal of the film studio. He had acquired them on the black market while on national service in occupied Germany and kept them in a safety deposit box. Now he needed to realise his asset. He insisted they were the real thing, repeatedly tapping at the authentic-looking seals, which he refused to let us disturb.

Without asking, Colin broke the seal, levered open a can and held the film up to the light. It wasn't Dietrich. It was her stand-in. The first frame said *Dietrich doppeltes*. The man refused to believe it. There was too much at stake for him to let go.

I stood at the window, looking out at the night. A phone rang downstairs.

I had kept my memory of Greer sealed. I'd preserved it, consoling myself with the thought that no matter what had happened since, nothing would take that one perfect night away from me. Greer's last night. It had happened, it wasn't an invention. Now it was corroding in front of me.

She had needed those tapes badly enough to do whatever it took to get them back. And everything that went with them. She'd given Anita the job. We'd been seen together in the hotel. She was known to the staff. No one would be surprised. Perhaps Greer thought it would only need as long as it took to empty two bottles of Chablis. But I had hidden everything too well. Anita needed more time.

Seeing the tape had triggered other images. I shut my eyes and replayed them. Back in the hotel after the interview. The shutters closed, the only light from the bedside lamp. I had filled out the labels and was sticking them to the Beta cassettes.

An open box file, scuffed and gnawed at the corners. The contents spread out on the bed. A bound foolscap ledger with a leather spine. Inside, pages of an unfamiliar knotted script waiting to give up its secrets. Black-and-white photographs bound with thread that had eaten a notch into the white borders spilled from a grease-stained envelope. A group of young men standing in a featureless desert landscape. They held their guns self-consciously, as if they'd just taken delivery and didn't yet know how to handle them.

A sheaf of loose papers – telegrams – lay inside a blue file. The letters on the thin strips of gummed paper were scrambled.

As an afterthought, just as I was leaving his boat, Rammal had handed me the box file, a bleary grin on his face.

The rest of the material for my obituary.

I hadn't taken any chances. I'd hidden the photographs under the carpet, the ledger in a space I found behind the drawers in the dressing table. I had slotted the blue file into a gap in the headboard. The tapes would have been hardest to find, behind a grille above the cistern in the bathroom, held in by corroded screws. It could have taken hours. It could have taken most of the night.

Anita standing at the bottom of the hotel stairs. Not in the new clothes I had bought her but dressed as she was the day she met me off the plane. The threadbare sandals and the worn shirt. I'd not wanted to look at her eyes. I knew what their message would be. I had felt the pain and shame they were projecting. If I had had the courage to meet her gaze, perhaps I would have noticed something else. The words on her note came back: *Believe me when I say I was given no choice.*

She had kept the tapes. Why? Because of me? *I still believe you wanted to make a difference.*

The night sky was empty except for a small squadron of clouds barely visible in the moonless night.

I would have to start again: a re-edit of the available material. A new version.

35

Colin had wound some of the tape out of the cassette and was examining it closely.

'Might be able to retrieve some more of it, but it'll have to go to a lab. There's a laser process that works on some older tapes, unless it's been near something magnetic. I'll burn these onto a DVD so you've got a copy.' He broke off. '*Try* to pay attention.'

I was looking at the lighter, turning it over between my finger and thumb.

'Who's Emma?' Colin was reassembling the cassette.

'What?'

'Emma. The girl he got set up with "before they *keeled* me".'

I shrugged.

The interview was an embarrassment. No wonder I had done my best to forget it. Had I realised at the time how plastered he was? I flushed at my own naivety.

'Harrop called.'

I made an effort to look attentive.

'Asked if you'd come along to our meet at the café. Wanted to know if you'd get his film back for him.'

I gave him a blank look.

'From Metro. The Northolt film. He wants to put it back into whatever MOD cupboard it fell out of.'

'Doesn't he know I'm gone from Metro?'

'I thought you'd prefer to break the news to him personally.'

For all his scorn, there was an underlying camaraderie between Colin and his community of film enthusiasts. Although he regarded some of the bin men as little more than thieves looking for a quick return, precious material would be lost for ever without them. To him they were at the vanguard of film archaeology, sifting through the debris of the modern world, saving precious footage for the nation.

'Anyway, I asked him about *Amerair*. He knew right away. I guessed he would. He's a walking archive of civil aviation trivia.'

'And?'

'A few months before Northolt, a gang of five posing as baggage handlers were apprehended at Frankfurt. They were going to put a bomb on a US-bound flight full of service wives and children. It was a big coup for British Intelligence.'

I thought of what Edge had found out about Tanager – his moment of glory.

'Am I boring you?' Colin gave me a look that said *get a grip, for fuck's sake.*

I shook my head apologetically. 'Sorry. Just a lot to take in. Wasn't Harrop curious?'

'What about?'

'Why you were asking.'

Colin threw back his head and laughed. 'Harrop's only curious about one thing – what planes landed when. He's a plane-spotter. He practically lives at the end of Heathrow where all the funny cargo planes berth. His mobile number is 077 AVIATION.'

I gave them Amerair. Malik had tipped someone off. Edge's words came back to me: *He wanted out.*

'Perhaps he had done a deal. That was why his death was faked after Northolt.'

Colin took off his hat and scratched his scalp. 'And given a new identity.'

He reached for the paper the Beta tapes had been wrapped in. 'Something else. This was with it.'

It was the small notebook. Inside was a list of the appointments Anita had made for our meetings with the peacemakers.

'And this fell out of it.'

A postcard of the Majestic Hotel. I turned it over. The message was short.

Happy Birthday M, Love B.

I had seen Greer's handwriting on notes she'd made for Anita. It had the same sweeping loops. There was an un-franked postage stamp on it, and a date: 5.3.95. The day before she died. I tucked it back in the notebook.

A copy of the *Daily Mail* lay open at a double-page spread. A row of children's portraits ran along the top, above a group-shot of their parents. THE NORTHOLT MOTHERS, ran the headline. STILL WAITING FOR THE TRUTH.

I stood up.

'Where's their HQ?'

Colin examined me over his glasses.

'If you're thinking what I think you're thinking – don't.'

I guestured at the frozen image on the screen. 'It shows that lies were told about Malik's death.'

'How?'

'There he is, alive in 1995.'

'Says who?'

'Me. Edge.'

'How can you verify it?'

'I was there. I can prove I was there. It's got my voice on. Look at the label.' I jabbed a finger at the top of the cassette. 'It's got the date on it.'

'Anyone could have put that on.' He leaned forward and rested his elbows on his thighs. 'You've got some tape of someone taken somewhere, sometime of a bloke who *seems* to look like Malik. How can you prove it?'

'We can verify the flash frame coming from the copy of *Face of a Terrorist.*'

'But it doesn't *prove* that it's him, dickhead. There are no pictures of him in circulation. No one knows what he really looked like.' Colin was waving a finger in front of me. 'So the Northolt people put your tape on show. The powers that be would demand to know where it's come from, where it's been all this time. They'd want you at the hearing.' He exhaled slowly then sat back and folded his arms. 'You may be an experienced archivist and all that, but you're also a thief on the run. Read my lips. You are wading in deep shit.'

I looked down at the notebook.

'I need to get to the bottom of this.'

He shook his head. 'What you need is a bath and a shave.'

36

Colin had laid out a pair of baggy cords and an army-surplus sweater with fabric patches on the shoulders and elbows. They would do. I changed the dressing on my chin for a small plaster.

I looked at myself in the mirror. Clean shaven, like the picture in Carrie's album – the one Saul must have removed.

Colin appeared in the doorway, a newspaper tucked under his arm, holding a mug of tea. He glanced at my reflection.

'You look like shit.'

'Must be the clothes.'

He hovered, his arms flapping at his sides. I looked round at him.

'Go on, spit it out.'

'I know I don't know the half of what's been going on and it's probably better that way …' He gave out one of his long despairing sighs. 'This crusade of yours; it's about a lot more than Northolt, isn't it? What do *you* want out of it?'

He put the tea on the edge of the sink and started work on another roll-up.

'None of my business, I know. But you had a bad time in Sri Lanka.' He stared into space for a moment. 'God knows, we've all got our regrets, things we wished we'd done differently. But it's a long time ago, and you can't change what happened.'

He held out the roll-up. I took it.

'What's that supposed to mean?'

He shrugged and waved his cigarette in the air. 'Don't make anything worse for yourself than it already is.'

I snorted. 'I don't think that's possible.'

He raised an eyebrow. 'If you are right – *if* – and you take your tapes to the Northolt people, they won't necessarily have your best interests at heart. How will you be able to control what they do with them?'

I lit the cigarette and blew a cloud of smoke at the mirror. He liked to compile and conserve. He hated the side of archive life that involved lending material to people who might misuse or damage it. Over the years, this had grown into a blanket suspicion about anything *out there*. Sometimes I thought he only kept up with the news to feed his conviction that everything was going to hell and the best response was to keep your head down.

He thought he had identified me as a kindred spirit, someone else who'd burned his fingers out in the world. He was right, at the time. Metro was his refuge; it became mine as well. And after he was sacked, this house became his last safe haven from the powers that be who had conspired to bring him down.

He wasn't finished. 'Even if you proved them all wrong about Malik, what does it really matter now? What difference is it going to make to anyone or anything? He's dead. Your … Greer's dead. Nothing's going to bring them back. Malik can't tell you what he did or didn't do.'

I watched him shaking his head. I saw now how different we were.

'You have a choice. You don't have to go on.'

I looked at my reflection again, the shaved face, the borrowed clothes.

He was wrong. I didn't have a choice.

He unfurled the newspaper. 'OK, my last try.'

He looked away as he held it out.

TV EDITOR FOUND DEAD.

I didn't move.

'Took his own life, apparently. Same day his wife died.'

37

The Northolt campaign HQ was in a house in an Islington square. A large poster hung in the front window: a montage of the EMA logo on the tailplane taken at the crash scene and the faces of the children that had appeared in the *Mail*.

I parked a few hundred yards away and zigzagged through the streets, doubling back on myself a couple of times. I paused on the opposite side of the square, with enough of a view of the building and the front door.

In the ten minutes I sat there it looked pretty busy. Several couriers came and went with packages. People who looked like students arrived on bicycles. A bouquet of flowers was delivered and a stack of pizzas.

I scanned the rest of the square. Cars were parked nose to tail. They were all empty. A Transit van stood a few doors away but it looked too conspicuous to be important. It had been painted orange, with what might have been a garden broom and flowers decorating the sides and bonnet. One of its tyres was flat.

Before I'd left Colin's I had looked up the Northolt Families' website. It was just a holding page with a contact number. I had dialled it on Colin's home phone and got a recorded message. There was a mobile number to ring 'Only in an emergency'.

'Yes?' The woman's voice sounded harassed.

'I'm sorry to trouble you.'

'Who is this?'

I gave her my name and explained I was a film archivist.

'The office is closed. You'll have to ring back.'

'I've got some material that might help you.'

'This isn't a good time. We're desperately busy.'

She sounded impatient but she didn't hang up.

'It's about Malik. Something you should know.'

She hesitated.

'Look, I'm sorry, but we're under a lot of pressure here.'

I took a deep breath.

'It's footage of him. Taken after he was supposed to have died.'

'OK. What's your number?'

I gave them the mobile number, but they hadn't rung back.

I got out of the car and set off across the square. The door opened and all the people I had seen arrive left at the same time, as if they'd just been let out of school.

I sat on a bench. After ten minutes a people carrier pulled up. The rear door opened and two men in fleeces started unloading silver boxes and a tripod. A television crew. I retreated to the car. A van arrived and lights were unloaded. They would be there for a while.

I felt for a cigarette and lit up. I turned Greer's lighter over between my thumb and forefinger. I took out the postcard. *Happy Birthday M, Love B*. It was Greer's handwriting, but she had signed herself *B*. Carrie had said Greer was Edge's invention.

Happy Birthday M. But the name on the card was Mrs Sarah Blaine. The address was in Surrey. I took a road atlas out of the door pocket.

38

Mayfield Lane might once have been a lane. It had been all but obliterated by a dual carriageway. A thin hedge shielded a small row of cottages. The house had a long front garden occupied by several identical vans in varying stages of decline.

A dog on a large rope alerted the occupants to my arrival. It was some time before the front door opened.

A man my age with a long ponytail stood on the step. He didn't speak.

'Sorry to trouble you. Is there a Mrs Blaine here?'

'You are troubling me. Fuck off.'

He slammed the door.

I stood there for a moment before rapping a second time. It opened again.

'I said fuck *off*.'

'I'm trying to find Mrs Blaine.'

A child started crying. The man stepped away from the door without shutting it. I stood in the doorway. I watched him bend down and slap the child on the leg, which raised the volume of the crying.

'Do you know where she is? I've got something for her.'

'Give it here.'

'I need to give it to her in person.'

He snorted and sat down in front of the television. The dog started barking again as another van bumped onto what was left of the lawn. A couple of children tumbled out of the passenger door, followed by a woman in a shaggy coat. She shouted at the dog and it retreated. She stopped when she saw me.

'Mrs Blaine?'

She laughed.

'You're joking.'

I explained I had some post for her, which had gone astray.

'She's been gone years.'

'Is she dead?'

'Good as.' She went round to the back of the van, flung open the doors and started unloading some sacks. 'Broadlands.' She gestured up the road. 'Opposite the BP garage.'

She stopped her unloading.

'Why's she so popular all of a sudden?'

'What do you mean?'

'You're the second this week.'

39

Broadlands was a large house dwarfed by a sea of lawn. I parked the Jag and walked up a path with a hand rail, clutching a bunch of chrysanthemums. The sun had come out for the first time in days and although it was cold a row of people in hats and overcoats sat in wheelchairs on a partly enclosed veranda. Those who weren't asleep stared out across the lawn. As I approached, the nearest lady looked at me with great enthusiasm.

'Good afternoon, young man.'

'Do you know a Mrs Blaine?'

One of the men groaned. 'Too right we do.'

'Now now.' The woman who had spoken first wagged a finger. 'It's not her fault.'

'Come on, Celia, she's in a bloody world of her own.'

'Well, you go on just as much.'

Celia looked back at me pityingly. 'Sarah does like to talk.'

'Thanks for the warning.'

'About the same bloody thing.' The man was hunched forward in his wheelchair. 'I've been here as long as she has, and do you know, every day at elevenses it's the same question.'

Seeing he had my attention he waved me over.

'Here, lad, give me a hand, I need to stretch.'

I offered my arm, which he grabbed with both hands. He shuddered as he worked himself up to a standing position. He moved his shoulders around and dropped back into the chair.

'Every bleedin' day.'

'Now, Stan, the gentleman doesn't want to hear your moaning. We all like to talk about our children.'

Stan waved at me.

'Son, do us all a favour, tell her once and for all her daughter's dead. D-E-A-D.'

Several of the others tutted.

'Stan! He might be family!' I smiled and shook my head, then moved on into the building.

I rang a bell on the reception and waited. There was a pervasive smell of disinfectant. The veneer around the desk had come away and there was a tear in the wallpaper where it had been scraped by some equipment. An odd assortment of chairs filled the area. Two male nurses came past wheeling a very old man on a trolley. He was curled in a fetal position.

'Be with you in a sec.'

A minute later one of them reappeared. He frowned at my bunch of flowers.

'Could I see Mrs Blaine?'

'Visiting's over for today.'

'It'll only take a minute. I've got something to give her.'

He looked unconvinced. I gave him my name.

'She doesn't usually have visitors. Are you family?'

'No.'

He turned away and consulted a large ledger.

'I'm afraid there's no unauthorised visiting for Mrs Blaine.'

'I'm sorry?'

He looked at me wearily.

'There's no unauthorised visiting for Mrs Blaine. It's a condition of her residency.' He held out his hand for the flowers. 'I'll see she gets them.'

'There's something else I need to give her, in person.'

'That's not possible.'

A buzzer sounded and a red light on a console adjacent to the desk flashed red. He threw a switch to silence it and headed up the corridor. I went back onto the veranda and gazed out over the lawn.

'No luck?'

Celia wheeled herself over.

'Seems not.'

She nodded at the other residents.

'Stan's right, I'm afraid, she does go on rather, about the daughter. Senile dementia, you know. I used to be a nurse.'

'I'd still like to see her.'

She shook her head. 'Poor Sarah.'

She made a disapproving noise with her tongue. I bent down.

'You couldn't show me where she is?'

She looked at me with mock disapproval. 'I could sneak you in. Would you like that?'

'Very much.'

'We'll have to go round the back. You push.'

She pointed to a far door in the sun room that led to a ramp and another path. It snaked across the lawn and round the main building. I hung on to the wheelchair as it gathered speed down the incline.

'Faster! We don't want you to get caught.' She giggled conspiratorially.

Behind the main building was a single-storey extension surrounded by bushes.

'So you've not been before?'

'That's right.'

'Apart from her doctor, no one comes to see her, poor thing.'

We were nearing the annexe. The paint around the windows was badly peeled.

'Most likely it was the shock that brought it on, you know. Couldn't accept what had happened. My brother was lost at sea. Mother always wondered, every time the doorbell went.'

The path sloped again. I concentrated on the task of keeping the wheelchair from running away. When we reached a door she pressed a number into a key pad.

'Pull! Quick as you can!'

The door was stiff.

'It's number eight.'

There was a CCTV camera in the corridor. My guide rapped hard on No 8.

'Are you decent, Sarah?'

There was no answer.

'Just go in. She'll not hear you.'

The room was very bare. A milky sun drifted in over the half net curtain. A pearl-handled brush and mirror set took pride of place on a small dressing table. She was sitting in a wing-backed chair, her hands folded in her lap, her eyes half closed. A dressing gown was tied tightly around her. She was slow to move but when she noticed me she caught a wisp of hair and tucked it back. The resemblance was unmistakeable. I felt my eyes fill and my throat tighten up. Her eyes settled on the flowers and she smiled.

'Oh, how nice.'

I introduced myself. She didn't hear me. All her concentration was on the flowers.

'Would you like me to put them in a vase for you?'

There was no response.

'She takes her time, don't you, Sarah?' bellowed the lady in the wheelchair. She had followed me in. I thanked her. 'I'll be in the lounge at the end if you need me.'

I sat down on the bed. It seemed inappropriate to suddenly raise the matter of her dead child.

I looked round to the other wall. There were three large photographs. Two were familiar, a BAFTA shot and a *Human Face* publicity still. The third must have been a school photograph, Greer's hair much longer and darker, a broad carefree grin on her face.

'Lovely pictures.'

Her face suddenly brightened. Perhaps she wasn't used to people paying attention to them.

'Oh, I'm glad you think so. I do think she comes over very well in them.' She spoke with an accent that sounded acquired. 'I have many more.' She reached towards a large plastic-covered album. 'Would you like to see them? I know her face is so familiar to everyone.'

'I have something that got lost. It should have reached you a long time ago.'

I took out the postcard and put it in her lap.

She picked it up and looked at it, smiling.

'Well now, that's a nice surprise.'

I relaxed a little. She seemed pleased to see it. She examined it closely and pointed to the date.

'Ah. This is the one.'

'I'm really sorry if this is in any way upsetting.'

She wasn't listening. She turned it over and looked at the picture of the Majestic Hotel.

'That looks like a nice place.' She smiled again. 'She *is* a good girl.'

She focused on me for the first time and waved the card at me.

'Thank you. You're very kind.'

She had the same serene, almost dreamy look. Perhaps she was on medication. She bent towards me.

'This is the lost one. They always come in the end.'

She reached forward towards a small chest of drawers, her hand shaking.

'Can I help you?'

She waved a crooked forefinger at the top drawer. I opened it. She reached in and her fingernails made a scrabbling sound as she moved aside a bag of cottonwool swabs and a hair-brush. Her thumb and forefinger curled round a pack of cards held together with an elastic band. She lifted them out. They were postcards, well thumbed. The top one was of Jerusalem. She held them suspended in mid-air. It was a moment before I realised she meant me to take them.

'Every year.'

She made a movement with her hands. I interpreted this as a signal to spread them out on the bed. Then she examined the one I had brought, pointing at the date.

'Nineteen ninety-five.'

She spread out the postcards, picture side up. There were at least twenty. Each came from somewhere different: Tunisia, Lebanon, Guadeloupe, Bahrain, Madagascar, Buenos Aires, Goa. She lifted one and looked at the date.

'In there.'

The sight of the cards seemed to have given her extra energy. She leaned forward and made a gap between Goa and Buenos Aires.

'It goes in there.'

In profile the resemblance between them was even stronger.

When I looked down again she had turned over two cards. They each carried the same identical message in the same handwriting:

Happy Birthday M, Love B

The card on the left was dated 1994.

I turned over the other. 1996.

I turned them all over 1997, '98, '99 and on. There were at least ten more. Each one carried the same message. I felt my pulse quicken. I picked up the most recent. My hands were trembling. It was of the Great Buddha in Kandy, Sri Lanka. I turned it over and examined the postmark: two weeks ago.

40

I stared at Sarah. She was beaming at the cards spread out on the bedspread. The one I'd just delivered in its rightful place.

'They always come in the end.'

I sat down heavily on the bed. All the strength left my legs. For a moment I thought I was going to faint. I put out my hand to steady myself. She took it, and clasped it in both of hers, a facsimile of Greer's smile beaming back at me.

'How kind of you.'

There was a knock at the door. Celia sat there, an apologetic look on her face. Beside her were the two male nurses.

'If you wouldn't mind, sir, the manager's waiting to see you.'

Sarah beamed. 'Do come again.'

I got to my feet and almost lost my balance as I bent to take her hand.

I was escorted back towards the main building, a nurse each side. Neither of them spoke. They were big. In different uniform they could have been bouncers. I thought I might just be shown off the premises, but they opened a side door and ushered me down a long corridor.

'She's alive.' I said the words to myself, as if I needed to confirm what I had just seen. Each postcard with the same message, in the same looped script.

They ushered me into a wood-panelled room. A large patch stood out on the ceiling, where the plaster had been repaired. The manager was dwarfed by the huge oak desk she was seated behind. She was writing something down. Eventually she looked up and smiled. She was wearing a kind of matron's uniform, dark blue with a black, elasticated belt. Her hair was scraped back into a tight bun.

She looked up. 'Elsa Keown. And you are?'

'Nick Roker.' My voice was barely audible.

'Sit down, Mr Roker.'

One of the nurses left the room.

Elsa Keown continued to smile, as if her face had been fixed in that position. Years of listening politely to the elderly had taken its toll.

'You are aware of our visiting hours.' Her smile seemed to stretch even wider.

'I'm very sorry.'

Did they know?

'And what is your connection to Mrs Blaine?'

'An old friend of her ... family ...'

'Mrs Blaine doesn't have any family.'

'I knew her daughter.'

She glanced up at the ceiling.

'So did a lot of people.'

She knitted her fingers together and rubbed her palms against each other. Beneath them was an open file. All I could see was the word *Medical*.

She stared at me for some time. I hoped she wasn't thinking of calling the police. 'I need to contact her representatives.'

The smile disappeared for a moment. She gave a tiny nod to the remaining nurse. We were alone. She looked down at the papers on her desk, weighing a thought. 'Do you have any identification with you?'

I took out my Metro ID card. She studied it. I hoped she wouldn't dial the phone number on it. Her mouth was clamped shut. She moved her tongue across her teeth.

'You were saying ... about her representatives ...'

'It isn't customary for us to discuss residents' details.' She coughed gently into her fingertips. 'Mr Roker, with wearying frequency, we get strangers here claiming to need to –' she drew a pair of quotation marks in the air – 'reacquaint themselves with residents, especially the ones without family.' Her smile widened still further. 'But I can assure you that you'd be wasting your time with Mrs Blaine. Not only have her standing-order payments ceased, the account it's paid from has been frozen.' She sighed. 'We are all very fond of Mrs Blaine. She has been here longer than I have. But we aren't a charity, Mr Roker. And we have a long waiting list. In such circumstances, we'll have no alternative but to hand her over to social services.'

A shadow crossed her face, as though she regretted this burst of candour.

She saw me glance at the file in front of her and folded it shut.

'Can I ask who the representatives were? I do need to contact them.'

Ms Keown's face didn't move.

'Has anyone else been to see Ms Blaine?'

She blinked twice and the smile finally disappeared.

'Does she have her own doctor?'

'Mr Roker, I think you should leave before I call the police.'

41

I'd expected at least one big nurse to escort me from the building, but the foyer was deserted. Several lights were blinking on the console. Celia waved at me from the conservatory. She made a sympathetic shrug. I did the same and smiled at her. 'Thanks for your help.'

I walked quickly to the car. I lit a cigarette and noticed that my hands were trembling. I inhaled deeply and gripped the wheel for support.

I had dreamed so often that I'd got it all wrong, that there'd been a misunderstanding, that Greer hadn't been on the boat when it exploded. She was somewhere safe, unharmed, and I hadn't witnessed her death. But now my elation was tempered by the knowledge that she had wanted me to be the witness to a giant hoax. I was the one who'd had to tell the world what happened.

And then it came, like a switch being thrown and light flooding into a dark space. *He's alive as well.* It explained so much; why Tanager was so interested in what I knew, wanting the copy of the film, the Government's reticence about what really happened at Northolt. *Malik's out there.* And as long as he was alive, he could tell the world who had set him up.

I was halfway round the mini-roundabout at the end of the drive when I floored the accelerator and headed back up to the main door.

Celia was still there, nodding in her wheelchair. She looked up, surprised. 'Hello again ...'

'You said Sarah's only visitor was a doctor.'

'That's right, she comes three or four times a year.'

'Do you know her name?'

One of the nurses appeared in the foyer, heading towards me.

Celia screwed up her eyes. 'Now I'd have to think ...'

She pressed her fingers against her brow.

'OK, sir, off we go.' The nurse gripped my elbow very firmly.

'An Indian girl. Very pretty ...'

I was being propelled towards the main door.

I twisted round. 'Anita?'

Celia's face lit up. 'That's it!'

I drove back to London, barely aware of the traffic around me. A pedestrian shouted when I over-ran a zebra crossing. A truck blasted its horn when I failed to move off at a green light. Then I saw a silver BMW do a U-turn and tuck in behind me. I made more of an effort to concentrate.

Rain spotted the windscreen. I switched the wipers to intermittent. They dragged the moisture into curved streaks that caught the oncoming headlights and blurred my vision of the road ahead. I fumbled in my bag for the phone and dialled Sivalingham's number without bothering to think what time it was in Sri Lanka. I put it on speaker and laid it by the gear stick while I listened to the unanswered ringing.

42

The grey evening had drifted into a misty wet night. I left the car a few streets away from Colin's house. There was no answer when I rang the bell. I called his mobile but it was switched to voicemail.

The café was tucked under the railway line I used to travel on every day to work. Colin went there when he needed a change from the takeaways he lived on. It was full of smoke and steam, which gave it a comforting fug that pulsed to a reggae beat.

I looked at the other customers. There was a group of office workers, all smartly dressed but dishevelled by an evening's drinking. Another three men sat hunched over their burgers, saying nothing. There were a few others sitting alone who looked like they might not have anywhere else to go tonight.

A teenage girl with a dog on a string sat near the door trying to make eye contact. All of them seemed to inhabit another world where human behaviour was predictable and there were certainties to cling to, however mundane. I was alone in my own space, where nothing was ordinary or normal.

Harrop was in a corner. He wore a fluorescent rain jacket with the hood still pulled up, the string tied under his chin, as if that was the way his mum always sent him out, even though he was well into his fifties. His fists were retracted into the cuffs. His expression was blank, trance-like. He was deep in his interior world, his own safe place.

'Where's Colin?'

'On his way, I expect.' I offered him a hand to shake. He looked alarmed but eventually released a fist from its burrow and took it. 'What can I get you?'

He looked mystified, as if he wasn't used to hospitality. 'A coffee would be nice.'

'Anything to eat?'

'A biscuit.'

He smiled nervously at the waitress. He had the round face and big eyes of a vulnerable animal.

'Colin says you're in trouble at work.'

He sucked in his upper lip. His head vibrated inside the hood. He was nodding.

'Because of the Northolt film?'

He sighed heavily.

'Let me guess. You didn't know it was going to be all over the news. And your colleagues in the MOD are asking how it got there.'

His head retracted into his hood, as if he'd sniffed danger.

'And you're worried that if they ask Metro—'

The waitress arrived with the coffee and a three-pack of bourbons.

Harrop unwrapped them and nibbled away at one.

'Three months off retirement – and that could be my pension gone.' He paused while he finished the biscuit and started on a second. 'I'd had that film out there, oh, a while. Showed it to a few of the lads, you know. Gave it a bit of a clean. If I hadn't spotted it in a Cold Box ...' He shook his head and breathed out through pursed lips, just as Colin would have, and made a tipping gesture. 'Into the fire.'

'Why's that?'

'Space. That's my job, isn't it? And space is money. Miriam – she's my boss, Head of Buildings and Services – her bonus depends on how well she uses the square footage.'

There would be no hurrying him. If I was going to learn anything I had to let him go at his own speed.

'They came our way about ten years ago, in the cutbacks after the end of the Cold War. Thought we'd have some spare aircraft hangar we could stash them in.' He leaned in again. 'Dead jobs. Stuff no one needed any more. No risk. All goes into a Cold Box. Files, tapes, film, artefacts. Box it all up, stick it somewhere and forget about it.' His head shook inside the hood. 'We were expecting a few hundred boxes. We got twenty thousand! Two cubic metres each. Mostly from the days of the Evil Empire. We had four warehouses full of 'em. But see, we've got our targets. Space is money now.' He examined my face to check I appreciated the gravity of the situation. 'Cremate. That's what Miriam says. If it's before 'eighty-five, off to the crematorium.' He giggled childishly. 'That's what we call the incinerator.'

'And you got to look in the boxes?'

His hands moved to his eyes then his ears. 'See no evil, hear no evil. That's what we always say. We provide facilities. That's our job. That's all.' He gave me his anxious animal look again. 'Well, there's the thing. The boxes themselves, they get recycled. They're aluminium. So you have to open them to chuck the contents.' His voice dropped to a whisper. 'That's why I volunteered to do the cremating. Can you imagine? Especially with my thing being the airports and that ... Well, I'm like a pig in shit. Soviet aircraft, all shapes and sizes. Ground footage, aerials, control towers, radar. And other stuff. Middle East. Hijack footage – brilliant. Tragedy of it – there was more than I'd got room for.'

He shook his head in awe, his eyes unfocused, recalling the undreamed-of treasure. The archive world I had inhabited suddenly seemed a long way away now.

'Several of them were so full of good stuff I put them by. No point sifting them.'

'Meaning?'

'I put them where I could keep an eye on them. On the premises.'

I thought of how I'd hidden the copy of *Face of a Terrorist* at Honor Oak.

'And that's how you came by Northolt?'

His face clouded. 'Like I said, I wanted to show it to some of the lads. Didn't seem any point taking it back.'

I brought him back to his current anxiety. 'So what's the problem?'

He dabbed his eyes. He didn't speak for a few seconds. Then he leaned closer. His voice was barely audible. 'Braintree.'

'Go on.'

'That's what's got Miriam all stressed. And when she's stressed, I'm stressed. Something big on. Scramble. Two days' notice, they want space for fifty bodies, all with terminals and telecoms. That means facilities – male and female, long-shifters – they're like beds for if they're working round the clock. And a canteen. Well, with all the cuts we've not got the space. So it's got to be Braintree. A hangar for the operatives, Portakabins for the boss. Bane of my life, I can tell you, Portakabins. Always trouble.'

'I can imagine.' It was all I could think of to say.

'So in they come – from all over the world. Talking all different languages, more like an airport than a chase. Next thing, they want to order up Cold Boxes. More stress for Miriam, No one told them they were being junked. *Where are the inventories for what's gone and what's not?* Why, that's not our job. We're not archivists.'

He blew out a long blast of coffee breath.

'Next day, the Northolt footage is on the telly. I'm keeping my head down cos I didn't realise about the inquiry or anything. To me it was just a good bit of footage. And Miriam says, "They want to speak to you in Braintree." So I've got to put a tie on and get down there.' He pushed the hood back and scratched his scalp 'Well, that's me finished, I think. Get your cards now, Harrop, old son. You may as well jump in the fire with all the rest of it. That's when I called Colin. I thought he'd know what to say. He's good at keeping out of trouble.'

The words echoed in my head.

He glanced at his empty coffee cup. I waved for a refill. The café had almost emptied. The group of silent men had gone. At their table was a couple poring over a *Time Out*.

'Talking to a *god*, I mean, that just never happens.' He repeated the see-no-evil gesture, his hands fluttering around his head.

'God?'

'God?'

'Those on high. The big boys. But the one at Braintree, he's a gentleman. He can see I've got the collywobbles, because straight away he's putting me at ease. "You and me," he says, "we're the old school, aren't we?" He puts his arm round me. "I need your memory." He's got a twinkle in his eye. He's not one of the self-important ones. More the sort you could have a joke with. And he offers me a smoke.' He shook an imaginary packet in his left hand, just as I had seen Tanager do. 'Which, by the way, is forbidden in the Portakabins. But just when he's got me starting to relax, right out of the blue he fixes me with this look and says, "Northolt." Well, I nearly shat myself there and then. It was like he knew just what I'd been up to.'

Moisture was collecting around the edge of Harrop's eyes. His breath had started to smell again.

'But then he says, "I'll bet you've got a good memory. See if you can remember what else was in the box?" Not "Where's the box?" Not "What have you done with the box?" Well, I'm not supposed to know, am I? He says, "Just between you and me, OK," and taps his nose.'

'What *was* in the box?'

I'd crossed a line. Harrop's face froze. High alert. Predator approaching.

'Oh, I don't think I can say.' He shook his head rapidly.

I smiled back. 'Of course not.' There had to be another way in. 'So, how were you able to tell him?'

'That was easy. Cos of the pictures they'd pinned up. In the main office, where all the terminals are.'

I left a silence, praying he would fill it.

He blinked a few times. 'Same couple; but with different hair and stuff.'

'Couple?'

'A man and a woman – shots of them at airports, mainly. The box was full of them.'

I pictured Tanager sitting in a Portakabin in Braintree, surrounded by surveillance photographs of Greer and Malik as they roamed the world in disguise. Goa, Buenos Aires, Dubai, sending Sarah a postcard when her birthday came around.

'Then he says to me, "Where's the box now?" Well, I didn't want to tell him, but I didn't have a choice.'

'Cremated?'

He gestured in a rough approximation of a westerly direction, and whispered, 'Washington.'

'The CIA?'

'No. An affiliate. Private Security Agency.'

He shook his head, slowly this time. 'The god's not pleased. Not happy at all. "Are you absolutely sure?" he asks. Sure as I can be. About nine months ago. They sent an armed special courier to accompany it. I did remember, because it had never happened before, a request for a Cold Box.' Harrop's eyes were full of tears now. 'I've never been in this sort of trouble. I've gone about my business, no one taking any notice – not even a please or thank-you. I don't mind about that. Last thing I need's attention …'

'But you've helped him – your "god".'

'But the *film*. If I could just get it back. Then they can't say I've taken it. Can't do me. Can't take my pension.'

He was like a small boy who'd been found out, wanting to make it all right, put back what wasn't his to take.

'How much did Darren give you?'

'Four hundred. But I blew it on a weekend trip to Ankara.'

He read my surprise. 'It's a great hub. Lost of flights east. Old stuff. The classics: Illyushins, Tupolevs, even Chinese stuff. All kinds of markings you never see at Heathrow.'

I looked at him, his head hanging down as if his neck had been wrung. His voice was very small.

'I thought perhaps you could get it back for me.'

'I'm not at Metro any more. You'll have to try Darren. He may be open to a deal, now he's had his moment of glory.' I took out my wallet, counted out five twenties and laid them on the table.

He looked at the money. And back at me.

'Really! Can I?'

As he reached towards the notes, I dropped a hand on his. 'What else was in the box?'

'Seven Network cans. *Human Face*. Some lever-arch files with date seals on. And all the photos.'

The material seized from Edge's production office. His eyes were still on the money.

'What are they doing? The staff in there, at the terminals?'

Harrop didn't speak. I started to put the money back in my wallet.

'OK, OK. They've got all the airline schedules, going back five years. They're going through passenger manifests. I only know cos I recognise them. I'm not being nosy. They've got all nationalities in there, all gabbling away in goodness knows what languages.'

'The pictures on the walls. Describe them.'

'All different. Clothes, hairstyles. You'd hardly know they were the same pair. And there's a big map. Lots of lines. Why do you need to know?'

I pushed the money towards him. 'Tell Darren there'll be an inquiry if you don't get it back. He's not supposed to take stuff from public servants. If he's difficult offer him the money. That should work. Thanks for the information.'

'None of my business, but why do you need it?'

'That's right.'

He nodded. 'Understood. None of my business.'

43

It was late. Colin's street was full of cars, parked nose to tail. The BMW a few houses along had nothing to distinguish itself from the other vehicles. A van's headlights picked out the two silhouettes inside, facing away from me. I turned and walked back the way I had come.

Halfway down the side street where I had parked was an alleyway that ran behind the back gardens. I had once helped Colin manoeuvre a second-hand washing machine along it in a shopping trolley, helpless with laughter as its wire frame sagged under the weight and finally gave out just as we reached his kitchen.

There were lights on. I banged the back door hard. Nothing happened. The spare keys were in their usual place, on a hook inside a long-vacated dog kennel. I stood for a few minutes, listening for any sounds, hearing nothing but the wind and the blood pounding through my head.

I knocked and listened some more. The lights were on. A radio was playing. I let myself in. A large soup bowl sat on the kitchen table. Beside it was an Indian takeaway. The lids had been removed, but the food was still in its foil trays. I held my hand over the rice. It was cold.

I moved towards the hall. Near the front door a can of lager lay on its side on the carpet, surrounded by a large damp patch. I looked into the back room. There was a pile of tape cassettes. Their open boxes, thrown into a corner, formed another pile. A brand-new video camera was still sealed in its box. The radio was coming from somewhere upstairs. 'Sailing By'. I climbed to the first floor, nausea rising with each step.

At first I didn't notice him. I allowed myself the faint hope that he had been urgently called away. He was in the spare bedroom where I had slept, crammed into the space between the bed and the wall, as if he had tried to take refuge there. His legs were drawn right up to his chest but his fingers, swollen and purple, were splayed out at odd angles.

His head rested on his knees. I took a deep breath and lifted his chin. His eyes stared out of a face frozen in fear. I stepped back and crashed into the wardrobe. The door swung open and a mirror shattered as it hit the wall. I swallowed hard. I heard Colin's voice in my head. *Don't be a prat. Get a grip!*

I had brought him into this. He had warned me from the start. He had been right all along. But I'd appealed to the other part of him. Fed his curiosity, played on his hatred of loose ends.

I put out my hand and touched his head. *Don't piss about. Get moving.*

I went down to the front room. Filing cabinet drawers yawned open. One had toppled over onto the editing bench. I cleared a space and knelt down in front of the fireplace. Colin detested banks. He liked his valuables around him. I lifted out the bar heater and took hold of the grate. I had seen him do this once. It moved after several tugs. Beneath it was a tile that lifted by depressing one edge. Below that was a shallow space about the size of a small briefcase. The can containing *Face of a Terrorist* just fitted. On top of it were Anita's notebook, a wad of cash and a white envelope. I tore it open.

If you're reading this, it means only one thing. Don't waste time blaming yourself. I could have opted out any time. The master's with Sargeant's. Ask for Tosspot. Take the money. If you don't, someone else will. Now fuck off out of here. C.

He'd used the old name for the lab. Sargeant's had been subsumed into another outfit in the eighties. 'Tosspot' was Colin's nickname for the irritating but diligent Eric, a technician who did under-the-counter jobs for him.

Hanging from the row of hooks in the hall was an ancient duffel bag. I put everything into it. I glanced up the stairs then left through the back door. I stopped where the passage met the street. I felt my legs start to buckle under me. I leaned against a low wall, gasping for air. The street started to tilt and the orange lights became smeary. *For fuck's sake, get a grip.* Colin's voice lifted me out of the vortex of rage and grief that swirled around inside my head.

I lit a cigarette, the wind blowing sparks off it. I stared at the ordered shapes of the paving stones, the dull sheen of frost on the car roofs stretching up the street, the row of curtained bay windows. Behind them, people were watching television, getting ready for bed, pouring a nightcap.

Then I was running, as fast as I ever had, putting as much distance as I could between myself and what I had just seen. When I couldn't run any further, I stopped and crouched, my hands on my knees, looking back the way I had come.

Cloud moved like bombers in formation over the city. I tried to stay focused, fighting the desire to shout into the darkness. When it came to it, Colin's cussed stubbornness prevailed. His attacker had tested it to the limit, one finger at a time.

44

A short while before I had made a breakthrough, now I'd lost my grip and slid down into a space I didn't recognise at all. The air was damp. The temperature had dropped. A fine mist blurred the edges of the buildings.

I walked for about twenty minutes, changing direction, turning back on myself, failing to convince myself that I wasn't being followed, but regaining enough composure to get me through the rest of the night.

I reached the tube, went down the escalators and stood on the platform. The station was being refurbished. Temporary lights strung along the pipes and girders gave off a dim glow. I was alone on the platform. The indicator showed the next train in four minutes.

A man in a leather jacket appeared at the other end the platform. He stood staring at the track. He looked up at me and turned. The train came in and its doors opened. He appeared to be debating whether to get on. His lips were moving.

I got on board, and saw that he had too, in the next carriage. He was standing at an awkward angle, as if trying to peer at me. Just as the doors were about to close, I leapt through them, sprawling alongside a row of seats. As the train pulled away, I could see he was on the platform too, halfway between me and the exit. He started in my direction.

I watched him come towards me. He had something in his right hand that I couldn't make out. With his left he started gesturing for me to come towards him. His mouth was working but any sound was drowned by the train arriving on the neighbouring platform.

It was Gareth from Metro. He was drunk. He peered at my chin.

'Wassapenteryerbeard?'

'I shaved it off.'

He thought about this. Then he shook his head.

'D'yer hear 'about the ray?'

'The ray?'

'The ray duh. Raid …' He repeated the 'duh' to be sure I'd heard it. 'Blokes looking for summat.' He put his hand over his mouth, as if stifling a belch.

'What did they take?'

He shrugged.

'We're laid off.' His expression changed, as if he'd found something to focus on. 'Cos of you! Nickin' stuff.'

I stepped back and he filled the space I'd just vacated.

'Your fuckin' fault.'

He took a swipe at me with the bottle in his hand. I ducked and the swing upset his balance. Another train arrived. He suddenly looked blank, as if he'd forgotten what he was doing.

'Comin' for a drink?'

'Thanks, but not tonight.'

'Aw, c'mon.'

He seemed uncertain where to go. I stepped on to the train. The doors closed and I watched him slide out of view as it gathered speed.

I got out at Victoria and climbed to the main station concourse. I saw a row of public phones. I went over to one, picked up a receiver and dialled.

'ID?'

'Where's Tanager?'

There was silence.

'Tell him it's Nick Roker.'

There was more silence, then a series of clicks.

'This is Tanager.'

There were sounds of a party in the background. A woman was laughing loudly. This was a mistake. I was still full of incoherent rage.

'You going to kill me as well?'

'I'm sorry about your friend.' He didn't sound it.

'Why?'

'Why what? Why am I sorry?'

'Why was he killed?'

'Where are you?'

I lit a cigarette to try to calm the rage.

'What happened to Edgington?'

'Died in his sleep, I read.'

'You expect me to believe that? And why Carrie?'

'I don't expect anything, Nick. Where are you?'

If I stayed on much longer they would trace the payphone.

'How are you getting on with your gaps? Filled any in?'

I didn't answer. His matter-of-fact tone was shocking. I felt a fresh stab of anger.

'What's happened to Anita?'

'Who?'

I immediately regretted mentioning her name.

'I've no idea who you're talking about.'

There was another silence. I couldn't tell if he was lying or not. My anger was turning into hysteria.

'You're fucking with me.'

'Oh, I think we're fucking with each other, Nick.'

I slammed the phone back on to its cradle and walked out of the station.

45

I was back at the Northolt Families building at eight in the morning. This time I walked straight up to the door and rang the bell. A dog barked. I clutched the bag to my chest and stepped back to look for any movement in the windows. All the curtains were pulled to. A fine rain was falling. I looked up and down the square. Pedestrians with cases and umbrellas were setting off for another day at work.

I'd walked several miles, ridden a night bus, stopped at an all-night burger bar where I'd fallen asleep and been told to move on. Then, at three, I bribed a hotel receptionist to let me have a room for what was left of the night so I could rest and clean myself up.

I tried to get my thoughts back under control. Carrie, Edge, now Colin. I hadn't led Greer to her death, but three others had been killed in the process. If I had done what Colin told me to do and laid low, would they still be alive? The call to Tanager had achieved nothing except give me somewhere to aim my grief and rage.

Would Anita be next? I rang Sivalingham's number again. Again there was no answer.

I've no idea who you're talking about. Tanager hadn't mentioned her when he retraced my movements in Sri Lanka over lunch. I hadn't included her on the Post-It notes when I was reconstructing my memory. Perhaps I could allow myself the hope that she at least was safe.

The temperature had dropped in the night. I'd left the hotel early and ridden an almost empty tube to Angel. From there I'd walked the rest of the way to the square, zigzagging through side streets. At one corner a car slewed to a halt right in front of me and a man got out – them slammed the door hard and shouted a stream of abuse at a woman inside who drove off with a screech. The man glared at me then laughed, embarrassed.

I rang the bell again. Curtains were tightly drawn behind the poster in the window, the faces of the children superimposed on the tailplane of the destroyed plane. There were five pints of milk on the doorstep.

The entry phone crackled. 'Who is this?' A woman's voice.

'I've got something for you.'

'Package? Post it through the letter box.' I glanced again at the big poster in the front window. A phone started to ring inside.

'It's more than a package.' A gust of wind picked up a swirl of litter and dropped it back on the pavement. I bent towards the speaker. 'Something that will help you. Something crucial for the inquiry.'

There were more voices inside. I heard locks being turned and the door opened a fraction. I glimpsed a woman in a dressing gown behind what looked like a nightclub bouncer. Esther Carr; I recognised her from the hearing. A dog's nose pressed through the gap, nostrils flexing.

'Sorry to call so early, but I've got something you need to see.'

They both stared at me. The minder held the door firmly, awaiting instructions. Water dripped off my hair and nose.

'Could I come in?'

Another phone rang. At least I wasn't the only one bothering them. Her hand disappeared into a pocket and pulled out a mobile, which she opened with a practised flick of her wrist. The minder held the door half open.

'Marla! You know what the time is here?'

I stepped out of the rain and into the warm.

The phone conversation continued. 'I know, I know. Hear me out. We can't let anything slow us down. No, no, I'm not trying to be stubborn. They won't grant an extension. They're saying any further adjournment's going to cost. No, I don't know, they didn't say. Thousands. Yes, pounds.' She nodded several times and clutched her brow. 'Yes, yes. Yes. I know he's got money.' She turned away from me and lowered her voice. 'But he can't testify. *Verboten.*'

She motioned to the bouncer to let me past. She moved further down the hall, but her voice was too loud to give her any privacy. The dog had lost interest in me and wandered after her, tail slapping the wall. She kneed it out of the way.

'You get back here, and soon. We need you on the stand. OK. OK, don't call so early next time.'

She snapped the phone shut and shook her head. The dressing gown turned out to be a silk kimono, which she hugged to her waist with one hand. Her hair was short and wiry and a large pair of rimless glasses had slipped down her nose. She pushed them back up with her phone hand and frowned at me.

'I phoned yesterday.' I held out the DVD. 'Something I have to show you.'

She looked blank.

'There's footage here of Malik, filmed after he was supposed to have been killed, saying he was set up.' She pursed her lips. 'Please – just have a look.'

The house phone rang. She shook her head. 'Israel's three hours ahead.' She backed into the living room and pressed a button that diverted the call. I followed her. The minder, lacking specific instructions, didn't try to stop me but kept close by.

The room ran from the front of the house to the back. It was lined with books. A baby grand piano stood by the rear window. An antique chaise longue and a bulbous sofa were draped with embroidered throws. Piles of paper surrounded an elderly computer on a large desk. Next to it stood an industrial-sized photocopier. A cat jumped down from a table and brushed itself against my legs.

She sighed. 'OK.' She raised a finger. 'We get a lot of nuts with conspiracy theories wasting our time. We've had it up to here.' The bangles on her wrist jangled as she raised her hand to her neck. 'So, I don't mean to be unpleasant, but we've got a lot of work to do just to keep this inquiry alive.'

'You're part of the legal team ...'

She laughed. 'Honey, I *am* the legal team.'

Her phone rang again. She flipped it open. 'Eda! Are you rested?' She listened, nodding, an arm extended as if she was about to perform an aria. 'OK. Just let me speak. We've tried their patience with the adjournment. We don't hold any cards.' She listened, nodding and rubbing her forehead with her thumb. 'So when will they let you fly?' There was a look of mounting frustration on her face. 'Honey, I've got someone waiting. Go and rest. Get in shape. We need you, soon as possible.'

She closed the phone and switched it off. Then she sighed heavily. The room was warm. I took off my jacket. She frowned, as if I hadn't had her permission.

'OK, so who are you?'

The urge to let everything spill out was almost overwhelming, to discharge all the pent-up grief and tension of the last few days. There was a loud crack and I jumped. A flaming log shifted in the nearby grate.

I gave her a sketchy account of my work for Metro and discovery of the copy of *Face of a Terrorist*. I told her I had other footage taken in Sri Lanka in 1995 that suggested Malik hadn't died after Northolt, that he was still alive several years later.

'Suggest? How?'

'It's an interview.'

'So?'

'The interviewee appears to be Malik.'

She raised her eyebrows. 'Impossible to verify. There are no known pictures of Malik in circulation. Believe me, we've looked.'

I took out the flash-frame image Colin had enhanced, and my shots of Rammal. I laid them on a small round table. I felt like a door-to-door salesman, willing a sale.

She glanced at the shots from her position in front of the

fire. The cat wandered over and brushed against her legs. The floorboards creaked above.

'Let me get this straight.' She folded her arms. 'You've got a film with one shot of Malik in it and some other footage that may look like him taken after he was supposed to have been killed.'

'In 1995.'

She looked at me over her glasses. She had already made up her mind that I was just another of the nuts.

'The man who made *Face of a Terrorist*. He's seen these stills. He agreed it was Malik.'

'I heard he died.'

I looked down. 'He said he always believed Malik was framed for Northolt.'

She was silent for a few seconds, measuring me.

'OK, Nick.' She coughed into her fist. 'Look, we really appreciate your interest. I'm sure you mean well—'

The phone on the desk rang. She raised a hand and moved towards it. She faced the window as she listened. It was almost filled with the poster. The paper was thin. The light shone through it. I could make out the shape of the tailplane and the EMA logo. My eye kept coming back to it, as if it was trying to get my attention. She pressed a button on the answering machine and turned back to me.

'We're grateful for your interest.' She folded her arms and took a deep breath. 'But right now we're getting nowhere very fast. The British Government's managed to put this inquiry off for years and years. Now it's happening, they're giving us nothing. Not a sliver. We asked the questions: what happened to the bodies of the gunmen on the plane? No one seems to know. Did the plane make a forced landing or was it directed to land at Northolt? No one knows. Where is the black box? Destroyed. But they're indestructible. Not this one. Who gave the order to refuel the plane? The person concerned is dead. Where is the hard evidence linking Malik to the hijack? In phone taps between him and intermediaries. Ah. Where are the phone taps? They're classified. Can we listen to them? No.

So we get a court order to hear them. Uh-oh. They've been lost.'

She clutched her brow.

'They've not given one inch' – she pinched a thumb and forefinger together – 'either because they couldn't give a shit or because they're shit scared we know something they don't want us to. And they're making the mothers look pathetic – like sad angry people in search of someone to blame. The papers are bored with us. One even said the mothers should move on.' She breathed out through pursed lips. 'We've got a week. Five working days. Then they pull the plug on us. That's it. Game over.'

She came forward and cupped my elbow. She was steering me towards the door.

'As things stand, a lot of unhappy people are going to go to their graves without any closure. If we don't get our act together Emma's going to end up just a footnote in the sordid history of terrorism.'

I frowned. 'Emma?'

'It's what they call it in Israel.'

I moved away from her cupped hand. The bouncer came forward, ready to deal with me.

They set me up with Emma, and then they killed me. Rammal's words. I glanced at the light streaming through the poster taped to the window. *E.M.A....*

Beside the fireplace was a small all-in-one TV and player. I handed her the disc.

'Please. Ten minutes. You'll thank me, I promise.'

46

Esther took the remote from me. She pressed Play and watched it through for the fourth time. When her mobile rang she ignored it. I could hear the bouncer pacing in the hall outside.

'Carl, make us some tea, would you, honey?'

She played it through again, freezing it every few frames. She stopped on the moment Malik lit his cigar.

'And you did this?' She looked at me and back at the screen. 'In 1995, right?'

I took out Greer's lighter and passed it to her. She turned it over in her hand.

'Jesus.' Her voice was barely a whisper. She shook her head slowly. 'How can you be sure it's him?'

I pushed Colin's enhanced print of the flash frame in front of her.

'That shot is a blow-up from this film.' I tapped the *Face of a Terrorist* can.

'And you can verify it's original?'

I nodded. A wave of elation washed through me – something I hadn't experienced since my days in television. I was making a difference, having an impact. I said a prayer of thanks to Anita.

'Who else knows about this?'

I shook my head.

'Are you OK?'

My eyes had filled with tears. I wiped them away with my finger tips.

Carl appeared with a tea tray. She snapped the TV off. She waited for him to leave, motioning him to close the door behind him. She grilled me about Sri Lanka and *Human Face* and how I had met Rammal. I told her about my trip to Jaffna, the meeting and the interview on the boat. She nodded to herself as she processed the information.

'You're in pretty deep, aren't you? Have you been contacted by anyone?'

I looked at her. I felt a spasm of doubt. What was I doing? How could I know to trust her? How could I stay in control of whatever I gave her or told her? This was Colin talking. I couldn't do this alone. What I'd discovered could make all the difference to them. Her eyes moved over my face.

'You know there are some people who really wouldn't want you to have these – and certainly wouldn't want you bringing them to us.'

I looked at her. Carrie's face; Edge in his chair by his dying wife; Anita in her surgery. Colin, crammed into his last desperate place of refuge. She put her hand on mine.

'You have something here.' She shook her head in disbelief. 'This could change everything for us.'

It was strange to be under such scrutiny. Over the years at Metro I had got used to people not taking much interest in me. It had been better that way. My life had been dedicated to not drawing attention to myself. I used to live in dread of someone recognising me from my former life. *Hey, aren't you the guy who was with Greer Harmon?*

I'd gone so far to erase that part of my life. But only so far, I now realised. The hidden copy of *Face of a Terrorist*, the Air Lanka bag with Greer's lighter and the photos of Anita; I hadn't lost them or destroyed them. I'd put them in safe places, as if in some remote part of my consciousness I'd known that one day I would be drawn back to them. All it had taken was one frame, one faint image, and the past had come crashing back into my life.

Anita had kept the tapes. Why? Was it the same for her? She'd left her past in Sri Lanka behind. She'd got away as I'd told her to, but she too was living with the consequences, keeping the secret about Greer and Malik, keeping up her visits to Sarah.

Esther's eyes narrowed.

'Is there anything else?'

I nodded. She waited, the same technique as Greer, creating a vacuum that would suck the answer out of me. All the saliva had gone from my mouth.

'OK, maybe I'm rushing you.' She smiled. 'You want to help us?'

I looked at her. 'Perhaps we can help each other.'

She digested this. 'I need to make a call. Are you due somewhere?'

I laughed for the first time in a long while, and shook my head.

She left the room for a few minutes. When she returned she was dressed in jeans and a leather jacket. She had a large bunch of keys in her hand and a lead. The dog leaped up and started pacing excitedly in front of her.

'Someone wants to meet you.'

She saw the suspicion in my face.

'It's OK. He's part of our team. He's come to help us, behind the scenes.' She looked down at my boots. 'You like to walk?'

I got to my feet and put on my jacket.

'Take the tube back to King's Cross, then switch onto the northbound line and come back to Arsenal. I'll pick you up from there. If you think anyone's following, stay on the train and switch again. And if it all goes pear-shaped, you've got my mobile.'

I ejected the disc and put it back in my bag, along with the film and the stills.

'You can leave them here.'

I didn't feel ready to do that.

47

The tube was nearly full. I felt everyone's eyes on me. When I got out at Arsenal I waited for the platform to empty before I left.

On the other side of the street was an ageing MG sports car. I crammed myself in beside the dog, which was panting with expectation. The windows had misted up, which gave an impression of security.

All Esther had told me was the name of the man we were about to meet.

'Jared. Is that first or last?'

She smiled. 'It's just the name he likes to be called.'

'What's his role?'

'If you don't mind, I'll leave him to explain that.'

We drove east, through Dalston and Leytonstone. At the edge of Epping Forest she pulled over.

'OK. Walkies.'

She took my arm and we crossed into a flat, frosted scrubland. The dog bounded ahead, into the monochrome landscape.

A sharp breeze flicked at the collar of my jacket and I thrust my hands deep into my pockets in search of warmth. There were few people about. We came to a lake and the dog splashed in, upending thin shards of ice that had formed around the edge.

A couple of men stood together, smoking. Another sat on a bench, studying a magazine. It wasn't the weather for relaxing. A woman in running gear came towards us, breath billowing from her every few paces. She nodded at Esther.

'To your left,' she said as she passed.

Esther changed direction and we walked towards a figure

jogging by the lake. She quickened her pace and we closed in on where the paths intersected. He didn't turn round. He was smaller than me. His wiry frame, encased in close-fitting clothes, looked like it belonged to someone younger, but his thinning hair, flecked with grey, suggested he could have been well over fifty. He appeared lost in thought. His pronounced brow shaded his eyes, which were trained on the ground.

'Good to meet you, Nick.' He thrust out his hand and raised his eyes briefly. They were dark and full of concentration. 'Hope you got your thermals on.'

He blew into his hands, which he had balled into fists. The men and the woman jogger we had passed earlier were keeping parallel with us. We walked three abreast, one of them on either side of me. He strode slightly ahead. Although he wasn't tall, he looked powerful and well maintained.

'Esther's briefed me.' He glanced back at me. 'Where are the masters?'

I hesitated. 'Safe.'

'There's no such thing as safe. Who knows where they are?'

I wasn't in any mood for an interrogation. I looked at Esther. She touched Jared's arm.

'OK, OK.' He raised a hand in apology. 'So, have you figured what's going on?'

'What do you mean?'

'Why we're here.' He gestured at the minders. 'With all this?' His expression softened. He looked at me properly for the first time. The skin round his eyes was etched with lines. 'Anyone follow you?'

'Maybe. How would I know?'

'Good question. So no one's tried to contact you or question you about what you've been doing, where you've been?'

I shook my head and looked towards Esther.

Jared laid a hand on my shoulder. 'OK. You want to know what you're getting into. How about I tell you what I know, and then you can tell me what you know?'

He cleared his throat. 'Here's how it is. On the twenty-seventh of June, 1989, three men boarded the EMA flight 157 from Tel Aviv to Oslo. Their mission, so we've been told, was to take passengers hostage until some of their comrades were released from jail. But they didn't get their act together until the plane was too far north to turn around and get to a friendly country.

'The pilot, a Brit, put down at Northolt, where the plane was surrounded by the military. The hijackers wanted to refuel. They started killing people. After three were shot and dropped on the tarmac the tankers arrived and filled the plane. But the pilot refused to put it back in the air so they shot him, right there in his seat. Then they put a gun to the co-pilot's head and told him to prepare for take-off.

'The control tower heard the commotion in the cockpit and someone took the decision to stop the plane by shooting out the tyres. Trouble was, they got there a bit late. So they decided to be a hero with a jeep. The rest is history.'

He took a deep breath.

'On the face of it, just another terrorist atrocity, orchestrated remotely, we were told, by a guy who called himself Malik. End of story.' He glanced at me. 'You believe that?'

I shook my head.

He smiled. 'Me neither.'

He took out a packet of cigarettes and offered me one. 'Let me guess where you're at, and stop me if I get it wrong. Right now you're pretty confused. You've got pictures taken in 1995 of a guy who's supposed to have died in 'eighty-nine. And you've figured out he's talking about Northolt. Her Majesty's Government, after years of stonewalling, are holding an inquiry. But they're sticking to their story that Malik was taken out in an ambush in Germany. Your tape's got your man talking about being set up with EMA and "killed". You poked into this a little and all kinds of shit started. Right?'

I'd said nothing to Esther about the last few days.

'OK, let me rewind a little.' He motioned for us to walk with him. 'After the Munich Olympics massacre in 'seventy-four it's a crazy time. Everyone's in shock. No one knows how to deal with terrorists. Security services are in disarray, all going their own ways. Covert operations, infiltrations, assassinations, no coordination between the Allies; it's a mess.

'Then there's Zarev, later to be one of the Northolt casualties. He's been retired out of Mossad, where his methods were a bit rich even for them. He decides to take matters into his own hands and starts busting not only terror cells but the bigger people financing them. Pretty soon he's man of the year in Israel. But all this is causing some people a big headache. His one-man crusade is playing hell with intricate networks of double agents and informers that Western Intelligence has been recruiting inside these groups. Someone decides those networks are more important.'

He paused to let the information sink in. All the muscles in his face tensed, his eyes focused somewhere in the distance. Esther watched him steadily.

'Meanwhile, a guy calling himself Malik has been making a name for himself. The US sees him as a threat, a Che Guevara of the Middle East, a poster boy to lend respectability to the armed struggle against Israeli oppression. He has to be discredited.

'Now comes the tricky part – the reason why we're here today and those poor ladies have had to wait all these years for this hearing.'

He swung round and looked at me hard in the face.

'Someone came up with a plan that's very beautiful. It deals with the twin problems of Malik and Zarev at a stroke. Malik's on Zarev's list. Get *Malik* to take out Zarev! Very clever, very controversial – and entirely plausible. Few people as possible can know. And it has to be done right.'

He shook his head.

'But it isn't. Just about everything that could go wrong does. What's supposed to be a surgical assassination turns into a blood bath. The gunmen are amateurs. Peasants. Goatherds from the Bekaa valley who've never even been on a plane before, let alone killed anyone. Britain ends up playing host to a major terrorist atrocity. And Malik isn't even there. He's stayed home. Sure, the Brits claim they caught up with him and killed him. But you and I, Nick, we know that isn't true.'

'Wasn't it mad to try and kill Zarev on a plane?'

'Zarev was hard to get at. Never slept in the same bed twice, or with the same woman.' He laughed and shook his head. 'Only way to get a fix on a guy like that is to catch him in transit. Besides, a surgical assassination would have aroused suspicion. They wanted it to look like an everyday, common-or-garden hijacking, with Zarev playing a bit part as a casualty.'

'Are you saying Malik *was* commissioned to do it, or that it was just pinned on him?'

'You're good. You've been thinking about this.' He shrugged. '"*They set me up with EMA.*" Could mean either.' His eyes flashed at me. 'Too bad we can't ask him.' He pressed his lips together and lines appeared on his cheeks. 'You've worked it out. That's why you're here, isn't it? You've figured out what all the fuss is really about. If he's dead, why would any of this matter? Case closed, mystery unsolved. But if he's alive ...'

He stood in front of me, gazing over my shoulder into the distance.

'I don't think I need to tell you there are people out there who badly want Malik to stay as dead as everyone else thinks he is. The same goes for his friends and acquaintances. And they'll do whatever it takes to ensure that.' He nodded towards the two men who had kept abreast of us. 'That's why we've got these guys watching out for us. People like you and me, Nick, going round with these ideas. We shouldn't be alive either.'

We had come to a fallen tree. I sat down. It had been days since I'd had a real night's sleep or a sensible meal, but my mind was on high alert. Esther sat beside me. The dog came and nosed at us.

'You've been busy.' Jared smirked.

I stared at him.

'We had you checked out. While you were on the way over here just now.'

I stiffened. Esther laid a hand on my arm. 'It's OK.'

He stepped closer. 'The stuff on the police intelligence database is sketchy; there are gaps you'll maybe want to fill in for us. Day One has your residence being searched by *S Ops*. That's dataspeak for Security Services. You're questioned about an item missing from your workplace. They appear to lose you after that, except for one phone contact at a South London address. They pick you up again in Sussex, two addresses, no action taken. The next posting is a *Person Unknown* murder suspect in hospital custody. Looks like local police failed to ID you at first. And by the time they'd contacted S Ops you'd busted out of there. Nice work.' He smiled. 'The next day is blank. You must have gone off their radar. But by now there's a *No Contact* directive. Even though you're down as a murder suspect, someone high up wants you left alone. Then two days ago you're sighted back at the South London address and there's a reference to a Jaguar car. And you make one trip out of London to a residential care home in Surrey.'

He looked at me, waiting for an explanation.

Nothing about my visit to Anita. Perhaps Tanager meant what he said. I met his gaze. 'How come it's so patchy?'

'It takes a team of forty to effectively cover one individual twenty-four seven. That's a lot of people to tie up. Maybe they don't have the resources. So they look out for hard points – CCTV sightings, known addresses, mobile phone contact, cash machines. Maybe you made it difficult for them.' He laughed to himself. 'They've underestimated you. With what you've got, you should be the most wanted man in England right now.'

I studied the ground for a while. Muddy footprints from warmer days had been frozen and crusted with white. Fallen leaves that should have rotted away had been preserved in ice.

'Why the killings?'

He rubbed his face with his hands. 'People who know stuff they won't let go of. People who know too much pose some kind of risk.' He shrugged. 'They want to erase, wipe the slate clean. No traces.'

'So why not me?'

He took his time to answer.

'Maybe you were lucky. Or maybe you've got a key – something to take us where we all want to go?'

'Where's that?'

He smiled. 'To Malik.'

He kicked at a splintered branch until it broke into pieces.

'You want to help us?' He fixed me with a cold stare.

I knew nothing about him, only his name, if it was his name.

'What's your stake in this?'

He absorbed my question. Esther turned and looked at him, waiting for the reply. Apart from the panting dog, and the occasional call of a crow, it was silent. He looked off into the distance.

'Zarcv was my father.'

48

The three of us sat on the fallen tree. Jared pulled off a glove and rubbed his face.

'He wasn't what you'd call a regular father. I barely knew him. I was a love child, I guess. One of several, most likely. He was married to his mission. He'd come out of Mossad, disillusioned but determined. He thought he could be more effective on his own.' He took a long drag of his cigarette and snorted. 'He was *too* effective.'

He gazed into the distance, his features drained of expression.

'I was in the forces when he was killed. I blanked it. I hadn't seen him for maybe four, five years. I'd hardly known the guy. Didn't think I needed to concern myself. I thought I could live without knowing what happened, just get on with my own life.' He turned and looked at me, as if he was reading the same thought in my own mind. 'But that didn't work. I'd gone into the same kind of business. Finally, I decided to take a look myself.' He shook his head. 'Nothing made sense. Nothing added up. We'd been had.'

I felt emboldened by his directness.

'Was he shot or did he die in the fire?'

'According to a survivor, as soon as Zarev knew what was happening on the plane, he identified himself. He was fluent in Arabic. He pleaded with them to spare the other passengers. That was all he cared about. He knew it was him they wanted. And he knew they'd screwed up. He offered to negotiate on their behalf, to help get them back to a friendly country. And he might have succeeded, until they shot the pilot.'

I heard a phone buzz. He reached into his jacket and listened, looking over at the two men, then snapped it shut.

'They're saying we need to move. We've been too long in the same spot. At least the bus'll be warm.'

He held his arm out to shepherd me along. Esther looked at her watch. 'I have to get back.' She started in the direction of her car then stopped when she saw me hesitate. 'You'll be a lot safer with him. You don't want to be out on the streets with all that in your head.' She patted my bag. 'Or with that.'

Jared took my arm.

'We need to talk some more.'

His grip tightened. We crossed the road that bordered the forest. A dark blue people carrier with tinted windows was parked there, its engine running. As we approached, the side door slid back. The minders had caught us up and we all got in. The air inside was warm and smoky.

Jared didn't speak during the journey. When I started to ask him a question he put up his hand and nodded at the others. He wasn't taking any chances.

We drove back towards London then veered off into an anonymous street of semi-detached, pebble-dash houses. At the far end was a small block of flats. A set of garage doors opened and swallowed the vehicle.

The flat was sparsely furnished for letting. There was nothing personal about it. In the kitchen a half-open dishwasher revealed a large number of mugs. A swing bin bulged with pizza cartons. Jared looked at his watch.

'Be back at four.'

The jogger and two of the men filed out. The remaining man started clearing up the kitchen.

'This way.'

Jared led me to a bedroom that had been turned into a makeshift office. There was a laptop and a TV and a large pile of newspapers. Opposite the window was a sofa-bed and an armchair. There was nothing on the walls.

'If you need to shower or nap go ahead. Or we can continue.'

I looked out at the garden, a square of lawn bordered by

a wooden fence. Beyond was a wide expanse of playing fields, pale with frost, and a plain grey sky. It felt as if I had travelled to the edge of somewhere, from which there was no way back.

I thought of my flat, Colin's house, my desk at Metro – the familiar places I couldn't go back to, in a world I no longer inhabited. The impact of the last few days had left me numb. I couldn't conjure up either fear or elation. It was as if I had slipped into neutral. I turned away from the window.

Jared was staring at me.

'So.' He smiled briefly. His aura of purpose and the organised way his team operated gave me some sense of security. I wondered what would happen if I tried to leave. 'You want anything? Coffee, tea?'

He seemed momentarily awkward, as if entertaining didn't come naturally. Perhaps he was used to having everything done for him while he focused on more pressing matters.

'You're CIA, right?'

He nodded. 'Was.'

'Don't you work together – you and the British?'

He chuckled. 'Not always.'

'Does Esther know?'

'I'm kind of on sabbatical. I need to get this out of my system, once and for all.' He took a breath and rubbed his hands together. 'OK, let's see it.'

I played him the DVD. And just as Esther had, he took the remote and reran it several times. He didn't move or comment. Eventually he ejected the disc and held it.

'It's good.' He shook his head. 'People get so hung up on their place in history.'

I reached for it. He hesitated then gave it back.

'I recognised him from the film – *Face of a Terrorist*.'

He frowned. 'But he was shown in silhouette.'

'In the final version that was transmitted, yes.' I took out the screen grab Colin had enhanced. I told him about the print, which had had all the shots cut out. 'This one got missed. And it's not full silhouette.'

A shadow of what looked like anger passed across his face.

'And you spotted it.' He nodded his approval.

'Otherwise I'd never have made the connection between Rammal and Malik.'

He stared at it some more. 'There's not a single image of him in circulation – and you've got this *and* the tape. Why do you think he let you film him?'

I made the same drinking gesture Tanager had used. 'He was unravelling. He'd been given a new identity and a new role. It bothered him that his "Malik" persona would go down in history taking the blame for Northolt. He thought he could tell me his story.'

Jared nodded. 'And round about the time you showed up, he'd decided he'd had enough, decided to disappear completely.' He picked up the disc. 'It's very good. But it's not enough.'

I waited for him to go on.

'They're using the inquiry as one great big fucking smoke-screen. Esther's people are doing their best but they're way out of their depth.' He tapped the print. 'Show this at the hearing and they'll shoot it down in flames. It'll create a bit of heat, a few headlines. They'll challenge the verification, then they'll want to interrogate us about where it's been all this time.' He shook his head doubtfully.

'Why have it at all then?'

'The inquiry? To let off a little steam. Be seen to be doing the right thing, after all these years. And once it's over they can say that's it. Case closed. The ladies will go home to Israel with compensation and whatever else they can console themselves with.' He sighed. 'The powers that be have got it well and truly under their control.'

Colin's phrase; how right he had been.

Jared sat down on the sofa-bed and pressed his hands together.

'What would change everything? Have Malik take the stand.' He closed his eyes. 'Imagine their faces. The notorious terrorist rises from the dead and breaks cover after all these years to tell the world. Have him point the finger. Hear him answer the question: "Who *really* killed Zarev?"'

He got up and went over to the window. He stared out at the dull sky, waiting for me to fill the silence.

'The clock's ticking, Nick. We don't have a whole lot of time.'

Harrop's description of Braintree came back to me. I saw Tanager in his Portakabin, the blow-ups of Greer and Malik on the wall. His team at their terminals.

'They'll be onto him. They'll want him dead – for real this time.' He rubbed his face with his hands. 'Talk to me, Nick. Help me find this guy before they do.' I followed him to the window and stood beside him. He put his hand on my shoulder. 'I've lived with this even longer than you have, Nick. We both need answers. We don't have a choice.'

I saw the postcards again. The last from Sri Lanka, three weeks ago. Anita's name, remembered by the woman in the care home. I was ahead of Tanager, perhaps. Ahead of Jared. I had the key.

He was silent, waiting for a response.

Outside, it was almost dark. Some cracks had opened in the clouds, letting through slivers of blue. I glimpsed a 747 as it climbed into the sky, a shaft of sunlight bouncing off its tailplane as it escaped the grey afternoon. The new passport was still in my bag. I took it out. He examined it.

'I know where to look.'

He stared at me.

'You get me there. I'll find him for us both.'

49

I sat alone in the back of the people carrier. The driver didn't speak. He might have been the twin of Esther's bouncer. I saw his eyes flick up to the rear-view mirror every few seconds. It was dark and raining. He drove fast then slow. Outside King's Cross he made a sudden U-turn and then a few miles on he stopped suddenly and waited for traffic to pass.

'Just a precaution.'

Jared wanted the interview tape masters as well as the stills and the DVD copy. He'd repeated his mantra: *There's no such thing as safe.*

ALC was the lab where Colin had taken the tapes. It was in an industrial estate in Kilburn. We pulled up across the road, watched and waited.

A fire engine trundled past. A white van pulled into a parking space. The driver got out and started yelling into his mobile.

'OK.'

There was no one behind the counter. I pressed a buzzer and a perturbed-looking woman waddled up. I asked for Colin's friend, Eric, and she turned away without comment. A few minutes later he appeared from another door and peered at me over half-moon glasses. Then, without any greeting, he waved me in.

The room was hot. Several grey boxes with keyboards and dials hummed and whirred. He opened a safe, took out a small stack of tapes and laid them in two separate piles on the counter. One set had my labels on, the others were blank. He tapped the unlabelled tapes.

'The ones we made to see if we could deal with the damage.' He shook his head before I had a chance to ask. 'Couldn't get anything more out of them. Fucked. Well and truly.'

I gathered them all up and started to put them in a bag, then changed my mind. I pushed the originals back towards him. 'Keep these for me, will you? Keep them safe. I'll pay.'

He shrugged. 'You're the customer.'

50

I lay on a bed in Jared's flat, watching the curtains sway in the draught around the window.

I swung between bursts of deep sleep and semi-wakefulness. Fragments of dream, so intense I couldn't distinguish them from what was real, splintered inside my head. The sight of Colin haunted me. I saw Tanager talking on his mobile, Edge sitting with his wife.

I saw myself alone in a hotel room at the Majestic, looking out at the sea. I thought it was Greer's but it wasn't. It was mine. I was alone, waiting for someone. My heart racing. There was a knock on the door. It wasn't who I'd been expecting. A concierge stood there with a note on a silver platter. I ripped it open.

Please don't take this the wrong way ... This is too soon for me. Please understand ...

I couldn't decipher the rest, but I knew who it was from.

Then I was falling through water. Red and silver explosions pounded the surface. I needed to breathe, but I knew there was only flame and choking smoke up there. I tried to swim away from it. I came to a wall and scrabbled at it with my fingers until all the nails were broken. I sat up in bed, gasping for breath.

I threw back the curtains and stared at the night sky. In a desperate bid to weave meaning from my tattered threads of memory, I'd allowed Greer to eradicate Anita.

I lay back down and drifted off again.

Please don't take this the wrong way ... Sleep sucked me down, but my mind was still racing. There was too much going on in my head to distinguish what was real from what was imagined. I was back on the train leaving Colombo station. Anita was at the window, trying to apologise. I wanted to change my mind, get out of the train. But a hand pressed my shoulder.

A voice came from somewhere above me.

'It's time.'

Jared flicked on the bedside light. He was in the same clothes as yesterday and looked as if he had slept as little as I had. He swept the covers off the bed. The clock on the side said four thirty.

'It's all arranged. There's a car waiting.' His expression was earnest. 'You have to leave. Now. Get dressed.'

I started to speak but he put a finger to his lips and disappeared. I heard the front door open and close. Outside, a car engine was idling.

I showered and dressed. Jared was by the stairs leading down to the garage. I stared at him. 'What's going on?'

'It's what you want. And you can't stay here. Your train's in half an hour.' He handed me a Eurostar ticket and a small laminated card. On it was a copy of my passport photo. There was no name beside it; just a series of letters and numbers. On the back was a magnetic strip. 'Show that first and they won't bother to check your passport.'

'What is it?'

'A tool of the trade. In Paris you'll be met by a woman. Her name is Cheryl. She'll give you everything you need for the next leg.' He grinned. 'Colombo. You're going back. Today.'

'This woman, how will she recognise me?'

'She will.'

He gave me a mobile phone. Taped to it was a charger with an international adapter.

'Keep it charged. And keep it on, so we can always talk.'

The cold forced me to focus.

'Go now. Don't miss the train.'

He pushed me towards the car. The garage door was sliding open.

'I'll call you when you get there.'

As soon as I was in the back seat the driver sped off.

The roads were empty. The driver said nothing and showed little interest in red lights. He deposited me at the Eurostar entrance of Waterloo station.

I fed my ticket into the machine at the gate and my pulse raced as I pushed my passport and the card Jared had given me under the glass partition. A woman smiled thinly as she glanced at the picture and handed them back. I rode the escalator up to the platform where the train stretched into the distance.

I watched Herne Hill station slide past. Bright white lights; empty platforms. Just a week ago I had been standing there, waiting to go into work. I ate some breakfast then fell into a deep sleep that lasted all the way to the Gare du Nord.

My head was throbbing when I woke. As I neared the exit, a pretty young woman swathed in a big scarf waved eagerly, as if she'd been missing me all winter.

'God, it's cold!' She kissed me and cuddled up against my arm as she led me out of the station to a waiting Range Rover. As soon as we were inside, her behaviour became more formal. 'No one notices couples.' The driver gunned the engine and we surged out into the traffic. 'OK, what've we got here?' She sounded American. She rummaged in her bag and took out an envelope. Under her Puffa jacket she wore a turtle-neck and jeans. She gestured at a bag in the load space behind the back seats. 'In back is pretty much all you'll need for the first couple of days.' She looked me up and down. 'It's a bit warmer out there. Do you have cash on you?'

'Very little.'

'OK, take this. They're big denominations so don't flash them around. Change some at the hotel. If you get in any trouble, use it to buy your way out. You're booked into the Oceania. The reservation is in the name of Swallow Travel. 'You all right?'

'Fine. Why?'

'You look kind of shaky. Try to look normal while you go through. Passport?'

I handed it to her.

'You look better without the beard.' She nodded her approval. 'I'll keep the card. You don't need it here on. Just keep cool and steady. Once you're on the plane, you're as good as there.'

'You work for Jared?'

'Sometimes.'

'Are there any instructions?'

'All I have is to put you on the plane. He said you'd know what to do. D'you have his number?'

'In the phone he gave me.'

'OK, so he'll be on your case the minute you land. Keep it charged. If something comes up you don't understand just call him. Any trouble, call him, day or night. Here are your tickets. The flight leaves in two hours.'

I examined the tickets. Air Lanka, to Colombo. So this was real.

'Why via Paris?'

'Waterloo isn't Heathrow. And at Charles De Gaulle they don't give a shit who's leaving. It's just bon voyage.'

A flaming-orange sun had broken over the city, filling the interior of the Range Rover with light. I watched the traffic moving fast along the Périphérique. All the cars seemed to be blurred at the edges. I blinked several times but it didn't help.

'You sure you're OK?'

Cheryl was frowning at me. I swallowed and my throat felt like sandpaper. 'Just a bit tired.'

The driver dropped us at Departures. Cheryl pulled the hold-all out of the rear compartment and the driver sped away.

'This is all happening so fast.'

She shrugged. 'I just do what I'm told.'

She led me towards check-in. There was no queue. I put the bag in the space by the desk. The attendant examined my passport and ticket.

'Did you pack this yourself?'

Cheryl nudged me in the back.

'Yes.'

'Anyone ask you to carry anything?'

'No.'

The bag disappeared behind a rubber curtain.

Just as I was about to go through Immigration, her phone rang. She opened it and listened, turning away from me.

'Got it. I'll check and get back to you.' She snapped it shut. 'Do you have any other cell on you?'

'I'm sorry?'

'Phone. You have another phone on you?'

'Why?'

'If you have more than one, someone could find that suspicious.'

'Who was that?'

'Jared. He doesn't want anything attracting attention. He's very fussy about detail.'

I felt in my bag. There were two: mine and Shirley's. I took out Shirley's and handed it over.

She smiled for the first time. 'Sorry to be a pain.'

We moved towards Departures. Again she snuggled up to me.

'OK, this is where we do a nice goodbye for the security cameras. Try not to look shocked.' She pulled me towards her and kissed me firmly on the mouth. When she pulled away her eyes were full of tears. She watched me go through, her face wearing a mask of bereavement. I blew her a kiss and she smiled back. As I queued for the X-ray machine I glanced over my shoulder. She was gone.

My throat was aching and I felt hot. I bought some aspirin and ordered tea at a bar and sat down at a window overlooking the apron. An Air France 747 was being pushed back from its stand. It was a long time since I'd been on an aircraft.

The tea made no impact on my throat. My legs had started to ache. The early-morning sun disappeared behind a thick ceiling of cloud. I watched a plane climb into the sky and curve away to the south. Elation and foreboding blurred together.

*

During my convalescence a therapist had recommended a return to Sri Lanka.

'You'll go back all the time in your mind, whether you want to or not. You won't be in control. Deciding to go back is taking control. You choose it – instead of it choosing you. Go to where it happened. It's cathartic. It's why soldiers revisit battlefields.'

I never did. I'd bottled it up instead.

The gate number went up on the board. There was no queue. The flight was only a third full.

The stewardess wore a sari and smiled at me as if I were an old friend. I sat in a window seat. I felt in the bag for Jared's phone. There was a text message: *Good trip. Call on arrival.*

I shut it off. Then I took out my own, the one I hadn't given to Cheryl.

51

The Airbus started to lose height. I lifted the plastic blind and stared into the darkness, broken only by the rhythmic flash of light from the wingtip. I looked at my watch. It was five a.m., Sri Lankan time. I tried not to think about the vast space between the plane and the ground.

Wisps of mist floated out of the air vents as the cabin depressurised. I could taste the moisture in the air. I looked at my clothes. Sweater and jeans. Maybe there was something more appropriate in the bag Cheryl had given me.

When I looked out of the window again the plane had dropped below the cloud. The sea was a dull grey; to the east, a ragged stripe of orange grew along the horizon.

Somewhere below were the people I was looking for. On a map it looked like a small island, a teardrop hanging off the bottom of India. From the window, it was a vast dark continent wrinkled with hills and forgotten valleys. An ideal place to hide and never be found.

Heavy, wet air hugged me as I stepped out onto the gangway. By the time I'd reached the bottom of the stairs I was covered in sweat. The smoky grey clouds above the tattered fringe of palm trees looked fat and ready to burst. Vast lakes of water stood on the airfield apron.

I had spent the last ten years of my life trying to escape from what happened here. Now I was back, pulled by an invisible force I had resisted for too long.

The sun broke through as I followed the straggle of passengers towards the arrivals hall. I half expected Anita to be waiting for me, clipboard in hand. A young soldier monitored our approach, his wrist resting casually on the barrel of a gun that hung from his shoulder. I jumped as another plane screamed past and slammed its wheels down onto the runway. The soldier laughed.

The baggage hall was heaving. A huge crowd had formed under the customs sign. One man carried a satellite dish wrapped in newspaper. A lady in a gold sari stood with a DVD player in a cardboard box balanced on her head.

The bag I had been given slid down a chute and onto the carousel. I took a deep breath to ready myself for Immigration. I was about to re-enter a country I had left on a stretcher.

'Mr Roker, is your visit business or pleasure?'

I hesitated. 'Just visiting old friends.'

'Pleasure, then.' He brought his stamp down on the first page of my passport and pushed it back to me. 'Enjoy your visit.'

Men offering taxis and even a limo surrounded me as soon as I had passed through the exit door. I remembered the lesson I had learned on *Destination* – never hesitate unless you want to be accosted. Look purposeful and keep moving.

The stalls in the men's had no locks but I shut the door and examined the contents of the bag: a lightweight suit, a short-sleeved shirt and a tie. I examined myself in a mirror. My hair was matted and my eyes bloodshot. They didn't go with the smart new suit. I took a deep breath and strode out into the concourse and changed some of Colin's cash. I would leave Jared's money for emergencies. Another driver broke away from the throng and sidled up to me as I waited for the money. I spoke without turning round. 'How much to the General Hospital?'

'Five hundred. I have air-conditioned Toyota. You will be in complete comfort.'

'Two.'

He hesitated, so I started to walk away.

'OK.'

The roads were thick with Japanese cars and minibuses. Billboards for Mobitel and Nokia lined the airport highway. I watched the throng of cyclists and tuk-tuks weaving along the hard shoulder and thought of Anita beside me, reading from the list of appointments she'd made at Greer's instigation and asking if something was wrong because I hadn't responded. I had been watching her but not listening. 'It's fine,' I'd said. 'Absolutely fine.' And her face had radiated relief.

The taxi's horn blasted me back into the present.

'You are doctor?'

'No. Patient.'

The traffic ground to a halt. I switched on Jared's phone and it rang almost immediately.

'What's happening? You OK?'

'Fine. Stuck in traffic.'

'Talk to me soon as you have anything. You don't sound too good.'

'Sore throat, that's all. I'll call you if I get anywhere.'

'No. I'll call you. It's a secure line.'

I paid off the driver. It was only eight thirty but the heat was building. I stood for a moment outside the hospital. I had no memory of the exterior. But as soon as I entered the lobby I knew the smell. It was dark inside. Large fans stirred the heat with little effect. About forty people, mostly women and children, sat on benches, clutching small tickets. There was a hand-painted sign above a grille in the wall: *Outpatients*. I went towards it.

A man in a white shirt waved me away.

'I'm looking for Dr Sivalingham.'

He continued to wave me away and someone pushed past to get to the window. I looked around for an alternative route. A nurse in a crisp fresh uniform came past, pushing a small trolley.

'Can you tell me where I can find Sivalingham?'

She pointed down a corridor. 'See the clerk in the end room.'

The end room had a sign on the door. *No Admittance*. I pushed it open.

A man looked up from a computer and frowned at me.

'Good morning. I'm here from London to see Sivalingham.'

He continued to frown. 'Have you an appointment?'

'It was just on the off chance. He told me to look him up.'

'Sivalingham does nothing on the off chance. His schedule is very full.'

'Is he here?'

'I'm not permitted to divulge his whereabouts. What is your business?'

'I'm a former patient. He told me to get in touch when I was here.'

'I will have to check. Fill this out.' He pushed a form towards me. It was all in Sinhalese.

'I spoke to him last week from England. He said to look him up.' I could hear the exasperation in my voice.

This man was Sivalingham's gatekeeper. He was in his element. He tapped the form. 'Name and patient number. And date of last appointment.'

I scribbled my name and pushed it back towards him. 'Could you just call him and tell him I'm here? I need to see him as soon as possible.'

'I already have noted your message.' He held up a phone. 'He doesn't take it to clinic.'

'Can I call him on a land line?'

He shook his head emphatically. 'No phone at Gardens clinic.'

I sat down on a bench.

'There is no waiting here.'

'Just a few minutes. I'm not well.' It was true. I rubbed my forehead. It was hot. I closed my eyes.

Staff came and went in a steady stream. Energetic exchanges in Sinhalese were punctuated by medical terms in English. I could hear the assistant's rising irritation. I wasn't the only one looking for Sivalingham.

A pretty young medic appeared, a strip of sari draped over her head. The assistant paid her more attention. Sivalingham's name was mentioned. I heard *Clinic* again, then *Gardens*.

The Gardens was a semi shantytown. Anita had taken me there.

'He has a clinic there?'

He didn't answer. It was as good as a confirmation.

The Oceania was a modern, featureless hotel. It could have been anywhere in the world. The lobby was like a giant mausoleum. I signed in and checked my bags. The air conditioning was fierce and froze me to the marrow. My eyes stung and the sweat prickled on my neck and forehead. I needed to lie down.

'Can anyone help me find someone in The Gardens?'

The receptionist's name badge said Pillai. He wore a stiff brown tunic buttoned to the neck and looked momentarily surprised. 'Cinnamon Gardens?'

Cinnamon Gardens was the smartest neighbourhood.

'No. I need to find a clinic in The Gardens. As soon as possible. A doctor called Sivalingham.'

'That's a Tamil name …'

'I know. I just need to find him.'

I put one of Cheryl's notes inside my passport and pushed it towards him.

'There'll be another one of those when I find him.'

He looked off into space for a moment and then at his watch.

'I get off in twenty minutes.'

We climbed into a tuk-tuk and buzzed out into the traffic. Pillai conducted a lengthy conversation with the driver who only too frequently took both hands off the handlebars to express his dismay at our chosen destination.

We wove through the traffic. Lorries blasted their multitone horns. I clung onto the chipped green grab rail behind the driver's seat and watched the road rush past inches from my feet. I had given Pillai a fifty-dollar bill. It was probably a month's pay, but if he got me to Sivalingham it would be worth every penny. The tuk-tuk dived off the main road and bounced down a rutted track.

I looked at my watch. It was already noon. The canopy of the tuk-tuk seemed to capture and hold the heat. I wanted to find Sivalingham and then lie down. Perhaps he could prescribe something for my temperature. I noticed Pillai glancing at me from the corner of his eye. The tuk-tuk suddenly slewed to a halt.

'Twenty-five rupee.'

I gave the driver fifty.

I steadied myself against an electricity pylon. Thick wires led out from it in all directions like a maypole. When I looked down again, Pillai was frowning at me.

'Do you want to continue, sir?'

'Of course.' I took his arm. 'The jet lag ...'

He nodded but didn't look convinced. He pushed away several children who were grabbing at my sleeve then beckoned the tallest and barked at him in a stream of Sinhalese. The boy pointed in several directions. Eventually Pillai wagged his head in agreement and gave him a few coins.

'Are you OK to walk? It's about ten minutes.'

It seemed like a strange question. I examined his face. He looked like he wished he were somewhere else. Then the ground smashed against my cheek and something sharp cut my temple.

'I'm fine,' I heard myself whisper. 'It's just my balance. At least I'm on my way to see a doctor ...'

Several adults had joined the throng of children. Pillai was clearly uncomfortable about the attention. I was used to it. I had stood in public places all over the world with a camera crew, to the fascination of myriad onlookers. Their faces swam in and out of focus. I had to be vigilant. One of them might be Anita. I considered this thought and wondered if it made sense. Sweat was running into my eyes.

Pillai grabbed my arm and I felt myself being hoisted onto my feet and propelled forward again.

I stopped him. 'I need to check ...'

I stepped away from him, towards a beautiful face framed in a green sari. The woman frowned and turned swiftly away. I called after her.

'Please, sir ...'

Pillai's grip on my arm suddenly got a lot firmer. We turned down a very narrow passage between huts made of pallets and corrugated metal. Colin squatted in a doorway, chopping a coconut with a cleaver. He lifted his face from his work and glared at me. I blinked. Colin's face dissolved.

Pillai held me closer to him. My feet seemed barely to touch the ground any more. We ducked under a sign I couldn't read and into a dark room lined with benches, every square inch of them taken up with people, either sitting or lying. Two electric fans stood on either side of the room.

I heard Pillai say Sivalingham's name amid a stream of Sinhalese.

'I go now.' I thought this wasn't a good idea, but Pillai nodded his head emphatically. I looked at the dirt floor. People lay on mats or pieces of banana leaf. I saw a vacant piece of leaf in a corner and made for it. Then I remembered the money. I hailed Pillai and brandished another note at him. All the waiting patients fell silent, as if someone had just fired a shot. Pillai strode back towards me. He bent towards my ear. 'I will look after this for you, I think, sir.'

'Good idea,' I said, not quite understanding what he meant. His hand closed round the wad of notes and gently took them from me. Then he was gone. I wondered whether I'd see them again, but I didn't mind. I had my eye on the banana leaf in the corner. I thought what a welcome place that would be.

I made it on my hands and knees while everyone watched in silence. I lay down and the ground floated pleasantly under me. All I wanted now was a drink. I lifted myself up to see if Anita was there. She'd bring me a drink. I tried to call her. But no one took any notice. I bet she was hiding there somewhere. I lay back down and examined the shapes of the beams holding up the tin roof. There was a flash of light, followed by a large crack.

The drumming began slowly, building in volume until it drowned out the hubbub of voices. I held my hands over my ears but it didn't make any difference. I called out her name as loudly as I could, but no one could hear me. I could smell the rain and a couple of drips fell on to my face. I could see her at last.

She smiled at me from her position on the balcony in front of the wrought ironwork. Behind it was a blaze of foliage. The sun must have either just risen or was about to set, for her face glowed gold. I hadn't seen her in the sari before and she had lined her eyes with kohl. I couldn't stop looking at her. And she held my gaze. I wondered if anything could ever be as good as this.

I blinked and the sequence of images replayed themselves. *Missing footage. Previously believed lost.* Each time the pain in my chest was getting worse. When I closed my eyes there were flashes. It was better to keep them open, even though the sweat seemed to run into them, whichever way I turned.

It was darker when my eyes were open. I was on my back now. Not curled up any more on the banana leaf. My mouth was completely dry and tasted acidic. For a moment I thought I was blind. Then I saw a small thread of light coming from beneath a curtain. Music was playing nearby, a high-pitched woman's voice meandering through a song in Sinhalese. I drifted off.

The next time I woke, I wasn't sweating any more. A woman was wiping my brow with a towel. I touched her wrist and she pulled away.

'I'm sorry. I thought you were someone else.'

She got up quickly and the curtains swayed. I could hear distant traffic, the throaty cough of the tuk-tuks' horns, a siren. A cockerel crowed. I sat upright and stared into the darkness. I gasped for breath. Minna stood in front of me. Minna, Anita's godmother.

'She tells me you are taking her to England. You better take care of her ...'

She melted away as the curtain swept back and a man stepped into the space beside the mattress. He made a tutting sound with his tongue.

52

Sivalingham sat at the end of the mattress, smoking a *bindi* and picking bits of leaf from his lips. He smiled a lot but it was clear he was not happy.

'You caused a great commotion.'

'I'm sorry.'

'The other patients thought you were a drug addict.'

I thought he was making a joke, but he was very serious.

'This facility is for the poor. The authorities tolerate it because we keep a low profile.'

'I'm very grateful to you for treating me.'

'Hardly.' He sniffed. 'We just put you in here and left you to sweat it out.'

'How long have I been here?'

'About twelve hours.'

I pulled myself up on my elbows to get a better look at him. His shock of wiry hair had started to go grey. Other than that he looked no older.

He shook his head. 'You do get yourself into the most terrible scrapes.'

'Anita. Is she safe?'

He looked down. 'As far as I know.'

'What does that mean?'

'What I said.'

'You gave me a message. I was very grateful to you. The package was very important.'

He put up his hands. 'No details, please. I don't want to be involved.'

'Are you interested in my progress?' He didn't answer. 'Last week when we spoke on the phone, you said you were very keen to know how I was getting on.'

'Perhaps that was rash of me. But you were an interesting patient ...'

'Why?'

'I'd not treated amnesia before. I didn't know what to expect.'

I sat up and swung my legs off the mattress so we were side by side. He fixed me with a look that seemed to go right through into my brain.

'You've got it all back now.'

I nodded.

'Is that difficult?'

I didn't answer.

'Did you *really* lose your memory?'

'It's possible for things to come back years later, isn't it?'

He sat down beside me. 'Sometimes a memory is gone for good and no amount of therapy or chemicals can bring it back.' He snapped his finger like a magician. 'Just like that. Here today, gone tomorrow. Nothing you can do.' He patted my arm. 'But that's not always the way. There are the things that for whatever reason people choose not to remember. Because the memory is sufficiently problematic or traumatic, sometimes the brain sets up its own firewall. Like the device on your computer that guards against viruses. It screens out the negative material it doesn't want.'

'How does it *decide*?'

'We all have an image of ourselves that we like to project. But most of us are more selfish than we care to admit. And sometimes we relegate things that we haven't faced up to. Very manipulative people can convince themselves that black is really white if it suits them. After even the most partial amnesia, learning to access your memory is a bit like learning to walk again – you have to do something consciously that you had used to do unconsciously. Along this road, significances get attached to certain memories. You may, for example, cling to the easiest explanation.'

He looked away for a second.

'And?'

'And ignore what's more ... difficult ...'

I looked at him. 'Go on.'

'When we first met, you were in a real mess. You had severe haematoma. We didn't know if you'd be a vegetable. When you started to speak it was all about the lady on the boat. With the film-star name.'

'Greer.'

'You had witnessed a terrible incident in which this woman, who was very important to you, had died. Maybe it didn't suit you to remember beyond that. After all, you had enough on your plate dealing with what you'd seen. Maybe you didn't have the energy to deal with other matters.' He stubbed the cigarette out under his heel. 'Anyway, you've recovered. That's the main thing. You have no further use for me.'

'Yes I do. Please.' I put my hand on his arm.

He looked at me over his glasses and sighed.

'Miss Jayarajah: you once made her a proposal. But you were young and ambitious, you were here to do a job. And the outcome put her in a compromising position with the authorities. I cannot comment upon the personal aspects of whatever passed between you; however, what is etched in my mind is the sight of her at your bedside when you were out for the count. Talking to you, willing you to recover. That's my memory.'

He paused while I took this in.

'You are a film-maker.'

'Was.'

'Well then, I am sure I don't need to tell you that no two points of view are the same. And when you put a film together, you make choices, no matter how objective you may fancy you are trying to be. You do what looks best. To tell your story. The bits that don't fit.' He threw the remains of his cigarette into a bin. 'What is memory but the stories we tell ourselves to remember?'

He looked at me and nodded.

'You had very much on your plate. Never mind the physical trauma – it was all you could do just to learn to function in the world again. Maybe some things did not get properly dealt with at the time.'

He picked up the linen jacket that had looked so new yesterday morning and tried to brush the dirt off it.

'I do have a message from her.'

He leaned closer.

'Go home. If you have any feeling or respect for her, go home. She gave you back what was rightfully yours. She does not want you to look for her. She put her trust in you, once. Don't hurt her any further. Surely if you have any respect for her, you will do this one thing.'

He got up and brushed his trousers with his hands.

'If you are now accepting some memories you put out of reach, then some good has been done. Denial is a corrosive thing. It traps the spirit. You know now what you couldn't face up to before. You're a better man for that. Maybe now you can start to rebuild your life. You feel shame, that's natural. But she doesn't need your apology.'

He lifted my hand from my lap and shook it.

'It is good to see that you are still making progress. My driver will take you back to your hotel.'

He swept back the curtain and was gone.

53

The driver held an umbrella over me as we splashed through the mud. I sat in the back of Sivalingham's Peugeot watching people moving through the rain. I looked at all the faces, hoping that I might see her. I still felt vague and fragile, but my temperature had stabilised and for the first time in days I felt like I had had some real rest. Perhaps he was right. The best I could do was honour Anita's wish and stay away.

'We are going to the Oceania, yes?'

'Yes. No. Drop me at the Majestic.'

Sivalingham's driver pulled in under the canopy and held the door for me. I thanked him and felt for some change. There was no money in my pocket. I shrugged an apology.

'Have a good day, sir.'

The vast lawn beside the hotel was deserted. Although it had stopped raining, the sky was still dark. The downpour had done nothing to clear the humidity and the air was thick with moisture. I walked to the wall and stared out at the brown sea.

'You want girl?'

A man in a silver shirt with a machete pattern was waving at me as if he was an old friend.

'I have very good new girl, just available.' He nodded and grinned. 'I use her myself.'

I stared through him while he continued to nod.

'OK. White sniff?' He tapped a forefinger against one nostril. 'Change money, very good rate.'

I shook my head and turned back to the Majestic. Although it was daytime, the darkness had triggered the floodlights, which gave the façade an eerie look, like a giant, yellowing wedding cake.

Anita had brought me here from the airport. I had told her I didn't want to stay in an air-conditioned concrete block.

'This is our least modern hotel,' she had said. 'It belongs to another time.'

While I checked in she had gone into a detailed list of royals and film stars who had stayed there.

'Would you like me to go to the room?' I had stared at her. On *Destination*, the local guides could be more than obliging in the line of duty. She blushed at her mistake and shook her head, annoyed with herself. 'To check it. That it is all right for you.'

'That's very kind of you, but I'm sure there'll be no need.' I smiled as warmly as I could.

A silver Jaguar and a black Range Rover waited under the canopy, a driver at the wheel of each, engines running and windows up to keep the air conditioning going. I felt the heat of the cars as I walked past them and up the steps into the lobby.

I heard the sound of a piano coming from the bar. A large banner had been erected between two pillars: *Majestic Hotel welcomes the Anglo-Sri Lankan Enterprise Congress.*

I stood in the spot where I had waited for Greer. Everything was just as I had remembered it. A cleaner in a loose blue smock was polishing the room key fobs with Brasso. Another was scooping butts out of the large marble lions with ashtray crowns on their heads. A concierge glided by, Dalek-like, in a white tunic and stiff damask sarong.

A man with a thinly clipped moustache was hunched over the piano, eyes closed as his white-gloved fingers slid across the keys. I looked over to the bar area and glimpsed the tables out under the sky. Rainwater lay in pools on the glass tops. The ashtrays had been inverted and the chairs tipped forward against them. The furled parasols were streaked with damp. I stared for some time at the empty table where I had sat with Greer. Then I turned back into the lobby.

I moved towards the antique lifts. The attendant swept back the gates.

'Two, please.'

He smiled broadly and pushed a lever with his gloved hand. 'The storm was bad.'

'Yes.'

His eyes registered my clothes. 'You need laundry?'

I managed a smile. The suit that was new yesterday had a large stain down one side of the jacket. One of the sleeves had a tear in it. 'And maybe a tailor …'

'I arrange for you?'

'It's OK, thanks.'

The lift stopped and he pushed the doors open. I had no coins to give him but he bowed theatrically and wished me a good day.

A cleaner's trolley stood on the landing. Another fragment of memory dropped into place with each step. I stood outside room 210. It was unlocked so I pushed it open.

A huge propeller-like fan stirred the air and murky light seeped through the closed shutters. The bed had been stripped. Fresh sheets were waiting to be put on. I went over to the window and pushed back the shutters. The sea and sky were identical shades of grey. It was as if I had stepped on to the set of a film I had once seen. It broke the spell, like discovering the secret of a magic trick.

I saw Greer's silhouette as I remembered it, looking out at the night. I stood in the spot from where I'd watched her, remembering now what I'd tried to forget that night, through the haze of wine – that what was happening was a mistake and a betrayal.

I had stepped away, embarrassed. I'd glanced at my watch and then at the door.

'*Don't.*' Greer's voice had been almost shrill. She had come over to me and pressed her mouth to my ear.

'Stay. Please. Don't leave me. Not tonight …'

I had tried to will Anita's face to go away, to erase the promises I had made to her. I was drunk, but not drunk enough to obliterate the lurking remorse. I had wanted to get away, but Greer was insistent, pleading for me at least to lie down beside her …

I stared at the unmade bed. I was sitting on it now, this space I had once been invited to occupy, my head heavy with the ache of remembering. I lay down and gave myself up to the fog of pain and shame that engulfed me.

There was a soft knocking sound. Two cleaners stood in the doorway with identical expressions of bewilderment. I got up, brushing the creases out of my soiled suit.

'Sorry.' I pointed at my head. 'Bad pain.'

I strode past them, out into the corridor, and took the stairs to the ground floor. I stood in the lobby, the energy drained from me. I had counted on Sivalingham's help. *Go home*. Was that really her message, or his?

A group of men in dark suits appeared, headed for the main doors. One of them was holding forth, clutching a small laptop. He paused and I met his gaze. Bernard Hinde stared back at me. One of his entourage looked in my direction, then back at Bernard, before they moved on to the waiting cars.

I watched the motorcade sweep out of the hotel forecourt. Hinde had a phone pressed to his ear.

I started back to the Oceania. I tried jogging, but my whole body still ached and the humid air was like treacle, resisting any attempt at speed. I felt in my pocket for Jared's phone. It was gone.

54

The Oceania reception area was filled with another suited party. I went to the desk. Pillai was on duty. He looked at me warily.

'I'm OK now. Much better. Thank you for your help.'

He handed me the key to my room. 'A moment.' He unlocked a drawer and passed me an envelope. Inside was the wad of cash he had taken from me in the clinic.

'I owe you for that.' I took out a fifty-dollar bill and passed it to him. Right now he felt like the only friend I had in the world.

My bag was in the room. The TV was on, tuned to a US Sport network: Detroit Pistons vs. the New York Knicks. In a box on the screen it said *Welcome Swallow Travel*. I turned it off.

I took out Anita's photograph and examined it. I had no idea how to find her. I put it in my pocket. I dialled Esther Carr's number on the room phone. It rang for a long time. I didn't leave a message.

The phone rang as soon as I replaced the handset. I moved to pick it up then hesitated. The display said *Foyer*. I let it ring. When it finally stopped, I dialled reception and asked for Pillai.

'A gentleman asked for you. I said you had left the hotel, but he's on his way up.'

There was a knock on the door before I'd put down the receiver.

I backed out onto the balcony. It was seven floors down to the pool below, and it had been drained. There was no sign of a fire escape.

I came back in. The room had a connecting door. It opened, but the second door was locked. I pulled the one to my room shut and flattened myself in the narrow space between the two.

I heard a key working in a lock. The room door opened. The sound of footsteps momentarily drowned out my echoing heartbeat. There was movement from the direction of the balcony, then silence. More footsteps; the unzipping of a bag – my bag, the contents being spilled out on the bed. He was much closer now, advancing towards the connecting door. A mobile phone buzzed. I heard it click open. He was so close I could hear the voice on the other end.

'Reception says he took a cab thirty minutes ago.' The accent was British.

There was another noise. He had got out his set of skeleton keys again. I could feel the door handle move against my groin.

'Where to?'

'Didn't know.'

The phone snapped shut. There was a knock on the room door.

'Turn down the bed, sir?'

I heard the rustle of notes.

'A few minutes.'

'Thank you, sir. Excuse me …'

Retreating footsteps. Things being moved about …

After a few minutes I heard the mobile being dialled.

'Nothing here.'

The door opened and closed.

I waited a full five minutes before letting myself back in the room.

My bag was exactly as I'd left it.

I called Pillai again.

'They asked me to call them when you came back. But I think there's another still here in the foyer.'

'Is there any way I can get out of here without being seen?'

'Turn left out of your room and you'll find a service elevator next to the laundry room. You'll need the code for the key pad.' He read me a stream of letters and numbers. 'From the basement you can access the car park.'

'Did they say who they were with?'

'No, but I've seen one of them before, escorting VIPs. A private security firm. The car park has a street exit. It's not for pedestrians, but the gate man should not be a problem.'

I gave him my mobile number. 'Call me if anything happens.'

The car park smelled of damp and drains and exhaust. A garbage truck was being loaded with sacks. The driver revved it and hydraulic rams compacted the refuse. I walked towards the ramp. At the top was a small glass booth. The man inside was asleep. My phone rang. It was Pillai.

'One has taken the main lift to the car park.' As he spoke the elevator doors slid open. A figure stepped out and looked around. I flattened myself behind a pillar. The refuse truck rocked as the driver revved the engine and the rams engaged once more. Then it started to move between my pursuer and the place I had tried to hide myself.

I ran towards the truck but just as I reached it, it speeded up. I veered back behind another pillar. The man pulled out his mobile and talked into it as he skirted around towards the exit.

'Here I am.'

The voice came from only a few feet away. I looked down into the car beside me. The woman's face was in shadow, but I could see the glint of teeth.

'You're early.' She rolled the window all the way down and smiled a knowing smile. Then she motioned towards the passenger door.

I hesitated.

'Come on.' She giggled and pushed open the door.

I looked back towards the exit. The man was bending down, talking to the guard in his glass box. I let myself in. A breath of chilled air and expensive scent wrapped itself around me.

The car engine revved and we surged forward.

'The hotel is very difficult. No meeting in the bar or lobby now.' She put her hand on my knee. 'You want a drink first? Something to relax you?'

'Good idea.'

She glanced down at my jacket and a trace of doubt showed in her expression. I was conscious of the smell of my sweat doing battle with her scent. We approached the exit barrier.

'It's fine. Just keep going.'

Something in my voice added to her suspicion. Her face clouded. The guard focused his attention on me. She gestured for him to open the barrier. He hesitated and then the bar lifted. The car lurched forward and stopped almost immediately, as the traffic on the street charged away from a light.

She looked at me again. 'Henri? You are Mr Henri?'

I nodded some more and smiled. She glanced past me, at something outside the passenger door. The man who had been looking for me was standing just a few feet away.

I pulled out the wad of dollars Pillai had given back to me.

'Just drive.'

'You're not Henri.'

'Look, it's OK.' I waved a fifty-dollar bill. The car forced its way into the traffic, braving a volley of car horns. Then the lights changed and there was a stampede. I watched in the rear-view mirror as the man flipped open his mobile and ran towards a Mercedes that was trying to make a U-turn. 'Fast as you can.'

'I don't want any trouble.'

The traffic thickened again as another set of lights loomed. I pointed at a narrow road off to the left. 'There.'

I grabbed for the wheel but she complied.

'OK. I'll get out here and you can even get back for your appointment.'

She glanced at me and then the money. 'I can be late.'

I gave her the fifty and ran down the narrow road. A huge billboard loomed ahead: a cinema poster, the faces of a wedding couple, the gold in the woman's sari standing out in embossed relief. They were looking into each other's eyes like it was the best day of their lives. In the background, a train curved towards them alongside a spectacular mountain-fringed bay. I ran across the road. The traffic swept around me, almost blowing me off balance. An elderly man gesticulated as I reached the far side.

'Mr Gentleman, you help for my daughter.' One of his pupils was swivelled up under an eyelid. A girl with a crutch hobbled after him. I stared into his face and whatever he saw caused him to lose heart before I had replied. Several more people were staring at me. The whole of Colombo might as well have been waiting for me to make my next move.

A flotilla of identical tuk-tuks came past. Each one slowed as they saw me. I sprinted to the nearest one.

'Go. Go ...' The driver looked dismayed, then saw the fifty-rupee note in my hand. 'Go left. That way.' I pointed and the driver leaned his weight into the corner. 'Now right.'

He laughed. 'Getaway!'

'That's right: getaway.'

The scooter engine under his saddle screamed as he revved it to its limit, sweeping left and right through the traffic. Anyone trying to follow would have their work cut out.

'OK. Station, please.'

'You need ticket? I can get very good price.'

'No thanks.'

Several men trotted up to me as I stepped out of the tuk-tuk. 'Welcome to Colombo, sir. You need guide, sir? Room, sir?'

'Thank you. No.'

They followed me into the concourse, gradually melting away as I ignored their offers.

The same dull red trains stood at the platform. There was a pervasive smell of diesel.

It had been early morning when Anita saw me off on the Jaffna train. A mist hung in the air, blurring all the hard edges, so the world looked slightly out of focus. In the taxi she had held my hand tightly, her face full of anxiety. I sat away from her.

Please understand ...

I'd looked into the misty dawn. I'd hardly slept. I wanted all my attention to be on the journey north. That was where my story would be. I had been given the chance of a lifetime. *Don't come back without a story. If there's any danger of that, don't come back at all.* Edge's parting words ...

I stood on the platform, aware that I was being watched. They were confused by my behaviour. I had no luggage. I'd declined more advice and guidance on directions, tickets, accommodation, food, drugs and girls. They stared at me as I stared at the platform and the empty track.

She had stood where I was standing. Eventually I had smiled at her, more out of pity than anything else, suppressing my irritation at something I couldn't quite identify.

'Don't expect things to come back in chronological order,' I had been told. 'There's no reason to what comes when.' I closed my eyes. 'It may have no form, just an emotion. When it comes, hold on to it.'

This is too soon for me ...

I stepped away, trying to grasp the splinter of memory, trying to draw it out from where it was embedded.

This is too soon for me. Please understand ...

The evening before, Anita had taken me to meet her godmother, Minna, a tiny bird of a woman with a powdered face, swathed in a sari. She had a big house that was in stately decline, circled with verandas. They sat together in a chair that hung on chains and groaned as it swung, which made them laugh. I'd watched Anita come alive in front of me in the hours after we'd been to the ruins of her house. She was wearing the sari I'd treated her to, and new sandals, though I'd failed to persuade her to throw away the old ones her mother had bought her. She'd put on make-up; she smoked one of my cigarettes and drank an arak cocktail. Her eyes were shining and every few seconds they settled on me. When she got up to get me a beer, Minna beckoned me over.

She grasped my hand with surprising strength. 'Get her away from here. Please. There's nothing for her.'

After dinner we walked in the garden. She showed me a den she'd built with her brother.

'This is where we hid during the anti-Tamil riots when I was a child.'

I'd ordered a taxi. We heard its horn blast in the driveway. I held her. 'Will you come later?'

Her hold tightened. When she released me, there was something in her face, but I was too intoxicated with excitement to pay it any attention.

Outside the station an ancient Opel taxi swerved to a stop in front of me.

'You know Ratnakara Place?'

The interior smelled of hot plastic. The footwells were covered in a dogtooth-patterned lino. A plastic fan in a wire cage was screwed onto the dashboard. The driver jerked the gear lever into Drive and nosed into the traffic. I checked the rear window. Any of the cars behind could have been in pursuit. If I was going to find Anita, I wanted to do it alone.

Headlights were coming on and the clouds seemed to be lowering themselves onto the city for the night. Every few minutes the car ground to a halt.

The driver cursed and shook his head. 'Rush hour, very bad.'

We drove for about twenty minutes. At one point the road ran alongside the water's edge. I could hear the sound of steel halyards clattering against the masts of yachts.

A large cruiser was moored close to a jetty. Under an awning a couple, drinks in hand, were leaning close to each other and laughing. What else had I chosen to forget?

I'd waited in my hotel room. I'd showered and changed. I'd already packed for the trip to Jaffna the next day. The train left at six. It would be an early start. I'd ordered a drink from room service. And then another. The soft knock on the door woke me up. I'd dozed off in an armchair. A concierge was there, holding a ludicrous silver platter with a small envelope. Anita's writing.

Please don't take this the wrong way ...

55

I stood in front of the plot where the remains of the house had been. The streetlights were partly obscured by the heavy foliage of the trees. Neat lawns ran down to a well-kept pavement. A tuk-tuk buzzed past and a sports car with its roof down turned out of a drive and sped away.

A new house had been built on the site. There was no trace of what had happened, no scar left on the neat suburban street. The house was more modern than those around it. Steel shutters blinded the windows.

The street was empty, the sky almost dark. Twilight was short-lived here. I moved off the pavement and squatted under a eucalyptus. The clatter of the cicadas surrounded me in the shadows. I saw her again, the day she brought me here, in her white shirt, freshly washed and ironed each day; her blue skirt, bag over her shoulder, the model student keeping up appearances in front of the shattered wreckage of her past.

I rewound and replayed what she had said. She had described her family: her father, a labour lawyer who was away from home a lot; her mother who had trained as a doctor, but had given it up when she married; her brother who was 'always naughty'.

'Mama realised he was never going to be a good student so she made me study extra hard. She so wanted me to be the doctor she hadn't become, right from when I was a child. There were no distractions. No TV. Mama disapproved.'

I imagined her at the dining table surrounded by books, her mother looking on. A tuk-tuk drove by slowly, hoping for a fare. I pressed my fingers into my eyes and stayed in the shadows.

'Minna always had TV. She watches everything. There was five minutes between the end of my piano lesson and the start of the evening programmes. If I ran I could get there for the start.'

I took out the photograph again. *Look into the corners.* The ornate wrought-iron balcony. Built by a railway engineer. Minna tapped it with her stick. It made an impressive clang. 'They can't burn this down.'

Five minutes away.

The roads were in a grid pattern. Minna's house was in a five-minute radius. I started up the street, heading north. The houses became a lot smaller and more modern. So I turned east.

The pavements were deserted. It was the sort of neighbourhood where everyone drove. And the sky looked like it was getting ready to rain. I kept walking, trying to keep my bearings. I covered four streets quite quickly. It was easy to eliminate those with modern, box-like structures. Maybe Minna's house had gone as well; maybe she had died.

I still had some residual dizziness from the fever and a couple of times I stumbled. I came to a wider road with much larger houses. They were further back from the street and I had to step onto their lawns to see their verandas and balconies. Several of the houses had gates and walls. I passed one and a dog barked. A guard strode up to the gates and I stepped back under a tree and waited for him to lose interest.

A tuk-tuk slowed and kept pace with me. 'Sir! Ride?'

'No thanks. I'm looking for a house.'

'I'll help you. What number, sir?'

'It's OK. I'm fine.'

I'd hardly finished speaking when my foot disappeared into a pothole and I stumbled. The driver dismounted. I put my hands on my knees while I recovered my balance.

'Oh. Good party! I take you home?'

Headlights appeared from nowhere and blazed across us. A police car. There was a sharp exchange in Sinhalese. I moved into the shadows. The talking stopped. A powerful torch swept the space in front of me.

Another car drew up. Doors slammed. Surely the Colombo police had more pressing matters than a lone drunk? I worked myself further into the bushes until I broke through into the grounds of a house that faced onto the next street. It was shrouded in darkness, but looked the right size and age. I skirted the lawn and got close enough to see an elaborate metalwork balcony. I scanned the houses either side; they were identical.

I stepped out onto the road and sheltered in a gateway as a car drove past. I didn't hear a sound above the swish of the tyres, but suddenly felt a threatening presence close by. I turned and saw two eyes inches from my face. The dog let out a sudden snarl and lunged at my neck. As I tried to roll away it caught my wrist in its jaws. I could feel the heat of its breath and flecks of saliva on my face.

A survival documentary I had once seen advised poking an attacking animal in the eyes. I plunged two fingers into the dog's face and it loosened its grip long enough for me to snatch away my arm. With a low growl, it lunged again – but only got as far as the limit of its chain.

I picked myself up and stepped back into the road.

Four identical houses stood in a curve, a high wall in front of each. A fifth, further away, was almost completely shrouded by trees. I walked towards it, my pulse racing.

It was much as I remembered it, though shabbier, maybe. There was no sign of life from within; no cars in the drive. A bright security light clicked on as I approached. I felt a warm, wet sensation between the fingers of my left hand. Blood was pulsing steadily from my wrist and dripping onto the road.

I took off my jacket and used the T-shirt to bind the wound. A dark stain immediately spread across it. I wrapped it again, tighter, but the blood continued to drip steadily. Another dog began to bark from somewhere below me as I climbed the steps up to the door and rang the bell.

There was the sound of running feet and two men appeared

on the veranda. They lifted me off my feet and I watched the house recede as they dragged me back down the steps. The front door opened. A tiny woman stood there, swathed in a shawl, her hair a white cloud and her eyes misty with cataracts.

There was a burst of Sinhalese from the porch. I recognised the voice straight away. A fist hovered above my face. A police siren sounded up the road. Both men were talking now, in low voices. I heard 'Come,' and 'Run'. I staggered with them down the side of the house and through the door of an out-building.

We waited in the darkness. The car moved slowly past, siren off. My assailants neither moved nor spoke. Apart from the cicadas, the only sound was the three of us breathing.

Then I heard footsteps on the gravel. A torch shone in my face.

'What a mess.'

56

I couldn't see her face. As she bandaged my wrist, a curtain of hair obscured it. She gave me an injection and checked my pulse. Then she sat at the end of the bed, her face averted, staring into the gloom. It was several minutes before she spoke.

They had brought me up to the room in the roof. Two big fans did their best to whip the heavy, humid air into submission. The only light came from a bedside lamp. One of the men started opening the small gable windows. She signalled for him to stop and leave us alone.

I lifted the bandaged wrist. 'Thank you.'

She frowned. 'Don't lift anything for a few days.'

I levered myself up on an elbow. We studied each other's faces. Hers was tearful.

'What happened to Carrie?'

'It was her old boyfriend.'

'*Saul?*'

'Do you remember anything about him?'

'Only that he had an American accent, and that she was all over him. It was so long ago. Why would he?'

'She's not the only one.'

She moved away from the bed and folded her arms. 'You shouldn't have come.'

'I know about Greer.'

Her mouth opened and closed.

'I saw her mother, I know you have too.'

She shut her eyes.

'I know she's with Malik. I saw the postcard she'd sent her mother. They're here, in Sri Lanka, aren't they?'

There was no sound except the thrash of the cicadas and

some music from another house wafting through the trees. She twisted the sheet between her fingers. 'Is that why you're here?'

'Partly. Why did you run?'

She took a couple of deep breaths. 'After you came, I checked with Carrie's doctor. He confirmed what you'd said.' She wiped a strand of hair off her face. 'There's a number Greer gave me, only for emergencies. It just takes messages. I'd never used it before. Greer called straight back and said I had to get out. "Leave now. Don't say anything to anyone. Just disappear." She'd warned me about the inquiry, that there would be things in the press. She asked me to tell her if anything "unusual" happened.'

'Like me turning up in your surgery?'

She closed her eyes again. When she breathed in I could see she was shaking.

'She'd made me promise never to have any contact with you.'

She let her curtain of hair fall again.

'But you left me the tapes.'

She stepped away and leaned against the wall, clutching her arms. All I could see was her silhouette, and the fans ruffling the light fabric of her dress.

'I couldn't leave them behind.'

'You took them from my hotel room – along with all the other Rammal material. She made you, didn't she?'

I saw a hand go to her face.

'She made you do it while she … distracted me. Then you helped her disappear.'

She winced. It was some time before she spoke again.

'That day, after the meeting in the office, she came here to the house. At first she was terrifying – this powerful, famous woman who I so admired, furious with me. She couldn't believe that I'd disobeyed her, helping you get to the north. "How could you let me down, after I've given you this great opportunity?" She was shrieking. I'd never been spoken to like this before. Ever. She was furious with you. "He should never have approached this man. He doesn't understand what he's done." She said it would be terrible for us all if it ever got out, worse than I could ever imagine.

'Eventually, I said, "You're his boss; can't you order him to give you all the material?" But she shook her head. "I can't do that," she said. I was lost. I didn't understand anything that was happening around me. I was utterly out of my depth. I just wished my parents were still alive and I could run home to our house and pretend none of this had happened.

'Greer's mood changed then. She calmed down. She even offered me a cigarette, which she'd never done before. She asked to see round the house. I had told her how Minna hid all her Tamil friends during the riots. She wanted to see where.

'I brought her up here. She paced up and down; she must have been working out what she was going to do. She became very calm and civil again, just like when I first met her. She sat down on the bed and beckoned me to sit by her. She took both my hands in hers. "You want to get away from here, go to England, to study? I'll help you. But first you'll have to do some things for me ..."'

Anita turned away from the window and came back towards the bed. She stood in front of me, staring into the gap between us.

'Greer said she needed everything you'd hidden in your room. Not just the tapes; photographs, papers, all of it, every trace of him. And I had to help her.' She dropped her head. 'It didn't feel like I had any choice. We went back to the hotel. She brought me up to her own room, above the bar. All her bags were packed. She put them in the wardrobe. She told me to wait there until I could see you both on the veranda. I watched through the slats in the blind, waited for you both to get settled. Then I had to go to your room. I knew the boy on reception, so getting the key wasn't a problem. I told him I had something to deliver for you. He just smiled, like he was saying yeah, yeah.'

She looked away and shook her head.

'At first I thought I couldn't do it, couldn't go in. I'd never done anything like this. It felt as if a steel gate was about to come down on everything that had gone before, and nothing would ever be the same.

'I prayed it would just take a few minutes. Going through your belongings, I felt disgusting. I couldn't see any tapes. After half an hour I came down and got the concierge to fetch her. She was insistent. "Just keep going. Don't come out until you've got it all." She said she'd keep you distracted, even if it took all night.'

She closed her eyes and shivered.

'At first I was very careful, trying not to disturb too much. By the end I was desperate, pulling everything apart. I had to go out and find a screwdriver. I thought I'd have to take up the floorboards. It was two in the morning when I left. On the way out, the night deskman gave me a knowing look and rubbed a finger and thumb together. I had to bribe him. My shame was complete.' She turned away. 'Greer told me to come back here, to the house, and wait for her. They arrived about five a.m. She was practically carrying him. I didn't know whether he was drunk or if she'd drugged him. He was in a terrible state, half conscious and rambling. He had fallen into the water and there was algae stuck to his suit. He struggled and she slapped his face quite hard. I'd never seen a woman do that before. It seemed to subdue him. After she got him up here she asked to see what I'd brought from your room. She looked through all of it, very methodically, then she said, "Burn all of it. Everything." She put her hands on my shoulders and drew me towards her until our faces were just inches apart.'

She used her own hands to replay the scene.

'"Never, ever, speak about this. Not to anyone. Your life will depend on it. So will your godmother's." I was too exhausted and shocked to protest. Then she sent me back to the hotel to wait for you with the message. "Just tell him that's what he has to do. Don't discuss it. Have a car waiting." She said I was never to see you again, ever, that you were the cause of all this and had betrayed my trust. And if I was in any doubt about that, to remember where you had spent the night.'

She turned away to the window and stared out at the night. Neither of us spoke. The rain started again, drumming on the tin roof.

'Later that morning, Bernard Hinde rang from the British Consulate. He was screaming down the telephone. That was the first I knew about the explosion. She said nothing about what to expect. I ran up here. Greer had Malik on a drip. She'd cleaned him up and he was laid out here. I told her you were in hospital. She said you should have stayed on the dock. You were only supposed to see what happened.'

Anita looked at me and chewed on her lip.

I waited for her to continue.

'They were here for three days. Then they left, very early one morning. A private ambulance came. She had it all organised. She'd dyed her hair and changed all her clothes. She'd bandaged him up like a fire casualty, unrecognisable. She handed me an envelope. Inside were details of a bank account in my name, my enrolment in college in London, air tickets, and a passport. How she did it all, I don't know. She pressed her finger to my lips. "This will be our secret."'

Anita walked over to the window again.

'But those few days they were here – it helped me understand, if that's the right word. Seeing them together. How much he meant to her. How much she loved him. She would have done absolutely anything for that man. I said, "But you're giving up your life for him." She just smiled and touched his face. "This is my life."

'I paid her back, of course. I didn't want to owe her anything.' She examined her hands. 'Even so, I never felt like my life was entirely my own. Not just because of what she'd done for me, but the thought that, because of the secret, someone might come asking and I'd have to drop it all and run.'

'And her mother?'

'Greer asked me to check up on her. Sarah thought she'd lost her daughter. I'd lost my mother.' She shrugged. 'I felt sorry for her.'

'Why did you keep the tapes?'

She closed her eyes and shook her head. 'An act of defiance? A moment's hesitation?' She stopped, as if she'd never really considered it. 'I didn't even know what was on them. It was what they represented.' She sighed. 'Your energy. Your determination. That's what I loved in you. They were a reminder of that.'

She gave an angry, desperate sigh and sat down on the edge of the bed.

'I'd burned all Malik's photos and papers – all the things from your room – in the stove in the yard. I was destroying his past. I'd left the tapes till last. Even then, I still believed you were only trying to do the right thing, because you cared, because you wanted to make a difference. They became part of what I carried with me.' Tears were running freely down her cheeks. She looked into my face. 'Aren't there things you've kept for no purpose, things that you can't bring yourself to let go of?'

She had moved nearer. I swung my legs off the bed and sat up. The movement startled her. I reached for my jacket, which was draped over a chair. I took out the photograph of her and laid it on the bed between us.

She glanced at it and smiled. The tears had gathered in her eyelashes so they glistened. 'After I got to England I so hoped you'd look for me. I couldn't break my agreement with Greer, but if you found me ... Then I saw you in the street.' She breathed in sharply and pressed her fingers against her eyes. 'The blankness in your face. As if everything had been wiped from your memory, and all life with it. I looked away until you'd passed. Then I watched you disappear into the crowd. I decided that it was amnesia. I even tried saying to myself maybe it's just as well, that knowing the truth would have been too painful for you to bear. But seeing you there, alone in the street, I thought: that was how you'd seen me the day I took you to the ruins of my house – someone with nothing. It bothered me for a long time. I called Sivalingham. I pretended I had a patient with amnesia and asked him about it. But I think he knew what I was really asking. He said he'd be surprised if you'd made a full recovery.' She leaned closer. 'Did you recognise me that day? Did you see me at all?'

I wiped a small tear off her cheek with my thumb. My voice was stuck somewhere in my throat. 'If only I had.'

She picked up the photograph. 'Do you remember what happened just after you'd taken this?'

She waited for me to respond.

'Do you?'

I flushed and nodded.

'Those were terrible times. My girlfriends and I, we put on such brave faces. My best friend Shirani, she became a prostitute – to raise enough for law school in India. She never got there. Her little sister – Rana – joined the Tigers. Became a suicide bomber. We'd all been such good girls, with top marks. We didn't have a clue. Life running on fast-forward. No time to think.'

She shrugged and looked towards the milky light that was starting to ease its way through the windows.

'A lot of me wanted to be with you, that night. Really wanted to. But I was still my parents' daughter, even though they were dead. I was still a virgin. It felt too sudden ...' She sighed and shook her head. 'In the end, I lost it at a student party in London. I didn't even know his name.'

She ran her forefingers round her eyelids, pushing away tears.

'I tried hating you, like the morning after you'd been with Greer, when I saw you on the stairs. But actually, at that moment, I was hating *myself*.' She pressed her fists to her forehead. 'It was supposed to be me. That was Greer's plan, that *I*'d be the one to take you away and distract you, while *she* searched your room. And when I saw you from the hotel window, the two of you, watching her work her magic, all I could think was, *That should be me*. But I'd refused. Not like that ... I just couldn't ...' She blew air out of her cheeks and blinked away some tears. 'So, now you know why I didn't want you to come.'

I didn't speak. I sat on the edge of the bed, looking at her, absorbing her version, adding the missing sequences to my own. The more I knew about Greer, the less painful it was. Realising how much I had lied to myself about Anita was much harder.

She reached out and touched my cheek. 'What are you thinking?'

'I'm thinking about "ifs" ...'

She waited for me to go on.

'If I hadn't been so put out that you wouldn't sleep with me ... If I hadn't gone to Jaffna ... If I hadn't let Greer seduce me ... If I'd seen you in the street ...'

'You're shaking.'

I drank some water. She helped herself to a cigarette. Although her eyes were red and some make-up had run, she still looked powerfully beautiful. We were both quiet. Eventually she looked at me.

'Thank you.'

'What for?'

She shrugged. 'Helping me escape these lies. Greer helped me to get away, get to England. I paid it all back, what she lent me. But ... I never felt I was really living my own life. I had to do a lot of pretending.'

A sudden gust of wind banged the shutters. She straightened up. The room came back into focus.

'What's going to happen?'

I told her about the Northolt people, what I'd learned from Jared, and my arrangement with him.

'Malik's ill. He may not have much longer. Greer wants him to go into hospital but he won't. I agreed to take them some supplies.'

She sighed. 'They're in the north. The Tigers control it. He wants to be there because it's where his mother came from. But they can't treat him. Greer asked me to get him to Colombo.'

'Is he really dying?'

She shrugged. 'I'll only know for sure when I take a look at him.'

She felt my pulse and her hand hovered over my forehead. I took it in mine.

For a moment everything around us, everything that had happened in the last few days, had vanished from sight, leaving us in our own private cocoon. I squeezed her hand like it was something I never wanted to let go again.

She looked into my face. 'Do you really have to do this?'

'If Malik dies, the truth about what happened dies with him.' I took her other hand. 'If he can speak, then it's all over. The truth will come out. Will you help me? I just need to know where to find them.'

She closed her eyes for a moment and took my other hand. Then she brought her face close to mine. 'I'm coming with you this time.'

57

I tried calling Jared but there was no signal his end. I called Esther again.

'He's on his way to you. He's in the air now. Don't try to meet him; he said he'd make his way to you.' She sounded distant. 'He's upset you didn't call.'

'I got separated from the phone.'

'Have you been successful?'

'Possibly.'

'We're depending on you.'

It was still dark when I heard the car. It slowed as it passed the house, the distinctive growl of a big V8. I had slept fitfully, my mind swirling.

The rain had stopped. None of the windows overlooked the drive but I leaned out of one to get a glimpse of the street. An American 4x4 slowed to a halt. The rear passenger window opened for a few seconds then the car moved off.

It was five thirty. I dressed and went downstairs. The house was already alive with people. The two men I had encountered the night before sat at a big kitchen table. They nodded and smiled when I came in. A woman was standing at an old Aga-like stove stirring a large pot. The air was full of spices. Behind the house I could see a minibus, its bonnet up, being worked on by another man.

'Lady there,' said one of the men, pointing to a room across the hall.

I went up to a large sitting room. There was one small light beside a vast old couch. Anita and Minna were seated together, talking, their fingers entwined. Behind them, through French windows covered in fine metal gauze, was the balcony where I had taken the picture. They fell silent when I approached.

Anita looked at me. She had changed into a T-shirt and jeans. Her hair was caught up in a loose bun. Seeing her there, by this balcony, I felt suddenly elated. I was about to be given a second chance, to rewind the years and take a different direction.

Minna swivelled round and with Anita's help lifted herself off the couch. She extended a hand and beckoned me forward, fixing me with her fogged gaze. Her grip was surprisingly strong. For a moment I thought she might strike me when she reached up, but she pulled my head towards her and kissed my cheek. Anita's phone rang and she left the room.

'She's not going back. She's staying here. She promised.' Minna's arm curved up as if she was preparing to take a bow. 'I grew up here. In the war, it was a hospital. During the riots I hid fifty-five people in the roof. It's always been a refuge.' She gripped my arm harder. 'It'll be hers soon.'

She held my face close to hers. Her eyes were fogged with cataracts but I felt the force of her gaze.

'You will look after her this time, won't you?'

Anita came back into the room. 'There's a problem with the minibus. Siva's working on it.'

I went out to look. The front was jacked up and half the wheel assembly lay in pieces on the ground. It reminded me of Colin. I wondered what he would have made of this. I imagined his low whistle of despair and the shake of his head. I saw now how different we were. So wary of involvement he'd tried to warn me off, and then paid the ultimate price for helping me.

The night was just beginning to lift. I lit a cigarette and walked out into the garden. The house had gone many years without a fresh coat of paint and creepers had colonised the ornate balconies. There was something stubborn and glorious about the way it had resisted change, like its owner.

I tried to picture Greer arriving here with Malik, hiding here, before they disappeared into their new life together. The singlemindedness with which she'd faked their deaths ... She'd used Anita, used me. Jared was right. *They set you up, big time*

. . . I had found Malik for her in Jaffna, and she had repaid me with a decade of guilt. Perhaps I should have felt more anger, but something else was driving me now.

Anita came out onto the balcony. She leaned on the balustrade, looking down at me, then turned and went back into the house. I stared at the empty space she'd left behind.

'Need a ride somewhere?'

Jared had come all the way up the side of the house and was standing under a eucalyptus, almost invisible. A pair of big black sunglasses obscured his eyes. Down the drive, parked across the gates, was the station wagon I had seen earlier. He moved towards me.

'I thought you'd given me the slip.' He made it sound like I'd meant to, but then his face broke into a smile. He strode up and gripped my hand. 'Have you found them?'

'They're in the North. He's ill. We're going to bring him down to Colombo for treatment.'

I hesitated.

'And?'

'Someone here recognised me. They tried to follow me.'

He took in the dismantled minibus and nodded at the station wagon.

'Then let's get this job done.'

Anita was back on the veranda, staring at Jared.

He looked at her then back at me. 'Aren't you going to introduce us?'

58

We crawled along with the northbound traffic. The early-morning sun had vanished into a thick blanket of purple-grey cloud. The windows were up and the air conditioning chilled the interior of the 4x4. It was already stickily hot outside.

The driver's name was Prem. Age seemed to have shrivelled him to the point where he was dwarfed by the big steering wheel. Jared sat next to him. Anita was beside me in the back. Apart from a burst of Sinhalese directions to the driver, she hadn't spoken. Whatever she was thinking she wasn't letting on.

Jared's stillness seemed to have left him. He drummed his fingers on the door, fiddled with his phone. He looked around a lot; every so often he glanced at Anita and me.

This wasn't what I had expected. I wanted to find them first, before summoning him.

When I'd asked how he'd found me, he just waved his mobile. I tried to lighten the atmosphere by asking him about his flight, but he gave only one-word answers.

I'd used his tickets and money. He'd seen Anita's hand in mine. Had he decided that I'd taken advantage of him – that I had my own agenda? Or was he just preoccupied with the prospect of meeting Malik, the man who'd carried the blame for the death of his father?

The outskirts of Colombo gave way to sodden green and brown fields. Although it was daytime, the clouds were so low that drivers kept their lights on, flashing each other as they came close.

Jared shook his head. 'Do they have to do that?'

He seemed much more American in these surroundings.

We passed a truck on its side where a whole section of road had given way. A crowd had formed round it and Prem slowed right down to look.

Jared slapped the dashboard. 'Keep it moving.'

The downpour came with all the force that the stack of clouds had threatened, hammering the roof of the station wagon. The big wipers spread their arms across the screen and back, fighting a losing battle with the rain. The only other sound was the occasional comment from Prem, the driver, in Sinhalese, gesturing at the road ahead.

Anita gave him more detailed directions. Prem waved his hand at the road and tapped his forehead as he spoke. Anita's response provoked another tirade and more slapping of the wheel.

Jared looked at Anita. 'What's he saying?'

'He's worried about going north. He didn't know where we were headed when he took the job. He's Sinhalese, so he's worried about going into Tamil territory.' Jared took off his sunglasses and frowned at Anita. She looked away.

The atmosphere in the car was changing. Anita had digested my explanation for Jared's sudden appearance, but she looked troubled. I wasn't surprised. She had kept the secret of Greer and Malik so long. Now she had let go of it. She was guiding us to them. Her breast rose and fell with short, sharp breaths, as if she was trying to contain something that kept threatening to burst out of her. She gripped my hand and covered her mouth.

Jared glanced at her again. 'What's up?'

Anita shook her head. 'It's OK.' She opened a window and a gust of hot, fume-laden air blew in. The car surged forward. She let my hand go. A few seconds later, I felt her finger on my thigh. She was spelling something. I looked down. An A, a U and an L. I looked at her. She did it again. Four letters. An S, an A, a U and an L. SAUL.

59

His eyes lingered on Anita a second while he tried to read her expression. Then his mobile rang. He pressed it to one ear, blocking the other with his finger. I leaned towards her and mouthed, *Sure?*

His phone snapped shut.

Her expression gave me all the answer I needed. She was sure. She turned away to her window. My lungs felt like they were on fire. I tried to focus. Colin's voice echoed in my head. *That was clever.*

Saul ... He had helped Carrie get the job with Edge; he had borrowed the *Face of a Terrorist* copy and cut out all the shots of Malik. Then he'd vanished out of her life for years, only to reappear a few days ago. *He'd killed Carrie. Colin as well? Edge?* Now I'd led him here. I gripped Anita's hand.

The car shuddered as it hit a pothole. In the side mirror, I could see his face, Saul's face, concentrating on the road ahead. *Like I said, nothing's what it seems.*

We joined the queue behind a truck full of cattle at a military checkpoint. Prem was talking and gesturing. Anita didn't respond. Saul wound down the window and drummed his fingers on the edge of the door. The air was treacly. Several cars and buses had been pulled over and were being searched, but we were waved through.

Prem put the gear lever in Park and opened his door. 'Toilet.' He darted away down the line of vehicles, clutching the carrier bag he'd had under his feet.

After a few minutes Anita spoke.

'He's not coming back. He didn't know he was going to drive into Tamil territory.'

Saul turned to me.

'You drive.'

It sounded like an order.

The cattle truck moved forward. The vehicles behind started hooting. I didn't move. He took off his sunglasses again.

'Is there a problem?'

He glanced at Anita, her face focused on something invisible inside the car. He sighed loudly and shook his head. The hooting from behind was accompanied by shouts. A soldier who had waved us on started towards the car. Saul reached into his bag.

'You don't have a choice.'

He gestured with his chin at what was in his lap. I looked between the seats. A slim gun with a long silencer lay across his thigh.

'You've got me this far. She can show me the rest of the way.'

'She won't.'

'She will.' He moved the gun between the seats so she could see it as well. 'Because if she doesn't, I'll hurt you. And she won't want me to do that.'

Anita was frozen, except for the tears running down her face. The hooting continued. Someone came up and banged the side of the car. Jared took no notice.

'That's right, isn't it, Anita?'

We all changed places. Anita sat in the front beside me, Saul in the middle of the back seat, leaning forward between us.

He brought his face up close. His voice was very quiet and very definite. 'Anything stupid, Nick, and I'll hurt her too.'

I fastened my seat belt, fired up the engine and started to pull forward. The soldier strode up to my window, looking irritated. I glared at him, hoping he'd make us all get out.

'Here.' Over my shoulder came Saul's hand, clutching a passport with a few dollar bills protruding.

The soldier smiled and withdrew the bills without even opening it. He nodded down the road. 'Good trip.'

We drove on in silence. The road was narrow, with a heavy

camber that fell away on either side into a deep ditch. We passed several wrecks, carcasses of cars and buses picked clean of whatever could be unscrewed. The station wagon was wide. Keeping it on the tarmac was a challenge when oncoming trucks hogged the centre of the road.

Anita was bent forward. I reached for her, but Saul rested the gun on my wrist.

'On the wheel.'

I glimpsed his face in the rear-view mirror. His expression was empty, like a commuter going to work.

He caught my eye and there was a brief flicker of a smile.

'You did well to get this far, Nick. Very determined, I like that. You were wasted in your archive.'

He used the patronising tone that had annoyed me when we first met in the forest.

'I saw Mom's postcards too. I was ahead of you there. But the one from Sri Lanka must have arrived later.'

'Why did you kill Carrie?'

Anita turned to me and shook her head. *Don't do this.*

There was a long silence. Saul sighed. 'She knew where all the bodies were buried. Well, almost all. We needed her diaries, the old contacts. But your visit had got her thinking. She'd gotten the idea into her head that I was more interested in Malik than her, maybe always had been ...'

I gripped the wheel. White spots appeared on my knuckles.

'And Colin? I saw what you did to him ...'

'Stubborn guy. And how was I to know you were about to bring everything right to me? You were way out in the lead, Nick.' He glanced at Anita. 'But then, you had what I didn't.'

I tried not to look at his face but it hung there in the mirror. The rage was boiling up inside me. 'And now you're going to kill them too. You and Tanager, you really want to keep Malik quiet, don't you?'

He was still for a moment. 'They fucked your life up, Nick. Don't you want to get even? After what they did to you?'

My mind was spinning back over the story he had told me in Epping Forest – the plan that was 'so beautiful'. I slowed and turned to face him. 'You started this, didn't you? It was your idea – to pin Northolt on Malik and then get rid of him. But you didn't finish the job. He got away from you, re-invented himself as Rammal and then disappeared in a puff of smoke. You're not Zarev's son – that was just your ticket into the Northolt campaign.'

His eyes looked dead ahead. 'Just drive the car, Nick.'

I reached for Anita's hand but he prodded it away with the gun.

I looked at her for as long as I could keep my eyes from the road. Her eyes shone with tears. There had been a moment in Minna's house, just a few hours ago, when I had glimpsed a future, known that after years of being lost, I'd arrived at the place I needed to be. And now it was being snatched away.

The road stretched into the distance then collided with a wall of charcoal-grey cloud. When we reached our destination, Saul would be finished with us. We drove on in silence.

We came to a fork. A group of buses were parked up on a piece of rough ground under a large Coca-Cola hoarding. 'Which way?' I slowed, waiting for Anita's direction.

'I'm not doing this.' She was hunched, strands of her hair hanging over her face. When she lifted her head, her gaze was blank. She had said she didn't want me to come looking for her ...

Saul's face was inches away from her neck. 'You don't have a choice.' His voice was almost a whisper as he put the gun against my neck. 'He's done his part. You, I still need.'

60

The rain had eased off, but the wipers revived themselves every few seconds and swept the droplets away. The road was empty. We were alone.

There were only a few more miles to the border with the Northern Territory. Surely there would be some kind of checkpoint. *You are in so much shit.* Colin's voice echoed in my head. Then I heard Tanager's mirthless laugh. *We're fucking with each other.*

Saul pressed the gun into my neck then withdrew it. 'Let's all keep our cool, now.'

An army truck was parked across the road. Two soldiers were squatting under a tree a few yards away.

'Keep going.' I felt Saul's breath on my ear.

But one of the soldiers had got to his feet and waved for us to slow down. Anything to prolong the journey, the time left.

I came to a halt. They were teenagers; their uniforms looked like hand-me-downs from their bigger brothers. Their guns dangled from long straps. As they wandered towards us, it was clear they were drunk or stoned. I heard a hiss of irritation from Saul.

The younger-looking one steadied himself with a hand on the mirror and motioned for me to roll down the window. The other opened Anita's door. He grinned at her and said something to his comrade that made him laugh. The younger one cocked his gun and rested the barrel on the sill of the window. His gaze settled on a point somewhere between us.

'Let's all keep our cool now. No tricks.'

Anita took out her ID. The older one scrutinised her, then he shouted something at her and both soldiers laughed.

She translated in a monotone. 'He's saying he's always wanted to bugger a filthy Tamil.'

He twisted his head and gestured with his gun. She got out and he walked her round to the front of the car. He issued another instruction and she put her hands on the bonnet and spread her legs. He started to search her, taking his time. Saul's hand gripped my shoulder.

'Nothing clever, Nick; let's not get them over excited.'

The soldier ran his hands slowly down her sides. He made another comment and laughed. His companion looked embarrassed. As he shifted his attention to the inside of her thighs, Anita fixed me with a cold gaze, like she had from the bottom of the stairs at the Majestic Hotel.

I was out of my seat before I'd thought about it. I smashed my door open and the gun that had been resting on the sill hit my soldier in the face. He lost his balance and fell. He tried to grab my foot as I passed but wasn't fast enough. The one who was groping Anita only looked up when I was two feet away. I kicked him as hard as I could and lunged for his gun. The air filled with a fine red mist. He stared at me for a moment then slid down behind the bonnet. I heard a second low *phut* and a dark red dot appeared like a caste mark in the centre of the other soldier's forehead.

Saul was by the car. He held his gun in both hands. It was trained on me but he addressed Anita. 'Leave them, Doctor. There's nothing you can do for them.'

She had dropped to a kneeling position over the one who had been exploring her crotch with his fingers a second ago. He gazed up at the sky like it was somewhere he wanted to get to. I wrapped my arms round her.

'Back in the car, guys. Let's not get side-tracked.'

Saul didn't look at the dead men. He looked at me and shook his head wearily. I'd allowed my emotions to get the better of me.

'I've waited a long time for this, Nick. If you fuck it up, it'll be worse for you.'

I didn't see how it could be worse.

'You're going to leave them here on the road?'

He shrugged. 'They'll blame the Tigers.'

I helped Anita back into her seat and fastened the seat belt around her. She didn't look at me. *If I hadn't followed you here; if you hadn't given me the tapes; if I'd never tracked you down …*

'Let's go.'

We crossed a causeway that straddled a large area of floodwater. Wrecks of several military vehicles poked above the surface. We passed through a high wire fence but there was no checkpoint. The other side, tall trees formed a canopy that blocked out the grey light.

'How far before we turn off?'

At first, Anita didn't answer. Saul pushed the gun into my neck so hard my head tilted over.

'Three or four miles.'

'And then?'

She didn't reply.

I let my left hand drop onto the seat and reached for hers.

'Hands on the wheel.'

A few more minutes.

We had been climbing since the causeway. I tried to imagine what lay ahead. I saw us pulling up at a house. He'd keep us with him, at least until he was sure he'd found Malik. Then he'd kill us both.

I looked at Anita again, trying to project all I felt. She smiled faintly. I forced my eyes back on the road, too late to avoid a large pothole. The passenger-side front wheel slammed into it, jerking Anita forwards. Saul's head hit the roof. He cursed and smacked the back of my head with his gun. We drove on in silence.

We reached the brow of the hill. The road ran straight down the side of the valley for two or three miles, then curved sharply to the left, past a low concrete wall and gateway, and disappeared into the trees.

Anita's hand shook as she pointed at the gateway.

'In there?' Saul was so close he seemed to be about to climb into the front seat. Anita nodded and put her face in her hands.

I glanced at the speedometer. Twenty-five. I let the incline add some speed and put a small amount of pressure on the accelerator. I looked over at Anita's seat belt. There was no way of warning her. I just had to hope she would be all right. My heart pummelled against my ribcage. At Metro I'd once catalogued a road-safety film. Its message was uncompromising: *At as little as thirty miles an hour, the unbelted rear passenger is launched, on impact, like an unguided missile.* I heard the blood pulsing in my head. I tried to tell my hands to relax their grip on the wheel as we sped downwards. All I had to do was aim the car at the wall beside the gate, but every muscle in my body screamed at me to stamp on the brake, to turn the wheel.

I heard a roar from Saul then everything exploded. The airbags deployed like giant boxing gloves, blasting my ears. My upper body was knocked sideways as Saul's body catapulted past my head. For several seconds I was blind as well as deaf. The air reeked of cordite from the airbag charges. When my eyes focused again, I saw the remains of the bonnet arched upward, shrouded in steam. There was a gaping hole in the windscreen and the wipers were splayed like the legs of a broken insect. I tried to breathe but only managed to produce a rattling sound, like a bath emptying.

I looked at Anita. She was unconscious, slumped against the passenger door. I pushed away the deflated airbag and unbuckled my belt.

I forced open the driver's door and went round to her side of the car. Her head leaned against the remains of her window. Her hair was matted with blood.

I released her belt and she fell against me. I felt her pulse and cradled her head as steam hissed from beneath the crumpled bonnet. I lifted her out and laid her gently on the long grass. I tore up my T-shirt and tied the pieces round her head. Blood spread across the fabric.

I reached into the footwell for my bag. It was covered in

glass. Beside it was Saul's gun. It was much heavier than I'd expected. I tucked it into my belt.

I looked over the wall. Saul's body was almost submerged in a ditch full of oily black water. His head was covered in blood. Anita let out a sharp cry. I turned back to her. Her eyes widened. 'Is it safe now?'

'I think so.'

'I don't want to die yet.'

I kissed her forehead. 'It's not going to happen. I won't let you.'

'Don't leave me.'

'I won't,' I said. 'I won't leave you.'

My mobile was still inside my bag. It flashed *Battery Low*. I hadn't charged it for days. Perhaps I could reach Sivalingham. I started to dial, but the zero button was jammed in its socket. I tried *Dialled Numbers*, but the display was blank. There was no sound from the earpiece.

Cradling her against me, I struggled to my feet then lifted her so her head rested against my neck.

'How far to the house?'

She didn't answer. I checked her pulse again. Still there. I hoped it wasn't a long walk.

61

I had lost all sense of time and distance. I looked at my watch. The face was smashed, the second hand stuck out like a torn fingernail. The sole of one of my trainers flapped and my toes stuck out. I was vaguely aware of the ground cutting into them with each step.

The red dirt track sloped upwards. I looked over my shoulder. I felt as if I had been walking all day, yet I could still see the steam billowing from the wrecked station wagon behind us.

Tall grass on either side made the track into a trench. A lizard ran out into my path. It stood for a few moments, watching me, before it darted back into the undergrowth. Beneath the relentless chattering of the cicadas there was another sound coming from the direction I was heading: the low, intermittent roar of the sea.

Anita was silent, inert. I could feel our sweat mingling where out bodies touched. It poured down my face and stung my eyes. My balance came and went, as if someone was constantly rearranging the ground beneath my feet.

The track curved to the left and climbed more steeply. I stopped by a second pair of ruined gateposts.

Anita stirred.

'Are there more?'

'More of what?'

'With him?'

The men in Colombo, Tanager's team in their hangar at Braintree; Saul must have alerted them ... 'I hope not.'

Her eyes closed again.

I didn't care about Greer and Malik any more. All that mattered was in my arms.

The roar was getting louder. I reached a break in the grass and saw waves breaking against sharp, black rocks about twenty feet below. The hint of a breeze was coming from the sea. The track widened into a turning area and came to a stop. I could see fresh tyre marks, but no vehicles. Beyond them, up a flight of overgrown steps, was an imposing house with a deep balcony overlooking the cliff.

I called out and saw a shutter move, but no one appeared. I paused to gather my last reserves of strength, and climbed the steps. A rotund man in a sarong and vest appeared on the veranda. He waddled towards me, gesticulating wildly.

I realised he had a mouthful of food that he was trying to swallow. Some bits of it sprayed out as he spoke. 'No here. Go.'

I pushed past him.

'Private here; no admittance ...'

'Show me somewhere I can put her down.'

'You cannot go.'

I walked on into the house. He waddled along beside me, flapping his arms uselessly.

'I have orders to admit no one.'

He tried to grab my shoulder but I shook him off. The muscles in my shoulders were screaming. There was a large cool reception room with high ceilings. The furniture was covered in sheets. I laid Anita down on a divan and knelt down beside her. We were both drenched in sweat.

'You have to help us.'

I heard a woman's voice behind me. 'It's OK, Sunil, do as he says.'

62

I didn't turn round at first. I saw Sarah's face, admiring the postcards, *She's a good girl.* I saw the three of us in the office in Colombo, Greer pacing to and fro, berating Anita and me between puffs of her cigarette. And on the veranda of the Majestic, listening to my story, while her mind must have been racing, racing …

I heard her breaths, short and fast. In some dark place, in my most fevered imaginings, I had once fantasised about such a reunion. *Grant me one wish; let her be alive.* Once or twice, after too much to drink, I had tried to conjure her up, some invisible breeze tugging at her muslin dress, smiling her forgiveness.

I looked at Anita. *Imagine if I'd stuck to our deal. Imagine if I'd never gone to Jaffna, never filmed the interview. Never gone to bed with the wrong woman …*

I turned. The pulse in my head was so strong it was warping my vision. All I could see was a silhouette in a doorway. She came forward, tentatively, hands clasped. Neither of us spoke. She stopped a short distance from me.

I got to my feet. Her hair and eyebrows were artificially dark and her loose-fitting sarong had a loud batik pattern that drew attention away from her face. Despite the disguise, and the passage of years, she had hardly changed.

She recognised Anita and her hand went up to her mouth. She sat down on the edge of the divan and touched Anita's face.

'What happened?'

'We came off the road. Is there a doctor nearby?'

She shook her head. 'How bad is she?'

'I don't know. She may be concussed.'

Anita stiffened. Her eyes flashed open and she gripped my hand. 'My bag. Drip and painkillers.'

Sunil was hovering at Greer's shoulder. I gestured at the doorway. 'The car's at the bottom of the track, by the road. It's a bit of a wreck ...'

Greer nodded and he waddled away down the steps. Then she turned back to me. Her mouth moved but no sound came out. Her eyes filled with tears.

I could see a staircase in the hall behind her. 'He's here. I know he's with you.'

Her shoulders sagged.

'Upstairs. He's sleeping.' There was real fear in her eyes. 'God, you must hate me.' She looked back at Anita. 'Did she tell you?'

I shook my head. 'She's been very loyal to you.'

Even with her right there in front of me, just inches away, I was having trouble absorbing this.

'It's a very long time to go on thinking someone's dead.'

She bit her lip. 'What's happening?'

'You're not safe here.' I bent over Anita. The strips of T-shirt were stiff with dried blood. 'And we need to change this.'

I cradled her head while Greer washed the wound.

'She was going to get us to Colombo. Get him to a specialist.'

She took out a pack of cigarettes from a small, embroidered purse that hung round her waist. I felt in my pocket. I'd forgotten about the gun. I took out the lighter and passed it to her. She stared at it in dismay.

'Present from him?'

She nodded. I looked at her eyes. The blue was slightly faded and the whites bloodshot. For someone who had once seemed so in control of her destiny, she looked anxious, hunted. She put her hand on my arm and took a deep, faltering breath. 'I had to save him.'

'Whatever it took?'

Her face flushed. 'You'd put me in an impossible situation.

He was in a bad way, wouldn't see me. I was going mad looking for him.' The words tumbled out.

I had come all this way for an explanation, but I already knew what she was going to say.

'And I found him. Just as he was getting ready to kill himself.' She hung her head. 'I know you must think me very cruel and calculating. You were supposed to wait on the quay.'

'And be the witness.'

She sighed. 'Wouldn't you have done the same – for someone you really loved? Don't you know what it's like when you feel that much?'

I looked down at Anita. Her eyes were open, looking at me.

63

Sunil had been gone more than thirty minutes. I walked out onto the veranda. The clouds were banking up, preparing for another downfall. I hobbled down the steps and started back along the track. As it curved towards the first set of gate posts I could see Sunil's body slumped to one side in the grass. Beside him was Anita's bag, the contents strewn across a muddy puddle. I was about to turn when I noticed a fresh set of tyre tracks and followed them to a Land-Rover parked amongst the trees.

I didn't need to see any more. I turned and half stumbled, half sprinted back to the house as the heavens opened once more.

Greer and Anita were gone. A gust of wind banged the shutters and something fluttered on the floor. A mosquito net had been torn down and there was a trail of muddy footprints across it. I took out the gun. Although I held it in two hands like Saul had, it shook absurdly.

Milky light spilled from an open door on the first-floor landing. Rain clattered on the tin roof and echoed down the stairwell. A gloved hand wrapped itself round the lower half of my face.

A familiar figure stepped out of the shadows. Tanager's voice was no more than a murmur. 'You've made this very hard for us.'

64

Tanager's men were right behind me, each holding an arm. Their grip was so strong my feet skidded as we mounted the stairs. One held Saul's gun against my neck.

Greer stood at the foot of the bed, a look of weary resignation on her face. Malik lay behind her. Only his head and shoulders were visible above the sheet. He was heavily bearded and quite grey. His eyes were almost obscured by the heavy lids that drooped even lower over his pupils than I remembered. The small triangular scar was still visible. His eyes widened as we appeared, but nothing else moved.

Saul's face was almost unrecognisable, blackened with mud and dried blood. Some of his teeth were missing and his jaw hung at an awkward angle. A strip of flesh had been torn loose from his forehead and a matted clump of hair hung down his cheek. But his strength was clearly far from gone. One hand was clamped across Anita's chest. His other held a knife against her throat. He adjusted his grip and her feet almost left the ground.

She mouthed a word it took me a moment to recognise: *Sorry* …

Tanager stepped out from behind us. Saul nodded at him. 'OK, let's finish this.'

Tanager moved over to the bed and peered at Malik.

He touched the scar on his cheek as if he needed to be sure. Then he looked at Greer. She reached out and gripped Malik's hand.

Saul waved the knife in my direction. 'My gun, please.'

Tanager said, 'You sure you're up to this?'

'It's what I'm here to do.' Saul pointed the knife at me then back at Anita. 'Them first.'

Tanager came towards me. I searched his face for a hint of emotion, and found none.

'You can have a few moments with her.'

He took the gun from his companion and walked me towards Anita. A gust of wind billowed the nets that hung in front of the windows. Saul lowered his knife and I scooped Anita into my arms. She was burning hot and taking shallow, rapid breaths. I buried her head as gently as I could against my shoulder.

Saul reached for the gun, steadied himself and took aim. His face was so battered it was hard to read his expression. He had reached the end of a journey that must have consumed most of his adult life. I tightened my grip on Anita and whispered, '*I love you.*' It was something I should have said a long time ago.

It was a small click but we all heard it, even with the sound of the rain. Saul looked at the gun and then at Tanager.

'What is this? Don't we want the same thing?' He dropped the gun and it clattered on the floor.

Tanager stepped forward and picked it up. 'Not entirely. Same ends, perhaps. But different means.'

The clip he had removed when they'd taken it from me downstairs was still in his fist. He slotted it into place and pushed it home.

There was no ceremony to what happened next. Saul lifted his knife a few inches, as if he couldn't find the strength to raise it any further. The determination that had driven him all this way had gone out of him. He didn't say a word.

There was a dull thud as the bullet entered his forehead, followed by another as he slumped to the floor.

65

No one moved for a second. Then Tanager had his phone out and was talking into it. I heard the crunch of gravel and a screech of tyres. More people came into the room. Malik was carried out by the two men who had held me. I clutched Anita tight, as if even now she could still be ripped away from me.

But my strength was seeping away. Whatever had been keeping my body moving, dulling the pain from the car crash, had stopped pumping and a fog of pain engulfed me. My arms were prised apart and Anita was lifted away.

When I came to, I was in a bed, propped up against a bank of pillows. I don't know how many days had passed. The room had a surgical smell and the fittings looked institutional. A French window opened out onto a balcony. I could see two figures sitting in folding chairs, fanning their sweat-streaked faces with British newspapers. Most of the day – at least for the parts I was conscious – the sun seemed to bounce off the sea, turning them into silhouettes. Occasionally they glanced back at me.

When I wondered out loud what the time was, they leapt to their feet and peered over me.

'Nick ... Are you with us?'

I recognised them now – the two men who had interviewed me in the police station in London, who I'd escaped from through the basement of my flat.

'Where's Anita?'

'Want a drink?'

'Where's Anita?'

'We're not authorised to discuss that.'

'Nick, you are still in a great deal of trouble. But we may be able to help you.'

'Show me Anita.'

'I'm afraid you're in no position to bargain.'

I don't know what chemical they'd filled me with, but I started to laugh. 'I think it's a bit late in the day to try and scare me. What are you going to do? Put me on trial?'

When I woke up again it was dark. A fingernail moon hovered above the horizon, casting a line of stepping-stone reflections across the sea. I could hear breathing, but it was a while before I traced it to a figure leaning against the wall at the foot of my bed.

'Cigarette? I'm sure it's forbidden.'

Tanager stepped out of the gloom and lowered himself onto the edge of the bed. His face lit up briefly as his lighter flared, then vanished again. He blew a long plume of smoke towards the open window.

'Perfect night.'

'Where am I exactly?'

'A base, about twenty miles south of Colombo.'

'Where's Anita?'

He stared at the sea.

'Is she OK?'

He nodded.

'I'll believe that when I see her.'

'That may not be an option.'

I hauled myself further up the bed. 'Does she know I'm here?'

He didn't answer at first. 'There are only three people who know you're alive, my two colleagues and me. The nurses here have absolutely no idea who you are. And even if they did, they wouldn't have any idea about the significance of your continued existence.'

'What *is* the significance?'

'Nick, my job is to put the lid back on this. We've made a bit of progress. But it's not over yet.'

'Why did you put me through that charade with the gun?'

'You kept your nerve. You were good.' He stood up and took a few steps towards the window. 'I needed to see him pull the trigger. It's hard to kill an unarmed, injured man. Easier once he's made no secret of the fact that he's a psychopath.' His face glowed red as he took a drag on his cigarette.

'You and Saul, weren't you supposed to be on the same side?'

He shrugged. 'Same side? Possibly. Though I sometimes wonder.'

'And Malik?'

'He hasn't got long. At least they don't have to run any more.'

'How did you find us?'

'Your phone. You finally switched it on.'

He threw his cigarette over the balcony and folded his arms.

'Nick, I need to know what you know.'

'You mean you've got some gaps?' I managed a smile. 'Last week, at your club, you seemed to know it all.'

His eyes narrowed. 'Let's not fuck with each other any more, Nick.'

'Did you lose me – or were you just keeping your distance?'

He shook his head. 'We live in an age of stretched resources, tight budgets.'

'I know. And it takes a team of forty to tail a man on the move. More if he thinks he's being watched.'

'Did Saul tell you that?' He paused. 'Frankly, I didn't think you'd be the one to lead us to them.'

'Greer was one of your people, at least to start with ...'

His eyebrows shot up. 'What makes you think that?'

'The way she arranged for the boat to explode when she wanted it to; how she managed to get Malik out afterwards. Why she was in Beirut when Edge bumped into her. She was there for you, wasn't she? *You'd* sent her to turn Malik. And that's when it all started to unravel.'

He looked at me for a long time. 'I underestimated you.'

'Maybe I underestimated myself.'

'And you convinced Saul. That was something.'

'He told me he was ex-CIA.'

'There's no such thing as ex.'

I shifted myself so I could see him better. 'Is this going to help me?'

He shrugged. 'It can't make things any worse.'

'It was Saul's idea, the hijack, to kill Zarev, wasn't it?'

Tanager didn't respond.

'And when it went wrong, it was his idea to blame it on Malik. The job of getting rid of Malik passed to you, because he was in your orbit – but you made sure it didn't happen.'

Tanager nodded. 'Very good. But what made Saul suspect Malik was alive after all this time?'

'Something he found in the Cold Box?'

'Your friend Harrop ...'

'When the inquiry could no longer be avoided, Saul had the box sent over to Washington. What he found inside was enough to confirm his suspicion that Malik hadn't been killed.'

Tanager shrugged. 'I was gone by then.'

I waited for him to explain.

'Early retirement is the usual euphemism.'

For a moment I thought of Colin. Old-fashioned loyalties, doing things his own way, whatever rules got broken.

'You were sacked?'

'Stick to the story, Nick.'

'When Malik, then known as Rammal, started to lose it, you weren't around to help. Greer was on her own. She took matters into her own hands. The explosion wiped the slate clean. Or did it?'

He shrugged. 'To be honest, I didn't know for sure. I wasn't exactly in contact.'

'But you must have wondered.'

He didn't answer.

'When the Government agreed to an enquiry, they brought you back to make sure nothing incriminating popped up.

And it was your chance to get to the truth about Malik and Greer. Once you'd found out the Cold Box had been sent to Washington, you realised you weren't the only one looking for them.'

He poured himself a glass of water and stared into it. 'It was smart of Saul to get inside the families' outfit. It was the best place to pick up stuff, while making sure they didn't get anything too useful. He must have thought Christmas had come early when you showed up with your little archive.'

'Which presumably he destroyed.'

He nodded. 'He wanted no traces. Neither of us did.'

'What's happened to the inquiry?'

He pursed his lips. 'Adjourned indefinitely. Lack of new evidence.'

I felt a flash of anger. 'Job well done, then.'

'The families got compensation. A goodwill gesture.'

'And you saved Malik from Saul. You felt you owed him, didn't you? For Amerair. Your moment of glory.'

He laughed and shook his head. 'You haven't missed much, have you? Yes. It was a brave thing to do, letting me know about that. He couldn't stay in the Middle East after that.'

He was quiet for a while, lost in thought, then he came back and sat on the bed. 'Nick ... understand this. They only let me back to do this one job then it's back to my watercolours. After that ...' He lit himself a fresh cigarette. 'The powers that be ... I can't protect you from them.'

Colin's phrase. He'd been right all along.

'And they want everything tidied up.'

He nodded. 'A clean slate. Nothing left behind.'

'Whatever it takes?'

'Pretty much.'

He looked at me. Years of subterfuge in far-flung places had moulded his face into a mask of inscrutability. In a business where decency could have been a handicap, he'd played a clever game to get his way.

'If you were anything like Saul, you would have finished me off by now.'

He sighed. 'There are plenty more where he came from.'

'And not many like you.'

He laughed. 'I'm practically extinct.'

He examined the glowing tip of his cigarette. 'There are elections coming up on both sides of the Atlantic. Nobody wants any more bad news about security service failures or nasty cover-ups. If, after I'm gone, they find any loose ends ...'

'And I'm a loose end.'

'It'll be out of my hands, Nick.'

'What about Anita?'

'She's less of a risk, given her track record in the secrets department.'

'You never knew about her?'

He shook his head. 'Completely slipped through our net.'

'So where does that leave me?'

'Well, let's take a long hard look at that, Nick. Edgington knew what he was doing when he hired you. You have to get to the bottom of things. You can't help yourself. No, it doesn't look good for you, I'm afraid. No government would want you loose on the streets.'

'You flatter me. I didn't exactly get the story.'

'You don't exactly come over as someone who's about to let go.'

'Maybe I've changed.'

I closed my eyes. I saw Edge in his kitchen, weighed down with regret for the wasted years he could have spent with his wife; Carrie, alone, walking on the sea front with her dog; and myself, in my flat, setting a table for one.

'Why are we having this conversation?'

'You tell me,' he said.

I looked into his eyes. I'd seen him kill. He'd almost certainly done it before. But something else lay beneath the well-honed world-weariness.

'When the order was given to take out Malik, you disobeyed it.'

He didn't respond. In his world, perhaps, a sense of fair play counted as a flaw.

'And you wouldn't have found him again without me.'

'I'm afraid that isn't enough.'

'You don't want the last act in your career as a spook to be getting rid of me.'

He looked away, out to the sea.

I hauled myself higher in the bed. 'If I came up with something, what would you be able to offer me in return?'

'You can't go home.'

'Here would be fine.'

He looked at me. 'It would have to be good. Something to make me believe that you'd really let go, that you wouldn't be any trouble later on.'

'Like the Rammal interview. The master tapes?'

The first hint of dawn was spreading across the sky. Tanager stood up. He didn't show any expression. All that moved were the muscles around his eyes. He peeled a fleck of tobacco from his lower lip and flicked it away.

66

The churchyard was tiny. It was so close to the cliff edge that it was crumbling in places into the Indian Ocean. The church itself had been freshly painted a blazing white, as if especially for the occasion. The rain and wind had left everything looking crisp and scrubbed in the blindingly sharp sunlight.

Greer leaned against the cliff wall, looking out to sea. A broad-brimmed hat and a fine net shielded her face. She straightened up when she saw me and smiled, relieved not to be on her own. I came and stood by her, sharing the view of the sea.

'Dutch settlers chose this site because they thought it would give the spirits …' Her voice faltered for a moment. 'It would give the spirits a better chance of finding their way home.'

I looked out at the endless expanse of water, imagining their journey. I didn't even know what Malik's real name was, or where he had come from. But none of that seemed to matter now.

She let her hand drop on to mine.

'I'm very sorry. For everything.'

I snorted. 'I should be comforting you.' If I felt any residual anger, this wouldn't have been the time for it. I looked round. We were still alone. Tanager's men, who had brought me here, had made themselves scarce.

I turned and looked at her. 'Tell me it was all worth it.'

She looked away for a moment then lifted the net. Maybe she wanted me to be sure she was being sincere.

'It was a ruthless thing to do. And I make no excuses. But you know … if it had been for just one year, one month even …' She took a deep breath. 'Yes. It was worth it. Every day felt precious. A bonus.' She looked hard at me and gripped my hand.

I felt a stab of envy.

A bleached wood coffin was being carried up the path, followed by a rotund, smiling priest, swathed in purple.

'Excuse me.' She touched my cheek and picked her way between mossy graves to the entrance of the church. There was something tentative about her movements, as if part of her energy had gone with him.

I glimpsed Tanager near the trees. He gestured at his mobile phone and gave me a thumbs-up. They had the tapes.

I wouldn't be going back to England, but I'd bought myself a future. I looked back at the ocean. It was fiery bright.

With the crash of the waves below and the rattling fronds of the palms above, I didn't hear her approach. But when I looked round again, she had come up right beside me, the scarf of her sari streaming behind her in the wind. I opened my mouth to speak but she planted a kiss on it then stepped back, holding my hand.

'I call it my Bollywood outfit. Do you think they'd give me a screen test?'

Anita slipped her arm under mine and I gripped it tight.

'Shall we go in?'

Acknowledgements

The origins of *Perfect Night* date back to 1984 when I was dispatched to Sri Lanka by the BBC for the *Real Lives* documentary series. Thanks to Peter Pagnamenta, Will Wyatt and Jeanne La Chard for giving me that opportunity. In Sri Lanka there were many people who thrilled and inspired me, most notably K Sivapalan. From the rest of my television life, *Crimewatch* creator Peter Chafer was a source of inspiration and much later Stephen Lambert recalled for me his own TV encounter with the LTTE (Tamil Tigers).

I received vital early encouragement from Richard Rayner, Paul Ensor, Angela Holdsworth, Karen Brown, Richard Beswick and Tiff Loehnis. Several people gave up time to read and comment on the work in progress: my mother-in-law Pat McNeill, Joanna Briscoe, Martin Rudland, Chris Hale, Olivia Lichtenstein, Katarina Petruscakova, Ruth Jackson, Patrick Tatham, Sara Beardsall, Dominic Minghella and Larry Finlay.

James Castle and Brian Trenery passed judgement on the finer points of TV archive and editing. Chantal Krishnadasan and Shirani Sabaratnam vetted all the Sri Lankan and Tamil detail. Richard McBrien cast an unflinching eye over the plot. And Lawrence and Lydia Calman-Grimsdale debated titles with me.

I am enormously grateful to Mark Lucas, a very special agent, for having so much confidence in me from such an early stage, providing an astonishing level of support and sending me to Bill Massey at Orion, whose enthusiasm and incisiveness makes him a delight to work with.

Finally, there would be no *Perfect Night* without the person who pestered, prodded, read and re-read more times than is natural – my wife Stephanie Calman.